The Captain's Angel

The Captain's Angel

BEST-SELLING AUTHOR ANITA STANSFIELD WRITING AS

ELIZABETH D. MICHAELS

SWEETWATER BOOKS
An imprint of Cedar Fort, Inc.
Springville, Utah

ISBN 13: 978-1-4621-4212-5

Published by Sweetwater Books, an imprint of Cedar Fort, Inc.
2373 W. 700 S., Springville, UT 84663
Distributed by Cedar Fort, Inc., www.cedarfort.com

Library of Congress Control Number: 2022933525

Cover design by Courtney Proby
Cover design © 2022 Cedar Fort, Inc.
Edited and typeset by Valene Wood

Printed in the United States of America

10 9 8 7 6 5 4 3 2 1

Printed on acid-free paper

To all of my devoted fans and readers that believed in me and stuck with me through my own personal and professional challenges. Your encouragement and support and prayers have always meant so much!

Other books written by

Elizabeth D. Michaels

The Buchanan Saga

Captain of Her Heart
Captive Hearts

The Horstberg Saga

Behind the Mask
A Matter of Honor
For Love and Country
The Tainted Crown
Through Castle Windows

For a complete list of this author's
books, go to anitastansfield.com.

We, we must go on now
Wherever people go who go on together.

—"The Border" by Mr. Mister

Prologue

1784

Garret Wentworth leaned against the rail of the *Phoenix*, watching the New England sun go down behind the silhouette of a typical port town. They'd all begun to look the same, and he was coming to hate them. He longed for home, and the motivation to stay there. But home was riddled with mixed emotions, and only the sea offered the irrefutable love that he ached for. The sea was in his blood, but even that was fast losing its appeal. His grandfather had advised him years ago that when he found a woman who could make him feel the way the sea made him feel, he should take hold of her and never let go—even if it meant giving up the sea. Well, Garret had long ago found such a woman—but she was married to his half-brother. Garret had diligently searched for a woman who could replace Kyrah Buchanan in his heart—as much as a man possibly could when his only contact with women came from brief visits to port towns around the world. But as of yet, no woman could fill his heart the way Kyrah did, and his love for her had even tainted his love for the sea.

Garret turned his back to the rail of the idle ship and looked out toward the distant horizon, where the ocean met the sky. He took a long drag on his narrow cigar and blew out a smooth line of smoke. He felt a tangible aching to be in Cornwall, amidst the walls of his brother's home, a place where he had found some of the happiest moments of his life. But at the same time, the distance between himself and

England felt safer somehow. He had expected the passing of time to ease these feelings that were so difficult to understand. But years had not diminished his feelings for Kyrah, and his frustration deepened steadily at not finding a love to replace her.

Garret wasn't surprised to turn and find Patrick standing beside him at the rail. In the absence of his brother, Patrick was the best friend he'd ever had. Their sailing together for years had deepened the bonds between them. Besides Ritcherd and Kyrah, only Patrick knew everything about Garret—even the deepest secrets of his heart.

"What is this?" Patrick grumbled, plucking the cigar from between Garret's fingers. Garret scowled as he watched Patrick toss it to the deck and crush it beneath the toe of his boot. "I can't begin to imagine why you picked up such a disgusting habit."

"I don't have a woman," Garret said. "I might as well keep company with a cigar."

"I don't have a woman either," Patrick countered, "but you don't see me sucking in foul air. It can't be good for you with the way it stinks."

"What are you?" Garret growled. "My nanny now?"

"I'm the ship's physician, and you—"

"And *I* am the ship's captain," Garret interrupted. "When I feel inclined to start taking orders from you, I'll—"

"You *will* take orders from me," Patrick said, only slightly humorous, "so long as your health is at stake."

Garret gave a scoffing laugh and turned back to look toward the port town over the stern. "I think you simply need something to nag me about," he said. "If I wasn't smoking, you'd nag me about something else."

"Maybe," Patrick said. "But if you'd find a woman and settle down, we could both quit the sea and have a real life."

"You are welcome to quit the sea any time you like, Doctor. If you wait for me to find a woman, you could die at sea."

Patrick sighed. His voice lost all humor. "What about Catherine?"

Garret snorted a harsh chuckle. "Yes, Catherine." He sighed loudly. "I was just trying to talk myself out of going to see her again before we sail."

Patrick raised his brows. "You have to talk yourself out of it? I thought you cared for Catherine."

"I do," Garret said, looking away.

A minute later Patrick said conclusively, "You told her good-bye."

"Of course I told her good-bye," Garret countered. "We're sailing in the morning."

"You know what I mean," Patrick said. "This is the end."

Garret looked sharply at Patrick. "Must you be so blasted perceptive?"

"I learned it from you," Patrick said coolly. "So, Catherine joins the ranks of Captain Garret's broken hearts. Let's see . . . there was Daisy, and Mary, and Lydia. And now Catherine."

"I know their names, Patrick. And may I remind you that Daisy is happily married? So is Lydia."

"Yes, they are," Patrick said, "but they didn't get married until *after* you broke their hearts."

"They're happy now. I did them a favor." Garret sighed. "That's why I had to tell Catherine good-bye."

"I thought there was hope . . . that she could be the one."

"There *was* hope," Garret said. "She's a fine woman, and I care very much for her. She's beautiful; she would make a good wife." His voice became gravelly. "But I cannot kiss her or hold her in my arms without having my thoughts stray to Kyrah. No woman deserves to be loved with only half a man's heart. Until I find a woman who can make me think only of her, I will have to be content with the sea."

"Never *quite* content."

"No," Garret said, his voice resigned, "never quite."

Patrick put a hand on Garret's shoulder and remained beside him, saying nothing for several minutes. Garret appreciated his silent compassion and the way he seemed to sense Garret's grief. But there was nothing to be said that might console him. Silence seemed preferable.

Patrick finally said, "So, now what? To England as planned?"

"Yes," Garret said firmly. "I need some time off."

"I won't dispute that," Patrick said. "But do you think it's a good idea to spend a few months living under the same roof with . . ."

He hesitated and Garret stated, "With Kyrah, you mean."

"Yes, I suppose that's what I mean." Garret scowled at him, and Patrick added, "Listen to me, Captain. Ritcherd's not here, so I'm the best friend you've got, and like it or not, it's evident that you're struggling with your feelings. You're frustrated and lonely—and occasionally your frustration and loneliness press you to anger, my friend."

For a moment Garret felt defensive, but Patrick's tone made it evident he had nothing but Garret's best interests at heart. He sighed and had to admit, "Yes, I know you're right. But I need to go home. Kyrah and Ritcherd are very much in love with each other. Being with them helps me keep perspective. They're both well aware of how I feel—and they love me anyway. I need to be with them—and with Celeste and Cetty. They're the only family I've got that means anything to me. I told them I was taking a vacation; they're expecting me, and we're already behind schedule after those blasted storms we hit in the islands." Garret sighed and looked toward the eastern horizon, the direction of home. "I just . . . feel like I need to be home."

"Then home you will go," Patrick said more lightly. "After all, you *are* the captain."

Patrick slapped him playfully on the shoulder and walked away. Garret squeezed his eyes closed as the memory of Catherine's tears mingled with thoughts of home. He lit up another cigar, wondering why he felt a formless urgency beckoning him to the shores of Cornwall. He prayed that the journey would go smoothly, and that he would find all well there when he arrived. He prayed that Catherine's heart would heal quickly. And he prayed that he might be able to avoid any more emotional entanglements until his own heart could be tangled completely and irrevocably.

Chapter One

The Absence of Light

Cornwall, England

*R*itcherd Buchanan pressed his stallion as quickly as it would carry him. The autumn wind was especially cold and bit at his face, escalating his desire to get home. His days of business in London regarding some long-time financial investments had dragged incessantly. His journey to the city had served a dual purpose in accompanying his mother-in-law, Sarah, to spend several weeks with a dear friend. Sarah was grateful for the opportunity to have Ritcherd see her safely there, but for him the extra time away from home had been frustrating. With his travel time back and forth, he'd been gone nearly a week. It was the longest he'd been separated from Kyrah through more than four years of marriage. He ached to be with her, and to see their little daughter, Cetty. But his deepest concern was for his sister.

Celeste had been ill off and on for months now, with no apparent cause. She had been slipping into another bad spell when he'd had no choice but to leave. The local doctor had offered to send for a specialist he'd heard of who had experience in rare ailments. But more importantly, this specialist had done a significant amount of research into the rare condition that Celeste had been born with. And now Ritcherd was completely preoccupied with wondering if the specialist had come in his absence, and what light he might have been able to shed on their concerns for Celeste.

Ritcherd heaved a deep sigh when his home came into view. Buckley Manor was beautiful, and his love ran deep for this place where he had grown up. But his heart was with his loved ones within its walls. He left his horse with the stablemaster and hurried inside, removing his gloves and cloak the minute he entered through the side door. He handed them idly to the maid who appeared.

"Good to see you home, Captain," she said with a quick curtsy.

"It's good to be home, Liza. Is—"

"Mrs. Buchanan's in the nursery with Cetty," she said.

"Thank you," he replied and moved quickly up the back stairs, removing his coat as he did.

Ritcherd's heart quickened as he pushed open the nursery door. He caught a glimpse of Kyrah turning toward him only a moment before Cetty ran and jumped into his arms. "Papa! Papa! You came home!"

"I did!" He laughed and turned with her in his arms. "And I think you missed me almost as much as I missed you!"

"Oh, I did," she said firmly. "Mama doesn't read stories as well as you." She glanced apologetically toward her mother and added softly, "She doesn't know how to do all the funny voices."

Ritcherd laughed and hugged her tightly. "Well, I missed you, too," he said, brushing a hand over her downy blonde hair that was so much like his own. Cetty was a bright and beautiful child, and Ritcherd could never put to words his gratitude for her very existence and the light she brought into his life. The fact that she was four and a half years old and her parents had only been married four years was something they'd simply had to accept. He had made some bad choices; he and Kyrah had suffered much from those choices, as well as from a series of circumstances that were still difficult to comprehend. The wounds left from those struggles were deep, and Ritcherd often felt twinges of pain when related thoughts came into his mind. But he did his best to force them away, knowing that life was good, and he had much to be grateful for.

Ritcherd's gaze was compelled toward Kyrah, and he wondered how she could manage to get more beautiful every day. He put Cetty down, saying gently, "Run along, darling. I need to talk to your mother." The moment his arms were free of his daughter, Kyrah filled them again, making it evident by her zealous embrace that she had missed him as much as he'd missed her.

"Oh, Kyrah," he murmured and kissed her as if he'd been gone a year. He looked into her eyes and touched her dark, curly hair that was barely managing to stay in the pins she'd put into it earlier in the day. "You've been out walking, I see," he said, knowing how the Cornish wind always tugged her hair out of place. He smiled and added, "You look most beautiful when you've had the wind in your hair."

She returned his smile. "It was too cold to walk far. I was hoping to meet you, but . . ." She touched his face. "Good heavens. You're practically frozen."

She pressed both hands over his face as if she could take away the cold. He kissed one palm, then the other. "I figured you could warm me up once I got here."

She laughed softly and kissed him again. As their lips parted, she felt his eyes delve into hers, and she recognized his unspoken question. She marveled at how well they could read each other. She knew what he wanted to know, but she didn't want to tell him.

"Kyrah," he said softly, "are you . . ."

She shook her head before he could finish the question, and she heard her own disappointment in his sigh. Cetty was still an only child. Pregnancy continued to elude Kyrah—a fact that troubled them both deeply.

She hurried to change the subject. "Did your business go well?"

"It did," he said. "I'm only grateful such matters don't require my attention very often. It was dull and tedious and I missed you dreadfully. All of you."

"And how is Mother?" she asked. "Did you deliver her safely to her friend?"

"I did," he said, "and she is well. I checked in on her again before returning. They were having a marvelous time."

"That's good then," she said.

With their greeting finished, his mind returned to Celeste. He saw Kyrah's eyes darken with concern and wondered if she had read his mind. "She's not doing well," Kyrah said before he could ask.

He hated the immediate dread that made his heart pound. "Did the specialist—"

"He came yesterday and spent considerable time with her. He was here again this morning. His name is Dr. Gates."

"What did he say?" Ritcherd asked when she hesitated.

She sighed and said, "He'll be back later this afternoon. He wanted to talk to you."

While Ritcherd was attempting to digest the severity in Kyrah's eyes, Cetty pulled on his arm. "Papa," she said, "will you read me a story?"

He squatted down and looked at her directly. "Papa needs to say hello to Aunt Celeste. And then I will read you *two* stories. You play with your dollies, and I'll be back."

Cetty grinned and skipped across the room to where she'd left a number of dolls of different sizes all perched around a tiny little tea set, as if they were engaged in a friendly chat.

Kyrah went with Ritcherd to Celeste's room. They entered to find Miss Benson seated close to her bed with a book. She had been Celeste's constant companion since the cradle, and the sad smile she turned toward Ritcherd in greeting only heightened his dread. Moving closer to the bed, he caught his breath and stopped. In the week he'd been gone, his sister had become pale and dramatically thinner. He squeezed Kyrah's hand in his and turned to meet the compassion in her eyes. While a part of him wanted to demand that she tell him what the doctor might have said, something deeper almost didn't want to know.

He prompted himself beyond his fears and hurried to Celeste's side. Sitting on the edge of the bed, he took her hand into his just as Miss Benson said quietly, "She was stirring some a minute or two ago. I think she'll be awake soon."

"She's been sleeping a great deal, I take it," he said.

"More every day," she reported and he sighed, at the same time uttering a silent prayer that this specialist would be able to solve whatever the problem might be and bring his darling sister back to life.

Ritcherd prayed with Celeste's hand in his for several minutes before she stirred and opened her eyes to look at him. Her smile was weak but still managed to light her eyes in a way that was so familiar to Ritcherd.

"There's my angel," he said and pressed a kiss to her brow. As he drew back, she weakly lifted her hands to take his face between them in a way that was common. She looked into his eyes with an intensity that was almost startling before she pressed a kiss to his nose. The gesture had become so comfortable that he'd not stopped for years to consider where it had begun, but looking into his sister's eyes at that moment, the memory became as clear as his arrival home only minutes earlier.

Ritcherd held tightly to Celeste's hand as they ran over the purple moors toward the church ruins, their favorite place to play and just be together. Celeste let go of his hand and ran ahead, giggling as she lifted her skirt higher, showing her little lace-up boots and dark stockings. She impulsively did a somersault then continued to run. Arriving at the church ruins, they both lay back in the grass and gazed toward the sky, counting the clouds while Celeste would spontaneously laugh for no apparent reason, as if she was simply incapable of holding all her happiness inside.

"Do you suppose heaven is beyond the clouds?" Ritcherd asked.

"Jesus lives there," she said as if she knew it with certainty.

"He does?" Ritcherd asked, sitting up. He certainly believed what she'd said, but her conviction intrigued him.

"He hugged me before I came here from heaven." She sat to face him. "He said the angels would watch over me and bring me back to Him." She looked into his eyes with an intensity that was not typical of her overly childish ways. It was as if her spirit was speaking to his, attempting to convey something very important.

When Ritcherd could think of no response, he simply touched the freckles on her nose and smiled. "That must be why you have so many angel kisses."

She giggled again, seeming more like herself, and touched his nose that was lightly freckled. "Angel kisses," she whispered, as if it were a secret.

In that moment Ritcherd felt such a perfect happiness, a perfect gratitude for having such an amazing little sister. He took her face into his hands, wishing he could tell her how precious she was to him. He settled for pressing a kiss to her nose, knowing she could never understand words he could likely never express.

"Angel kisses," she repeated, still whispering. She took his face into her hands and returned the gesture by kissing his nose, repeating still again, "Angel kisses."

Ritcherd looked into his sister's eyes while the memory consumed him with a torrent of emotions. It had only been days later that Celeste and her nanny had been sent to live elsewhere because her condition had been a source of anxiety and social disdain for Ritcherd's parents. They'd not bothered to give him any explanation, as if her absence would mean nothing to him. His devastation had only been eased when he'd met seven-year-old Kyrah Payne at the church ruins soon afterward. Celeste had not come back into his life until many years later. A few weeks after their reunion, she had taken his face into her hands and pressed a kiss to his nose, whispering, "Angel kisses." It had become a common habit between them, something special and secret that only the two of them shared. It linked their childhood to the relationship they shared now. But looking into Celeste's eyes in that moment, he felt decidedly afraid.

Not wanting to upset her or mar these moments together, he forced a teasing smile. "What are you doing lying around all day? I thought you were going to draw a picture for me while I was gone."

"I'm sorry, Ritcherd," she said in a way that reminded him of Cetty. He knew their minds were very much on the same level. "I've been too tired."

"That's all right," he said gently. "When you get feeling better, we'll draw a picture together."

She smiled and asked, "Did you bring me a present from London?"

"I did," he said. "When I get my bags unpacked, I'll bring it up to you. Are you hungry? I could go to the kitchen and find some of that cake you like and—"

"No," she said and closed her eyes, "I'm just thirsty."

Miss Benson set a glass of water into his hand, and he lifted Celeste's head to help her drink. The evidence of her weakness deepened a dread in him that he didn't care to define. She actually drank very little before he laid her head back on the pillow and she insisted quietly, "I'm tired now, Ritcherd."

Before he could say anything more, she had drifted back to sleep. Ritcherd sat numbly watching her for several minutes while his mind screamed silent protests. He refused to accept the evidence before him that whatever ailed his sister was serious. He finally turned to Miss Benson and asked, "How long since she's eaten?"

"A few days," she said. "She simply refuses anything we've offered. She insists she's not hungry."

Ritcherd just nodded and resisted the urge to take out his frustration on the nanny. She was kind and good and always had Celeste's best interests at heart. He knew Celeste had been given the best medical care available, but he wondered if this specialist would have any insight that might give them a hope the doctors in the area had been unable to give them. He lost track of the time until Kyrah put a hand on his shoulder, saying gently, "You promised Cetty some stories."

"Of course," he said and came to his feet.

In response to his concerned gaze at Celeste, she added, "I'll come for you if there is any change."

He nodded and said, "And let me know the minute that doctor gets here."

Ritcherd did his best to block out his concerns and enjoy his time with Cetty. She was bright for a four-year-old and had a wry sense of humor. And she was one of the lights in his life. Still, he was distracted by the reality that one of his other lights was growing dim, and he felt so helpless—so desperately helpless.

He'd been in the nursery for nearly an hour when Kyrah peered in and said, "Dr. Gates is here."

Ritcherd jumped to his feet and left Cetty to play with the promise that they would share another story at bedtime. He entered the drawing room with Kyrah to see this doctor come to his feet. He was nearly as tall as Ritcherd, with white hair that gave a wise distinction to a face that didn't show the years he'd been at his profession.

"Dr. Gates," Kyrah said, "my husband, Captain Buchanan."

"Captain," the doctor said, extending a hand. "I assume, then, that you served in the military."

"Some years ago, yes," Ritcherd said. He didn't add that he preferred the military title over his aristocratic title that meant nothing to him. "We appreciate your coming," he added, wanting to get to the point. "We know you've traveled far."

Ritcherd motioned to the sofa and the doctor took his seat again. Ritcherd and Kyrah sat close together, facing him.

"The journey has been well worth it, Captain. The time I've spent with your sister has been memorable. She has that indescribable special quality about her that is characteristic of those with her condition—although I believe Miss Buchanan is likely one of the sweetest people I've ever met."

"She has that effect," Ritcherd said, hearing the adoration in his own voice. He had to ask, "What do you know of her condition?"

"Very little, actually. As far as what causes it, there's no beginning to know. But from my opportunity to spend time with a number of people much like your sister, myself and my colleagues have established certain similar characteristics."

"Such as?" Ritcherd asked, wishing he'd known that such a specialist existed years ago. He'd believed that no one else in the world had such a condition.

"Well," Dr. Gates said, "of course there are the physical characteristics that distinguish them as different from the rest of us. The flatter face, smaller head, shorter arms and legs. Then there are the mental difficulties that keep them very much like young children through their entire lives. But the most startling similarity among all of them is the tender personality. They are completely without guile, absolutely pure in heart. Any negative behavior in these kind of people is mostly due to a very childlike frustration. But as I said, I believe your sister is especially gifted in that regard. I have become well acquainted with nine others like her. But she is a living miracle."

"Why is that?" Ritcherd asked, wanting to bring the conversation around to Celeste's health.

"How old is your sister?" the doctor asked.

"Twenty-six, I believe."

Dr. Gates smiled and shook his head. "She is almost twice as old as any others I have known."

"What are you saying?" Ritcherd asked, feeling the dread inside him deepen. When the doctor looked at him carefully but hesitated to speak, Ritcherd pressed firmly, "What's wrong with her, Doctor?"

"She is dying, Captain."

Ritcherd sucked in his breath. In spite of the evidence he'd seen of how poor her condition had become, he didn't want to believe it. "Dying?" he echoed. "Of what? What's wrong with her?" He felt Kyrah's hand on his arm, as if to keep him calm.

"There's nothing *wrong* with her, Captain. I have never seen anyone with her condition live beyond twenty. The average age of death is much younger. We know very little, in essence, but it would seem that they just have a weaker body system. Basically, she's dying of old age."

Ritcherd pressed a hand over his mouth to keep from crying out. He was aware of Kyrah's arm coming around him while the doctor allowed him a few minutes to absorb what he'd just heard. *He couldn't believe it!* He thought of a hundred questions he wanted to ask, but the only one that made it to his lips was, "How long does she have?"

"Very little time, I'm afraid. Her body is shutting down. Her condition has deteriorated dramatically in the last twenty-four hours. I doubt she'll make it until morning."

Ritcherd hung his head and groaned. Suddenly he had no questions, nothing to say. It took everything inside of him to keep from visibly crumbling in front of this man who was practically a stranger. Dr. Gates's experience in dealing with such matters became evident when he rose and moved toward the door, saying gently, "I'll leave the two of you alone while I go and check on her. I was planning to stay close through the night . . . or as long as you need me."

"Of course, Doctor," Kyrah said. "Thank you." After the door closed, she added with a quiver in her voice, "I'm so sorry, Ritcherd. Nothing will ever be the same without her."

Hearing her express the raw truth of what he felt, he laid his head in her lap and cried like a child. *He just couldn't believe it.*

With the stark realization that his time with Celeste was brief, Ritcherd finally got control of his emotions. Kyrah went to check on Cetty while he went to Celeste's room. Dr. Gates was seated next to a little table, jotting notes in a book. Miss Benson reported that Celeste hadn't shown any response since the few words she'd spoken to Ritcherd. He sat in silence with her hand in his, just watching her while his mind vacillated between the memories they'd shared and the horrible pall before them now. Kyrah checked in regularly while trying to keep Cetty happy. She brought Ritcherd some supper and insisted he eat it. Until smelling the food made his stomach growl, he'd honestly forgotten that he'd not eaten any lunch. At Cetty's bedtime he slipped away long enough to read his daughter her promised story, and he stayed beside her until she slept. Then he hurried back to his sister's side, too dazed to even believe this was really happening.

Ritcherd took Celeste's fingers into his right hand until he realized he was unable to sense her touch. He shifted his chair and switched to his left hand, more aware of his war injury than he'd been in years. Having been shot in the lower arm at close range, he'd lost a great deal of feeling in his right hand, and its abilities were minimal. He'd grown accustomed to the problem and hardly thought about it, but right now he wanted to feel every sign of Celeste's life and he preferred to use his left hand.

Keenly aware of Celeste's hand growing cold, Ritcherd's mind became absorbed with the light she had brought into his life. In fact, she had a way of lighting up everything and everyone she came in contact with. Everyone who knew her loved her, and there would be a great hole left in the world in her absence. But Ritcherd knew there was no one who would feel her loss more keenly than he. In spite of being separated through the majority of their lives, the bond between them had been deep. The entire household would miss her. The community would be mindful of her absence. Kyrah, and Cetty, his brother Garret, and Kyrah's mother would mourn her death deeply. But for Ritcherd, the loss would be incomprehensible.

Ritcherd insisted that Miss Benson get some rest while he sat with Celeste. Kyrah came in to sit with Ritcherd once the household was settled for the night. She took his hand but said nothing. He concluded there was nothing to say. After sitting in silence for more than an hour, aware of Celeste's shallow breathing, he finally said, "Isn't Garret supposed to be here by now?"

"Yes," Kyrah said. "He said very plainly that he planned to be here by early October, and he intended to take a few months off, and give the crew some time off with pay. He said he wanted to be here for Christmas. He made a rather big fuss about getting in on all of the preparations. Considering he's never actually been with us for Christmas, I'd say it would be good for all of us."

Kyrah hadn't told him anything he didn't already know, but he appreciated the way her words filled the torturous silence.

"So he's what?" Ritcherd asked. "More than a week overdue?"

"At least," she said. "But you know how common setbacks can be at sea. He's likely encountered some nasty storm that's blown them off course or something." She sighed and expressed his own thoughts when she added, "I only hope and pray it's simply a setback and not something more serious."

"Amen," he said and allowed his thoughts to briefly wander to his half-brother. The circumstances that had brought him and Garret together were memorable, to say the least. It was more accurate to say that the experiences leading to Ritcherd's discovery that he actually *had* a brother were among the most profound of his life. He had no doubt that God had brought them together to strengthen each other's lives and to answer each other's prayers. No man had ever had a degree of the influence and impact on Ritcherd that he had gleaned from Garret. Their bonds ran deep. And although Garret spent the majority of his life at sea, heavily involved in world trade, nothing ever seemed quite right in Garret's absence. And now, he couldn't fathom getting through this impending doom without his brother at his side. He knew how much Garret cared for Celeste. And Garret's visits had always been a bright spot for her. But with Garret's arrival overdue, and Celeste's life now being measured in hours, he had to accept that Garret would never see his half-sister alive again.

As the hours of the night wore on, Ritcherd marveled at how he didn't feel at all sleepy. Dr. Gates, Miss Benson, and Kyrah took turns resting and being in the room with him until just past three, when the doctor declared that it wouldn't be much longer, and they all gathered around Celeste's bed. While Ritcherd had expected some great, dramatic event to bring her life to an end, instead she simply stopped breathing and passed silently on. He sat in a dazed stupor, just staring at his sister, attempting to comprehend the life that had slipped away and the empty shell she had left behind. When the reality of her death finally penetrated the shock blanketing him, his emotion gushed out in torrents. Kyrah held him while he cried, and he was vaguely aware of her crying as well. While he knew she loved Celeste deeply, he wondered if she could ever begin to understand the hole that had just been cut into his heart.

She finally insisted that he go to bed and try to rest. She held him close and whispered reassuring words. But nothing—not even Kyrah's perfect love—could ever rekindle the light that had just been extinguished inside of him.

Ritcherd slept half the day, and spent the other half facing the necessary task of arranging his sister's funeral. He was grateful for the blanketed shock that had settled in to numb his emotions, which kept him from bawling like a baby through the course of tasks he had to be about. First—and most difficult—was telling Cetty that her Aunt Celeste was gone. With Celeste's childlike mind, the two of them had been good friends. Cetty shed tears and asked questions, then she looked into Ritcherd's eyes and said firmly, "It's all right, Papa." She wiped his tears away with her little fingers. "Celeste's gone to live with the angels in heaven."

Ritcherd nodded, unable to speak. It was a pleasant thought, and he was glad for the concept that gave his little daughter peace. But finding peace for himself would not be so easy. In spite of his belief in God's existence, and the numerous times in his life when he'd seen clear evidence to strengthen that belief, he suddenly found himself confronted with questions about life and death that seemed to have no answers.

A short while later, Ritcherd was startled to come across the little doll that he'd bought for Celeste in London. Apparently one of the maids had found it among his luggage and left it on the bureau. For a long moment he just held it in his hands. He contemplated giving it to Cetty, even though she had far more dolls than any little girl needed, and he'd already given her the gift he'd brought her from London. Feeling suddenly angry without fully understanding why, Ritcherd tossed the doll into the fire and watched it burn, the same way he'd watched Celeste's life fade away.

Through the days leading up to the funeral, Ritcherd felt a deep restlessness growing inside of him. The house seemed darker and colder. The world had become bleak and dreary. The light was gone.

He could look around and see that he had much to be grateful for, but the reality of his gratitude couldn't seem to penetrate the walls around his heart. He didn't feel grateful. He felt cold and scared and alone. And for the love of heaven, he just didn't know how he was going to keep putting one foot in front of the other.

Chapter Two

The Captain's Return

Days after Celeste's funeral, Kyrah's thoughts were drawn away from her grief by a startling concern for her husband. She had expected him to grieve deeply. They had suffered losses before, and she clearly expected the adjustment to be difficult. But in the past, they had shared their grief. They had talked and cried together, and found comfort in the affection they shared. Now there was only a growing despondency in Ritcherd that was very unlike him. They'd been close since their childhood, and she'd certainly seem him struggle with the difficulties that life had dealt him. But the years they'd been married had been filled with a peace and happiness that was close to perfect. For the first time since she'd become his wife, Kyrah felt detached from Ritcherd. This man she had known heart and soul had become very much like a stranger in the days since his sister's death. And she couldn't deny being afraid.

She had hoped that when the funeral was over, he would open himself to her and allow her to help him through this. But that evening he shut himself in his sitting room until long after Kyrah had gone to bed. And several days later, the only thing he'd said to her aside from necessary exchanges was an occasional, "Where do you suppose Garret is?" He became almost ghostlike, usually hovering near her and Cetty without interacting at all. His mind was obviously elsewhere, and his heart broken.

At Kyrah's suggestion, Ritcherd gave Miss Benson a retirement bonus that was more than sufficient to keep her in comfort for the rest of her life. He and Kyrah both felt certain she had earned it, and now that Celeste no longer needed her, Miss Benson could do some of the traveling she'd always wanted to do. Ritcherd felt a deepening of his sadness at seeing the nanny go. He recalled how kind she had been to him in his youth, and her tenderness with Celeste had been remarkable. Once Miss Benson was gone and his business with her complete, he sank back into the dark cloud that had surrounded him since Celeste's death.

Kyrah observed Ritcherd withdrawing further from her and Cetty. She prayed night and day that she would be able to reach her husband, that he might allow her to help him carry his burden of grief. As her concern deepened by the hour, she felt certain that nothing short of divine intervention could bridge the chasm that had opened between them in so short a time.

A ray of hope appeared when the local vicar came to see how they were adjusting to the loss they had suffered. Kyrah showed him to the drawing room and went to find Ritcherd, praying that the vicar could give Ritcherd some peace and comfort that might help him come to his senses. She missed her husband desperately and felt a lonely ache from the reality of how he had closed himself off from her.

"Ritcherd," she said, coming into the doorway of the nursery to see him leaning against the window frame, staring outside at nothing. Cetty glanced up at her mother from where she sat on the floor playing. Her expression betrayed that she shared Kyrah's frustration and loneliness when her father would hardly give her so much as a glance. He made no response and she moved toward him, touching him on the shoulder. He started and turned toward her, his eyes distant and hollow. "Ritcherd," she repeated. "The vicar is here. He would like to speak with both of us."

Without responding, he followed her out of the room and down the stairs. Not a word was spoken between them as they walked side by side. Kyrah couldn't help thinking of how he normally would have held her hand in such a situation, but he made no attempt to touch her. In truth, he'd not touched her at all since he'd initially cried in her arms immediately following Celeste's passing.

The vicar came to his feet as they entered the drawing room. He was more short than tall, a wiry man with dark, graying hair and a subtle twitch in his lanky fingers. "Captain," he said, reaching out both hands. Ritcherd took them for only a second and quickly let go. "How are you doing?"

"I'm fine," Ritcherd said, and Kyrah wanted to hotly accuse him of lying. "And you?"

"I'm very well," the vicar said, and they were all seated. "I simply wanted to see how you're coming along with the loss of your sister, and to see if there's anything I can do."

"There's nothing anyone can do," Ritcherd said.

"But you're obviously very troubled," the vicar said. "You must find peace with this, my son."

Kyrah watched Ritcherd expectantly, biting her lip, praying that he would respond to the vicar's plea. He looked firmly at the vicar and asked, "How exactly would you suggest I go about that?"

"Through prayer you can find peace, Ritcherd, and come to terms with the fact that your sister is gone."

"Gone?" Ritcherd echoed, visibly bristling. "How can she just be . . . *gone?* Surely her spirit lives on in a better place than this. You have spoken of paradise yourself many times."

The vicar looked decidedly nervous, which seemed to pique Ritcherd's attention. He wrung his twitching hands, saying, "Yes, but . . . you must understand, my son, that paradise is reserved for a select few. You must not concern yourself with your sister's whereabouts now, Ritcherd. You will never find peace if you trouble yourself over such things."

Ritcherd absorbed the countenance of this man sitting before him, and the implication of his words, and everything inside of him screamed in protest. His only grain of comfort in losing Celeste had been the belief that her perfect spirit would have gone directly to a place of perfect peace and happiness, and now this man was suggesting otherwise. Reminding himself not to jump to conclusions, he asked carefully, "What are you implying, Vicar?"

"You must accept the truth, Ritcherd," he said. "Your sister's condition makes it difficult to know exactly what her eternal fate would be."

"Her *condition?*" Ritcherd snarled. "What does her *condition* have to do with anything?"

"I don't have all the answers, Ritcherd," the vicar said nervously.

"If you don't, then who does?" Ritcherd shouted.

"Ritcherd," Kyrah put a hand on his arm, a gesture that often reminded him to stay calm and think clearly, but he tersely brushed her hand aside and scowled at her before facing the vicar as if he might tear him to pieces.

"There are some things that we simply cannot understand from our mortal perspective," the vicar said.

"Well, at least I agree with you on that," Ritcherd said, "which makes it evident that you are more of a hypocrite than I realized. How can you sit there and tell me that my sister is eternally damned through circumstances completely beyond her control, and then tell me there are things we can't understand from our mortal perspective? What gives you the knowledge of my sister's eternal judgment?"

The vicar looked angry now; his voice was barely calm. "The Bible states it plainly. 'For I the Lord thy God am a jealous God, visiting the iniquity of the fathers upon the children.'"

It took a moment for Ritcherd to feel the implication settle in. He heard Kyrah gasp and knew she'd grasped the vicar's meaning in the same moment. Again, he told himself not to jump to conclusions. He swallowed carefully and asked, "Stop beating around the bush and just come out and say it, Vicar. What truth is it that you think I need to accept?"

The vicar drew up his chin, showing visible courage. "Your parents were guilty of many sins, Ritcherd. The results of those sins are all around you. Your sister's ailment was clearly a result of those sins, and—"

"By whose definition?" Ritcherd growled, erupting to his feet. "Who are you to stand there and pretend to know the hearts and souls of my parents? You have no idea the matters of forgiveness and repentance that took place within these walls, and whatever they did or did not do had *nothing* to do with my sister."

"As long as you believe that, you will never find peace," the vicar said with a vindictiveness that didn't ring true with the character that Ritcherd believed should be present in *any* clergyman. A part of him knew this man was only human, and that each vicar put his own interpretation to the scriptures. A part of him knew that he was hearing more opinion than doctrine. But something deeper in him, something raw and frightened and hurting, wanted to strangle the man. Knowing that anger would only leave him looking like a fool, he swallowed hard and forced his emotions below the knot gathering in his chest.

Barely calm, Ritcherd retorted, "I will never find peace as long as you're standing there trying to tell me that my sister is rotting in hell because of circumstances that had nothing to do with her. Get out of my house and don't ever come back."

"Ritcherd, my son," the vicar protested, "your own salvation is at risk if you refuse to accept that—"

"My salvation is between me and God, and I don't give a *damn* what you might think about me *or* my family. Now get out!" The vicar hesitated and he shouted. "Now!"

The vicar scurried from the room, closing the door behind him. The moment he was gone, the anger Ritcherd had been fighting to suppress rushed up and exploded somewhere between his heart and his head. He reached for the nearest tangible object, which happened to be a small porcelain statue. He hurled it at the wall, where it shattered. Kyrah's breathless scream reminded him that he wasn't alone. He turned to see the terror in her eyes and a dozen disjointed memories flitted through his mind, leaving him with the formless sensation that he had been born to suffer, and those he loved would suffer right along with him. Perhaps he too was cursed because of the sins of his parents, and inevitably destined for hell. Looking into Kyrah's eyes, he briefly recalled the horrors she had endured as a direct result of his poor choices, his anger, the life he'd been born to, and he wondered what she had done to deserve being sentenced to live her life tethered to a man like himself.

Her eyes softened with the same love and concern that she'd given him unquestioningly for most of his life, but he felt so undeserving, so thoroughly ashamed. "Ritcherd," she said gently, stepping toward him, "you must know that what he said isn't true. This particular vicar has always been prone to putting his own interpretation into his sermons, and—"

"Don't patronize me, Kyrah," he snarled, wondering how such words could come from himself.

She lifted her chin and spoke firmly. "I have *never* patronized you, Ritcherd. And I don't care how hurt or angry or confused you might be, you will not speak to me that way. I have done nothing to deserve your disdain."

Ritcherd knew she was right, but he couldn't find the words to tell her that he didn't know how to feel anything *but* hurt and angry and confused. So he just turned on his heel and left the room, slamming the door behind him.

Kyrah slumped into a chair and cried for only a few minutes before she convinced herself that no amount of tears would solve this problem. With a prayer in her heart, she went upstairs to spend some time with Cetty, hoping to buffer the effect of her father's neglect. She was grateful for Pearl, the young governess, who was gifted at not only caring for Cetty, but keeping her distracted and happy much of the time. While Kyrah was careful not to let Pearl take her place as a mother, it was good to have someone see that Cetty was cared for and secure, especially with such difficult circumstances going on in her life. While Pearl took a break, Kyrah played with her daughter, wondering where Ritcherd was and what he might be doing. While she longed to seek him out and talk with him, she felt certain that such efforts would only leave her more frustrated.

He appeared at dinner, as quiet and despondent as he'd been for days, but there was an added darkness in his eyes that increased her inner fear. He rose from the table before she was finished eating, and she didn't see him again until she crawled into bed that night and found him already there.

"Are you awake?" she whispered. He grunted in response but kept his back turned to her. "Ritcherd," she said gently, putting her hands to his back, "we need to talk. We can't go on this way."

"I don't know what to say, Kyrah." He sounded angry.

"Just . . . tell me what you're feeling. Let's talk about it. We've been through so much; surely we can get through this—together."

"Kyrah," he sounded more calm, but his voice was tight, almost forced, "I appreciate your concern, but I don't want my struggles to be a burden to you."

"You could never be a burden to me, Ritcherd. I love you. I love you more than life."

He sighed loudly. "For that I am grateful," he said, "but I need to deal with this on my own."

Following several minutes of silence, Kyrah took a deep breath and pressed her hands around to his chest. She felt him tense but put her lips close to his ear. "Ritcherd," she whispered, "it's been so long. You've not even held me since you returned from London. We'll never get a baby this way."

"Forgive me, Kyrah," he said, gently pushing her hands away, "but I'm just not up to it."

Ignoring her previous conviction that crying would do no good, Kyrah eased away and turned over, weeping silent tears into her pillow. She'd never felt so completely alone in all her life.

Garret glanced around the captain's cabin of the *Phoenix* and determined that he had everything he needed to leave the ship in the care of others for the next few months. Home was so close he could almost taste it. The months since he'd been in England had left him starving for the company and affection of those he cared for most. His delays at sea had been more frustrating than usual, and he'd felt an urgency that told him his plans to spend these months at home likely had more purpose than his initial desire to simply be with his family. The *Phoenix* had docked with the evening tide, and Garret had stayed up late going over last-minute details with the crew. He'd risen at dawn to finish his packing, and now that breakfast was over, he was counting the minutes until he could be within the walls of Buckley Manor. He removed the gold earring he wore when he sailed and tucked it away, wanting to look more civilized for the next few months.

A light knock at the door preceded the entry of George Morley, his first mate and a close friend. "Good, you're here," Garret said, throwing his saddlebags over his shoulder. "Did you get me a horse from the livery?"

"I did," George said in an unusually somber tone that caught Garret's attention.

"What?" Garret demanded.

"I'm afraid you won't be leaving just yet."

"What's wrong?" Garret growled, wondering what evil force was trying to keep him from going home.

"We've been boarded."

"Boarded?" Garret echoed, his voice gravelly. "What on earth would . . ."

"I don't know," George said. "There's a Mr. Thayer who wants to see you, and he's got a couple of mates that don't look very friendly. He introduced himself as an investigator with His Majesty's Committee of National Security."

"Good heavens," Garret muttered, not liking the sound of this at all.

"You'd do well to hurry, I think," George said.

"This is just what I need," Garret growled with sarcasm, tossing his bags onto the bed.

He hurried to the deck with George just behind him. His first impression of the three men waiting for him was their intimidating demeanor. Garret knew well how to be intimidating when he wanted to be; it had been a matter of survival through certain endeavors of his past. But coming face-to-face with these men, he felt intimidated. He was also quick to notice their refined manner. These were not third-rate thugs.

"Joe Thayer," the man in the middle said, extending a hand as if this were going to be a friendly chat. "I assume you are Captain Garret."

"That's right," Garret said, cautiously shaking the man's hand. At such moments he was grateful that he'd established himself in this business with only the use of his given name. Practically no one knew his full legal name, and he liked it that way. "What might I do for you?"

"I'll just need to have a look at the ship's records," he said, "while these men have a look around. They'll start with the cargo holds."

Garret countered firmly. "I'll just need to see some proof that you are who you say you are."

Mr. Thayer calmly pulled a folded paper from the inside pocket of his coat and handed it to him. Garret took his time looking it over. It certainly looked legitimate. Mr. Thayer's bored confidence compelled him to agree to the search. He handed the paper back and motioned with his arm toward the stairwell.

"Mr. Morley," Garret said, "would you and Patrick please give these gentleman a tour." He nodded toward Mr. Thayer. "If you'll come with me . . ."

Garret led the way to his cabin and motioned toward the ship's log left open on his desk. While Mr. Thayer was thumbing through its pages, Garret opened a cabinet and said, "Everything else is here."

Garret paced quietly while this man took his time looking through one record book after another. "Your record keeping is impressive," he commented. Garret just grunted and kept pacing, hating the violation he felt at having his records canvassed by a perfect stranger.

Garret finally forced himself to sit down, since Mr. Thayer was obviously going to keep taking his time. He smoked a cigar until it was far too small to hold, then he smoked another. Nearly two hours after entering the cabin, this man slammed the book closed in his hands and said, "There are no records prior to the end of the war."

Garret's heart quickened as he heard a clue as to what this might be about. He looked at Mr. Thayer firmly and spoke in an even voice. "They were lost in a fire. The *Phoenix* was attacked at sea and left burning."

"I see," he said. "And what exactly was the *Phoenix* engaged in during the war?"

Again Garret kept his voice steady and his eyes firm. "The same thing she is engaged in now. World trade. We buy things in one country and sell them in another. It's a simple equation."

"It is indeed, Captain. Unless, of course, you're buying the goods of war and selling them to the enemy. That would not be world trade, Captain. That would be treason."

"It would be," Garret said coolly.

"The *Phoenix* is registered as a British vessel. If she had been engaged in any activity in favor of the American colonists—and against the crown—that would be a shame."

"It would be," Garret repeated. "But I can assure you that's not the case."

"Well, we'll see about that," Mr. Thayer said, moving toward the door. "The *Phoenix* is officially grounded until further notice."

"For what purpose?" Garret demanded, erupting to his feet.

Mr. Thayer turned toward him with his hand on the door. "This ship and her owners are under official investigation for treason against crown and country during the American Revolution, Captain. You and your partner, Captain Buchanan, would do well to cooperate. The two of you are now officially linked to a thorough investigation into British citizens aiding the colonist cause during the Revolution. We will be contacting you within the next few weeks. In the meantime, if the *Phoenix* leaves this spot, she will be permanently confiscated."

Garret swallowed carefully and took a deep breath, knowing better than to argue with this man. He settled for saying, "I will not be on board. I'm on my way home to—"

"I know where you're going, Captain. And I'll expect to find you at your brother's home should I need to talk with you—or him. Enjoy your visit. You can save me the trouble of informing Captain Buchanan of the charges against him."

"Charges?" he countered. "You just said it was an investigation."

"Give it time," Mr. Thayer said and hurried from the cabin.

"Blast!" Garret muttered into the empty room before he followed the messenger of doom back to the deck.

Once Mr. Thayer and his mates had left the ship, Garret called the top members of his crew together to discuss the situation, then he left the ship in their care and rode toward home. He relished the Cornish wind in his face, wishing it could drive away the horror of what lay ahead. He wondered how he would break the news to Ritcherd. He wondered, too, if they would ever be able to prove their innocence. Or was this simply the beginning of a problem that would end at the gallows?

When Buckley Manor came into view, Garret forced all dismal thoughts from his mind. He was home, and he would be staying long enough to fill his starving soul with the presence of those he loved most. They could deal with accusations of treason later on.

Garret rode into the stables of Buckley Manor and gladly relinquished his horse to the stablemaster. He was so anxious to get inside he could hardly bear it.

"Thank you, Kendall," he said as he dismounted.

"It's good to have you home, Captain," he said.

"It is *so* good to be here," he replied, then practically ran to the side door of the house. He tossed his cloak and gloves onto a chair and took the stairs three at a time. His first destination was always the nursery. Not only did he always look forward to seeing Cetty, but Celeste was often there playing with her, and one or both of Cetty's parents were usually nearby. He'd learned long ago that the heart of Buckley Manor was its nursery. He hesitated at the door to catch his breath, then he pushed it slowly open. It was only a matter of seconds before he got the expected greeting.

"Uncle Garret!" Cetty squealed and ran toward him. He scooped her into his arms and laughed, turning in circles. "Did you bring me a present?" she asked when he finally stopped spinning.

"I did," he said and reached a hand into his coat pocket. He pulled out a closed fist and held it in front of her. "What do *I* get?" he asked. She kissed him loudly and he opened his hand.

Cetty gasped and lifted the finely crafted little brass bird out of his palm. "It's beautiful, Uncle Garret. Where did you get it?"

"Guess."

"Italy."

"No. Not even close."

"America."

"No."

"China."

"No, but you're getting closer."

"I know. It's the place with the elephants."

"That's right," he said. "It came from India. And we can tie it on a string and hang it above your bed so you can watch it flying when you wake up in the morning."

"I'm going to show Mama," she said and he set her down. "Mama! Mama!" she called, running into the hall.

He watched her leave, then turned to see Ritcherd leaning in the doorframe that led from the adjoining sitting room. "Well, hello," he said an instant before he realized something was terribly wrong. When Ritcherd said nothing, he stated the obvious. "You don't look so well. Is something—"

"It's good to see you, Garret," he said tonelessly. "I'm glad you're safe." He turned away and went back into the sitting room. Garret followed and found Ritcherd gazing out the window, his hands clasped behind his back. He took a sharp breath when he noticed the black armband around Ritcherd's upper arm. *Mourning?* His heart quickened as he quickly made a tally. Ritcherd was here. Cetty had gone for Kyrah. Could it be Kyrah's mother? *Or Celeste?*

Garret fought against the knot gathering in his throat, knowing he had to ask. Before the words could form, Kyrah rushed into the room—wearing black.

"Oh, you are here!" she exclaimed, sweeping him into her embrace. She held him so tightly that he could feel her arms trembling.

He took hold of her shoulders and looked into her eyes. "What's happened?" he asked quietly. His dread deepened when the tears he saw in her eyes were not of grief, but of fear. When she said nothing, he searched her eyes and found there a definite plea for help. She discreetly glanced toward Ritcherd, who was still staring out the window, his eyes hollow and distant. She gave a slight nod, and he felt relatively certain she wanted him to pose his question to Ritcherd.

Garret nodded in return and stepped toward Ritcherd. "What's happened?" he repeated.

Ritcherd glanced briefly toward him, then at Kyrah, as if he were somehow angry with her for not providing the answer.

"Well?" Garret pressed. "Do I have to slap it out of you?"

Ritcherd turned back toward the window. His voice was raspy as he stated, "Celeste is gone."

Hearing the reality, Garret felt a little queasy. He reached out a hand toward the wall to steady himself. *He couldn't believe it!* There were a hundred questions he wanted to ask, but he couldn't even form a cohesive sentence. He finally managed to sputter, "What happened?"

"What difference does it make?" Ritcherd growled. "She's gone."

"She's my sister!" Garret retorted. "I have a right to know what happened!"

"You probably do," Ritcherd said, moving toward the door, "but I'm not going to be the one to tell you." He left the room abruptly.

Garret swallowed hard and turned to find Kyrah with a hand pressed over her mouth and tears streaming down her face from beneath closed eyelids. *Kyrah.* She was so beautiful! He felt momentarily distracted from his grief as he soaked her presence into himself. His vivid memories and constant thoughts of her never did justice to the reality of being in her presence. Seeing her in pain was likely more difficult for him to endure than any other trial life could dish out to him. And keeping his feelings for her in perspective was no doubt harder than any other challenge he had to conquer. The fact that he was hopelessly in love with his brother's wife was no secret in this household. Ritcherd and Kyrah were both well aware of his feelings. The situation had initially stirred up a great deal of grief and contention, but once Garret had made it inescapably clear that he would never do anything to hurt either one of them, they had all taken a relaxed stand. His feelings were now addressed with a certain amount of humor. But he'd only been home five minutes, and there was nothing humorous about the situation he'd just stepped into the middle of. Celeste was dead. Ritcherd was angry. And Kyrah was hurting. The urgency he'd felt to get home now made perfect sense, but now that he was here, he wasn't sure what to do about it.

Kyrah opened her eyes to see Garret watching her. He looked the same as he always had. His dark hair was pulled back into a fashionable ponytail, albeit he wore his hair longer than most men. An equally dark, neatly trimmed beard framed his firm features well. His eyes were still the most intense she had ever seen. She had hoped and prayed for many long months that he would find someone to love, a woman who could fill his heart and erase the fruitless feelings she knew he held for her. But the love in his eyes was as evident as ever. While she had learned to ignore his feelings, and she'd never once felt uncomfortable with them since her marriage to Ritcherd, she now felt somehow comforted to see such blatant adoration. She'd seen nothing at all in Ritcherd's eyes for weeks.

"What happened, Kyrah?" he asked gently.

Kyrah glanced down to see Cetty standing close by. She quickly wiped her tears with a handkerchief and held up a finger toward Garret to indicate that he give her a moment. She distracted Cetty with a picture book she'd not looked at in a long time, and left her in Pearl's care before she took Garret's hand and led him down the hall to her personal sitting room. Once inside, she closed the door, but Garret immediately opened it, giving her a hard stare. She'd forgotten how careful he had always been to never be alone with her behind closed doors. He'd assured her in the past that it was simply a matter of principle because he had no intention of ever crossing inappropriate boundaries with her. He knew she and Ritcherd loved each other, and their marriage was strong and good. She wondered now if he sensed the rift between her and her husband.

Garret sat down and watched Kyrah do the same while he tried to convince himself that Celeste was really gone. He felt a burning in his eyes that barely overpowered the heat growing in his throat. When Kyrah said nothing, he repeated his question. "What happened?"

Kyrah took a deep breath. "She . . . uh . . . had been ill off and on for quite some time, but it got dramatically worse and . . . the doctors could tell us nothing. We finally got word of a specialist who worked with conditions such as Celeste's. We were able to get him to come the same week that Ritcherd had to go to London for business. He came the day before Ritcherd returned and spent some time with her. By the time Ritcherd returned, Celeste had eaten nothing for days and she was sleeping most of the time. Dr. Gates told us that she was a living miracle."

"Really?"

Kyrah nodded. "He'd never known of anyone with her condition to live to the age of twenty. In essence, she was dying of old age."

Garret drew a sharp breath and let it out slowly. "I see," he said, his voice breaking. He was no longer able to hold back the tears, and they fell steadily down his face as Kyrah went on.

"She died that night. She just . . . went to sleep and never woke up. The funeral was beautiful. It was evident that everyone who knew her, loved her. For myself, I was able to find great comfort. As I see it, these years that she lived since her mother's death have been a gift, a miracle. Rather than resenting her absence now, I feel blessed to have had her in our lives at all."

"Well put," Garret said and sniffled. He wiped his face with a handkerchief and muttered, "I can't believe she's gone. I've thought about her so much. I've looked forward to spending time with her as much as anyone." He sighed loudly. "If only I could have gotten here sooner."

"You did the best you could," she said. "I'm just grateful that you're here now."

"Yes, so am I." They both cried silently for several minutes before Garret added, "Where is Sarah?"

Kyrah dabbed at her reddening eyes. "She's in London, actually. She went to spend some time with her friend, Miss Hatch. You remember; she was the schoolmistress in the area who mostly raised my mother. She's getting on in years and struggling with her health. Mother felt she should spend some significant time with her. Ritcherd accompanied her there when he went to London. We notified her of the death, but she felt she needed to stay with Miss Hatch, so she missed the funeral. She'll be back for Christmas."

"I see," Garret said, unable to hide his disappointment. Kyrah's mother was another of the lights in his life. Having her absent through the bulk of his stay was a definite drawback. He felt a momentary longing to be back on the *Phoenix,* somewhere at sea, oblivious to the heartache he was now feeling. But turning to look at Kyrah, he could see that his presence here was needed. He wasn't certain what exactly was going on—beyond the death of a family member—but he knew something wasn't right. He felt certain that with time he'd figure it out. For the moment, he felt compelled to approach another subject— however sensitive.

"Forgive me, Kyrah, but I expected you to look the way you did when I first met you." She looked disoriented and he added gently, "You were pregnant when I left six months ago. I expected you to be about ready to deliver."

Kyrah looked intently at her hands that were wringing her handkerchief. "Yes, well . . . so did I, but . . . we lost the baby." New tears showed in her eyes. "It was a girl. We lost her about halfway along. The doctor couldn't tell us why. Ritcherd took it very hard."

"And you?" he asked with a tenderness in his voice that heightened her flow of tears.

"And me," she stated.

"But there's still hope for more children?" he asked. Again she looked confused by the question and he clarified, "You're all right . . . physically? It's still possible?"

"Yes," she said, then her voice turned subtly acrid. "Although at this rate, there will *never* be another baby." Garret's astonished expression made Kyrah realize what she'd just said. "I'm sorry," she added. "You really didn't need to know that."

"Or perhaps I did," he said curtly. "What are you saying, Kyrah?"

She sighed and looked down. "He's not so much as kissed me since the day he returned from London."

"And how long is that?"

"More than a month."

"Well, he's a fool," Garret muttered.

"He's struggling with Celeste's death," she said in Ritcherd's defense.

"And how are you, Kyrah?" Garret asked. "And don't lie to me."

"I've never lied to you."

"I know. But I have a feeling you'd like to now."

"Why is that?" she asked without looking at him.

"Because you're hurting. You're scared. But worst of all, you're lonely."

"You've only been home twenty minutes, Garret. How can you possibly know what I—"

"And I figured out that much in the first two minutes. Am I right or not?" he asked and she only looked away. "And you don't want to talk to me—at least not about that. I'm the last person you want to admit such things to—especially the lonely part . . . because you know how I feel about you."

Kyrah's sharp glare let him know that he'd pegged the situation accurately—at least to some degree. When she turned just as abruptly away, he said gently, "Kyrah, you know me better than to think that I would take unfair advantage of a difficult situation. You should know I would *never* do anything to hurt you *or* Ritcherd."

"I know that," she said firmly.

"Then why won't you talk to me?"

She looked at him with a determination in her eyes that he'd been trying to coax out of her. "Yes, Garret, you're right. I am hurt, and scared, and lonely. But don't think I'm sitting around feeling sorry for myself. It's Ritcherd I'm worried about, and it's Ritcherd you should be talking to—if you can get him to talk at all. God knows I've tried. He's completely shut me out, Garret. He won't talk to me beyond the most minimal exchange. He won't even look at me. He's so lost in some kind of horrible pain that I can't even reach him. He's reminding me very much of his behavior aboard the *Phoenix* before we were married." Garret's eyes widened. He knew that Ritcherd's behavior then had been deplorable. He felt a bit relieved when she quickly added, "Of course, he's not been nearly so angry as he was then."

"That's somewhat of an improvement," Garret said.

"Although he did throw a porcelain figure at the wall after the vicar left."

Garret's eyes widened further. "At least he didn't throw it at the vicar."

"I think he would have liked to, but then . . . I've felt angry enough with the vicar since that day that I think I'd like to throw something at him myself."

"What did the vicar say?"

"Maybe you should get Ritcherd's version of that. Perhaps it would get him talking; perhaps it would give you some insight into what's going on in his head. I'm hoping beyond hope that he'll talk to you. If he doesn't talk to somebody, I fear . . ."

"You fear what, Kyrah?"

Kyrah looked away, feeling her chin quiver as he prodded too close to her deepest concerns. "Maybe my fear is disproportionate, Garret. It probably has a lot more to do with what my father did than any valid concern I should have with Ritcherd. But I never expected my father to shoot himself in the head, and he did."

"Do you really believe it's as bad as all that?"

"I don't know, Garret. When he's not shared *anything* with me for more than a month, how can I have any idea how bad it is?"

Garret blew out a long breath. "I'll do my best to talk to Ritcherd," he said, and she sighed audibly. "But if it's as bad as you say, I'm not sure he'll want to talk to me either. Why don't you tell me what the vicar said, and then I can compare his version to yours—if he'll tell me at all."

Kyrah's expression became immediately agitated, and he felt certain she'd meant it when she said she wanted to throw something at the vicar. "First of all," she said, "let me say that this particular vicar is a good man, but we've been well aware—as have many people in the community—that he often takes a slightly distorted approach to certain doctrines. But people like him and they're generally willing to overlook his shortcomings and appreciate the good in him. Sometimes we just have to separate human weakness from the man's calling."

"Sounds reasonable," he said.

"Well, Ritcherd was already struggling when the vicar came by to check on us. To put it succinctly, he told us that we would never find peace if we concern ourselves with where Celeste is now. He implied quite strongly that her condition made her eternal fate questionable."

"What?" Garret retorted in a voice that was uncharacteristic of his usual controlled demeanor.

"He quoted scripture, Garret. He said, 'For I the Lord thy God am a jealous God, visiting the iniquity of the fathers upon the children.' And then he said that Ritcherd's parents were guilty of many sins, and he implied that Celeste's condition was some kind of curse that resulted."

"He didn't!"

"Oh, he did," she said firmly. "Ritcherd told him exactly what he thought about that and told him to get out and never come back. Then he threw that porcelain statue at the wall, and what was bad has been worse ever since. Needless to say, he's not been to church. In fact, he's not been anywhere at all since the funeral. I've tried to get him to go into town with me, or for a walk . . . riding, anything. It's almost as if he's . . ."

"What?" Garret demanded when she hesitated.

"Like he's afraid to leave the house."

Garret stood up abruptly and moved toward the door.

"Where are you going?" Kyrah demanded.

"I'm going to find a Bible, and then I'm going to have a little talk with my brother."

Kyrah sighed and watched him go, praying with all the strength she had that Garret could get through to Ritcherd, and this horrible torment could be over.

Chapter Three

The Trigger

Ritcherd sat on the edge of his bed, just wanting to climb in it and never get out. He pressed his head into his hands and sighed, wishing he could find a way to be free of this inner torment. No matter which direction he attempted to steer his thoughts, they always ended up in dark caverns of difficult memories, which circled back to the present emptiness he was feeling. He felt helpless and lost, and certain that, given Kyrah's present frustrations with him, she would likely be better off without him.

"May I come in?" Garret asked.

Ritcherd looked up to see him standing in the open doorway. "Sure. Come in."

Garret walked to a chair and sat down, holding a book with his finger tucked between the pages. "What did the vicar say?" he asked.

Ritcherd let out a disgusted sigh. "Don't beat around the bush, Garret," he said with sarcasm. "Just get straight to the point."

"Just answer the question."

"You've been talking to my wife."

"Of course I've been talking to your wife. Next to you, she's my best friend. Now tell me what the vicar said."

"It's irrelevant."

"I don't think so. Maybe what he said is irrelevant, but how it affected you is highly relevant—at least it is to me. So, what did he say?"

"He said that Celeste would go to hell because of her parents' sins."

"That's pretty nasty," Garret said, "especially considering that *I* am one of her parents' sins. Of course the vicar is well aware—as is everyone else in this community—that you have an *illegitimate* half-brother living under your roof. I'm certain that my existence has contributed to his judgmental theories."

"Perhaps," Ritcherd said, "but I don't really care *what* he said."

"Oh, I think you do. Or perhaps . . . the fact that he quoted the Bible to you makes you care. I know you believe in the book and respect it." Garret saw the tiniest glimmer of intrigue showing through the darkness of Ritcherd's eyes. "So let me tell you something about the Bible, Ritcherd," Garret went on. "A line or two taken out of context can be twisted to mean just about anything a person wants it to mean. It's important to look at the full perspective. Now, I'd like to talk about Celeste for a moment, if I may. Do you have any comprehension of what a miracle her very existence was?"

Ritcherd squeezed his eyes closed and his expression betrayed overt pain.

"Yes, I'm sure you do. Everyone who knew her loved her. She shed light and joy. She touched lives for good. She taught us all a great deal about what's important in this world. Would you not say that her purpose in this world was good and right?"

"Absolutely," Ritcherd said with conviction.

"Read this," Garret stood and handed the open book to Ritcherd, pointing at a particular spot. Seeing that it was the Bible, he felt momentarily hesitant. "Verses one through three," Garret added. "Read it out loud."

Ritcherd cleared his throat and tried to focus. "And as Jesus passed by, he saw a man which was blind from his birth. And his disciples asked him, saying, Master, who did sin, this man, or his parents, that he was born blind?'"

Ritcherd stopped and looked up at Garret, who said, "Keep reading."

Ritcherd read on. "'Jesus answered, Neither hath this man sinned, nor his parents: but that the works of God should be made manifest in him.'"

"And then Jesus healed him. So you see," Garret said, taking the book from Ritcherd, "Celeste was born into the world with a perfect spirit that remained perfect so that she could be an angel on earth and spread a little bit of God's love around. That's how I see it. And I think the vicar ought to have his head examined."

Ritcherd sighed. He couldn't deny that Garret's perspective helped immensely on that one count, but he still felt as if an impenetrable cloud had settled over his mind. He said curtly, "Or maybe I should have *my* head examined."

"Why is that?" Garret asked, sitting back down and setting the Bible aside.

"I don't know. I just feel . . . crazy. I don't know why I can't just . . . get past this and . . ."

"It's not been so long. You're entitled to grieve for your sister. But I get the feeling there's more than that going on."

"Whatever gave you that idea?" Ritcherd snarled sarcastically.

"Oh, your snappy attitude, for one. So, maybe you ought to just tell me what's eating at you, instead of having your head examined."

"Well, I don't want to talk about it," Ritcherd said and left the room.

Garret sighed and picked up the Bible, thumbing through the pages while he muttered to himself, "Am I my brother's keeper?" He made a dubious noise and slammed the book closed.

Kyrah vigorously scrubbed one potato after another while the kitchen maids chattered nearby. She enjoyed the distraction of their conversation and laughter, and she appreciated the satisfaction she found in doing ordinary tasks that had once been a way of life for her. Setting a clean potato aside and picking up another, her mind wandered to her own simple upbringing, and the years she'd had to work every waking hour just to keep herself and her mother fed and sheltered. She was grateful beyond words to have the financial security of being Mrs. Ritcherd Buchanan, but she'd never been comfortable with being Lady Buckley. She'd insisted from the start that the servants call her Mrs. Buchanan, as opposed to the aristocratic title she'd gained upon becoming Ritcherd's wife. After all, she was married to Ritcherd, not his title.

Soon after her marriage, the servants had all been surprised by her insistence on helping with household chores, rather than simply overseeing them. But they had gradually become accustomed to her desire to work *with* the staff, as opposed to having them work *for* her. She marveled that the bulk of the aristocratic people she knew spent their time doing nothing of any value. There seemed to be some prestige in being considered ladies and gentlemen, with no need to work or be busy, but Kyrah didn't understand it. Ritcherd had generally agreed with her theories, and she had seen him work very hard in the gardens or the stables. But lately he'd taken to doing nothing at all. She felt sure his idleness was contributing to his ongoing depression. She wondered, if he'd had no choice but to work in order to provide for his family, he might be less inclined to feel sorry for himself. But she'd already had that particular conversation with him, and he'd paid her no mind. His hiding in idleness was completely incompatible with her hiding in hard work. And in truth, he paid no mind to anything she said these days; she'd become invisible to him, and the reality broke her heart. Deep inside, she couldn't help wondering if the social differences they'd grown up with had finally come between them, as she'd always feared they might.

Kyrah scrubbed more vigorously as her thoughts became more tormented. She was startled to hear Garret say, "Are you cleaning it or wearing it out?"

Kyrah looked down to see that the potato in her hands had turned white since she'd completely scrubbed away the skin. "Wearing it out, apparently," she said, setting it aside. She wiped her hands on her apron while Garret washed his own hands at a nearby sink. She knew he'd been out in the stables the better part of the afternoon, likely for the same reason she'd been working in the kitchen. On his visits home he usually spent time each day in the stables, doing whatever might need doing. Ritcherd would generally accompany him, but Ritcherd hadn't gone anywhere or done anything for weeks now.

When Garret had finished washing up, he flirted with the kitchen maids and teased them until they were all giggling and blushing. Kyrah couldn't help smiling to observe their interaction. Garret was so thoroughly genuine, even in his teasing. His playfulness was touching, but at the same time it evoked an undefinable heartache in her.

She wondered how long it had been since she'd seen Ritcherd laugh or tease or even smile. A familiar burning crept into her eyes and throat but she fought to hold it back. As the maids scurried back to work, Kyrah felt Garret's eyes come to rest on her. "And how are you, Lady Buckley?"

His use of her title was subtly facetious, so she retorted in the same tone, "I'm well, Sir Garret. And you?"

"It's good to be home," he said.

"It's good to have you home," she said, not prepared to have her emotion force its way back to the surface rather suddenly. She forced a smile toward Garret and left the kitchen, removing her apron as she left and hanging it near the door. Her hope that Garret would remain in the kitchen was dashed when she heard his footsteps behind her.

"Now that we're alone," he said, catching up to her, "you can tell me the truth."

She scowled at him and kept walking. "I have much to be grateful for," she said, her voice quavering only slightly.

"Yes, and so do I," Garret said, "but that doesn't eliminate the fact that we are both terribly concerned about your husband. I think this situation is a lot more difficult than you're letting on. Your courage is admirable, Kyrah, but there's no need for pretenses with me."

"Courage?" she scoffed. "I feel anything but courageous. While Ritcherd is completely lost in his own concerns—whatever they may be—I'm becoming very adept at feeling sorry for myself."

"I think it's Ritcherd feeling sorry for himself," Garret countered.

"Whatever it is," Kyrah said, "I hate it, and I don't want to talk about it."

Kyrah quickened her pace as if to say that she'd said all she intended to, and she wanted to be alone. Garret let her go, watching her walk away while his heart threatened to crack wide open. For the hundredth time since his return home, he told himself that he needed to mind his own business and keep his distance. But, oh how he hurt for her! And the entire situation made him just plain angry. He simply didn't know what to do about it, so he went outside and enjoyed a lengthy visit with an expensive cigar.

Over the next few days, Garret felt the evidence deepen that Ritcherd was deeply troubled and not handling the situation well at all. Kyrah's unhappiness was readily evident, even though he knew she was working hard at putting up a brave front. Ritcherd wandered the house like a ghost, unwilling to talk or interact. He appeared at meals but said practically nothing. Garret attempted to make light conversation with Kyrah, but gradually even that became too much work. He kept telling himself that he needed to stay out of it; he needed to let Ritcherd and Kyrah work this out between themselves. But he wondered if that was his own fear talking. Was he simply afraid to get too involved, knowing that he was far from indifferent toward both of them? More accurately, toward Kyrah. He didn't want to admit—even to himself—that seeing her hurt this way made his feelings for her doubly difficult.

Through his own attempts to deal with the fact that Celeste was gone, he found himself struggling with his own grief. He had loved Celeste dearly, and her absence in the house was keenly felt. Still, he had not interacted with her day in and day out as Ritcherd had done. He just wished he could find a way to reach whatever was *really* bothering Ritcherd. Occasionally Garret would recall the situation with the *Phoenix* and feel tangibly ill. He didn't want to even think about it, let alone talk about it. But he felt relatively certain that Mr. Thayer and his friends would be showing up with more questions, and they had to be prepared.

Garret found Ritcherd in the library. It wasn't an unusual place to find him. Ritcherd loved to read, and the collection of books here was exceptional. But Ritcherd wasn't reading. He sat at one end of a long sofa, his ankle crossed over his knee, his elbow leaning on the arm of the sofa, his head in his hand. Garret made no effort to enter the room quietly, but Ritcherd made no indication that he was aware of his presence.

"Daydreaming?" Garret said, and Ritcherd raised his head abruptly, startled.

He looked up at Garret with an expression of total indifference. "Not exactly," he said, his voice toneless. "Did you need something?" he asked with a clear insinuation that he wanted to be alone.

"I'm afraid I do," Garret said, sitting down across from him. "There's something I need to tell you. I hate to even bring it up. Under the circumstances, I don't want to add to your burden."

"What's wrong?" Ritcherd demanded with the first real interest Garret had seen in days.

"I'll just get right to the point. The *Phoenix* was grounded the morning after we came into port."

"Grounded?" Ritcherd echoed breathlessly.

"That's right. She is grounded pending the investigation."

"What investigation?"

"Her owners—specifically you and I are—"

"I know who her owners are," Ritcherd interrupted tersely. "What investigation?"

"Treason."

A long minute of deathly silence preceded Ritcherd's stunned response. "Heaven help us."

"Amen," Garret muttered.

"But . . . why . . . and how?"

"I do not know," Garret said. "I was told nothing except that our names had come up as the result of some thorough investigation into British citizens aiding the colonist cause during the Revolution."

"But the war is long over."

"It would seem that to these people, the war being over is irrelevant."

"*What* people?"

"The officials who boarded and searched my ship, thoroughly canvassed the records, and disabled the helm."

"Good heavens," Ritcherd muttered and rubbed a hand over his face.

"You know what bothers me most?" Garret said.

"What?"

"The fact that we're guilty."

Ritcherd sighed. "Yes, that bothers me, too." He turned to Garret. "So, what are we going to do?"

"We're going to keep a straight face, be cooperative, and answer all the right questions in the right way."

"You mean we're going to lie to save our hides."

"That's exactly what I mean," Garret said.

"And I thought we were men of integrity."

"We are," Garret insisted. "Men of integrity who fought for and believed in a cause; a cause that stood up against tyranny and oppression. I'd do it again and I believe you would, too."

"Yes, I would," Ritcherd admitted.

"And if we go to the gallows and all of our property is confiscated, where does that leave your family?" Ritcherd took a sharp breath and Garret added, "You'd better believe we will lie, dear brother. We will do whatever we have to in order to keep what we have—including our necks."

Nothing was said for several minutes and Garret could easily imagine this giving Ritcherd one more reason to hide in his depression. Hoping to get him to think about what he was doing, he decided perhaps it was time to provoke him to a broader perspective.

"So, how's your wife?" Garret asked.

"You see her as much as I do."

"And why is that?" Garret asked. "Seeing that she's *your* wife, I would think you'd be spending a whole lot more time with her than I do. Judging from what little time I've spent with her, I'd say she seems awfully unhappy." Ritcherd said nothing and Garret added, "So, what are you going to do about it?"

"My relationship with my wife is my concern," Ritcherd said indignantly.

"Relationship? Is that what you call it? Is glancing at her over the breakfast table what you consider a relationship? That sounds suspiciously like the *relationship* you once shared with your mother."

Ritcherd bristled visibly but his voice maintained its acrid tone. "Kyrah is nothing like my mother."

"No, she's certainly not—at least not the mother you knew most of your life. But apparently you are still the same man. Kyrah does not deserve to be shut out of your life because of whatever you might be carrying around in your deluded head." Garret saw Ritcherd's anger deepen, but he leaned forward and added firmly, "She does not deserve to be punished for your mother's sins."

A barely perceptible flicker of enlightenment showed in Ritcherd's eyes before they hardened further. "You have no idea what you're talking about."

"Maybe I don't. But I know that Kyrah is hurting—and I know it's your fault."

"Whether she is or not, Kyrah is my concern."

"If either one of us truly believed that, then you would be doing something about this problem. As it is, she certainly *is* my concern, whether you like it or not."

"And how is that?" Ritcherd countered snidely.

"I love Kyrah," Garret said with no hint of apology or remorse.

Ritcherd's eyes widened. "You just had to remind me of that . . . now."

"It seems you need reminding. Does knowing there's another man under your roof who is in love with your wife make a difference? It should."

"What are you implying?" Ritcherd asked firmly.

"I'm not implying anything, my dear brother. I'm making it very clear that I will not stand by and see her hurting and lonely, while you are unwilling to do anything about it."

Ritcherd's eyes widened further. "You once told me that you were a gentleman, a man ruled by your head, not your heart. You made it clear that you would never do anything to hurt either of us, that you would never come between us."

"I also told you that if you ever hurt her, I would give you a fat lip. I'm a gentleman, not a saint. And I'm not going to lie to you, Ritcherd. My head grows weaker when my heart sees her in such anguish. And you should be man enough to realize that the only way to truly keep a woman from straying is to keep her happy. If you would come out of the hole you've carved for yourself long enough to take notice of her, you would plainly see that she is *not* happy. You married her. You pledged your heart and soul to her—for better or worse—to honor and cherish her. You're shirking your duties, man."

Garret expected Ritcherd to get angry. He *wanted* him to be angry. Perhaps anger would incite him to do something about this problem, but Garret's heart sank. A recently familiar indifference clouded Ritcherd's face, prompting Garret to say, "You have much to be grateful for, Ritcherd. You have a beautiful wife and daughter who need you. Do you have any idea how I envy what you've got?"

"So you mentioned a moment ago," Ritcherd said, his voice acrid.

"That's not what I meant," Garret countered, but again Ritcherd only showed indifference. Feeling suddenly angry, he heard himself saying, "What if I told you that Kyrah came to my room last night?" Ritcherd turned toward him, his eyes wide with a fury that completely dispelled the apathy. "She was lonely and desperate. She knew that I would actually take notice of her existence. We talked. She cried. Things got out of hand."

Garret was well prepared for the fist Ritcherd threw toward his face. He grabbed Ritcherd's arm to stop the blow and twisted it behind him. He spoke hotly behind his ear. "At least I know you're still alive. We were beginning to wonder. Now, before you get all upset, I was just trying to get your attention. You should know me better than that. You should know *her* better than that. But as I said, I'm not a saint, Ritcherd. And she's only human—and lonely and hurting. You can't keep shutting her out this way." He let go and Ritcherd turned to face him, his eyes still angry. But Garret wondered if it was enough to provoke him to action. "Again I ask you," Garret said, "what are you going to do about it?"

"What *can* I do?" Ritcherd asked just passively enough to make Garret *really* angry, but he fought to keep his expression steady, as well as his voice.

"You can stop feeling sorry for yourself and let her help you work through this grief, instead of shutting her out."

Ritcherd sighed loudly. "I'm not sure I can do that."

"You can do anything you have to do, and you *have* to do this."

"I can't," he repeated, hanging his head.

"You're a fool, Ritcherd," Garret said and hurried from the room before his growing anger pressed him to say something he'd likely regret—and to give Ritcherd a fat lip at the same time.

Ritcherd looked up to see Kyrah enter the bedroom, where he'd been sitting on the edge of the bed for nearly an hour, just staring at the floor. The determination in her expression made it clear that she'd not come here just to get something and leave again. She wanted to talk, and the very idea made his stomach tighten into knots. How could he ever explain to her what was going on inside of him, when he didn't begin to understand it himself?

"How are you?" she asked gently.

"I'm fine," he lied.

She sighed loudly and her eyes flicked downward briefly before she gazed hard at him, lifting her chin to a courageous tilt. "If I even remotely believed you, I would turn around and leave you in peace. As it is, there's something I need to say."

"I'm listening," he said, wishing it hadn't sounded so caustic. At times he felt as if his self was divided starkly, and while a part of him ached and screamed silently for help and understanding, a more powerful component of his character held back any such pleas, allowing nothing but rancor and indignation into the open. He could feel a tangible black cloud hovering between his heart and his head, a barrier that had refused to allow his fear and vulnerability to be assuaged by his ability to love and be loved. And now he truly wondered if it was possible for love to break through that barrier at all. But he didn't know how to fix it, and he didn't want to talk about it.

Kyrah looked at her husband closely, wishing for the millionth time that she could see in his eyes even a trace of the man she loved, the man who loved her. She'd come here determined to air some of the thoughts that had churned in her head for days now. She feared if she didn't voice them, they would tear her to pieces. She had struggled to find the words to begin, and she had prayed that she might be able to reach his aching spirit. But she reminded herself that she could not penetrate the walls around his heart if he wouldn't allow her inside. All she could do was try.

"Ritcherd," she said, her voice tender, "do you remember what you said to me when I agreed to be your wife?"

Ritcherd bristled and straightened his back. He recalled the gist of the conversation, and already he had no desire to be reminded of it. He said nothing and she continued, "You told me that I was the security of your life, that I was your heart and soul. You said that you couldn't promise difficulties wouldn't come up, or that you would always be agreeable, but you promised that you would never, ever forsake me, that you would never be ashamed or embarrassed to have me by your side. You said you would be committed to me as long as there was breath in you, that you would sacrifice all that you have to keep me safe and happy, and you would do it with joy in your heart." She paused and drew a deep breath. "I remember it well, Ritcherd, because at the time my doubts and fears were many. My deepest fear was that you would become disenchanted with me, that you would regret making me a part of your life because of the differences between us. I knew then as I know now that the social barriers between us are no small thing." She tightened her gaze on him. "Is that what's happened, Ritcherd? Have you come to regret it? Are the barriers between us too wide after all? Do I not fill your life enough for you to want anything to do with me?"

"You misunderstand me, Kyrah."

"Then make me understand, Ritcherd." Her voice broke. "Make me understand why you have not so much as looked at me with anything but indifference for many weeks now. Help me know why I no longer have any value to you."

"You are more valuable to me than anything else in my life," he said, but he said it dispassionately, and she could see something almost patronizing in his eyes.

"Then prove it," she insisted.

When he only looked away abruptly, Kyrah fought back the hurt and frustration consuming her and attempted to focus on her purpose for this conversation. She hoped and prayed with everything inside of her that she could remind him of the love they had once shared, of the promises they'd made. Fearing her hurt and frustration would drive her to anger, she took a full minute to focus her mind and calm her feelings.

"Ritcherd," she said, attempting to will back the tears burning into her eyes, "do you remember when you gave me the diamond necklace and earrings?" He looked at her with the tiniest glimmer of something warm in his eyes. "Remember how we danced in the church ruins? How you . . . held me . . . and kissed me? I felt as if you were my air to breathe." Her tears refused to be held back and they trickled down her face. "I still feel that way."

Ritcherd watched her crying and wondered how many tears she had shed as a result of the pain he'd brought into her life. Could she not look at him and see that he was no good for her? He wondered what kind of woman she was to put up with such nonsense for so many years.

"Tell me you remember," she said.

"Of course I remember," he snapped. "And do you remember what happened only a matter of hours after that?" He saw in her eyes that she knew what he meant, just before she turned them shamefully away. How could either of them ever forget how he had allowed his passion to be ruled by his fear and anger, and he had crossed boundaries with Kyrah that he never should have crossed without first giving her his name? Cetty had resulted from that indiscretion, and the hell that he and Kyrah had gone through before they had finally been able to marry was indescribable. He doubted he could ever forgive himself. And that was just one of many poor choices he'd made through his life, choices that marched through his head incessantly, making him wonder why God had not just completely destroyed him years ago—a solution that would put him and those he loved out of their misery.

"Of course you remember," he said with a cruel edge to his voice that tightened Kyrah's stomach and made her throat go dry. "How could you forget when it was the beginning of your worst nightmare?"

"And yours," she pointed out, sounding less calm.

"And mine," he agreed. "But I'm not the one who ended up married to some degenerate cretin who beat me senseless."

"It was *my* choice to marry Peter, not yours," she insisted. "And I haven't the slightest notion what that has to do with this conversation."

"You're the one who started reminiscing, my dear. And I can't help noticing that you seem terribly unhappy these days." He came to his feet and started pacing but kept his eyes pinned to hers. "Obviously I'm not man enough to keep you happy. Obviously I have broken many promises to you." His voice raised to a shout that Kyrah felt certain could be heard by others in the house. The servants would certainly have something to talk about now. She only prayed that

Garret had gone outside. "Maybe you should be questioning your *own* choices, my dear," Ritcherd shouted louder.

"I have no regrets," she insisted, but he gave her a scoffing laugh.

"How could that be possible when I have brought so much utter misery into your life?" he growled, as if *she* had somehow wronged *him*.

Kyrah stood frozen, watching her husband pace, ranting about the mistake she had made in marrying him and committing her life to him. Instinctively she knew that the real problem was not related to the words coming out of his mouth. Attempting to figure where the true source of his accusations might lie, she came to one horrifying conclusion. He *did* regret marrying her! The social barriers that had existed between them truly had come to a breaking point. What other explanation could there be for his obvious efforts to convince her that they weren't right for each other? As her darkest, most intrinsic fear from the past boiled up from the deepest part of her, she felt an inner burning that threatened to explode.

All through her childhood, and through the years Ritcherd had been away at war, she had been looked down upon and snubbed by those who considered her far beneath a man like Ritcherd Buchanan. While they had done their best to ignore it, she was well aware that many in the community were still disgusted by Ritcherd's choice in a wife. And she knew that the situation had to be difficult for Ritcherd. She had feared that eventually their differences would come between them, and looking into his angry eyes, as he raved on, doing his best to convince her that she had made a mistake, she read easily between the lines. Was this his way of twisting the truth around because he didn't have the courage to face up to what he *really* felt? Did he regret the choice he'd made to lower himself to her standard? Had the years of social disdain finally become too much for him? Had Celeste's death pushed him to a breaking point where he was no longer able to temper his feelings and keep the truth from her?

From his sitting room, Garret overheard Ritcherd shouting and hurried to the hallway outside of Ritcherd and Kyrah's bedroom, where they were obviously arguing. He paced the floor frantically, barely keeping himself from kicking the door in and busting Ritcherd in the jaw for even daring to talk to her like that. He reminded himself that this was between Ritcherd and Kyrah, and he had no right to intervene. Still, he couldn't force himself to leave while his every instinct urged him to stand between Ritcherd and Kyrah and protect her from Ritcherd's anger. He was at least grateful to know that the governess had taken Cetty for a walk in the garden, and she would be spared hearing her parents engaged in such an angry confrontation.

Kyrah suddenly found it difficult to breathe as Ritcherd raged on, telling her all the reasons she would be better off without him. How could she not believe that what he meant, in truth, was that *he* would be better off without *her?* When she could bear his disdain no longer, she felt her fear leap out of her in a scream that she'd never fathomed could come from her own throat. "How dare you stand there and say such things to me! You lied to me, Ritcherd Buchanan! You told me it would never come between us! You promised to love and cherish me, no matter what!"

"Well, maybe you married the wrong man!" he shouted back, while her words and that tone of voice triggered a hundred ugly arguments from the past—with his mother.

"Maybe I did!" she screamed. "The man I married would never have been so cruel and unfeeling . . . so insensitive and heartless!"

"Then why do you put up with it?" he bellowed. "You're a fool, Kyrah Payne!"

"I'm not Kyrah Payne!" she screamed. "I'm Kyrah Buchanan! I'm *your* wife! And *you* are an aristocratic snob!"

Her words triggered a deep, festering hurt in Ritcherd. He drew back a hand and slapped her hard across the face before he even realized he wanted to. The instant his hand connected with her flesh, the horror of what he'd done reverberated back into him, shocking him from the blindness of his anger into an abyss of regret and repulsion that threatened to consume him in a lake of fire and brimstone. The next few seconds seemed eternal as he heard her scream and watched her stagger from the blow. She almost gained her footing, then sank onto the carpet, gasping for breath, holding the side of her face with one hand and breaking her fall with the other.

As Kyrah absorbed the reality of what had just happened, she felt her knees buckle beneath her, not so much from the force of the blow as the memories that came crashing down around her, sucking her to the floor. *Peter. Her first husband. He'd hit her once. And then again, and again, leaving her battered and bruised and alone. She'd wanted to die.* Turning to look at Ritcherd, standing above her, she had no reason to believe that he had not somehow turned into the same kind of horrible monster.

"Oh, Kyrah," he muttered, his voice hoarse and raspy. "I don't know . . . why I . . ." He stepped toward her, his hands outstretched.

"No!" she screamed and recoiled. "Don't *touch* me! You . . . You . . ." Her breathing became so sharp she couldn't speak. Ritcherd took a step back and watched in horror as she pressed her face to the floor and wrapped her arms over her head, shrieking "No!" over and over.

Ritcherd didn't know where Garret had come from, but he felt more grateful than angry to see him there, even given the accusing glare that Garret tossed toward him as he rushed to Kyrah's side. He knelt beside her, gently touching her arm, but she screamed louder and again recoiled.

"It's Garret," he said, taking hold of her shoulders. He shook her gently to stop her ranting as he said more loudly, "Kyrah, it's Garret. It's all right. Everything is all right."

Kyrah lifted her head and opened her eyes to look at him. Garret's inner seething, that had begun when he'd heard the slap and the scream, magnified tenfold when he saw the evidence come into view. Her reddened cheek and the terror in her eyes made him angrier than he'd ever felt in his life. When her eyes focused on him, she gathered his shirt into her fists and cried, "Don't let him hurt me! Please, don't let him hurt me!"

"I promise," he said gently. "I'll never let him hurt you again. I promise."

In response to his promise, she pressed her face to his chest and sobbed. Ritcherd stood frozen and stunned, unable to move, unable to speak, observing through some kind of haze as Garret scooped her into his arms and carried her to the bed. He sat close beside her, holding her in his arms, attempting to calm her down. Her crying finally diminished to an occasional whimper, and her breathing gradually became more steady, while Ritcherd wondered what kind of evil had possessed him to do such a horrible thing. He was startled from his own thoughts when he heard Kyrah speak, her voice muffled against Garret's chest. "Where is Peter?"

Ritcherd took a step back as if he'd been slugged in the stomach. Her response made perfect sense now—perfect, abhorrent sense—even before Garret turned to look at him with piercing eyes, speaking in a voice that was punishing. "It would seem you've taken her back in time."

Still Ritcherd couldn't move, couldn't respond. A thousand memories swirled in his mind while a tangible pain gathered in his gut. Never had he felt such regret, such unfathomable horror. When Garret was able to ease Kyrah away from him, she curled up on the bed, wrapping herself around a pillow. "Will you be all right?" Garret asked with a calmness that defied the anger in his eyes when he tossed Ritcherd a firm glance.

Kyrah nodded and Garret came to his feet, facing Ritcherd as if he'd like to tear his head off. Ritcherd met his gaze, wanting with everything inside of him for Garret to just belt him in the jaw. He'd done it before when he'd thought Ritcherd deserved it. And he certainly deserved it now.

Garret stood for a long moment facing his brother, willing his anger to a place where he could handle it reasonably. He wasn't a man to lose control. Even when he'd given Ritcherd a fat lip in the past, it had been controlled and with purpose. He was not going to lower himself to Ritcherd's level now and allow his anger to be lured into violence. Still, he *wanted* to hit him! Oh, how he wanted to! But there was something in Ritcherd's eyes that took the edge off Garret's anger. *Regret.* The regret was so blatant that Garret almost felt sorry for him. Almost. But whether Garret was angry or not, there was one thing he needed to make perfectly clear. He was searching for the right words when Ritcherd broke the silence by saying, "Go ahead and hit me, Garret. I deserve it."

"You bet you do," Garret growled.

Ritcherd felt Garret's words startle him from the dazed stupor that had held him bound. He sidestepped to keep from falling as his head spun from dizziness and his stomach smoldered. He groaned and put his head down, pressing his hands over his thighs to keep himself steady. "Oh, God help me," he muttered. "What kind of man am I?"

"That's what I was wondering," Garret snarled. "I should have come in here and knocked you out cold when you first started shouting at her."

"Yes," Ritcherd muttered and sidestepped again, "you should have. I . . . I don't know what happened. I . . . I . . . just . . . She deserves better . . . so much better."

Garret's smoldering anger refused to be reined in any longer. He took Ritcherd by the collar and pushed him back against the wall. "You'd better believe it!" he growled. "She *does* deserve better. But *you're* the one who vowed to keep her safe and happy. So, what are you going to do about it?"

Ritcherd only hung his head in shame and groaned in self-punishment. Garret slammed him against the wall. "Look at me!" Garret said from low in his throat. Ritcherd groaned again and Garret slammed him once more. "Look at me!" he shouted, and Ritcherd reluctantly lifted his head to meet Garret's eyes. "Now, you listen and listen well. If you *ever* lay a hand on her to hurt her again, *ever,* I will steal her away from here, and you will *never* see her again. Do I make myself clear? Vows or no vows, no woman deserves what you just did to her—especially not Kyrah. I have fought every day since the day I realized she was yours to keep my place, to be perfectly proper and appropriate because she was yours first and she loved you best. And that's the way it should be. But by heaven and earth and all I hold sacred, if you ever hurt her again, I will consider her fair game, and I will do everything in my power to lure her away from you as surely as the sun rises in the east. Do I make myself clear?"

"Impeccably clear," Ritcherd said. "But maybe it would be better . . . for her . . . if you just took her now."

Garret slammed him against the wall still again, and Ritcherd groaned. "You're not going to get out of it that easily. She is your *wife.* You committed your heart and soul to her." With his fury vented, Garret absorbed the remorse in Ritcherd's countenance and felt his anger replaced by compassion. "I love her, Ritcherd," he went on in a voice that was more calm, "but *you* are my brother. And in spite of whatever is going on inside of you right now, I know you're a good man, and I know you love her, too." Garret let go of him and stepped back, tugging on his waistcoat to straighten it. "As God is my witness, we are going to get through this, and we are going to fix these problems. But you have got to learn to control your temper. Are you hearing me?"

Ritcherd nodded and squeezed his eyes closed with a self-punishing grimace. He hung his head and groaned as his strength left him and he slid to the floor, wrapping his arms up over his head. "Dear God above," he muttered, "what have I done? What kind of man am I?"

"I'll tell you what kind of man you are," Garret said, squatting beside him. "You're the kind of man who is going to do the right thing. You're going to find the strength inside of you to talk through whatever is eating at you, and you're going to come to terms with it and overcome it. You're the kind of man that loves your wife enough to be willing to change and become a *better* man." Ritcherd looked skeptically at Garret and he added, "And I'm the kind of man that's going to stand by you, no matter what."

The skepticism in Ritcherd's eyes deepened. He looked abruptly away and muttered, "I need to be alone."

"I won't be far if you need me," Garret said and stood up straight. "Do you need anything right now?" he asked. Ritcherd shook his head. Their eyes both moved toward Kyrah in the same moment. She was still curled up on the bed, crying quietly. "Take her with you," Ritcherd insisted. His voice broke as he added, "Keep her safe."

Ritcherd watched Garret speak softly to Kyrah and help her to her feet. Without so much as a glance in his direction, she left the room with Garret's arm around her shoulders, closing the door behind her. He stared at the door while the episode with Kyrah reviewed itself in his mind, over and over, each time deepening his revulsion to what he had done. Memories littered his mind of another time in their lives when his anger and depression had put a rift between him and Kyrah. Then, just as now, Garret had been there for her—always appropriate and proper, but giving her the sensitivity and compassion that Ritcherd was unable to give her. At the time, Ritcherd had only been able to feel jealousy and anger. He'd given Garret a fat lip without even asking first what was going on, and once Garret had left the room, Kyrah had let Ritcherd know exactly how she felt. Her words rang in his ears as clearly as if she'd spoken them today.

"Sooner or later you're going to have to learn to ask questions before you start swinging. How do I know that I won't be the next victim of your anger? Or Cetty, perhaps?"

"No!" he protested. "I would never—"

"Don't expect me to believe that! After what I have been through, I will not live in fear of your temper. So, if you must hit me, do it now and have it over with." She pushed her face close to his. "Go ahead and hit me, Ritcherd. If that's how you handle your anger, just go ahead and do it. Give me the excuse I need to just turn my back on this whole mess and run away. Do it! I can take it! I've been hit so many times that I stopped counting after an hour. So, just do it!"

Ritcherd recalled the anger he felt toward Peter Westman for the beating he'd given Kyrah, and he recalled feeling queasy at her insinuation that he would ever take his temper out on her. He recalled once slapping his mother, the way she had often slapped him. Her behavior had been so appalling that he'd felt justified in doing so. He'd felt certain that he could never treat Kyrah that way—but he had. All these years later, he had crossed a horrific line and behaved deplorably. In that moment, his betrayal of her trust surrounded him so thickly that it threatened to choke him. He felt deeply certain that she could never forgive him, never trust him again—and he couldn't blame her. Thinking of her now in Garret's care, he felt more sorrow than jealousy. It was easy for Ritcherd to see how he had lost the right to have Kyrah in his care. She was better off with Garret; of that he was certain. Still, facing his future without Kyrah in it was more than he could bear, and he wished the darkness surrounding him would just swallow him whole and get it over with.

Chapter Four

The Retreat

Garret walked with Kyrah down the hall to an empty sitting room. He left the door open and guided her to a small sofa where they were both seated, his arm still around her shoulders. "Are you going to be all right?" he asked gently.

She nodded but pressed her face to his shoulder and cried like a frightened child. When her tears finally quieted, Garret murmured, "Talk to me, Kyrah."

"I was so scared," she admitted. "I'm still scared."

"I think that's understandable, but tell me why."

"It all came back to me—the way Peter hit me, and then he kept hitting me. I thought he was going to kill me. He'd been so kind and tender and then he just . . . turned into this horrible monster." She sobbed and clutched his arm. "I love Ritcherd so much," she cried. "Why would he do that to me? What have I done to make him hate me so much?"

"You haven't done anything, Kyrah, and he doesn't hate you. His regret is evident. I'm certain he's as frightened right now as you are." She drew back, looking confused, and Garret clarified, "I believe he's having trouble understanding why he would do something like that when he loves you so much."

"I'm wondering that myself," she said, coming abruptly to her feet. Anger overtook her hurt and confusion as she paced the floor, wringing her hands, while Garret leaned back and crossed a booted ankle over his knee, watching her closely.

"So, now what?" he asked when she said nothing for several minutes.

"I don't know. Now what? Can I even be in the same room with him and not be afraid? Can I ever trust him again?"

"I don't know," Garret said. "You tell me. You've lived with him for years. You've loved him since you were a little girl. Do you think one bad episode wipes away all that's good between you?"

Kyrah countered hotly, "Do you think all that's good between us can wipe away the fact that he is capable of becoming angry enough to physically do me harm? What about Cetty? How can I be sure it won't happen again?"

Garret put both feet on the floor and leaned his forearms on his thighs. "It could happen again, Kyrah. If he chooses not to face and overcome the source of that anger and learn how to control it, then today's episode could very well happen again. If it happens once more, then he's a fool. If it happens twice more, then *you* are a fool."

"What are you saying?" she demanded and stopped pacing to look at him directly.

"In my opinion, Kyrah, his obvious regret and the fact that it has never happened before warrants giving him another chance. But he needs to understand that he gets one—and only one—such chance. There is no place for that kind of behavior in a marriage, Kyrah. If you can't trust him and feel safe, then you should not be living with him. If you stay around long enough to let it happen still again, then you're a fool, Kyrah. If I were you, I would make it very clear to him that you are *not* a fool, and if he chooses to behave that way—ever again, even once—you will leave him."

Kyrah gasped and took a step back, pressing a hand to her heart. "You're talking about Ritcherd."

"Yes, I'm talking about Ritcherd. He's my brother and my friend. At heart he is one of the best men I have ever known. I'm also talking about the man who just hit you."

Kyrah sighed and looked at the floor. "It frightened me more than it hurt me," she said, touching her face where the redness had almost disappeared. "He didn't really hit me that hard or—"

"Don't you dare try to minimize what happened and justify away his behavior!" Garret growled. "He *hit* you, Kyrah. And he could do it again. I pray to God that he doesn't, but it could happen, and you're going to have to accept that."

"But how could I ever . . . leave him?"

"How could you stay, always wondering when or if he might do it again? And what happens the first time Cetty gets a little sassy and sets him off? Can you live with that?"

Kyrah slumped into a chair and pressed a hand over her eyes.

"Don't get me wrong, Kyrah," Garret went on, "I think you should give him another chance—but only one. And I really believe that if he knows he only has one chance, he'll do the right thing. But I think he needs to know exactly where he stands while the problem is still fresh." He paused a long moment then said, "So you know what I think. What do you think?"

Kyrah moved her gaze to his. "I think I need some time to think."

"Of course."

"But I think you might be right; you usually are." She reached out a hand toward him. He stood and took it, pressing her fingers to his lips. "You are the dearest friend in all the world, Garret—to both of us."

Garret forced a smile in response, wondering what she would think if she knew that deep inside, an aching, lonely part of him wanted very badly for Ritcherd to drive Kyrah away. But a more civilized, compassionate part of him knew that he could only be truly happy when Ritcherd was happy, and he prayed that this mountain could be conquered—for all of them.

"Kyrah," he clarified, still holding her fingers tightly, "whatever you do, whatever you tell him, it must come from your own heart. I've given you my opinion, but you are a sound, intelligent woman with good instincts and a strong heart. You must handle this in the way you feel is best, and I will do whatever I can to support you." He squatted down in front of her, adding in a firm whisper, "I want you and Ritcherd to be happy, Kyrah, but you need to understand that I meant what I said to Ritcherd."

"What did you say to Ritcherd?" she asked quietly.

"Did you hear me? In the bedroom just before we came in here?"

Kyrah recalled hearing a few words here and there, but she'd been too absorbed in her fear and emotion to pay attention. She shook her head slowly.

"I told him if he *ever* hurt you again, I would steal you away and he would never see you again." Kyrah gasped and he went on. "I told him that I had always been proper and appropriate with my feelings for you, but if he ever laid a hand on you again, I would consider you fair game and lure you away from him."

Kyrah looked abruptly away, and Garret clearly read the meaning in her eyes. To Kyrah, he was her brother, her friend, her confidant. But she was not now—and never had been—romantically attracted to him. She loved Ritcherd, and he was glad for it. That was the way it should be. He hurried to clarify, "Kyrah, I want you and Ritcherd to be happy. I want more than anything for all of this to work itself out so the two of you can go back to the happiness you once shared. I just want you to know that there are always options. And if you could never feel for me the way I feel for you, I would still do everything in my power to help you and keep you safe."

Kyrah smiled, and moisture brimmed in her eyes. She touched his face, saying, "There is no truer friend in all the world than you. Thank you. I'm sure Ritcherd will be fine."

Garret stood up straight, letting go of her hand. "I'm sure he will be," he said with conviction, "as long as you can be strong enough to make him deserve you." He took a step back. "But it's always good to have options."

"Yes, it is," she agreed. "Thank you, Garret."

He nodded. "I'll check on Ritcherd. With any luck, I can talk him into coming down to supper."

Kyrah smiled again and watched him leave the room, praying with all her heart and soul that Ritcherd would be fine.

After slipping outside for a cigar, Garret knocked lightly at Ritcherd's bedroom door and got no response. He turned the knob and pushed the door slowly open to find the room growing dim with the setting sun. Ritcherd was sitting on the floor exactly where he had left him, his head pressed into his hands. Garret stood directly in front of him and still saw no movement. "Ritcherd," he said, and his brother looked up, startled.

Ritcherd groaned when he saw Garret, and put his head back into his hands. "What?" he mumbled.

"Are you all right?"

"Should I be? After what just happened, I don't believe I will ever be all right again. Sometimes I think of Kyrah's father—Stephen—looking down on me, wondering what kind of idiot he left in charge of his precious daughter."

"Stephen knows you love her."

Ritcherd made a dubious noise. "Do you think Kyrah knows I love her?" he snarled with sarcasm. "Do you think Kyrah would ever dare be in the same room alone with me again—ever?"

"Yes, I do. It might take a little time, but she's a forgiving woman."

"Maybe she shouldn't be."

"Forgiveness does not equal trust, my friend," Garret said, sitting beside him and putting his arms on his knees. "I daresay you're going to have to earn her trust, but I'd bet money she'll forgive you. I think the problem lies more with you forgiving yourself."

Ritcherd lifted his head to look at Garret, his eyes were hard and skeptical. "Can *you* ever forgive me?" Ritcherd asked.

"For what?"

"For hurting the woman you love," Ritcherd said.

Garret's eyes narrowed. "You love her, too."

"Apparently not enough."

"I suppose that remains to be seen."

"What?"

"If you love her enough to actually get past whatever made you do what you did and be a good husband to her."

Ritcherd grunted and put his head back down.

"It's nearly supper time, my brother," Garret said. He came to his feet and took hold of Ritcherd's arm, dragging him along. "Come on. You must eat."

"I doubt I can," Ritcherd insisted, coming along reluctantly.

"You've got to try," Garret said, and they walked in silence down-stairs to the dining room, Garret keeping a firm hold on Ritcherd's arm.

Ritcherd's heart quickened as they entered the dining room, where Kyrah was already sitting at her usual place, toying idly with her napkin. The horror of what had happened earlier came rushing over him and he froze in the doorway. Garret stopped beside him and Ritcherd whispered, "I can't face her. I can't. Not right now."

"Now is just as good a time as any," Garret whispered back. "Come along. She's your wife, for heaven's sake."

Ritcherd sighed and watched Kyrah closely as Garret urged him toward the table. She glanced up as they moved closer. Ritcherd was relieved to see no visible sign of his assault on her face, but the evidence of what he'd done showed clearly in her eyes. Their eyes met for only a second before she looked overtly away, saying, "I was beginning to think I would be eating alone."

"Perhaps you would prefer the peace and quiet," Ritcherd said with a subtle edge as he took his seat.

"Never," she said without looking at him.

The meal progressed with Garret working very hard to provoke clever conversation. Kyrah ate slowly, rarely lifting her eyes from her plate. Ritcherd mostly stirred his food around, feeling progressively more sick to his stomach. When Garret finally gave up on his attempts to get them to talk, Ritcherd pushed back his chair abruptly and came to his feet. "Forgive me. I'm not hungry," he said and hurried from the room, slamming the door.

Kyrah winced, then watched Garret stand up and go to the door. He opened it wide and returned to his chair.

"I'm worried about him, Garret," Kyrah said.

"Yes, so am I," he agreed. "I'm also worried about you."

"I'm fine," she insisted, wishing she could explain that the only thing really wrong with her was a deep concern for her husband, and the abject loneliness and confusion that was a direct result of his behavior. If only she knew what to do about it.

A few minutes after Ritcherd left the table, Kyrah rose to do the same. Garret came to his feet as she did.

"I fear I don't have much of an appetite myself," she said.

"Do you need to talk," he offered, "or—"

"Thank you, Garret, no. I think I've already got far too much to think about. I believe some time alone would help me sort my thoughts."

"Of course," he said. "If there's anything I can do . . ."

She forced a smile toward him and hurried from the room. Even though it was terribly cold outside, and the sun had long gone down, Kyrah pulled her cloak tightly around her and wandered into the gardens. She ambled slowly among the rows of dormant roses and shrubberies, finally settling herself onto a little bench.

Taking her mind through the course of her life with Ritcherd, she found it impossible to grasp the present situation as real. She had seen his temper flare in the past, and she had seen him go through times of frustration and depression. But never like this. And never would she have dreamed that their relationship would come to this. Recalling their heated, angry words—words that had only come to a halt when he had struck her—she still couldn't believe it. Her husband, her lover, her lifelong friend had actually raised a hand and struck her. Still, she couldn't bring herself to condemn him. She had said some awful things, even if she felt they were mostly true. She'd allowed her own anger to rise against his.

For nearly an hour, Kyrah sat in the cold, dark garden, attempting to justify and excuse Ritcherd's behavior. She convinced herself that he would never turn into the animal that Peter Westman had been—and in her heart she knew he wouldn't. But he *had* hit her, and he was capable of doing it again. As much as she loved him, she could not change him if he didn't want to change, and she simply could not allow such a thing to become a pattern between them. She finally came to the conclusion that Garret had been right. Ritcherd needed to know exactly where he stood, and she couldn't bluff. If she threatened to leave him, she had to be prepared to do it. And that was the thought that provoked her tears. How could she? How could she turn her back on him and walk away after all they had shared, all they had been through? But it was just as Garret had said: How could she stay, always wondering when or if he might do it again? And what about Cetty? Could she live wondering if he might turn on their daughter next as she got older and more independent? She wasn't always going to be a sweet little girl.

When emotion threatened to consume her, Kyrah prayed. She prayed perhaps harder than she ever had in her life, that she would instinctively be able to know the right course to take, the right things to say, and that she could feel calm and confident in saying them—and following through, if necessary.

After sitting in the garden another hour, pondering and praying, she came to some firm conclusions and walked toward the house. She was nearly to the door when she heard Garret say, "Are you all right?"

Kyrah turned to see something glowing in the darkness, and it took her a moment to realize he was smoking a small cigar. "What is this?" she demanded, taking it from him. "When did you take up such a disgusting habit?"

"You're sounding a lot like Patrick," he growled with irritation.

"Patrick knows what's good for you," she countered and tossed it to the ground, crushing it beneath her shoe.

"Surely I'm not the first man you've known to smoke a little and—"

"No, my father used to smoke, if you must know. And my mother hated it. Those nasty cigars stink and they make everything else stink. It can't be good for you with the way it stinks."

"You *are* sounding like Patrick."

"Well, obviously I haven't talked to Patrick for several months, but if I ever see you with one of those things again, I will . . . I will . . ."

"You'll what?" he challenged with severity, taking a step toward her.

"I don't know." Her voice softened as she suddenly felt a bit unnerved by how close he was standing. "But I'll think of something."

Garret chuckled, easing the tension somewhat. "Well," he said, "if anyone could get me to stop smoking, it would be you."

"Good then," she said, moving on toward the door. "We'll consider it done."

Kyrah hurried into the house and found Pearl just tucking Cetty into bed. Kyrah felt badly for leaving Cetty in Pearl's care more than usual of late. But at least the child could be spared from her parents' foul moods. Kyrah had spent most of the afternoon with her daughter, but she'd not seen her since Pearl had taken Cetty out for a walk and Kyrah had gone to find Ritcherd, wanting to talk—and the episode had ended in disaster. Now, Kyrah sat close beside her daughter and they talked for a long while before Kyrah kissed her good night. Cetty said nothing about the change in habits between her parents, but

Kyrah felt certain she sensed the growing tension—and she couldn't help noticing that her father paid her no mind at all.

With Cetty sleeping soundly, Kyrah went to her own bedroom, wondering if she would find Ritcherd there, or if she would have to go looking for him. Pushing open the door, she found the room dark and reached for a candle on the bureau to light it. As the dim glow illuminated the room, she saw Ritcherd leaning against the window frame, looking out into the night. He glanced toward her, surprise showing in his eyes before he turned back and settled more comfortably into the windowsill.

"Hello," she said, her voice gentle.

"Hello," he replied tonelessly. A minute of silence preceded his saying, "You're actually stepping into the lion's den. I wasn't sure you'd ever step into a room alone with me again."

"Is there a reason I shouldn't?" she asked, and he turned to look at her with an expression that clearly told her it was a stupid question.

He turned again to look out the window, and Kyrah felt a tangible aching in her chest. The years they had shared—and even this horrible rift between them—had not lessened his effect on her. Even now she felt momentarily taken aback by the overall impression of Ritcherd Buchanan. In a word, he was breathtaking. She noted his most comfortable boots, how they rose up over his calves, as if the leather had been made for him and him alone. His narrow breeches eased beneath a brocade waistcoat with crisscross lacing partway up the back. The white sleeves of his shirt billowed over his arms. His golden hair hung over his collar in a haphazard ponytail, tied with a dark satin ribbon. Physically he looked as he usually did; his attire was typical, his stance all male. But even in the dim light with his back to her, she could see the difference. His normally confident and happy aura was completely absent. And the weeks she had spent living with the ghost of Ritcherd Buchanan were beginning to tell on her. She ached with loneliness, and the uncertainty and heartache of the situation only made her heavy heart more disconsolate.

Kyrah felt compelled to be close to him and pushed away the horror of their last encounter in this room. She stood beside him, watching his face closely while he seemed completely unaware of her.

Praying she wouldn't regret it, she reached up a hand to touch his face. "Ritcherd," she murmured, and he squeezed his eyes closed with pain in his expression—if only she understood its source. When he didn't recoil from her touch—as he had done many times through the past several weeks—she pressed her hand into his hair, marveling at how familiar it felt, and how long it had been since she'd been this close to him. Impulsively she pulled the ribbon from his hair and watched it fall over his shoulders as he tilted his head forward, his eyes still closed, as if he were trying to block out the thoughts in his head—or her attention to him. Perhaps both. But *why?*

Holding the ribbon in her hand, Kyrah pressed her fingers gently through his hair. She heard his breathing sharpen and saw his shoulders rise and fall. "Ritcherd," she said again, moving subtly closer, pressing her other hand over his chest. He gasped at her touch but still didn't open his eyes.

Ritcherd felt almost dizzy from the confusion pounding through his head as Kyrah eased even closer, pressing a kiss to his cheek. She was so beautiful, so incredible, but he couldn't even bring himself to open his eyes and look at her. He felt completely incapable of even moving, let alone taking her in his arms. While a part of him ached to hold her and kiss her in a way that had become such an indelibly familiar part of his life, something more powerful—something dark and ugly—bound his heart tightly, leaving him too crippled to respond to the attention she was giving him. How could he take her in his arms when all he could see in his mind was his despicable behavior with her earlier? How could he kiss her when he was so completely unworthy of her? How could he hit a woman, then turn around and make love to her, in spite of how desperately he wanted to? Oh, how he wanted to! But the hypocrisy of even entertaining such an idea threatened to choke him. Images of hypocrisy catapulted forward from his childhood into his mind, where they swirled into the moment, leaving him formlessly angry. He felt Kyrah's lips over his and turned his face abruptly.

"Is my kiss so repulsive?" she asked, but her voice was tender and her fingers eased through the buttons of his waistcoat.

"No, Kyrah," he muttered, "your kiss is anything but repulsive."

"Then kiss me," she urged, but he made no response.

With his waistcoat unbuttoned, she pressed her hands over the shirt covering his chest. She kissed his cheek and worked open the top three buttons of his shirt before he abruptly took her wrists into his hands to stop her. "No, Kyrah, please," he murmured.

"Why not?" she countered, and he finally looked at her. "I'm your wife. We're alone. Does my affection displease you, Lord Buckley?"

Ritcherd felt his nerves tighten to hear her actually call him by his aristocratic title. He *hated* the title, and hearing her speak it so caustically brought back the stinging memory of her calling him an aristocratic snob. He couldn't even begin to fathom how deeply such words cut into his heart. While he fought with everything inside of him to stay calm and not allow his behavior to be affected by his emotions, he heard her whimper and felt her trying to free her wrists from his grasp. He focused on her eyes just as she said, "Let go, Ritcherd. You're hurting me."

Only then did he realize how tight his grip had become as he'd struggled internally with his anger. He opened his hands and let go as if the contact had burned him. He watched her as she rubbed her wrists, looking at him much the same way she had earlier after he'd hit her.

"Oh, God help me," he muttered and stepped back, putting his hands in the air, wondering if he would ever dare touch her again. He staggered into a chair and wrapped his arms up over his head, groaning from deep in his chest.

Kyrah felt her heart breaking to watch him. While she struggled to know what to say, she felt compelled to remind him of the most important thing. "I love you, Ritcherd."

"How can you?" he asked, pressing his hands brutally into his hair.

Kyrah chose her words carefully, knowing they needed to be said. "Because the man I love is not the same man I've encountered today. I believe the man I love is still in there somewhere. We need to work together to bring him back, Ritcherd, because I miss him—I need him."

Ritcherd leaned back in his chair and looked at her skeptically. "And what if the man you love doesn't exist anymore, Kyrah?"

"That's the most ridiculous thing I've ever heard," she insisted. "Whatever is wrong it is fixable, Ritcherd. But not if you shut yourself off from me and allow your anger and frustration to build until it breaks." Their eyes met for a full minute while Kyrah hoped for some kind of response, but he said nothing.

Ritcherd took a good, long look at his wife and wondered what had gone wrong. While a part of him longed to reach out to her and respond to her pleas, he felt crippled and completely incapable of reaching beyond the fog clouding his brain. As he grew increasingly uncomfortable in her presence, he asked, "Is there something you wanted to say?" If nothing else, he wanted to get this conversation over with and be alone in his misery.

Kyrah looked into his eyes, seeing a trace of defiance, and she felt deeply grateful for the voice of reason she had in Garret. His advice came back to her, and instinctively she knew it was the right course. However difficult it might be, she needed to let Ritcherd know where he stood; she could not allow him to believe that his hurtful behavior would be tolerated.

"Yes, there's something I need to say, but it's not easy for me." He motioned for her to go on. She took a deep breath and began carefully. "Ritcherd, I love you. I love you more than life itself, and—"

"Maybe that's where your problem is, my dear."

Kyrah was momentarily too astonished to speak. She found her voice enough to say, "*My* problem? I don't have a problem, Ritcherd, except for—"

"Except for me," he insisted, "and the fact that you were fool enough to fall in love with me at all. If you had any brains, you would—"

"Do you hear what you're saying?" she countered. "Loving you is the best thing I ever did, Ritcherd, and I will love you until I die. I will not, however, put up with your ill treatment. Whatever struggles or challenges you might endure—now or in the future—I will stand beside you unquestionably. I will do everything in my power to give you the love that you need and help you through, provided that . . ." she paused and lifted her chin courageously, ". . . that I can feel safe with you." She saw him bristle but pressed on. "I will not live in fear of your temper, Ritcherd. I have thought this through very carefully, and what I'm saying I say of my own free will. I'm giving you another chance—but only one. If you ever—ever—do me, or Cetty, harm . . . I will take her away from here, and you will never see us again." The blatant sorrow and disbelief that rose in his eyes tempted her to take it back, but she knew in her heart that she couldn't. "I will never say it again, but you need to know that I mean what I said and I will not back down. Once more, Ritcherd, just once and it will be over between us. I was prepared at one time, when I was married to Peter, to be a divorced woman. Don't think I'm not capable of doing it now."

While Ritcherd attempted to perceive that she was serious, he had to admit that he felt some relief in her ultimatum. Questioning his own sanity, he couldn't be certain that he would never hurt her again, and he was glad to know that she wouldn't put up with it, that she would protect herself and Cetty. But he felt he had to say, "Perhaps it would be better if you just leave now."

"What are you saying, Ritcherd? That I should start divorce proceedings?"

"If that's what you think you should do, Kyrah, then you should do it. I'll sign anything you want me to. I'll give you everything I have."

"I don't want everything you have, Ritcherd. I want *you*. I want our marriage to be the way it used to be—the way it should be."

He turned to look at her with hard eyes. "Well, maybe that's just not possible. I don't know what's wrong with me, Kyrah. And I don't know if it's fixable. If you can't live with that, I certainly understand."

"Well, I *don't* understand, Ritcherd. Why can't you just *talk* to me—or to Garret? Why can't we work this out *together?*"

He stood and moved again to the window. "I don't know, Kyrah. I just . . . can't."

"Can't what?"

"Can't . . . anything. I feel like my mind . . . my emotions . . . have become completely crippled. And I don't know what to do about it." Again he turned a hard gaze toward her. "I don't know what's wrong with me, Kyrah. I fear I'll only end up hurting you . . . again . . . worse."

Kyrah took a deep breath. "So, you're saying that our leading separate lives is the only option to keep me safe? Is that what you're saying?"

"Perhaps."

"Well, I don't believe it. And I won't stand for it. I'm not leaving, Ritcherd. I married you so that we could face life's challenges *together*. Maybe you're telling me to leave is just the easy way out for you. If I leave, then you don't have to talk about it, you don't have to fix it, you just . . . what, Ritcherd? Then what? You spend the rest of your life holed up in this huge home, alone and going crazy? Is that it?"

"Maybe I already am crazy," he insisted.

"You're not! You're just indolent and selfish. Or you're too afraid of facing your fears. Do your fears mean more to you than your love for me, Ritcherd? That's what it comes down to, you know. Either you face up to the problem and do something about it, or I will assume your fears are more powerful than your love for me."

"Maybe they are," he said as if he'd resigned himself to his fate.

Kyrah hurried from the room, fearing she would either burst into tears or fall down on her knees and resort to petty begging. Either way, she would make a fool of herself, and she was growing tired of trying to give him her whole heart while he made it clear that he didn't want to—or wasn't capable of—taking it.

For more than an hour Kyrah sat in Cetty's room watching her daughter sleep, praying with everything inside of her that Ritcherd's heart could be reached. Exhaustion finally urged her back to her own room. Ritcherd had gone to bed and the room was dark. She changed into her nightgown and quietly slipped into the bed, relatively certain that Ritcherd was awake, even though his back was turned to her. While he rarely snored, he had a certain way of breathing when he slept that she was well accustomed to. After staring at the ceiling for several minutes, she asked quietly, "Are you asleep?"

"Yes," he said immediately. Normally she would have chuckled at such a comment, but she could find no point of humor in this rift between them.

"I love you, Ritcherd," she added gently.

Following a long moment of silence while she wondered if he would respond at all, he finally muttered, "I know."

Kyrah turned her face into the pillow and wept silently, wondering if the best years of her life were over. In that moment, she couldn't comprehend ever getting beyond this horrible pall.

The following morning, Kyrah awoke to find Ritcherd gone. She went down to breakfast to find him there, but he didn't speak, and she didn't see him eat anything at all before he left the table without a word, leaving her alone with Garret.

"Did something else happen last night?" he asked.

Kyrah looked at her plate as she spoke. "I gave him an ultimatum, just as you suggested. He said it might be better if I just left now. He said he would sign divorce papers without question, that he'd give me everything."

Garret leaned back in his chair and sighed loudly. She repeated the gist of the conversation then turned to look at him. "So, now what do I do?"

"You take it one day at a time," he said. "You can't force him to talk to you, Kyrah. You can do your best to let him know you love him, and hold your ground."

"That's easy to say," she muttered, throwing her napkin on the table, "but if something doesn't change soon, Ritcherd's not the only one who will be questioning their sanity."

An hour after breakfast, Kyrah couldn't find Ritcherd and began to feel panicked. She finally found him in their bedroom, curled up in the bed, apparently asleep. At lunchtime she checked again and found him staring at the wall. She nudged him and told him it was time to eat. He insisted he wasn't hungry. She spent most of the afternoon with Cetty, and peeked in on him three more times. When supper time came, he still insisted he wasn't hungry. When she attempted to firmly tell him he had to eat, he snapped at her, "I know where the kitchen is, Kyrah. If I want something to eat, I assure you I can find it. Just . . . leave me in peace!"

"Fine," she snapped back, and hurried from the room to share another meal with Garret. She refused to discuss Ritcherd with him any further, and every other attempt he made at clever conversation for the sake of distraction fell flat.

Late that evening Kyrah climbed into bed again beside Ritcherd, knowing full well that he was awake. But she said nothing. Again she cried silent tears until she slept. She woke in the dark and realized she was alone. A distinct uneasiness crept over her as she scrambled to light a candle. Holding the flame near the clock, she realized it was past four in the morning. A quick search made it evident that Ritcherd's boots were accounted for, but a dressing gown was missing. At least that left her relatively certain he was in the house. But it was an awfully big house. After searching for an hour, the uneasiness inside of her had heightened to an undeniable panic. She finally went to Garret's room and knocked at the door. She was about to knock again when Garret pulled it open. He wore a dressing gown that hung nearly to the floor and was left hanging open to reveal his bare chest and bare feet and his most comfortable breeches. The ribbon that held his ponytail had loosened, leaving his hair mussed and barely in a ponytail at all. For a moment she was taken aback. She'd simply never seen him look that way before.

"What's wrong?" he demanded, and she felt certain he sensed her panic.

"Ritcherd's gone. I've searched the house. I don't think he's gone out. Maybe I just missed him, but . . . if we split up and look we could . . ."

"I'll look downstairs," he said and hurried toward the stairs.

Twenty minutes later, Kyrah came out of one of the many guest rooms to find Garret standing in the hall. "I found him," he said in a gravelly voice that let her know something was wrong.

"Is he all right?" she demanded. "Is he—"

"He's passed out drunk." Garret's voice betrayed his anger. "He's in the library. You probably didn't see him since he's on the floor on the other side of the sofa."

Kyrah moved around Garret with the intention of going directly to Ritcherd, but he caught her arm to stop her. "I think you need to go back to bed and let me handle this," he said. Kyrah opened her mouth to protest and Garret put his fingers over her lips. "I know where to find you if I need you. I'll make certain he's all right. Now, go to bed," he ordered, and she did. But she didn't sleep.

Drunk? *Ritcherd?* She'd never seen him drunk. He'd told her more than once that he'd struggled with some heavy drinking right after he'd returned from fighting in the colonies. But he'd quickly gained control of the problem and had never indulged in more than a little drink here or there and the usual wine with dinner. And now he was drunk—passed out, no less. Was that his only choice besides giving into anger or despondency? The very idea made her sick to her stomach. She could feel Ritcherd retreating further and further into a place where she was not allowed, and she didn't understand. She forced her mind to prayer, knowing that nothing short of divine intervention could ever undo all that was wrong with her husband.

Chapter Five

The Betrayal

By dawn, Garret finally managed to rouse Ritcherd enough to help him to his feet, but he still had to practically carry him up the stairs.

"Come along," he urged. "We're going to let this wear off someplace where the servants won't find you."

He opted to take Ritcherd to his own room, rather than Ritcherd's room, where Kyrah would be trying to sleep. Ritcherd groaned as Garret pushed him onto the bed.

"Snap out of it, my friend," Garret said, gently slapping his face.

"I just want to sleep," Ritcherd said in a slurred voice without opening his eyes. "Just leave me alone and let me sleep."

"Later," Garret said, lifting him to a sitting position by holding to his shirt collar. "If you think I'm going to let you get drunk and actually enjoy it, you are quite mistaken."

Ritcherd groaned again and hung his head. "I think I'm going to be sick," he muttered, clutching his middle.

"I shouldn't wonder," Garret snarled and reached for the chamber pot, grateful to find it clean. After Ritcherd had thrown up twice, Garret added, "Drinking that much brandy on an empty stomach would make anybody sick." Ritcherd just scowled at him and threw up again.

When it became evident that Ritcherd's sickness had passed, Garret poured some water into the basin and washed the sweat away from Ritcherd's face and chest before he finally left him to rest. He went to Kyrah's room and knocked lightly at the door. She opened it so quickly that he knew she hadn't been asleep.

"How is he?" she demanded, tying a wrapper around her waist.

"He'll be fine. Right now he's miserable, which is exactly what he *should* be. He's been quite ill, but he's resting now. Could you sit with him while I take care of a few things?"

"Of course."

"He's in my room," he said, already moving down the hall. "I'll get back as quickly as I can."

Garret found the majority of the servants gathered in the kitchen for their usual early breakfast.

"Good morning, Captain," Mrs. Hawke, the head cook, said warmly. "Would you care to join us?"

"No, thank you," he said, "but there is something I need to say, if I could have everyone's attention." The room became silent, all eyes turned to him. "Forgive me for interrupting your meal, but there is something you need to be informed of. I'm certain you're all well aware that Captain Buchanan has been struggling since the loss of his sister. Your discretion in keeping the matter within the household is greatly appreciated. Unfortunately, my brother has decided to take up drinking, and he's made himself rather sick. Within the hour I want all of the liquor in the house either disposed of or hidden and locked carefully away. Anyone who allows the captain to find liquor in the house will be let go. Do I make myself clear?"

A number of noises of agreement responded. "Good, then. Thank you." He then asked that a hot bath be prepared in his room, and hot coffee be taken up to the same place as soon as the captain came around.

Garret quickly took care of a few other things, then returned to relieve Kyrah of her vigil. When she seemed reluctant to leave, he said, "You go and be with Cetty when she wakes up. I can handle this, and it would be better if you weren't here when he comes around. It won't be a pretty sight."

"You mean he'll be sick to his stomach again?"

"Probably. But what I really mean is that I'm probably going to bust him in the jaw for being such an idiot."

Garret sat with Ritcherd for most of the day, attempting to get lost in a long novel without much success. Kyrah checked in occasionally and brought Garret some lunch, but he insisted that she stay away and let him handle Ritcherd. When he finally came around, complaining of a horrible headache, Garret simply said, "Your head's going to hurt a lot worse if I bust you in the jaw for being such a fool. What possessed you to personally dispose of all the brandy you could get your hands on?"

"Oh, leave me alone," Ritcherd snarled.

"I would if I thought you could behave like an adult, but as long as you're going to act like a child, I'm going to have to be your nanny."

"Oh, that's just what I need," he said with sarcasm, attempting to sit on the edge of the bed. "Thank you, but no thank you. I don't need you or anyone else to take care of me."

"If you could see yourself now, you wouldn't be saying such stupid things. And you smell as bad as you look. If you don't want me following me around, then start acting like a man. I'm going to tell them you're ready for a bath now, if you think you can manage on your own for that long."

Garret moved toward the door then turned back. "Oh by the way, most of the liquor in the house has been dumped out, and what's left has been locked up with strict instructions to the servants that anyone who allows the lord of the manor to have anything more to drink than wine with dinner will be immediately fired."

Ritcherd groaned and Garret left the room, resisting the urge to slam the door. According to a familiar pattern of late, he prayed silently that he would be guided to the means to help Ritcherd get beyond this. But so far, he just kept coming up empty.

Three days later, Ritcherd had managed to stay sober and he appeared in the dining room for most of his meals. But he said practically nothing to either Garret or Kyrah. He was like a ghost, barely existing. Garret sensed Kyrah's growing concern, in spite of her efforts to talk about anything else when they were together. He continued to pray—as he knew Kyrah was doing—that something could snap Ritcherd out of this stupor and give him the motivation to solve this problem, and to go on living.

Four days after Ritcherd's drunken episode, Kyrah found Garret in the library. He saw a familiar panicked concern in her eyes as she announced, "Ritcherd is gone. His horse is missing. And yes, I'm going to let you handle it." Tears showed in her eyes. "I can't take this anymore, Garret. I can't."

"Go read Cetty a story or something," he said, giving her a quick embrace. "I'll find him."

Garret quickly saddled his own stallion once he had established that Ritcherd's was indeed missing. He rode first to the ancient church ruins, a place that he knew was a common respite for Ritcherd, but he wasn't there. He galloped the surrounding area and saw no sign of him. On a hunch he went to the house that stood empty near Buckley Manor. It was the home Kyrah had grown up in, although its history was rather complicated. As Garret understood it, Kyrah's father, Stephen, had won this estate in a card game, and several years later had lost it the same way—after which he had shot himself in the head, leaving Kyrah and her mother destitute. Kyrah had gone to work for the man who had won the estate—Peter Westman, a villain and a blackguard in the truest sense. Kyrah had eventually been taken in by Westman's manipulation and had agreed to marry him—a story that in itself was complicated. He'd beaten her senseless and abandoned her, and eventually he'd met justice and lost his life in a fair fight, but not before he'd shot and killed Ritcherd's mother in the skirmish. Being Peter Westman's widow, Kyrah had inherited the estate at his death, but the house had been empty since that time. Garret walked through it now, wondering if Ritcherd might have come here to find solace. Ritcherd had spent more time in this home than his own through his youth, finding a place in Kyrah's family that he'd never found in his own. Garret found the house a little eerie and needing some work, but he couldn't help pondering its potential as he went from room to room.

Concluding that Ritcherd wasn't there, he checked the cottage on the estate as well, then he rode toward town, not wanting to admit that his next logical conclusion would be that Ritcherd had gone in search of liquor. Garret checked three pubs before he found him, his face pressed to a table, barely coherent. Garret paid his bill and helped him into the saddle before he mounted behind him to keep him upright. They rode slowly toward home with Ritcherd's stallion in tow, while Ritcherd grumbled and complained and Garret ignored him, if only to keep his own anger in check.

Back at the manor, Garret dismounted and helped Ritcherd down. "Are you sober enough to hear what I'm saying?" Garret asked.

"I hear you," Ritcherd said as if he resented it.

"Good. I want you to remember this in the morning." Garret belted him in the jaw, then deftly caught him when he fell.

He left the horses in care of the stablemaster and helped Ritcherd to his room. Kyrah met them in the hall and said nothing, but her tears made it clearly evident what she was feeling. Garret helped Ritcherd to bed and stayed close by while he slept it off. He finally came awake late in the evening, growling about his sore jaw.

"You do remember *why* it's sore, don't you?" Garret countered.

"Yes, I remember," Ritcherd said with an angry scowl.

"Good," Garret said. "I'm going to keep belting you in the jaw until you wise up enough to stop drinking. I thought you learned a long time ago that drinking will never solve anything. It's only likely to land you in a whole lot of trouble when you lose your senses and do something stupid."

Garret expected him to argue, but he admitted humbly, "Yes, I know you're right."

"That's something, I suppose. But is it enough to make you stop drinking?"

Ritcherd hung his head and sighed. "Yes. I'll stop drinking."

"Is that a promise?" Garret asked.

"Yes," Ritcherd said and sighed, "I promise to stop drinking."

"Good," Garret said with exaggerated joy. "Now could you promise to start talking to me so we could get all of this worked out, once and for all?"

Ritcherd just scowled at Garret and said, "I need to be alone, if you don't mind."

"Fine," Garret said. "You just stay here alone and wallow in your misery, but eventually you're going to find that cutting yourself off from everything you love is going to get you exactly what you're working for."

"And what's that?"

"You're going to be cut off from everything you love." Garret lifted his finger. "You've been blessed with people who love you—people who are willing to help you through this. But we can't do it for you, and quite frankly we're getting tired of living with your ghost."

"If you're trying to make a point, make it and get out of here," Ritcherd said.

"Your wife is hurting and sorely neglected. Every time I see her, she's crying."

"My wife is none of your concern."

"*Someone* needs to be concerned about her," Garret said.

"Why don't you just . . . go back to sea or something, and let me worry about my wife."

"As if you would," Garret growled. "But I can't go back to sea, even if I wanted to. My ship is grounded, as you'll recall."

"Are you finished?"

"Apparently I am," Garret said and left the room.

A few minutes later, Garret found Kyrah sitting in the formal dining room, surrounded by a huge array of scattered Christmas decor that had obviously just been removed from several scattered boxes. He left the door open and approached her quietly. His heart tightened when he saw the tears streaming down her face. She caught sight of him and glanced up abruptly before she looked away and wiped frantically at her face.

"Do you think it will do any good to hide your tears from me now?" he asked, stepping closer.

"My tears are none of your concern," she said.

"Well, at least you still have one thing in common with your husband. He told me that you were *his* concern, not mine. But he doesn't seem to be too concerned about anything—least of all your tears."

Kyrah said nothing, but he could easily read in her eyes that she shared his helplessness. They were both startled when a maid entered the room, saying, "Excuse me, Captain, but there's someone here to see you."

"Who is it, Liza?" he asked, his heart quickening with dread.

"A Mr. Thayer," she said and his stomach tightened. "He wishes to speak to you and Captain Buchanan. Should I go up for him or—"

"No, thank you, Liza. You tell Mr. Thayer we'll be there in a few minutes. I'll get the captain."

"Very good, sir." Liza curtsied and left the room.

"Who is Mr. Thayer?" Kyrah demanded.

"It's nothing," he insisted.

"I know you better than that, Garret," she said, coming to her feet. "Something's wrong. What is it?"

Garret sighed and moved toward her, taking her shoulders into his hands. "I'll tell you everything, Kyrah, but not right now. You just . . . stay out of sight and let me handle this. With any luck, I can get Ritcherd to show his face and act like a man for five minutes."

He hurried from the room, leaving Kyrah to wonder what she would do without Garret. More and more it seemed he was handling *everything*.

Garret took the stairs three at a time and rushed into Ritcherd's room without knocking. "Put your boots on and comb your hair, Captain." Ritcherd opened his mouth to protest but Garret didn't give him a chance. "Our accuser is downstairs; he wants to see us." Garret pulled a clean shirt out of Ritcherd's closet and threw it at him. "So, try to act like a man for a few minutes—and for the love of heaven, try to act innocent. Just let me do the talking."

Ritcherd just looked stunned and Garret added firmly, "Hurry it up, Buckley. Whatever you've got inside of you . . . this would be a good time to bring it out. I need you."

Ritcherd pulled on his boots and changed his shirt. While he was fastening the buttons, Garret smoothed his hair with a comb and tied it into a ponytail. "Now you are acting like my nanny," Ritcherd grumbled.

"Anything to get you to hurry," Garret said, and they walked together downstairs. "I hope you're praying," he added as they approached the drawing room.

"I'm just trying to think straight," Ritcherd admitted. "That's the best you're going to get at the moment."

"Good enough," Garret said and lightly slapped him on the shoulder.

Garret took a deep breath and shot Ritcherd a concerned glance before he pasted on a smile and pushed open the drawing room doors. "Ah, Mr. Thayer," he said with false enthusiasm. "How good of you to pay us a visit."

Mr. Thayer gave a suspicious smile. "I was beginning to think you'd run out the back way."

"No need for that," Garret said. "Captain Buchanan's not been feeling well. It took him a few minutes to get dressed."

"I see," Mr. Thayer said, eyeing Ritcherd. "So, this is your partner, then."

"Ritcherd Buchanan," he said, reaching out a hand toward Mr. Thayer. "What is it that we can do for you?"

Mr. Thayer said, "I assume your brother informed you of the pending investigation of the *Phoenix.*"

"He did," Ritcherd said, "but I must confess that I'm confused over the issue. I can't begin to imagine why our travels on the *Phoenix* would be of any concern to anyone."

"Would you like to sit down," Garret said, motioning with his arm.

"Thank you," Mr. Thayer said and turned to find a seat. Garret shot Ritcherd a cautious glare that he either missed or ignored. Garret didn't know whether to be pleased to hear Ritcherd talking at all, or scared to death that he was going to ruin everything by actually being talkative in his present state of mind.

When they were all seated, Mr. Thayer said, "The *Phoenix* was apparently seen in many American ports during the war."

"I had no idea it was a crime to dock a ship in the colonies," Ritcherd stated in a tone of voice that made Garret realize, until now, he'd not seen the real Ritcherd Buchanan since he'd returned home.

"It certainly was not," Mr. Thayer said with a little chuckle. "But your activity in those ports is under investigation. A ship does not make that many stops without a purpose. If you were in any way aiding the colonist cause, then the both of you will surely be convicted of treason. I can guarantee it."

Ritcherd leaned forward and said with calm confidence, "Well, let me tell you about our activity in the colonies, Mr. Thayer. The *Phoenix* normally did trade between the islands and Europe, but in seventy-nine, the woman I love—who is now my wife—was illegally deported to the colonies. My brother and I sailed for many months, stopping in nearly every port in our attempts to find her. Now, if locating a woman is a crime, I should very much like to see where that law is written."

Mr. Thayer eyed them both and stated, "That's a clever story, Captain, but not very likely."

"I know it sounds bizarre," Ritcherd said, "but the truth is often bizarre. Feel free to question any members of the crew who were sailing with us at the time. Question people in the area here who were well aware of what happened."

"I intend to," he said and came to his feet. "So, is that your official statement?"

"It is," Ritcherd said, standing also. "Only because it's the truth."

"Captain?" Mr. Thayer questioned Garret as he rose to his feet. "Do you concur with your brother?"

"Absolutely," he stated.

"Well, I'll be back," he said as if it were a threat. "We will be doing a thorough combing of many records that we've acquired since the war. But most importantly, my gut instinct tells me that you're guilty—both of you. I've been in this business a long time, gentlemen. I know how to see the truth in a man's eyes, and I know how to read between the lines when it comes to evidence." He moved toward the door. "Watch your backs, gentlemen. This is not over yet."

Long after the front door closed in the distance, Ritcherd and Garret stood in silence. Garret moved into the open doorway of the drawing room and leaned against the doorjamb, staring at the front door where Mr. Thayer had just left. "That was pretty impressive," he finally said, turning to look at Ritcherd. "Amazing how you can suddenly be yourself again when your life is on the line."

"Frankly, Garret, I don't give a damn about my life, but it wouldn't do Kyrah or Cetty much good if I go to the gallows and all my property is confiscated."

"No, it certainly wouldn't," Garret said, "but has it ever occurred to you that Kyrah and Cetty would very much like to have their husband and father back? I daresay if Kyrah could have seen that little performance, she'd be asking you what Mr. Thayer's got that she hasn't got."

Ritcherd gave a scoffing chuckle. "You just don't get it, do you."

"Apparently not."

"Kyrah deserves better than me, Garret."

"No, what Kyrah deserves is for *you* to treat her better, for you to actually be a husband to her."

"I refuse to discuss this with you," Ritcherd said, leaving the room.

Garret grabbed his arm as he walked past. "Fine. Don't discuss it with me. But for the love of heaven, discuss it with somebody, because you're tearing this family apart and none of us knows what to do about it."

Ritcherd scowled at Garret and twisted his arm out of his brother's grasp before he hurried up the stairs. Garret sighed and hung his head, squeezing his eyes closed. He groaned aloud as the threat of hanging for treason spun in his mind with this horrible, unexplainable pall that hung over Ritcherd. His concern for Kyrah and Cetty ached tangibly inside of him until he didn't know whether to scream or cry. So he just groaned again.

"I know exactly how you feel," Kyrah said, and he shot his head up to see her standing in the hallway.

"I thought I was alone," he said.

"Well, you're not." She moved into the drawing room and motioned for him to sit down. "And now would be a good time to tell me about this Mr. Thayer, don't you think? Especially since . . . how did you put it? I should be asking what Mr. Thayer has got that I haven't got? Was that it?"

Garret bristled visibly and pushed his hands behind his back. "That conversation was meant to be private."

"Well, it wasn't. I was waiting in the next room for Mr. Thayer to leave. I did not intend to eavesdrop."

"And did you hear our conversation with Mr. Thayer as well?" he asked.

"No, I only heard what you said to Ritcherd after he left. So am I to assume that Ritcherd actually *talked* to Mr. Thayer?"

"That's right."

Kyrah lost her attempt to stay calm as the full extent of what she'd overheard came back to her. "Sit down, Garret," she said, her voice quavering, "and tell me why Ritcherd's life is on the line, and why he is talking about going to the gallows." He hesitated, and she added through clenched teeth, "Tell me, *now!* I've already got one man who won't talk to me!"

Garret moved to a chair and sat down. Kyrah closed the door and sat across from him. Garret stood up and opened the door before he returned to his chair. She became momentarily distracted by his reasons for always leaving the door open, and she was startled when he said, "There's no easy way to say it, Kyrah. The *Phoenix* and her owners are being investigated for treason."

"What?" she gasped. "But . . . the war is long over, and . . ."

"Apparently that is irrelevant. If they can prove that Ritcherd and I aided the colonists, all of our property will be confiscated—including the *Phoenix*—and we will both go to the gallows."

Kyrah's breathing became raspy and she pressed both hands over her heart. "Good heavens," she muttered, then pinned her eyes on him. In little more than a whisper, she said, "But Garret . . . you and Ritcherd are—"

"Don't say it, Kyrah." He glanced toward the open doorway as if to imply that servants might overhear.

Seeing a helpless frustration on her face, he moved to sit beside her, taking her hand into his and putting an arm around her shoulders. Whispering close to her ear, he said, "Yes, Kyrah, Ritcherd and I are guilty of treason. What they are saying is true. We can only hope and pray that they can't find proof."

She turned to look at him, clearly astonished and afraid. "Can they find proof, Garret?" she demanded in a whisper.

"I don't think so," he said quietly, "but I don't know what started this investigation to begin with. I just don't know, Kyrah."

Emotion bubbled up from Kyrah's chest, and she pressed her face to his shoulder to muffle the sound of her tears. When she was able to calm down, she muttered quietly, "Oh, Garret. I can't even imagine losing one of you. If I had to lose both of you . . . I couldn't. I just couldn't."

"It's going to be all right, Kyrah. It just has to be."

Kyrah held tightly to him, wishing she could believe him. At the moment everything seemed all wrong, and she simply couldn't fathom anything ever being right again.

Ritcherd came down to supper, but as usual, he said practically nothing. While Kyrah's fears over the pending investigation threatened to consume her, she felt a growing anger toward the distance between them. Following several minutes of silence, Kyrah said to him, "So, I hear you're being investigated for treason." Ritcherd looked abruptly toward her. "Funny, that I should have to hear such a thing elsewhere." He said nothing and she added, "That must be weighing heavily on your mind."

Ritcherd sighed. "It doesn't help any."

"No, it certainly doesn't help any," she retorted, her voice only slightly terse.

Again there was silence until Kyrah had to say what was on her mind or scream and throw something. "So," she said, looking directly at Ritcherd, "should I just accept that I was born to survive by doing manual labor? Should I start looking for work now?"

"What on earth are you talking about?" Ritcherd demanded.

"If you hang and we lose everything, I have to assume that I will be left to fend for myself and Cetty. So I want to know how serious this is. Should I start looking for—"

"Don't be absurd, Kyrah," Ritcherd said, none too kindly. "Even *if* they could prove I was guilty of treason, you should know I would not leave you with nothing."

"Yes, I should know that. But I don't. My father promised he had not left us with nothing, but I still had to work every waking hour to keep food on the table. And quite frankly, I don't know *anything* anymore. How can I, when the man I thought I knew so well has become a complete stranger to me?"

Ritcherd gazed at Kyrah long and hard, anger visibly brewing in his eyes. Just when she thought he might actually answer her question, he threw his napkin to the table and left the room.

"That went well," Garret said with sarcasm.

Kyrah glared at him and left the room as well, deciding that Cetty's company was the only place she could find any solace at all. She found her in the nursery with Pearl, and the three of them had a delightful little tea party with several dollies. Kyrah would have thoroughly enjoyed the experience, if not for the ever-growing dread in her heart. She could only think that whether Ritcherd was convicted of treason or not, her life with him was over.

When Cetty was all ready for bed, Kyrah held the child on her lap and read her one last bedtime story. They were nearly to the end when Garret came into the nursery. Cetty jumped off Kyrah's lap and ran to him, giggling. He laughed and picked her up, twirling her around as he said, "How's my favorite princess?"

"I'm glad you came to see me," Cetty said. "Papa won't come to see me anymore."

Garret exchanged a discreet glance of concern with Kyrah. "Well, your papa hasn't been feeling well," Garret said. "I know for a fact that he loves you very much, even if he doesn't come to see you."

"He's sad that Aunt Celeste died," Cetty said.

"Yes, he is," Garret said, "although I think that his being sad over Celeste has reminded him of other times in his life when he was sad, and now he's just so sad that he can't remember how to be happy. But we'll keep praying for him, and I'm certain that everything will be all right."

Cetty nodded and returned to Kyrah's lap. "We're just finishing a bedtime story," Kyrah said.

"Don't let me stop you," Garret said, taking a chair across the room.

When the story was finished, Cetty hugged Garret once more then went to her room with Kyrah close behind. Once Cetty was tucked in for the night, Kyrah returned to the nursery to get her shawl and found Garret still sitting there.

"I'm certain Cetty wouldn't mind if you played with the toys," she said, pulling the shawl around her shoulders.

Garret smiled and glanced around the room. "It wouldn't be any fun to play without Cetty."

"Something you do every day, I've noticed," she said, sitting on the edge of a chair. Garret didn't comment and she added, "I'm grateful, Garret, for the effort you make on Cetty's behalf."

"It doesn't take any effort, Kyrah. I love to be with Cetty."

"Nevertheless, your spending time with her eases the difficulty of her father not giving her any time at all."

"Cetty seems to be doing all right," he said. "But what about you?" Kyrah steeled herself to give him a courageous answer, but he quickly added, "And don't lie to me."

She sighed. "I'm trying very hard to . . . be brave, to not allow his depression to bother me, but I feel . . ." Her voice broke. "I feel . . . cut in half, Garret. I feel severed and incomplete. It's as if he is half of my flesh and blood, and seeing him suffer while I'm left so helpless is just . . ." Kyrah swallowed hard and gathered her composure. "I fear that eventually I will have nothing more to give him, that I will be forced to sever myself from him completely in order to survive emotionally. In the meantime, I just have to . . . pray that he will come around."

"Yes," he said in a tender voice that warmed her, "we must pray very hard and do our best to let him know that we love him."

Kyrah nodded and offered him a wan smile, wishing she could begin to tell him how she appreciated his optimism, his wisdom, his sensitivity. He returned the smile, looking into her eyes in a way that was plainly familiar. Still, she felt startled to see such blatant adoration there. She knew it had been there all along, but she wondered if she'd been too caught up in her own sorrow to pay any attention to the deeper meaning in his gaze. Looking into Garret's eyes now, she found the contrast startling. She'd not seen the tiniest glimmer of affection or love in Ritcherd's eyes for many weeks, yet Garret's eyes shone brilliantly with a love and admiration that she knew he worked hard to keep within appropriate boundaries. For a moment Kyrah became lost in his eyes, then she forced herself to look elsewhere, reminding herself where her commitment lay. She'd never felt remotely attracted to Garret. She appreciated his wisdom and sensitivity. They had been good friends for many years. And that was all. The strain between her and Ritcherd changed nothing.

"I should try and get some sleep," she said, standing abruptly.

Garret stood to face her, taking both her hands into his. "Sleep well," he said, pressing a quick kiss to her a brow in a way that was familiar.

"And you," she said, squeezing his hands tightly. "Thank you, Garret . . . for everything."

"I wish I could do more," he said, and she left the room.

An hour later, Kyrah lay staring into the darkness above her while her husband slept on the far side of the bed. She hadn't felt any more lonely than this when there had been an ocean between them, and she'd had to wonder if he would ever find her. Now she was his wife, but she couldn't help wondering if the best of all they would share was now in the past. She wished desperately to reach his aching heart, but each passing day made it seem more inevitable that she never would. As much as she tried to keep her mind from wandering to her conversation with Garret, she simply couldn't help recalling his tenderness, his concern, his sensitivity. But what frightened her most was that overt adoration in his eyes, and how she couldn't seem to stop thinking about it. Oh, how she longed to see even a degree of such affection in her husband's eyes!

Kyrah finally drifted into a fitful sleep, and somewhere in the darkness she rose from her bed and left Ritcherd sleeping. Carrying a lantern, she wandered the endless halls of her home with no particular destination in mind. Then, for no apparent reason, she found herself in the library. She set the lantern near the door and stood at the window, staring at the closed draperies, feeling they were somehow symbolic of the shroud surrounding Ritcherd's heart.

Kyrah heard a noise and turned abruptly to see Garret standing in the doorway, wearing a long dressing gown, hanging open to show that he wore his most common breeches, just as he'd worn when she'd awakened him to help search for Ritcherd. A quick glance told her that his feet and chest were bare, but she kept her focus on his face, feeling his eyes delve into hers.

"I couldn't sleep," he said. "I saw the light." While she was wondering what to say, he added, "Why are you crying?"

Kyrah touched her face to find it damp. "I didn't realize I was."

"You're always crying," he said. "I'm growing tired of seeing you cry." He closed the door as he said it, and Kyrah's heart leapt into her throat. She stared at the closed door, contemplating the implication, and then he locked it. She struggled for words to protest their being alone this way, while she willed herself to move toward the door, imagining herself leaving through it and returning to her bed—where her husband was sleeping. But her feet became as frozen as her tongue. She was startled from her attention to the door when Garret touched the tears on her face and she realized how close he was standing. Looking into his eyes, her heart quickened with a longing that she'd not even realized she felt. The warmth of his fingers on her face was hypnotizing, and she couldn't find the will to protest when he put his lips there, pulling her tears away with his kiss.

"Garret . . . no," she muttered, well aware of her own lack of conviction.

"I love you, Kyrah," he said, and she could feel his lips move against her face.

"I know, but—"

He pressed his fingers over her lips to stop her protests, then he replaced them with his lips. Kyrah was startled at how quickly she succumbed to the pleasure of his kiss, a kiss that went on and on, filling the aching hole in her with the love and affection she'd been starving for. He set her lips free only to press his kiss to her throat. "Garret . . . we mustn't," she murmured.

"I know," he said but made no effort to curb his passion. The room began to spin as he held her closer, kissed her harder, touched her as if he had a right to. She found herself looking up at him, wondering how she had allowed herself to let this happen. Mingled with a perfect rapture was the memory of Peter Westman beating her senseless while he'd repeatedly called her a whore. Realizing what she had just done with her husband's brother, she had to wonder if it was true. Garret drowned her desire to protest with a consuming kiss. She only wished that the moment could last forever, that the consequences would never have to be faced. But the reality bubbled out of her in a stifled cry. "Garret, no!"

Kyrah pushed him away and sat up abruptly. She came awake with a gasp and felt the darkness of her own room surround her. Ritcherd was snoring softly beside her. Her relief that the incident had only been a dream was starkly counteracted with the horror that her mind would conjure up such an experience at all. An undeniable tingling tempted her to believe that the experience had been real. Images of Garret's affection catapulted through her mind while she attempted to ban them from her thoughts and convince herself that the experience had not been real. Attempting to catch her breath and calm her racing heart, Kyrah wondered where such thoughts had come from. Never once had she even mildly contemplated such betrayal. She'd been comforted by Garret's sensitive words and tender understanding.

But she'd felt no yearning for his affection. She could almost imagine Lucifer himself planting such images in her mind, and now she had to be plagued by memories of an experience that had never happened.

Chapter Six

Temptation

While Kyrah's mind churned with the memory of her dream and the distance she felt from Ritcherd, she turned toward him in the bed, feeling a desperation she could never explain. "Ritcherd," she muttered, nudging him. "Ritcherd, wake up."

"What is it? What's wrong?" he asked, almost sounding like himself.

"I had a dream," she said. "A horrible dream."

"Tell me," he said as she pushed her arms around him and laid her head on his shoulder.

Kyrah hesitated. Certain that Ritcherd would see nothing in her dream but one more reason to be depressed, she simply said, "It's not worth repeating. I just . . . I need you, Ritcherd. Hold me," she pleaded. "Talk to me."

She felt more than heard him sigh as his arms came around her, but his embrace felt guarded, cold, almost patronizing. After several minutes of silence, he eased away, murmuring softly, "Forgive me, Kyrah. I know you deserve better than what I can give you. I just . . . don't know how to get past this."

"Past what, Ritcherd? This is much more than losing your sister. Talk to me," she pleaded. "Let me help you through this."

For a moment she allowed herself to believe that he would answer her plea, that he would open his heart to her and together they could get past this. But he eased farther away from her and out of the bed.

"Where are you going?" she demanded, wishing she'd never awakened him.

"I need to be alone," he said, and a moment later she heard the door closing softly.

Kyrah wrapped herself around Ritcherd's pillow and wept until her head pounded and her eyes burned. The light of morning filled the room while the aching loneliness consumed her. Attempting to be rational, she knew there was only one option to get through this. She would face this day with determination and keep putting one foot in front of the other. She was committed to Ritcherd, for better or worse, and she refused to let this setback undo them. Memories of her dream paraded through her mind, but she forced them away, certain that just as with most dreams, she would hardly be able to recall it by lunchtime.

Once she was bathed and dressed, Kyrah spent some time with Cetty before breakfast. She arrived at the dining room with a cheerful countenance, resigned to keeping her mind free of inappropriate thoughts, and to find a way—somehow—to reach her husband's grieving heart. Her courage faltered the moment she walked into the room to find Garret there, reading a London newspaper—and Ritcherd absent. She was contemplating a gracious escape when he tipped the corner of his paper down and smiled at her. She cursed inwardly at the way butterflies fluttered inside her and she was assaulted with a clear memory of how it had felt to have him kiss her. *But he hadn't!* she reminded herself. *It was a dream! Only a dream!* She forced her eyes elsewhere and coerced her mind to thoughts of Ritcherd.

"Good morning," Garret said. "I was just beginning to wonder if I would be eating alone."

"Perhaps I should go and find Ritcherd," she said without looking at him.

"He knows what time breakfast is served," he said.

Kyrah wanted to tell him her concerns, that he'd left their bed in the middle of the night. But she didn't want to tell him anything. She didn't even want to look at him. When Ritcherd came in and sat down, she felt equally reluctant to look at him. While vivid memories of her dream littered her mind against her will, she felt as if she had betrayed Ritcherd in her heart—even though she certainly had no control over the dream, and she was doing her best to fight away the memories of it.

As usual, Garret attempted to make some light conversation. Normally, Kyrah was grateful for his efforts, but today she didn't even want to acknowledge his presence in the room. After she'd managed to evade several polite questions, he asked, "Is something wrong, Kyrah?"

"I'm fine," she snapped, wishing it hadn't sounded so defensive. She glanced at Garret, then Ritcherd, startled to realize they were both surprised. At least she had Ritcherd's attention, she thought as she rose abruptly from the table, tossing her napkin in her chair. "I'm fine," she repeated and hurried from the room.

Ritcherd watched Kyrah leave then turned to look at Garret, who simply smiled and shrugged as if he had no idea why Kyrah was so testy. While Ritcherd continued to pick at his food, he was surprised to find his mind wandering to Kyrah's odd behavior. He'd spent weeks grossly preoccupied with his own dismal thoughts, but he'd not been totally unaware of Kyrah's moods. Of course, he knew he was likely to blame for her gloomy countenance and touchy emotions. He'd felt helpless to do anything about it and had hoped, if nothing else, that she might reach a point where she could stop worrying about him and be happy. But there was something odd about Kyrah's behavior this morning that piqued his interest. He almost forgot about it through the next few hours as his mind traveled through its habitual paths of self-degradation and misery. But at lunch Kyrah was even more terse toward Garret. She only glanced at Ritcherd once, and then she looked away as quickly as if his looking back at her was somehow painful.

Through the next few days, Ritcherd became so preoccupied with the changes in Kyrah that he found himself distracted from his own fears and grief. Her tender efforts to coax him out of his low spirits had completely ceased. In fact, she wouldn't speak to him at all, and she'd not looked him in the eye for days. Observing Kyrah and Garret interact, something uneasy began to smolder inside of him. The comfortable friendship shared between his wife and brother was completely absent; something between them had changed. How long had they been this way and he hadn't even noticed? Lying awake far into the night, he attempted to figure what possibilities could have created such tension between Kyrah and Garret—and between Kyrah and himself. He finally slept with the realization that his brain was too clouded to come to any feasible conclusions.

The following morning, Ritcherd came to terms with his concerns by coming to the same deduction he'd already come to—that Kyrah was likely better off without him. Over the next few days, he continued to observe Kyrah and Garret while his belief deepened that she would do better with a man like Garret. Without giving Kyrah any explanation, he began sleeping in a guest room. He contemplated filing for a divorce himself, knowing it was a relatively simple process if they were both in agreement. The social taint for both of them would be eternal, but that was something they'd both become accustomed to long ago. Then other complications that he'd almost forgotten about came to his mind, and he felt the answers to several problems were the same. He thought the situation through carefully, then waited until dessert had been served at supper before he brought it up.

"I've been thinking," he said, provoking astonishment from both Garret and Kyrah. "I don't wish to sound impertinent or difficult, but I've been thinking about the challenges we're facing, and I believe I've come up with a viable solution to every aspect of the problem."

"What problem exactly are you referring to?" Garret asked curtly.

"Accusations of treason, of course," Ritcherd said. He glanced at Kyrah and added, "And other . . . difficulties."

"We're listening," Garret said with a scowl, as if he already knew he wasn't going to like what Ritcherd had to say.

"It's all quite obvious, really. I'll transfer all of my property and assets to your name, and then I will simply tell the officials any treasonous activities were my doing, and you were just an ignorant pawn. If I tell them you're completely innocent, then you can be here to . . ." he glanced at Kyrah, "make certain all is well."

Following a long moment of bewildered silence, Kyrah rumbled, "You can't be serious!"

"Quite serious," Ritcherd insisted quietly.

"So, what are you saying, Ritcherd?" Kyrah came to her feet and gripped the table with both hands. "Is going to the gallows a favorable choice over living with me?"

The question cut Ritcherd deeply, but he fought to keep his emotions out of this. Glancing subtly toward Garret, he simply said, "Perhaps you would be better without me, my dear."

"And that's it?" Kyrah growled. "My husband cannot find the determination to even fight for his life—to fight to have a life with his wife and daughter? Well, maybe you're right, Ritcherd. If having me in your life is so meaningless to you, then maybe I would be better off without you. I really thought you were more of a man than that."

Ritcherd stood as well and leaned toward her. "Maybe I am man enough to see what's obvious."

"And what is that?"

"That it would be better if there were only one man in your life."

Kyrah's response was cut short by Garret saying coolly, "I have to agree on that point. But if anyone is going to take the blame for treason, it's going to be me. I got you into the privateering business. I don't have a wife and daughter who need me. If anyone is going to the gallows, it will be me."

"No," Kyrah insisted, "neither of you is going to die for this. You once lied to protect yourselves because you believed in the cause and there was no other way. The war is over, but you still believe in the cause. And you will both do whatever you have to in order to stay safe."

"And lie to save our hides?" Ritcherd countered.

"Yes!" she shouted.

"And what if there is evidence against us?" he retorted. "What if we can't worm our way out of it? Better that one of us dies so that you're not left alone to—"

"And it should be me," Garret said firmly.

The defiance in Ritcherd's eyes prompted Kyrah to the *real* problem. Her voice softened as she asked, "Why are you willing to die, Ritcherd? Why are you willing to leave me in Garret's care?"

Ritcherd looked at the floor as he answered, his voice resigned, "Perhaps you would be better off in Garret's care."

Kyrah gasped and took a step back as Garret shot out of his chair, took Ritcherd by the collar, and pushed him against the wall. She felt chilled from the intensity of the gaze they shared as Garret hissed, "I thought we already had this conversation—years ago. I thought you had learned this lesson. Do I need to bust you in the jaw to help you remember?"

"Maybe you do," Ritcherd said, his eyes intense, his voice passive.

"If you're trying to provoke me, it's working," Garret said, still holding him tightly against the wall. "Tell me how you can willingly let her go. Tell me how you could choose death over a life with her. I envy what you have, Ritcherd; night and day it nags at me. But I do not covet her. She is *your* wife. You spoke vows with her, and now you're telling her that you would choose to honor only the 'till death do you part.'"

Garret drew a sharp breath and went on, "Look at her, Ritcherd." Ritcherd only squeezed his eyes closed. "Look at her!" Garret growled and slammed Ritcherd against the wall. Ritcherd opened his eyes and looked over Garret's shoulder to see Kyrah silently weeping. "She is more precious than anything else this world or the next has to offer. She deserves every happiness. She deserves to be loved and revered beyond compare."

Ritcherd's eyes shifted to Garret. "Yes, I know, Garret . . . which is why she would be better off with you."

"How can you say that?" Kyrah cried just as Garret calmly stepped back and threw a fist that connected to Ritcherd's jaw.

"Stop it!" Kyrah demanded, pushing her way between them.

"You're a fool, Ritcherd Buchanan," Garret said. Ritcherd touched his lip, then looked at the blood on his fingers.

"I love *you*," Kyrah said through a stifled sob while she pressed her handkerchief to his bleeding lip. "You're the one I chose, Ritcherd. You're the one I committed my life to. It is you—and only you—who holds my heart. If I had to choose all over again this day, I would choose no differently."

Ritcherd's eyes showed the first glimmer of anger since he'd entered the room. He gazed hard at Kyrah, then Garret, then Kyrah again before he said, "Forgive me, my dear, but I'm not certain I believe you."

Ritcherd hurried from the room, slamming the door behind him. Garret turned to meet Kyrah's eyes. She looked abruptly away, speaking her most prominent thought. "When did all of this become my fault?"

"Your fault?" he echoed dubiously. She found her feelings difficult to define, and was relieved when he added, "Whatever he may or may not imply, Kyrah, it's clearly evident that you've done nothing wrong."

Kyrah wanted to believe him, but she felt the shame rise into her face. Her attention was drawn to the closed door. She became so focused on it that she was startled when Garret opened it. She expected him to leave, but he returned to the chair he'd been sitting on earlier.

"Talk to me, Kyrah," he said gently.

"What is there to say?" she asked, turning her back to him.

"We never had a problem in the past coming up with something to talk about. We are friends, Kyrah—brother and sister. There have never been any secrets between us. We've been through similar struggles in the past, and we may go through them again. But this is the first time in all the years I've known you that you wouldn't talk to me—you won't even look at me. And I want to know why."

Kyrah turned to look at him abruptly, tempted to be angry at his gumption. But his eyes were so genuine, so perfectly concerned, all she could do was look at the floor and try to force the images out of her mind. How could she tell him that she'd been plagued with the memories of a dream that tempted her feelings for him far beyond friendship? She felt tempted to leave the room and leave his plea unanswered. But she missed him. She needed his sound advice, his wisdom, his strength. But she felt hesitant to confide the whole truth to him. She didn't have to wonder if he might take unfair advantage of her vulnerability. She knew he wouldn't. She was more concerned with voicing her feelings and allowing them into the open. Attempting a different approach to the same problem, she admitted quietly, "I feel . . . lonely, Garret."

"Then talk to me," he said with a blatant compassion that made her heart swell.

Kyrah knew she only had two choices. Garret *was* her friend, and she knew he would never betray her trust—or Ritcherd's. She either had to be completely honest or continue shutting him out the way Ritcherd was shutting her out. She looked into his eyes and carefully weighed the risks. Then she sat down. "Garret," she said in little more than a whisper, "I'm well aware of your feelings for me. As you said, there are no secrets between us."

Kyrah watched him squeeze his eyes closed, as if hearing his feelings acknowledged was painful for him. "And what relevance does that have to anything?" he asked.

Tears trickled down Kyrah's cheeks as she admitted, "What I see . . . in your eyes, I long to see . . . in Ritcherd's, but . . . he won't even look at me. I know it's not been so many weeks, but . . . it feels like forever, and at times I fear that . . . he'll never come around, that the best of my life has already passed. I have to wonder if . . . he'll ever look at me that way again. If he'll ever want to touch me . . . or hold me. And now he tells me he would rather die than give me the love I need." She sniffled and wiped her face with the same handkerchief she'd used on Ritcherd's bloody lip. "Now he tells me that he doesn't believe me when I tell him that I love him. What have I done to deserve his disdain?"

"You've done nothing wrong, Kyrah. This problem is in Ritcherd's heart, but he will never solve it on his own. He's going to have to trust you enough to let you help his heart heal."

"And what if he never does? What if his hurt is too deep this time?"

"I can't answer that, Kyrah. But I really believe everything will be all right . . . eventually."

Kyrah met his eyes, then quickly darted her gaze elsewhere when memories of him holding her catapulted into her mind. She felt her breathing sharpen and closed her eyes, attempting to force her thoughts elsewhere. "What is it, Kyrah?" Garret asked in a voice that only heightened her difficulty in putting him out of her head. Fearing she'd said too much already, she stood and rushed toward the door until he caught her arm with his hand. She looked down at where he held her, then up at his face. She saw his eyes widen before he said, "You look absolutely terrified." He tightened his grip and eased her closer. "What have I done to make you afraid of me, Kyrah?"

"You've done nothing, Garret," she said, looking away.

He touched her chin with his finger and lifted her face to his view. "Then talk to me. Tell me why you won't look at me."

Kyrah knew he'd not let her go until she told him the truth. She closed her eyes to avoid looking at him. She cleared her throat carefully while searching for a safe place to begin. She finally asked, "Do you ever . . . struggle with . . . thoughts of me? With . . . temptation?"

She deeply hoped that he would tell her no. But his voice was gravelly as he said, "Every day."

Kyrah swallowed carefully and tried not to think too hard about that. "How do you deal with it, Garret? Isn't there something in the Bible about our thoughts and the way that—"

"Proverbs, twenty-three," he said. "'As he thinketh in his heart, so is he.'" His tone was subtly self-recriminating, and Kyrah wondered how much time he had spent studying Proverbs twenty-three. Then he added with a deepening terseness in his voice, "And in Matthew, chapter five, it says, 'That whosoever looketh on a woman to lust after her hath committed adultery with her already in his heart.'"

Kyrah sucked in her breath and teetered slightly. Garret steadied her arms with his hands and asked, "What is it? What's wrong?"

"That's your answer, Garret."

"What?" he asked, looking into her eyes.

Kyrah looked away and added, "That's why I can't look at you."

She heard him draw in a sharp breath then let it out slowly. "I see," he said and let go of her, taking a step back. His voice was toneless as he added, "And what exactly brought this on? I was under the impression that it was never a problem for you. Is Ritcherd's neglect of you so bad that—"

"Yes, his neglect is tearing me to pieces, but that's only part of the problem." She heard anger in her voice and wondered who exactly she was angry with.

"What's the other part?" he asked.

Kyrah turned her back to him. "You must understand me," she said.

"I'm trying to, but I can't if you don't tell me what's going on."

"I've always cared for you, Garret. Always. But my affection for you has never been remotely inappropriate. You must understand what I mean when I say that you are an extremely attractive man, but I never felt attracted."

"I understand," he said as if they were discussing the purchase of supplies for the *Phoenix*.

"I love Ritcherd."

"I know."

"I married him for better or worse. My commitment includes lengthy periods of grief or anger or detachment."

"I know."

"I have never even remotely entertained an inappropriate thought about you or any other man."

"Until . . ."

Tears bubbled out with her confession. "I had a dream . . . about you." She turned to look at him, seeing only confusion on his face. She attempted to clarify without being inappropriate. "I woke up feeling as if . . . it had really happened . . . between us."

"It?" he questioned, and she hardened her eyes on him. "Oh!" he said with obvious enlightenment, then he gave an embarrassed chuckle. "I see. And I missed it," he said with a trace of humor. "How tragic for me."

"Garret!" she scolded and he chuckled.

"Sorry," he said.

"I've tried to push the . . . memories out of my mind, but I have nothing to replace them with. And quite frankly . . . it frightens me."

"Frightens you?" he asked. "Why? Did you think I would take advantage of your loneliness?" He almost sounded angry.

"In my dream you did."

"Well, it wasn't real. It wasn't me."

"I know," she cried as her tears resurfaced. "But . . . the thoughts . . . plague me. Will my thoughts lead me to do something I'll regret? Have I committed adultery in my heart because the image is so clear in my head?" She lifted her eyes to his and felt a piece of her heart crack. It was clearly evident that he knew *exactly* how she felt. If nothing else, she had certainly learned to feel the poignancy of his position in this situation.

As if to clarify her own thoughts, he said in little more than a whisper, "I have asked myself those very questions a thousand times, Kyrah."

"And what are the answers, Garret? How do you deal with such thoughts and feelings?"

"I pray," he said firmly, matter-of-factly. "I pray very hard—sometimes constantly. I pray for the thoughts to relent, for the feelings to be tempered. I do my very best to make it clear to God that I did not choose these feelings and I would prefer to be without them, that my desire is to do what's right—by Him and by those I love. As I've said before, a feeling is just a feeling. It's how we act on our feelings that proves our character. So I do my best to keep my feelings properly reined. I pray for strength and discipline—and forgiveness because I struggle daily to be strong and disciplined."

He looked into her eyes and Kyrah returned his gaze, wondering why Ritcherd couldn't seem to love her half as much as Garret did. In spite of his resolve, the love in his eyes was blatantly evident—and it frightened her.

"You don't seem convinced," he said.

"Convinced of what?"

"That I would never do anything to hurt you—or Ritcherd."

"We can never be too careful."

"No, we can't. That's why the door is open. That is why I will *never* be alone with you—except in broad daylight with the door open and plenty of people in the house. I'm not naive enough to believe that we're beyond temptation, Kyrah. I know you see desire in my eyes, because it's there and I grow tired of trying to hide it. But look deeper, Kyrah. Look into my eyes and tell me what else you see. I'll tell you what you see. It's conviction. I have felt the destroyer in my life, Kyrah. I have a firm belief that Satan is real and he relishes destroying lives, families, relationships. He stirs up storms of greed, jealousy, anger, and hatred. And I believe the only way to ride such storms is by holding fast to our integrity and what we know to be right and true. I have seen firsthand the grief that comes from infidelity, Kyrah. I grew up knowing I was the product of my mother's affair. I hated my parents for their selfishness, and I hated the man who raised me for never accepting me as his own. I long ago came to terms with those feelings, but I will *not* make choices in my life that could leave you or anyone else vulnerable to such atrocity. My conviction is stronger than any temptation, Kyrah. And I will never cross such lines with you or any other woman. I love you, Kyrah, I do. And don't think for a moment that I don't see the loneliness in your eyes, and I ache to ease it. I struggle with such feelings every day, but I've not struggled with them this way since we were aboard the *Phoenix,* before you were married, and Ritcherd was so full of anger. He got through the problem then, and I believe he will again. I love Ritcherd. He's my brother and my friend. And we will ride this storm, the three of us, because we are *all* in this together—for better or worse."

Kyrah took a deep breath, inhaling his strength, his wisdom. She could never tell him how grateful she was for his conviction, because at the moment, she felt absolutely no conviction at all. She just felt lonely and weary. "Thank you," was all she could think to say, but his smile showed that he understood. He kissed her brow and left the room. Kyrah fought back a fresh rise of tears and went upstairs to be with Cetty. She was the one bright spot in Kyrah's life, and she was grateful for the distraction of being with her daughter.

The following morning, Kyrah went down to breakfast to find Garret at the table with a newspaper. He stood when she entered and helped her with her chair while they shared typical morning greetings—and pretended that they weren't both struggling with forbidden attraction.

Kyrah had barely begun her breakfast when one of the maids entered and said, "Captain Buchanan won't be joining you. He asked that breakfast be brought to his room."

When the maid left, Kyrah said to Garret, "Did you hear that? *His* room?"

"What do you mean?" he demanded.

"He's sleeping elsewhere."

Garret's eyes widened. "How long?"

"Days now. Except for our little conversation about his resigning himself to martyrdom, he's not said a word to me for . . . I don't know, it seems like forever. Oh, he says, 'Hello, dear,' when he passes me in the hall or sits down at the same table to eat. Now he's taking his meals in his room. How am I supposed to interpret this, Garret? I don't know which is worse—having him stay on his side of the bed, or leaving me alone in my bed altogether. He's made it clear that he would rather go to the gallows than be my husband. Now he's leaving me either alone or alone with you more every day."

Garret made no comment, and they ate mostly in silence, but a few days later Kyrah was tempted to eat in her room as well. Her loneliness was beginning to tell on her, and she was beginning to feel that thoughts of Garret were far more pleasant than wondering what had gone wrong between her and Ritcherd. In fact, she had hardly seen

Ritcherd at all since he'd told her he intended to go to the gallows and leave her in Garret's care.

Looking down the table at Garret while they silently shared their supper, she couldn't help wondering if it was in her to cross boundaries she never would have imagined being capable of. She didn't even think the words through before they rolled off her tongue. "Come to my room tonight, Garret," she said, and he choked on his wine. "Stay with me."

Once he'd stopped coughing, he said firmly, "What are you doing, Kyrah? Testing me?"

"Maybe," she said. "Or maybe I'm just lonely, or desperate, or . . . *angry* enough that I would actually consider giving Ritcherd exactly what he wants. He may not realize it consciously, but it seems readily evident that he's trying to give me away, and you're the most likely candidate to scrape me up off the floor once he's tossed me aside like an old pair of gloves. Right now I feel unloved, unwanted, unneeded . . . by the one person in this world who means more to me than any other—the man I love, and want, and . . . need." Her voice cracked. She squeezed her eyes closed and her lashes became wet with the tears that crept through. "Right now it's easy to believe that whatever I may have shared with Ritcherd is over, and the only way to feel loved and needed is . . . to be with you." She took a careful sip of her wine and absorbed his cautious countenance that couldn't begin to mask the desire in his eyes. She knew beyond any doubt that he was using every measure of self-discipline he possessed to keep from accepting her offer. And she admired him for it. She wasn't sure she could be that disciplined, given her present state of mind.

The ongoing silence compelled her to ask the most prominent question on her mind. "Does that make me a whore, Garret?"

"No!" he insisted. "It makes you human."

Garret watched Kyrah's eyes fill with fresh tears while an angry frustration mounted inside of him. He felt angry with himself for feeling this way about a woman forbidden to him, and he felt angry with Kyrah for putting him in a position where the battle between his heart and his head had become fierce and unnerving. But most of all he felt angry with Ritcherd for creating this situation that left him and Kyrah both feeling so completely helpless. He tried to force his anger back, but when a tangible desire filled him in its place, tempting him to just bolt out of this chair and take what Kyrah was offering, he lured the anger to take over. In this case, being angry seemed safer. He wondered if Kyrah really had any idea of the fire she was dabbling in. And he wondered if letting the subject drop now would only make her delusions grow deeper. And while he wondered, his indignation roiled inside him. Impulsively he heard himself testing her, as well. "Kiss me, Kyrah," he said, amazed at the fury he heard in his own voice. "Give me a taste of what I could expect if I came to your room tonight."

Kyrah glanced around uneasily, her eyes wide with astonishment. "We're in the dining room, Garret. We can't just—"

Garret shot out of his chair and took her arm, urging her to her feet. He rushed her into one of the side parlors, tossed the door closed, and turned her to face him. "Kiss me," he muttered. Her heart quickened with a combination of fear and excitement, but she couldn't bring herself to do it—as much as she wanted to. He took a step closer and pressed his lips to her throat. Her uneasiness increased and she eased away, saying, "Garret, no."

"You see," he said almost spitefully, looking into her eyes, "you can't go through with it. You could *never* go through with it."

Kyrah turned her back to him, finding it difficult to breathe beneath his intense gaze. Her heart threatened to pound right out of her chest when he shot one arm around her waist, then the other, pulling her back so tightly against him that she could feel his heart pounding, too.

"When you come clean with Ritcherd," he whispered behind her ear, his breath hot, his voice husky, "be sure to tell him the truth."

"What truth is that?" she muttered breathlessly.

"That when the opportunity was staring you in the face, you couldn't go through with it. Tell him that his brother cornered you alone in a room. Tell him he was even more desperate, and lonely, and . . . angry than you were. Tell him he'd had enough of seeing you hurting and alone when he'd been longing for too many years to just . . . have you." His voice lowered further. "But you couldn't go through with it."

Kyrah hung her head and wept while abject shame battled with an intrinsic desire to simply feel loved and cherished.

"Kyrah," he muttered, close to her ear, "do you have any idea how I want you? How I ache for you? Every night and day for as long as I've known you, I've fought away the temptation." His voice lowered and he tightened his grasp. "Oh, Kyrah, I love you. My love for you lures me to madness, to throwing all reason aside until I believe I could give up all that I have just to be with you for an hour." He sighed and moved his lips closer to her ear. "But I love you, Kyrah. How can I do something that would only bring pain into your life, when my deepest wish is to never see you hurt? How can one desire so directly contradict the other?"

"All that I feel is pain, Garret," she said, leaning her head back against his shoulder. She wrapped her arms around his where he held her, as if she could prevent him from ever letting go. "All I have felt for months now is pain. Even if the result were pain, how would I know the difference?"

He tightened his embrace as if to offer compassion for her pain, then abruptly he let go and turned her to face him, holding her shoulders in his hands. "Oh, you would know the difference, Kyrah. Stop thinking with your heart and use your head. Your heart is too battered right now to be fair to you. Think, Kyrah. Think. Imagine the day that Ritcherd suddenly comes back to his senses. Imagine his apologies, his humility, the evidence of his love for you. Imagine his helplessness when he doesn't understand why he feels the way he does. Imagine the way he punishes himself a hundredfold for the things he's done to hurt you. Now imagine looking him in the eye and telling him that you betrayed him when he needed you most." Kyrah moaned and hung her head. Garret went on, his voice growing husky. "Imagine trying to explain the selfishness that drove us into each other's arms. Think how it might feel to tell him there's a baby and it's not his." Kyrah whimpered and pressed a hand over her mouth. She attempted to free her shoulders from his grasp but he held her tighter, saying hotly, "Try to imagine looking at that child every day of its life, knowing its conception was a mistake. How do you make that child feel loved, Kyrah? Would Ritcherd love that child as his own? Or would he banish it from his heart, and banish me from his life?" He tightened his hold and lowered his voice. "That's how I grew up, Kyrah. No father to claim me and a mother who was ashamed of my

existence. Trust me when I tell you that you would know the difference. The possible pain we could create by selfishly taking what we
want now is indescribable."

Kyrah slumped against his hands and sobbed. She felt his arms
come around her, but it was only her friend, her brother, holding her
now. When she had managed to calm down, he lifted her chin with
his finger, forcing her to look at him. She was surprised to see anger
still brewing in his eyes when his demeanor was so calm. In a severe,
quiet voice, he said, "This is what we are going to do, Kyrah. We are
going to keep sleeping in our own beds, and we are going to keep
praying very hard. We are going to pray that Ritcherd finds his way
out of whatever inner prison is holding him, and we are going to pray
that in the meantime you and I will be able to withstand any temptation we are presented with. Right now you are going to walk away
from me and open that door and leave the room, so that when the
time comes, you will be able to look your husband in the eye and tell
him that you made the choice to leave the situation. But before you
leave, you are going to look me in the eye and promise me that you
will never—*never*—confront me with such a proposition again." He
sighed and the anger in his eyes deepened. "Next time I may not be
so noble." His gaze tightened on her as he growled quietly, "Promise
me, Kyrah."

Kyrah looked into his eyes while her mind wandered to a conversation they had shared years earlier when they had barely known each
other. She had begged him to make a promise to her and keep it. And he
had. She had seen evidence over and over since that time of the depth of
his integrity and the strength of his character. She reached up a hand to
touch his bearded face, murmuring quietly, "I promise, Garret."

He sighed and pressed a lingering kiss to her brow before he said,
"Go, Kyrah. Now." She hesitated and he snapped, "Go!" She stepped
away from him, startled. His expression became as fierce as his voice.
"Go before I change my mind."

Kyrah hurried from the room. Garret stared at the open door,
resisting the urge to curse aloud. He felt like finding Ritcherd and
giving him a fat lip—or worse. He knew he needed to talk to Ritcherd,
but he felt sure it would be better to wait until he'd cooled off a bit.
He couldn't recall ever feeling so angry in his life. He sank into a chair

and sighed loudly, rubbing his aching brow with his fingers. It took several minutes to work his way through the thicket of anger and find the underlying truth. He wanted Kyrah so badly that it hurt, and he was just plain scared that if Ritcherd didn't come around soon, he was either going to have to leave or end up doing the very thing he'd just convinced Kyrah would only bring more pain into their lives. He was only human, and the strain was beginning to tell on him. So he went outside and slowly savored a cigar.

The following morning, Garret skipped breakfast and went for a long ride. He spent some time in the stables, and purposely waited to go into the house until he knew lunch would be over. He got something to eat in the kitchen and went back to the stables, wondering if he could hide here until bedtime. He was alone in the stables with dusk settling in when he heard Kyrah's voice behind him.

"So, now you're avoiding me, as well," she said.

Garret glanced over his shoulder to see her holding a shawl tightly around her shoulders. Her expression revealed the torment she'd been struggling with. The quickening of his heart reminded him she wasn't the only one struggling. "Perhaps it's safer that way," he said, returning his attention to the horse he was currying.

"I see," she said, and he could hear the hurt in her voice. Better that he hurt her feelings than her, he reasoned. "Did you think I would back down on the promise I made to you?"

"No," he said quickly and firmly. "I just needed some time to . . . cool off."

Kyrah wondered if he was referring to anger or passion. He glanced briefly toward her, and she concluded that it was both. "And have you?" she asked.

"I'm working on it," he said. "How are you?"

"I'm . . . praying very hard," she said. When he said nothing and silence settled around them, Kyrah knew she had to say what she'd come here to say. "I must ask your forgiveness, Garret." He stopped currying but didn't look at her. "What I said was wrong."

Garret sighed. "What you said was understandable, Kyrah."

"Still wrong," she insisted. "I can never tell you how grateful I am for your . . . insight, and . . . your discipline."

Garret gave a scoffing laugh. "Don't go making me the noble one, Kyrah. Don't lose sight of the fact that I'm in love with another man's wife, and if I were not, we would not have a problem. If something doesn't change soon, I will be leaving."

Kyrah felt so startled that she was grateful he kept his attention on the horse. She forced a steady voice and asked, "Where will you go? If the *Phoenix* is grounded, then—"

"I don't know where I'll go. It doesn't matter. I feel like Ritcherd needs me, but if he refuses to let me help him, then I'm only making the problem worse by being here."

"And what about me?" she asked.

Garret gave her a sharp glance. "You would be better off crying on someone else's shoulder." He watched Kyrah's eyes fill with mist then turn downward, and the anger came rushing back into him. He tossed the currycomb down and moved toward the door.

"Where are you going?" Kyrah asked, turning to watch him go.

"I think it's time to have another little chat with your husband."

"Garret," she said as he neared the door. He turned to look at her. "You haven't told me if you've forgiven me," she said, her voice breaking as she looked down shamefully.

Garret stepped toward her and took her hand, pressing it to his lips. "Of course I have," he said. "It's all right, Kyrah. I understand."

"Yes, I know you do, but I have to say . . . thank you . . . for being strong enough for both of us."

"Kyrah," he said, briefly touching her face with his fingertips, "you must save yourself for Ritcherd. One day something's going to snap him out of this madness, and the two of you will be divinely happy."

"And you?" she asked.

"Me?" He laughed softly. "I'm saving myself, as well. I'm dreaming of the day when I find an incredible woman who will make me—"

"Forget all about me?"

"Never," he said. "You're far too unforgettable, Kyrah. It will take an incredible woman to take your place in my heart. And she will put my feelings in perspective, and the four of us will live happily ever after."

Kyrah smiled. "That's a nice thought."

"Yes, it is," he said, kissing her hand once more. Kyrah watched him, praying that he was right. But at the moment, it was difficult to comprehend any kind of happy ending for her. She felt more prone to believe that Garret would soon find the love of his life, and she would be doomed to a strained marriage for the rest of her days.

It took Garret nearly half an hour to find Ritcherd as he combed the ridiculous number of guest rooms in the house. He found him sitting in a chair, typically staring at nothing.

"So, what is this?" Garret asked, leaning in the door frame. "Now you've not only stopped eating meals with us, you've left your wife to sleep alone?"

"Did you come to say anything pertinent, Garret? If so, do it and get it over with."

"Fine, I will," Garret said, coming into the room. "I was going to talk to you last night, but I was so angry I was afraid I'd kill you. Now that I've calmed down, I came to tell you that you're an even bigger fool than I thought you were."

"Oh, well, thank you very much, Garret," Ritcherd said with sarcasm. "That's exactly what I needed to hear."

"What you need to hear is the truth, my brother. Do you have any idea the message you are giving your wife?"

"That she deserves better than me?" Ritcherd countered.

"Under the present circumstances, that's absolutely true. But that's not what she is getting from all of this. Your sweet wife has been put onto a list of priorities somewhere beneath whatever is eating at you. She figures—for good reason—that you would even prefer death over being her husband. She's certain that her happiness is all in the past and you have tossed her aside like an old pair of gloves. You won't even sleep in the same bed or eat at the same table with her—let alone show her any affection."

"Well, it's not true," Ritcherd said angrily. "I love her more than life . . . which is why I think it would be better if I just—"

"Oh, stop the self-pitying drivel and act like a man. You are plenty capable of giving her the love she needs. If you'd lower your pride and ask for some help to work through whatever is eating at you, perhaps you could get beyond it once and for all. But as long as you keep yourself locked up and away from those who love you, this will only get worse, and you *will* lose her. And when that happens, you will wonder what on earth you were thinking. You're going to wake up one day and find her gone, Ritcherd, and you're going to remember this conversation and hate me almost as much as you'll hate yourself."

Ritcherd looked hard at his brother while something sparked inside of him. While he was trying to figure out what it was, Garret asked, "Is that what you want? Is that *really* what you want, Ritcherd? You keep saying things to imply that you're trying to get rid of her. But I don't think you mean it. You know what I think?"

"I'm sure you're going to tell me."

"You bet I am," Garret said. "I think that deep down you're just desperately wanting her to assure you that she *does* love you, that she wants to be with you in spite of all the bad behavior you can dish out. Well, she *does* love you, Ritcherd, but eventually you're going to convince her that what you're saying is true. And what will you do when she finally says, 'You're right. I would be better off without you?' Then what?" Garret lowered his voice and tightened his gaze on Ritcherd. "You're losing her, Ritcherd. Be careful, my friend, or you will lose her completely. If you don't start showing up in her life and paying attention to what's going on, you are going to get exactly what you've asked for."

Ritcherd stared at Garret with an expression that was either dumbfounded or bored. Weary of trying to figure him out, Garret turned and left the room, figuring it was up to Ritcherd to decide if he would actually absorb the reality of what had been said. For himself, he was determined to put his own feelings aside, to put the past episodes behind him, and to be there for Ritcherd and Kyrah as far as it was possible.

Ritcherd watched Garret leave and attempted to push away his words. But hours later they were still churning in his head, while something deep inside lured him to believe that Garret was right. Were his own declarations to Kyrah only a backdoor effort to find proof of Kyrah's love and commitment to him? Was he inadvertently driving her to do the very thing he feared most? Attempting to look at his feelings honestly—instead of merely hiding from them—he had to admit that facing life without Kyrah was unthinkable. Only death could ease the pain he would face in losing her. Was that why he was so willing to lay down his life? Only because at some level he'd already accepted that he'd lost her? But how could he lose her? How could he possibly live without her? Garret was right—as usual. Ritcherd was a fool, a complete and utter fool. He didn't know what was wrong with him, but he knew he'd never get through it without Kyrah. He could only hope that it wasn't already too late to mend all that had come between them.

Chapter Seven

The Assumption

The following morning, Ritcherd got cleaned up and went down to breakfast. He'd slept very little as he'd contemplated Garret's warning. He'd struggled with how he could possibly get beyond the darkness clouding his mind and undo all that he'd done. He'd finally come to the conclusion that he had to ask for help. Garret and Kyrah had both told him over and over that he needed to open up to them, to talk about what he was feeling and work it through. The very idea was terrifying, but not as much as the idea of actually losing his wife.

Kyrah was alone in the dining room when he entered. Her surprise at seeing him there was evident, but when she barely glanced at him, he was reminded of earlier concerns that he'd dismissed by reverting to his old habits of wallowing in his grief. Garret entered the room while he was still attempting to put his thoughts together.

"Well, good morning, Ritch," he said brightly.

"Good morning," Ritcherd said.

Ritcherd's uneasiness increased as he observed his wife. Days ago he'd come to the conclusion that something had changed between her and Garret, but he'd given up his attempts to figure out what it was. Now, the tension was so thick in the room that Ritcherd could barely see his wife through it. But her attention was elsewhere. When she wasn't closely studying the food on her plate, her eyes were definitely elsewhere. Her eyes were on Garret.

Kyrah absently stirred her food while her mind was raging a battle between good and evil, between thoughts of a husband who wanted nothing to do with her, and a man who had quickly become an obsession to her—even against her will. She was more grateful every day for Garret's convictions when her increasing loneliness and frustration lured her thoughts easily to Garret and the memories of an indiscretion that was nothing more than a product of her imagination. Still, the images had settled comfortably into her conscious mind, and she was daily becoming weaker in fighting away those images when there was so much in her life that she didn't want to even consider. Garret's advice to keep praying was all well and good—and she certainly *had* been praying, harder than she ever had in her life. But the reality of fighting these feelings day in and day out, when her husband wouldn't so much as glance at her, was growing more difficult by the hour.

For a long moment Kyrah allowed herself to look at Garret while she wondered what it might be like. He caught her looking at him over the table. She saw his brow furrow and his eyes intensify, as if he were attempting to gauge her thoughts. He continued to hold her gaze while empathy and compassion shone brilliantly in his eyes. Her heart quickened and her mouth went dry. She abruptly squeezed her eyes closed against the images in her mind, only to have them become more clear. Opening them again, she saw Garret glance toward Ritcherd, and his eyes turned cautious. Kyrah turned abruptly to see Ritcherd watching her, his eyes wide with astonishment. He'd hardly glanced at her for weeks, and he just had to be looking at her in *that* moment. She felt shame rise into her face and quickly looked down, consumed with guilt and contrition.

Ritcherd's heart began to pound before he consciously realized what he'd just seen in Kyrah's eyes. Everything suddenly made such perfect sense that he found it difficult to breathe. He felt as if a fire had just erupted in the center of his chest and was threatening to burn him alive from the inside out. He rushed from the room with no explanation, fearing that any attempt to speak would betray the horror he'd just been confronted with.

Ritcherd hurried into the nearest empty room, which happened to be the library. He closed the door and leaned against it, gasping for breath. He pressed both hands over his chest as if he could force air into his lungs. "No!" he growled from low in his throat and slid to the floor. "They wouldn't do this to me. They *wouldn't!*" He pressed his knuckles to his mouth to keep from screaming aloud.

Ritcherd told himself to be rational and not go making gross assumptions. But logically adding up the circumstances only deepened the evidence. The blatant guilt in Kyrah's eyes. The obvious tension between her and Garret. And the memory of Garret's words . . . *I'm a gentleman, not a saint . . . My head grows weaker when my heart sees her in such anguish. And you should be man enough to realize that the only way to truly keep a woman from straying is to keep her happy . . . I will consider her fair game, and I will do everything in my power to lure her away from you . . . You're going to wake up one day and find her gone, Ritcherd, and you're going to hate me almost as much as you'll hate yourself.*

"No!" Ritcherd muttered again, tugging at his hair with his hands. "Oh, God help me. What have I done? What have I done?"

Ritcherd recalled a time in the past when he had initially discovered Garret's feelings for Kyrah. He'd been angry and hotheaded, and Garret had quickly put him in his place. But Ritcherd didn't feel angry now. He only felt a deep, irreparable heartache. It was easy to see that he'd driven her away. He'd hurt her deeply and he knew it. Garret and Kyrah had both tried repeatedly to reason with him, and he'd stubbornly resisted their advice and their efforts to help him through his heartache. Instead, he had closed himself off. He had sorely neglected, even abused his wife. And now he could not deny the part he had played in driving her to another man's arms. But why did it have to be Garret? The one man he loved and trusted more than any other? He couldn't believe it. He just couldn't believe it.

Ritcherd became so thoroughly upset that he forced himself to calm down and think clearly, fearing he would truly go over the edge to insanity if he didn't. Sitting on the floor for more than two hours, he convinced himself that he was jumping to conclusions and assuming the worst. Perhaps their changed behavior was for an entirely different reason. When he realized it was lunchtime, he forced himself to his senses and quickly freshened up before he went to the dining room. He'd spent weeks wanting only to hide and wallow in his anguish. Now he felt suddenly desperate to be with Kyrah, to see if he could somehow undo the damage that had been done—if such a thing was possible. Deep in his heart he hoped and prayed that spending time with Garret and Kyrah would prove his assumptions foolish and ridiculous. As the meal commenced, he discreetly observed them. Garret was keenly aware of Kyrah, in a circumspect and perceptive way that Ritcherd knew well. And Garret's feelings for her showed clearly in his eyes. That was nothing new. He'd never made any attempt to hide the truth, making it clear to Ritcherd that he felt complete honesty was the best way to handle the situation. The irony of such a statement now made Ritcherd's stomach churn. Again, Ritcherd tried to tell himself that he was letting his imagination overtake him. But as he watched them closely, the evidence deepened. Garret appeared overly concerned by Kyrah's blatant avoidance of his gaze. When he looked at Ritcherd he didn't look guilty, rather defiant—but subtly nervous.

What really caught Ritcherd's attention, however, was the way Kyrah blatantly avoided looking at either one of them. Wanting to get a good look at her eyes, he asked, "Are you all right, Kyrah?"

She looked up at him, astonished. Of course, he'd not inquired over her well-being for several weeks. Still, she only looked at him a long moment before her eyes turned shamefully away—but not before he'd clearly read the guilt there. She had betrayed him and he knew it.

"I'm fine," she insisted in a tone of voice that completely contradicted the statement.

A part of Ritcherd wanted to jump out of his seat and bust Garret in the jaw. He wanted to kick him out of the house and tell him to never come back. He wanted to hold Kyrah painfully tight and remind her who her husband was. But Ritcherd knew that no amount of anger would solve this problem. In fact, his anger had only helped create it. He was mostly to blame and he knew it. And in the deepest part of his heart, he had to wonder what he'd wondered all along. Perhaps she was better off without him. Perhaps he should be grateful that a man as fine as Garret was there for her, to scoop her up off the floor—quite literally—when her husband caused her such pain.

Ritcherd took a good, long look at Kyrah, then Garret, then Kyrah again. And before he even realized what was happening, he felt tears slide down his cheeks. He'd not actually cried tears since the night Celeste died. Since that time, he'd kept his emotions locked away while he'd only felt hollow and dead inside. And now—now—he was crying. He was startled from his thoughts when he realized that Kyrah and Garret were staring at him. They appeared as astonished as he felt. The irony of the situation settled in more deeply as Kyrah's eyes filled with guilt and turned away. Ritcherd wiped at his face with his shirtsleeve and hurried from the room. Again he found himself alone in the library while torrents of emotion rushed out of him in tortured sobs. He fought to keep his tears silent as he knelt in the center of the floor, wrapping his arms around his middle, groaning in anguish. He wondered when it had happened between them. Where? *Why?* He groaned again. He *knew* why. He'd been a fool. He'd driven her away.

"Oh, God help me," he muttered as a physical pain threatened to completely devour him. He prayed and cried for what seemed hours until he ended up lying on the floor, looking at the ceiling, wondering what he was supposed to do now. For the first time since Celeste's death, he felt as if he could actually *feel.* And what he felt was pain, regret, perfect sorrow. No wonder he'd chosen to block such feelings out of his mind, his heart. Or had he? Looking back over the past several weeks, he felt as if he'd been existing in a dark cloud of confusion and despair. He didn't see how he'd had any choice at all in the way he'd felt. Then it occurred to him that he certainly had a choice now. He felt alive again—the pain was a good indication of that. He marveled that emotions could cause such literal, physical pain. Still, he *did* have a choice. What had Garret said in their last conversation? *You're losing her, Ritcherd. Be careful, my friend, or you will lose her completely.* Did that mean he'd not yet completely lost her? Did that mean there was still hope? Only if he could be man enough to let her know how he loved her, how he would die without her. Surely it wasn't too late.

Ritcherd tried to stand but only made it to his knees. Deciding he needed all the help he could get, he stayed there a long while, praying for forgiveness, for fortitude, for understanding—and for his head to remain clear of the fog that had held it bound. He needed to get on with his life.

Determined to let Kyrah—and Garret—know exactly where he stood, Ritcherd hurried from the library, hoping he could find them without too much effort. His strength was drained. He'd not gone far down the hall when he heard them talking and realized they were in one of the parlors, with the door open. At first he was unable to catch any words, but he could distinctly hear Garret's tender tone of voice as he spoke to Kyrah. Again he felt tempted to anger, but he knew the damage his anger had done in the past. Surely he could be a better man than that; surely he could be civilized and noble and rise above the beast within himself to solve this problem with these people he loved so dearly. Moving closer, but staying out of sight, Ritcherd wondered if he might hear evidence that his assumptions had been ridiculous. Oh, how he wanted to! But as the conversation evolved, Ritcherd slid to the floor and pressed his head into his hands, wondering how it had come to this—and how it could ever be undone. And then Kyrah's words gave him something he'd not expected—hope. Tangible, definable hope. Still, his hope mingled with his anguish until he felt as if a volcano might erupt inside of him. Since Celeste's death, he had struggled inwardly over every hurt in his life. But only now did he feel those hurts. Fearing he would create a scene if he stayed here another second, he rushed down the hall and out the side door, wanting only to be alone. Completely alone.

The moment Ritcherd left the dining room, Kyrah rose and did the same, wanting only to be alone. At times her burden simply became too much to bear, and this was one of those times. Her heart ached for Ritcherd, while at the same time she felt so thoroughly confused and abandoned by her husband that the heartache rushed out of her in torrents. She quickly hurried to one of the parlors and closed the door, crying for what seemed forever, then she curled up on one of the sofas and prayed with all the energy of her soul that the Ritcherd she knew and loved could somehow reach beyond this cloud of oppression that stood between them.

Kyrah wasn't aware that she'd drifted off to sleep until she was nudged awake. "Are you all right, Kyrah?" Garret asked gently. She glanced to the door, not surprised to see it open.

"I'll be fine," she said, forcing herself to sit up.

He told her that he'd been with Cetty and talked of the things they'd been doing. Kyrah expressed her gratitude for all that he did, then silence fell between them.

"What's wrong, Kyrah?" Garret asked softly.

"That's a stupid question, Garret." She couldn't help sounding angry. "You know as well as anyone that Ritcherd is—"

"I'm well aware that Ritcherd is struggling." His tone was equally terse. "I want to know why you won't look at me without looking terrified. I thought we'd talked all of that through and put it behind us."

"It's all very well and good to say that I should be able to will feelings and memories out of my mind, but it's much easier said than done. I have prayed to put it behind me, Garret, but I'm not so sure my prayers are being heard."

"And why wouldn't they be?" he asked more gently.

"I don't know," she snapped. "Maybe it has something to do with the way I keep hearing Peter Westman in my head, calling me a whore."

"That's ludicrous," Garret insisted. "The man's been dead for years."

"Well, he came back to life the same moment I—"

"Kyrah, listen to me. You've got to calm down. You can't blame yourself for being human. I think you're making far more out of this than it warrants." His voice softened considerably. "You are *not* a whore. Do you hear me?"

"Then why do I feel like one? You're the one who was quoting scriptures the other day. How exactly do you define adultery according to Matthew, chapter five?"

"You'd do well to keep your voice down, Mrs. Buchanan. Do you want the entire household gossiping about us?"

"I don't care. I don't care what anyone thinks . . . except Ritcherd. And what I wouldn't give to know what he's thinking these days!"

"You need to tell him what happened, Kyrah," Garret said gently.

Kyrah responded with a bitter laugh. "Tell him? Oh, that ought to lift his spirits! He would never understand, Garret." Her voice saddened. "Or maybe he simply wouldn't care. If I had any reason to believe he cared about me whatsoever anymore . . . if he would talk to me at all . . . if he would even look at me with half as much love in his eyes as I see in yours . . . Oh, Garret! If only he could know how I love him—how I have always loved him. If only he could forgive me and we could start again."

"You must tell him," Garret urged.

"I suppose I must, but . . . I can't. Not yet. I already lie awake at night, fearing he'll do something rash. I've had nightmares about him confessing his crimes and hanging for them, all for the sake of attempting to put an end to the heartache he's feeling. Oh, Garret," she muttered and was overcome with tears. She found herself in Garret's arms while her heart ached for Ritcherd and she wondered what it would be like to feel his arms around her. She honestly couldn't remember what that was like, it had been so long.

The sound of hurried footsteps and a door slamming in the distance brought Kyrah to her senses. "That can't have been one of the servants," she muttered, looking at Garret with panicked eyes. She rushed to the window and saw Ritcherd running across the lawn toward the stables, his cloak flying behind him.

"Good heavens," she said and moved into the hallway with Garret close behind her. They each grabbed their cloaks on their way out the side door.

"Why don't you let me handle this?" Garret said as they entered the stable.

"No," Kyrah said, grabbing a bridle from a hook on the wall. "Why don't you let *me* handle this?"

"You have no idea where he's even gone." Garret took the bridle and put it on her favorite mare. "You can't just go wandering the countryside looking for him in this cold. You'll—"

"I know exactly where he's gone," she said, and mounted bareback with his help. Looking into Garret's eyes she added, "I just feel like I need to handle this alone. Give me an hour. If I'm not back by then, come find us. Start looking at the church ruins."

"I will," he said, albeit reluctantly. "Be careful."

"Of course," she said and heeled the stallion into a gallop.

It only took her a few minutes to arrive at the church ruins. She saw Ritcherd's horse tethered there and her heart quickened. Tying her horse beside his, she heard evidence of his emotion and prayed with all her heart that she would be able to reach him, that somehow they would be able to find something they could hold on to together.

Kyrah made no effort to enter the ruins quietly, but she soon realized that Ritcherd was completely unaware of her presence. Her heart broke to see him on his knees, wrapped in his cloak, sobbing like a lost child. Silent tears fell down her own cheeks to witness his anguish. She moved quietly to one of the few remaining stone pews and tried to comprehend what might have provoked such grief in Ritcherd when he'd been mostly emotionless and despondent for more than two months.

Minutes passed while Kyrah attempted to get control of her own emotion and allowed him the time he needed to vent his. Three different times he muttered, "Dear God, what have I done?"

"Ritcherd," she finally said, unable to witness his anguish any longer. His head shot up and he stood abruptly. Their eyes met for only a second before he glanced away, looking ashamed. "It's all right," she said, stepping closer. "I've seen you cry before, Ritcherd." Still he wouldn't look at her. "What *have* you done?" she asked.

Ritcherd squeezed his eyes shut and swallowed hard. He'd been praying that he could reconcile with her, that everything could be brought into the open. But he hadn't expected the opportunity to present itself so quickly, and he wasn't certain how to handle it. Praying now for courage, he reminded himself that she was his wife, and she certainly *had* seen him cry before. But never like this. He couldn't recall ever being so emotional. The deaths of loved ones, and the heartaches of his life, all fell into perspective with the reality of what he had lost with Kyrah. He only prayed that he could get it back. Slowly he turned to face her, and he felt freshly taken aback by her beauty. How long had it been since he'd noticed how beautiful she was? Garret had noticed. The thought provoked fresh pain. He forced away the images in his mind and prayed for a place to begin.

"What have you done, Ritcherd?" she repeated gently.

It took him a moment to recall what she'd overheard him saying. He cleared his throat and kept his eyes focused on hers. "I pushed you away. I shut you out. I drove you to him." She said nothing and he forged ahead, telling himself to just get it out and get it over with. "You don't have to tell me what happened, Kyrah, because I already know." He paused to gauge her reaction, and couldn't tell if she looked scared or confused—or both. He forced himself to keep going. "I've seen the guilt and shame in your eyes, Kyrah, and the way you look at him—and he at you. I cannot even begin to tell you the . . . horror I feel . . ." He closed his eyes and choked back a sob. "To think of you . . . with him . . . that way, but . . . I know I'm at least partly to blame." He sobbed again but couldn't look at her. "I know he loves you, Kyrah, and I have to assume that you love him, too, but—"

"I love *you*, Ritcherd," she said with conviction and a surge of tears that made it impossible for her to come up with the words to clear up this misunderstanding. Had he overheard something? Misconstrued the situation so grossly?

Ritcherd opened his eyes, searching for sincerity in her eyes, and quickly finding it. "Do you, Kyrah?" he asked. "Do you really? There's a part of me that just can't imagine someone like you loving someone like me, especially with the way I've treated you at times. I just couldn't believe it when you told me, but I overheard you telling Garret that you love me. Oh, Kyrah, I pray to God that you love me, that you can put this behind you, because I can't bear the thought of giving you up to him. I need you, Kyrah. I know I've been a fool. I know there's something wrong inside of me, and I need to work it out. I need to talk it through. You were right when you said I can't fix the problems myself. I need you. I need your help to get through this, and I'll never shut you out of my heart again, Kyrah, I swear it."

He stepped forward with a desperation that she felt in his grip as he took hold of her shoulders. "Please tell me that you love me, Kyrah, that you will still be mine, that you will put whatever you shared with him behind you. Please tell me that you can forgive me, because I would gladly forgive you if you would only give me another chance. Even if there's a baby, Kyrah, it's all right. I'll raise it as my own. The child will never know the difference. Please, Kyrah, tell me we have another chance."

Kyrah was momentarily too stunned to speak. "Oh, Ritcherd," she whispered and wiped the tears from his face with her fingers. Looking into his eyes, she could see the love and conviction that had once been so familiar to her.

Ritcherd held his breath, waiting for some kind of response. In spite of his anguish over all that had come between them, he felt as if his very life depended on her willingness to put her relationship with Garret aside and give him another chance.

"You're back," she said and smiled with fresh tears showing in her eyes.

When she said nothing more, he tightened his grip on her shoulders and pleaded, "Kyrah, tell me there's still a chance for us. Tell me that—"

"Ritcherd," she put her fingers over his lips, "there has been a horrible misunderstanding. I have shared nothing with Garret beyond what you have seen with your own eyes. He's not so much as kissed my lips since our wedding day when he insisted on kissing the bride."

Ritcherd sucked in his breath and held it. The conviction in her eyes lured him to believe she was telling the truth, but his mind tallied the evidence and he felt the need to protest. "Something changed between the two of you, Kyrah. I could see it, feel it. I saw the guilt in your eyes. I heard the two of you talking."

"When?" she asked.

"Just . . . before I came here." He tried to recall exactly what had been said, and he couldn't, except for that word; that horrible word. "You said something about . . . a reference in the Bible. Adultery, you said."

"Oh, Ritcherd," she muttered, her voice cracking. "I had a dream— a very . . . disturbing, vivid dream . . . about Garret. I couldn't get it out of my mind. That's the source of the guilt you saw in my eyes. That's the reason I couldn't look at Garret, or speak to him without feeling ashamed. He finally forced me to tell him what was wrong. He admitted to often struggling with the same thing." She leaned closer to him. "Matthew, chapter five. I've read it a dozen times since we talked a few days ago. 'That whosoever looketh on a woman to lust after her hath committed adultery with her already in his heart.'"

Kyrah became unnerved by the intensity in his eyes. She could well imagine how disgusted he must feel to know that she and Garret had been thinking that way about each other. Looking away, she added in a tentative voice, "So you see, Ritcherd, there is cause for the guilt you see in my eyes. But not for the reasons you believed. I've prayed very hard to be free of the images in my mind, and Garret is doing the same. You must forgive me for—"

Ritcherd lifted her chin with his finger and looked into her eyes. His voice broke as he asked, "I need to know if I understand. Are you telling me that nothing happened between the two of you? Nothing?"

"Nothing beyond a dream that I've had trouble forgetting. Nothing."

With the assurance that her explanation was indeed valid, a tangible relief flooded from the deepest part of Ritcherd's chest, coming into the open on an unfathomable sob. He hung his head and sobbed again before he sank to his knees and cried without restraint. He felt Kyrah's hands in his hair and he clutched onto her, pressing his face into the folds of her skirts until she knelt to face him, silent tears coursing down her face. Gaining a degree of control, he wiped his face with his sleeve and looked into her eyes. Taking her face into his hands, he felt the need to clarify something he found difficult to believe. "He didn't even kiss you?"

"No, Ritcherd."

Ritcherd laughed with perfect relief and wrapped her in his arms. Kyrah held to him and wept against his chest, grateful beyond words to feel her husband hold her close, but more importantly, to feel his love for her. She found her lips beneath his and whimpered from the comfort. His kiss was so thoroughly familiar to her, yet through many weeks of going without his affection, it felt captivatingly strange. She took his face into her hands and welded her mouth to his, as if she could never get enough to replenish the drought she'd experienced through his absence of spirit.

While Ritcherd absorbed a tangible sustenance from Kyrah's kiss, he wondered what kind of madness had lured him to initiate such distance between them. He honestly had to wonder if he'd become victim to some measure of insanity. What else could possibly explain his recent state of mind and the wedge it had driven between him and his wife? And to think of the damage it had very nearly done in their lives made him tremble from the inside out. His gratitude that Kyrah had remained loyal to him was beyond description. But his own behavior of late frightened him. When Kyrah lay back on the cold earth, her cloak beneath her, urging him to lie beside her, he forced his mind to the present and pushed all else away.

"I love you, Kyrah," he murmured close to her face, "more than life itself." She cried audibly and held him closer in response to his words, and he began to comprehend the anguish he had put her through. "Forgive me," he whispered close to her ear as he drew her more closely into his arms.

"Of course," she said. "You must forgive me, as well."

He lifted his head enough to look into her eyes. "But you just told me you did nothing wrong."

Kyrah measured her words carefully. "If we're going to get beyond this, we have to be completely honest with each other."

"I would expect nothing less from you," he said.

"I wanted to do something wrong, Ritcherd. The temptation was great. My heart was with you, but my head was elsewhere. If not for Garret's conviction . . . it might have happened."

Ritcherd took a sharp breath then rolled away from her, looking toward the sky. Her admission that nothing had occurred between her and Garret had relieved him so deeply that he'd not stopped to ponder the implications of her explanation. He reminded himself that she was being open with him, and asking his forgiveness. He had to handle this maturely. Their relationship was too fragile to endure more strain. He swallowed carefully and said, "You've told me many times that you weren't attracted to him."

"I never was . . . before."

"Before?"

"Before . . . that dream," she admitted. "But you must understand, Ritcherd. Such a dream at any other time might have been disturbing, but I doubt its effects would have stayed with me long. But under the circumstances, I . . ." Kyrah hesitated, not wanting to upset him or undo the progress they'd made.

"You what?" he demanded gently.

Reminding herself of what she'd said moments ago, that they had to be completely honest with each other, she forced herself to just say it. "I saw love in Garret's eyes, Ritcherd. I saw nothing in yours. You wouldn't touch me, or even look at me. You made it clear that you preferred to die than be a part of my life, and you told me that I would be better off with Garret."

Ritcherd squeezed his eyes closed in self-recrimination. "Maybe you would be."

"No!" She took his face into her hands and shook it gently, startling his eyes open. "I love you, Ritcherd. It's you that I need, you that I want. But I was lonely . . . and hurt. Even angry. Since you seemed eager to toss me aside and leave me in Garret's care, I reached a point where I could find little reason not to give him everything that you would not take. I'm not going to keep any secrets from you, Ritcherd. You need to know that I asked him to spend the night with me."

Ritcherd's breathing became sharp and he turned his face away. Even in his belief that they had been intimate, he had somehow assuaged his own pain with the assumption that Garret would have been the initiator, that he might have taken advantage of the situation. He had to admit now that with what he knew of Garret's character, it didn't ring true. But to know that Kyrah would not only entertain such thoughts, but act on them, was difficult for him to swallow. He forced himself to the fact that nothing had happened between them. For that he was truly grateful. He was also grateful to have a wife who would still love and accept him, in spite of his atrocious behavior. A wife who was honest and courageous enough to face this squarely instead of brushing it under the rug to fester unspoken between them.

"Only minutes ago you told me you would forgive me for committing adultery, that we could put it behind us and start over. Surely you can forgive me for merely wanting to."

Ritcherd sighed. "Forgiveness is not the issue, Kyrah. Of course I forgive you. How could I not, when you are always so eager to forgive me of my every shortcoming, even when I hurt you?"

"So, what is the issue?"

He swallowed carefully and looked into her eyes. "I can keep him out of your bed, but I can't keep him out of your mind—and your heart."

"You *can!*"

"How?" he demanded. "Tell me how and I'll do it. I'll do anything if it will keep you mine—all mine!"

"You can do it the way you always did before. You kept my mind and my heart so full of your love that there was no room for Garret, there was no reason to have him there. I love him as my brother, my friend.

But I do not need him in any other way so long as I have you. Keep me in your heart, Ritcherd. And let me keep you in mine. No matter what troubles you, please . . . promise me . . . that you will keep me close to you, that we will share our burdens as we always have before."

"I promise, Kyrah. Oh, I promise. Forgive me."

"It's in the past," she said, and kissed him long and hard.

He drew her back into his arms, holding her as if he might never have the chance again. The passion they shared was brief but intense, filled with the desperation they'd both encountered in fearing they might never share such intimacy again. And when his passion was spent, Ritcherd pressed his face to her throat and wept. He wept for the losses that had catapulted him into an internal hell that he still didn't begin to understand. He wept for the grief he had caused for Kyrah— and even Garret. And he wept for the relief he felt now in knowing that his marriage had been spared in spite of his stupidity. Or was it insanity? He forced the question away and allowed the tears to flow out of him, praying they might take all of his grief and fear with them.

A perfect stillness overtook them, beyond the familiar howl of the Cornish wind playing among the church ruins. They held each other in silent contemplation until Kyrah nuzzled closer, saying, "It's cold out here."

"I hadn't noticed until a minute ago," he said.

"Me neither," she added with a little laugh.

"It is winter, after all."

"We must get back," she said, sitting up abruptly.

"Did you have an appointment or something?"

"No, but . . . Garret was worried. I told him if we weren't back in an hour, to come and find us."

"Well, I'm glad he didn't find us a few minutes ago," Ritcherd said, helping her to her feet. "I love you, Kyrah." He touched her face and hair.

"I love you too, Ritcherd. I always have. I always will."

"For that I am truly grateful."

He helped her mount the horse she'd come on, then he mounted his own and they rode toward home, side by side. A few minutes later, he said, "Wait a minute." And they both halted.

"Is there anything else I need to know?" he asked.

"No." She shook her head.

"One thing, perhaps," he said intently.

"What? I'll tell you anything . . . everything. Just ask."

"What did Garret say . . . when you invited him to spend the night with you?"

She sighed loudly. "He told me we'd do well to keep sleeping in our own beds, and to keep praying very hard."

"*Keep* praying?" he asked. "About what?"

"He'd told me earlier that the only way he could deal with his feelings for me was to pray. And perhaps you would like to know what else he told me."

"I'm listening," he said, while a mixture of emotions made him wonder if he *did* want to know. While he couldn't help respecting Garret for his choices and his wisdom, it was difficult to feel comfortable with the open knowledge that his brother was deeply in love with his wife.

"I'm certain I can't say it as eloquently as he did, but I remember the gist of his words well; they left a profound impression on me." Kyrah took a deep breath. "He said that he firmly believed that Satan is real and he works very hard to destroy families and relationships, that he stirs up storms in our lives through our hatred and anger and jealousy. Garret said that he believes the only way to ride out such storms is to hold to our integrity, and to do what we know is right. He talked about the grief he had personally experienced from infidelity, growing up as he had, and that he would never make choices in his life that could leave anyone vulnerable to such horrors. He made it clear that his conviction was stronger than his temptation, that he would never cross such lines with me or any other woman." Kyrah's voice broke as she finished with vehemence. "And he said that he loves you . . . as his brother, and his friend. He told me that we would ride this storm together, the three of us, because we are *all* in this together—for better or worse."

Kyrah studied his stunned expression before she added softly, "Was there anything else you wanted to know?"

"Only one thing. What did I ever do to deserve such love and devotion from the two most incredible people I've ever known?"

Kyrah reached out a hand to touch his face. "Garret is no more incredible than you, Ritcherd. He's simply found peace with himself."

"I'm not certain such a thing is possible for me," he admitted. "But I'm willing to try."

"And I will be beside you, so long as you want me there."

"Forever," he insisted and bent toward her to kiss her before they rode on.

Chapter Eight

The Awakening

Ritcherd and Kyrah were nearly to the stables when Garret emerged at a full gallop. He drew back the reins abruptly when he saw them, and the horse turned an impatient circle before coming to a halt. Ritcherd and Kyrah halted beside him as he questioned firmly, "Is everything all right?"

"Yes, actually," Kyrah said, unable to keep from smiling.

"She's smiling," Garret said to Ritcherd. "I've not seen her smile in weeks. Whatever did you do to make her smile?"

Ritcherd tossed a smirk toward Kyrah and said, "I think we should not discuss such things in polite society."

"I'm not polite society," Garret said lightly. "I'm your brother."

"All the more reason we shouldn't discuss such things," Ritcherd added and trotted on toward the stable with Kyrah coming beside him. Garret turned and followed after sharing a warm glance with Kyrah. It was evident he sensed the changes in Ritcherd, and he was clearly happy about it. Ritcherd helped Kyrah dismount and pressed a quick kiss to her lips.

"I should go and check on Cetty," she said, glancing quickly at Garret, then at Ritcherd again. He didn't miss the implication that she was purposely leaving them alone with the hope that the air might be cleared between them. With no servants present in the stables, it was a perfect opportunity. Ritcherd watched Kyrah walk away, then turned to find Garret standing beside him, holding the reins of his horse, observing Ritcherd skeptically.

"What?" Ritcherd finally said.

"I'm just trying to figure which Ritcherd Buchanan I'm dealing with."

Ritcherd led the horses to their stalls, not liking the way he'd put that. "The sane one, I hope," Ritcherd said.

"I take it something's changed. *You've* certainly changed since I saw you last. You're almost yourself."

"Almost, perhaps. I guess you could say I had the hell scared out of me, but I think I've got a long ways to go to be myself—if such a thing is possible."

"Anything is possible, but not if you insist on trying to battle your dragons all by yourself."

"Yes, I'm sure you're right. You usually are."

While Ritcherd unbridled the horses he and Kyrah had ridden, Garret took up a brush and began smoothing it over his horse's coat. Ritcherd knew he'd get no better chance to say something that needed to be said. "I need to thank you, Garret."

"For what?"

"For not going to bed with my wife." Garret stopped brushing but didn't look at him. "I'm assuming that you wanted to," Ritcherd went on, "and I understand the opportunity presented itself." Garret drew courage and turned to meet Ritcherd's gaze, but he couldn't come up with anything to say before Ritcherd added, "She told me everything."

"Did she tell you that she never could have gone through with it?"

"What makes you think so?"

"It's obvious," Garret said, returning his attention to brushing the horse. "Her thoughts might have convinced her she wanted to be with me, but her heart was always with you."

"Her heart has been deeply wounded, I believe," Ritcherd said, "as you pointed out the last time we talked."

"Yes, I believe it has," Garret said without looking at him.

Following several minutes of silence while they finished caring for the horses, Garret asked, "So what exactly scared you back to your senses?"

Ritcherd looked at him firmly. "I had every reason to believe that you were making love to my wife."

Garret's eyes widened. "And you didn't beat my face in?"

"No, surprisingly enough, I wasn't angry. I was just . . . devastated."

"As you should be. But then, you did practically give me a gilded invitation to take her from you."

Ritcherd looked at the ground. "Yes, I suppose I did. But it would be nice if you'd wait until I'm dead before you start sleeping with her."

"Are you planning on dying soon?" Garret asked with a seriousness that reminded Ritcherd he had good cause to be concerned over that very thing.

"Not if I can help it."

"Well then, I'll just have to keep searching for a woman of my own."

"You do that, and when you find her, I shall very much enjoy flirting with her."

"You do that," Garret said. "But keep your hands to yourself."

They both chuckled before Garret asked, "What exactly made you think we were . . . you know?"

"I felt something change between the two of you, and she wouldn't look at me without guilt showing in her eyes."

"You noticed that too, eh?" Garret asked and Ritcherd nodded. "So you were with us more than you let on."

"I suppose. And you should know that I also overheard your conversation with her earlier."

"Really? What did we say? Remind me."

"I'm not sure I can recall the words, but she talked about trying to put something behind her, and she was obviously feeling a great deal of guilt. It was that word 'adultery' that clinched it for me." Garret looked confused and he clarified, "I believe she asked you how adultery was defined in Matthew, chapter five."

"Ah, yes," Garret looked away, "the conversation comes back to me now." He looked again at Ritcherd. "Are you sure you don't want to hit me?"

"Is there a reason I should?"

Garret drew a ragged breath and admitted, "I struggle with thoughts of her, Ritcherd. I have to pray very hard to keep my mind where it belongs."

"Well, you keep praying," Ritcherd said almost lightly. "As long as you keep your hands to yourself, what goes on in your head is your business."

"Perhaps, but . . ."

"But?"

"According to Matthew, chapter five, Kyrah and I are both guilty. Doesn't that bother you?"

"More than you could possibly imagine," Ritcherd admitted. "But a few hours ago I had believed that it had *really* happened between the two of you. I'm deeply relieved, and I'm trying to keep perspective. But you might have to be patient with me—perspective hasn't been a strong point with me lately. Still, I'm going to try very hard to never give her a reason to think about you that way again."

"That sounds more like the Ritcherd Buchanan I know and love."

"Well, let's hope he stays. To be truthful, I have my doubts."

"What do you mean?" Garret asked, his brow furrowed.

Ritcherd was surprised by the emotion that came with just contemplating an answer. His voice broke as he admitted, "I don't know what's wrong with me, Garret. I can't even begin to fathom what made me behave the way I did. You know better than anyone that it's not the first time I've been out of my mind with . . . who knows what. This time I nearly lost Kyrah. What will happen next time? There are moments when I truly wonder if there's something wrong with my head. Maybe I suffer from some measure of insanity, and eventually I'll just—"

"That's ludicrous," Garret said. "You're not crazy."

"Then what am I?" Ritcherd countered. "The fear of losing Kyrah finally got hold of me today, but I can't be sure I won't return to that state of mind when I don't even understand the cause."

"You're aware of it and you're talking about it. That's a good start. Just promise me that you'll keep talking about it."

"Just promise me you'll keep listening," Ritcherd said.

Garret smiled and reached out his left hand. "It's good to have you back, my brother."

"It's good to be back," Ritcherd said and took it firmly. They shared a familiar brotherly embrace and walked together toward the house.

Entering the side door, it occurred to Ritcherd that Kyrah had said she was going to check on Cetty. *Cetty.* His sweet, beautiful little daughter. He felt as if he'd been separated from her for months, and yet she'd been under the same roof all along. The separation had been self-inflicted, and again he wondered how he could be such a fool. His desire to see her became suddenly desperate and he quickened his pace, hurrying up the stairs while Garret came more slowly behind him.

Ritcherd quietly pushed open the door of the nursery to see Cetty watching her mother put a dress on one of her favorite dolls. He watched for a long moment, absorbing the scene into his consciousness. He felt an unfathomable joy to simply see them there, and to know that they were his—and his alone. At the same time he felt an equivalent sorrow to recall his horrendous behavior and the hurt he'd inflicted on his wife and daughter. Thankfully, Cetty's only hurt had been neglect; she had been spared from his angry outbursts and sharp words. Still, his regret was profound. He told himself that he couldn't change the past, and the future at this point only felt dark and frightening. But right now, in this moment, he could do everything in his power to let them know how he loved them.

"Hello, Cetty," he said, momentarily fearing she'd want nothing to do with him.

"Papa!" she said with such excitement that it broke his heart to think of how he'd avoided even seeing her these many weeks. She took a step toward him then hesitated, uncertainty showing in her eyes. Ritcherd glanced at Kyrah and found strength and encouragement radiating from her countenance. He squatted down and focused on Cetty. Not knowing what to say, he just opened his arms and without another moment's hesitation she rushed into them, holding to him tightly, laughing near his ear.

"Oh, Cetty," he muttered, holding her as if it had been a year. He felt tears course down his cheeks and looked up at Kyrah to see that she was crying, too. They exchanged a tender smile before he drew back, taking Cetty's little shoulders into his hands. "I love you, Cetty. I want you to know that. I'm so sorry that I haven't been a very good father for you."

Cetty wiped at his tears with her little fingers, just as she'd done after Celeste had died. "It's all right, Papa. Uncle Garret said you weren't feeling well, but he said he knew everything would be all right."

Ritcherd chuckled. "What would we do without Uncle Garret?"

"I'm certain you'd manage," Garret said, and they all turned to see him leaning in the doorway.

Without moving away from Ritcherd, Cetty said brightly, "Papa's feeling better now."

"So I see," Garret said, sauntering into the room. "Didn't I tell you everything would be all right?"

Cetty said to Ritcherd, "Uncle Garret told me that I needed to keep praying very hard for you, and I did—every night and every morning."

Ritcherd exchanged a long glance with Garret before he turned back to Cetty, pressing a hand over her hair as he said, "That explains why I'm feeling better then, doesn't it."

Cetty nodded and hugged him tightly again, seeming reluctant to let go. Ritcherd stood with her in his arms. "I think we're terribly behind on reading stories," he said, and Cetty giggled.

Ritcherd settled himself into a big chair with Cetty on his lap. She scrambled away and returned moments later with a stack of books that she set at his side. "This one's your favorite," she said, handing a book to Ritcherd as she climbed back onto his lap.

He chuckled and opened it to begin reading, then he glanced up to see Garret and Kyrah watching him. "Don't the two of you have something better to do?"

"Not really," Kyrah said.

"I like to hear you do the funny voices," Garret said with a smirk.

"Get out of here and let me spend some time with my daughter." He glanced at Kyrah and added, "Why don't you have a long talk with my wife, Garret? Maybe the two of you could figure out how to keep me sane."

Kyrah noted the severity in Ritcherd's eyes when he said it, and she knew he truly feared that his present state of mind would not last. She couldn't deny that she shared his fear, but for the moment she reveled in the joy she felt to see his attention to Cetty, to feel the pure love in his eyes.

Ritcherd met Kyrah's eyes and wondered for a moment if she was hesitant to leave Cetty alone in his care. He couldn't blame her. Still, he wanted more than anything for the trust between them to be rebuilt. He was wondering how to assure her that he would not behave rashly when she smiled and said, "Enjoy yourselves, then. I'll check back before supper."

"Good-bye, Mama," Cetty said cheerfully.

Ritcherd watched Kyrah leave the room with Garret following. He appreciated the trust they were giving him to be with Cetty this way, and he hoped they understood the gesture of trust he was giving them in return. Once they were gone, he turned his attention to the book in his hands and the child on his lap. Her perfect love and forgiveness warmed his heart, and he couldn't hold back a little laugh as he began to read his favorite story to her.

Garret followed Kyrah down the hall and around the corner, surprised when she stopped suddenly and turned to face him. With no warning she pushed her arms around him, hugging him tightly while she cried against his chest.

"What is it?" he asked softly, lifting her face to his view. "I thought you'd be happy."

"Oh, I am happy—that's just the point." She sniffled and accepted his handkerchief. "I'm so grateful, Garret. I'm grateful that some unexplainable miracle has brought him back to me, and I'm even more grateful . . . now that we've arrived at this moment . . . that I have nothing to regret. If not for your conviction, Garret, I very well might have."

Garret shook his head. "No, Kyrah. You never could have gone through with it. I just saved you the trouble of having to tell me no when I actually showed up at your door."

Kyrah looked into his eyes and wasn't so sure he was right. But it didn't matter. She was grateful nothing inappropriate had ever happened between them, and equally grateful to realize that her difficult thoughts of him were completely gone. Ritcherd had replaced them with the tangible evidence of his love for her.

"Nevertheless," she said, "I'm grateful—not only for all you've done for me, but for your friendship with Ritcherd. With you we might actually be able to get through this."

"Through what?" he asked in a tone that made it evident he knew exactly what she was talking about.

"It's not over yet."

"No," he said, looking down, "it's not over yet. But at least his heart is open now, his spirit is receptive. We just have to keep praying and stay close to him. I'm not going to intrude on your time together. Heaven knows you need it. But you know where to find me, Kyrah, any time of the day or night. If you need me to be with him . . . if he gets upset . . . or scared. Or if you get scared . . ."

"I know, Garret. Thank you." She went on her tiptoes to kiss his brow. "There is no truer friend in all the world." She smiled and added, "I think I'll go see if they need some help in the kitchen."

"I'll see you at supper then," Garret said, and she walked away.

More than two hours later, Kyrah peeked into the nursery to find Ritcherd lying on his chest on the floor, arranging toy soldiers along the parapets of a castle made from wooden blocks. Cetty was building block towers at the corners of the castle.

"And which one is the captain?" Kyrah asked, and they both looked up at her.

Ritcherd grinned in a way that melted her heart, then he pointed to a toy soldier in a red uniform. "This one right here," he said lightly. "It might look like he's a redcoat, but he's actually a turncoat."

Kyrah felt her joy falter. With the happiness she'd felt over having her husband back, the accusations of treason had not even crossed her mind. Ritcherd had often joked about being a turncoat, but suddenly it wasn't funny anymore. He *was* guilty of treason. And somebody was on to him.

Ritcherd glanced up at Kyrah to investigate her silence. Her tear-filled eyes revealed an unmasked terror. He tried to remember what he'd said just before she hurried from the room.

"I'll be back," he said to Cetty and jumped to his feet. He had to run to catch up with Kyrah before she started down the stairs.

"What's wrong?" he demanded, taking hold of her arm.

Kyrah looked into his eyes, warmed by his genuine concern, and terrified of losing him to a force that had nothing to do with his internal struggles. When it became evident that he expected an answer, she felt briefly disoriented, as she'd become accustomed to him showing her no concern whatsoever.

"Well?" he asked softly.

"You *are* a turncoat, Ritcherd. You *are* guilty of treason."

Ritcherd sighed loudly. "I know, Kyrah."

"Oh, Ritcherd," she touched his face, "I couldn't bear to lose you now—not after we've come this far."

"It will be all right, Kyrah. Personally, I think Mr. Thayer is just a bag of wind."

"And what if he's not, Ritcherd? What if he *does* have proof of your guilt?"

He sighed again. "I don't know, Kyrah. I can't answer that. My brain is trying to catch up with simply existing in the real world again. I do know this, however—I will do everything in my power to prove my innocence, and to stay alive." He kissed her brow. "I have too much to live for, Kyrah."

Kyrah eased into his arms, unable to hold back her tears. He pressed her face to his shoulder and whispered, "What is it, Kyrah? Talk to me. I know I don't deserve to have you talk to me, but I'm asking you to do it anyway."

Kyrah reasoned that she had to be honest with him, as difficult as it was to say. "How can I believe you, when not so many days ago you told me you were ready to go to the gallows?"

Ritcherd held her tighter, groaning with self-punishment. "I don't know how you can believe me, Kyrah. I can only say that I wasn't myself then."

"And how do I know if you will be yourself tomorrow?" she asked, looking up at him.

She was surprised to see moisture brim in his eyes. "I don't know, Kyrah. I keep wondering the same thing, and it scares me. I can't go back to that . . . darkness, Kyrah—I can't. And I pray to God that I can find a way to keep it at bay, to keep control of my senses. I want to live, Kyrah. I want a life with you and Cetty—a good life."

Kyrah wiped his tears away and smiled. "Then we will keep praying, and we will find a way—together."

Ritcherd shook his head in disbelief. "How can you say such things and mean them when I have been so—"

Kyrah pressed her fingers over his lips. "I married you for better or worse, Ritcherd. I love you more than life itself." She replaced her fingers with her lips, kissing him the way she'd wanted to a thousand times through these weeks of distance between them. He responded immediately, eagerly, and she clutched onto his shoulders, fearing she might collapse otherwise.

"Kyrah," he muttered, pulling her completely into his arms. He pressed her back to the wall and kissed her as if his very life depended on it. While he felt tempted to carry her to the bedroom this very moment and make up for lost time, he exercised enough self-discipline to ease away. "I told Cetty I'd be right back," he said and kissed her again.

"I think we're late for supper," she added, and he kissed her once more.

"Just give me a minute," he said and kissed her still again before he hurried back to the nursery. He found Cetty just beginning to eat her supper with the governess. Her face lit up when she saw him. "I'm going to eat my supper and I'll be back before you go to bed," he told her. "I promise."

Cetty nodded and hugged him tightly before he left the room to find Kyrah waiting in the hall. He took her hand and gave it a lingering kiss, resisting the urge to kiss her lips again, certain they'd never make it to supper if he did.

Garret hurried up the stairs in search of Ritcherd and Kyrah. After sitting alone in the dining room for several minutes, he had begun to wonder if something was wrong. He came around a corner in the upstairs hall and stopped abruptly to see the two of them engaged in a kiss so passionate that Garret almost felt embarrassed. He immediately turned away then slipped back around the corner, undetected. But he had to lean against the wall to catch his breath and collect his thoughts. "Please God, help me," he muttered under his breath while he consciously willed back any feelings of desire or jealousy. She was Ritcherd's wife, and being in his arms was exactly where she should be. He couldn't deny the deep peace and joy he felt to see them together this way after all that had happened. He was happy for them—truly happy. But oh, how he loved her! As difficult as Ritcherd's behavior had been, Garret had found some gratification in Kyrah's need for him—however innocent. Of course, now he could stop struggling with Kyrah's feelings for *him*. Her heart was obviously with her husband—exactly where it should be. And he would simply have to keep his feelings in perspective and pray very hard for strength and discipline—just as he'd done all along.

Garret hurried back down the stairs, figuring he would rather eat alone than interfere with Ritcherd and Kyrah's getting reacquainted. He'd only been seated a few minutes when they entered the room, holding hands, their faces glowing much as they had when they'd been newly married. The joy he felt on their behalf went a long way toward assuaging his own heartache.

Ritcherd helped Kyrah with her chair and pressed a kiss to her cheek before he sat in his own chair. Supper was pleasant and more comfortable than it had been since Garret had returned home to learn of Celeste's death and Ritcherd's subsequent depression. There was no talk of death, or treason, or the darkness Ritcherd had struggled with. Just refreshing conversation that reminded Garret of his previous visits home. But when supper was over, Garret watched Ritcherd and Kyrah leave together, and he was left alone. He began to wonder if his idea to stay here for months was a mistake. But then, he felt they needed him. He knew Ritcherd's struggles weren't over. Garret had been where Ritcherd was now, and he wouldn't feel comfortable leaving until he knew that Ritcherd had come to terms with his inner turmoil. And even if Ritcherd and Kyrah didn't need him, his ship was grounded. He was stuck, and he was going to have to live with it. So he went to the library in search of something he hadn't read, then he went to his rooms to be alone. Always alone.

Ritcherd and Kyrah both spent the remainder of the evening with Cetty, not leaving her until she was sleeping soundly. They walked across the hall to their own room. The moment the door was closed, Ritcherd pulled her into his arms and kissed her as he'd done earlier in the hall.

"Oh, how I missed you," he murmured and kissed her again.

"I was here all along," she replied, pressing a hand into his hair.

"I know," he said, "and I pray that I am never fool enough not to see you when you're right in front of me. You're beautiful, Kyrah. You are the most amazing woman ever born to this world, and I love you with all my heart and soul."

Kyrah couldn't keep from crying as his words penetrated her neglected heart. Her tears turned to laughter as he scooped her into his arms, carrying her to the bed. She relished the way he made love to her as if he had been as starved for affection as she. And she loved the way he held her close to him far into the night while they talked and kissed and just soaked up each other's presence. She eventually fell asleep in his embrace, feeling more safe, more comforted, more loved than she had since Celeste's death.

Ritcherd fell asleep more quickly than he had in weeks. He'd grown accustomed to lying awake for hours while disturbing thoughts assaulted his mind without mercy. He drifted to sleep, holding Kyrah close to him, feeling more content and at peace than he had since he'd lost his sister.

But somewhere in the darkest part of the night he awoke, consumed with a familiar darkness. "No!" he whispered into the silent room, and only Kyrah's even breathing responded. Negative memories paraded through his mind against his will, gradually merging into negative beliefs, finally resulting in a negative voice, coming from somewhere within, telling him he wasn't worthy of holding this incredible woman in his arms. He'd hurt her deeply, and surely he would hurt her again. He wasn't worthy of the life he was living, the people who loved him. He wasn't worthy of peace or serenity. Ritcherd felt his breathing become sharp, and a tangible pain burned in his chest. He almost woke Kyrah, but he desperately wanted to hold onto the precious, tender mood between them. He felt crazy, and if she thought he was crazy maybe she would follow through on her threat to leave him. As his desperation mounted, Ritcherd did something he'd stubbornly avoided doing all these weeks. He slid to his knees beside the bed and silently poured his heart out to God, begging Him to relieve this anguish and remove this darkness. He fell asleep praying and woke with his back and knees aching, shivering from the cold. He stoked up the fire and crawled into the bed to realize he felt better.

"Are you all right?" Kyrah murmured, easing into his arms.

"I am now," he said, and kissed her before they both drifted back to sleep.

He woke to morning light and slipped out of the bed to get cleaned up and dressed. He was with Cetty when Kyrah woke. They were playing toy soldiers again when Kyrah appeared in the doorway, her expression filled with panic then relief.

"What's wrong?" he asked.

"I woke up and you were gone," she admitted, pressing a hand to her heart. "I was afraid it had only been a dream."

Ritcherd stood and moved toward her. He took both her hands into his and smiled before he kissed her. In a quiet voice he said, "No, my dear, unlike your experience with Garret, it was real."

Kyrah resisted the temptation to feel guilty. She had been completely honest with Ritcherd—it was in the past. Instead she smiled back at him, saying, "Garret who?" He chuckled and she added, "Oh . . . you mean Garret. Your brother." She gave Ritcherd a lingering kiss. "I've not given him a second thought since you took me in your arms yesterday at the church ruins."

Ritcherd grinned and lifted his brows. "Well, maybe you should, my dear." He glanced at the clock. "He's probably all by himself in the dining room again, wondering if we'll ever show up."

"Then we should go to breakfast," she said. "But first let me get dressed."

"That would be a good idea," he said, glancing down at the wrapper she wore. "I don't think it would be wise for Garret to see you dressed like that."

Kyrah smiled and hurried back to her room to change. Ritcherd went back to playing with Cetty until Kyrah returned and they went together to the dining room. They entered holding hands to find Garret reading a newspaper.

"Good morning," Ritcherd said brightly, and Garret folded down one corner of the paper.

"Good morning," he replied, eyeing them with comic skepticism. "The two of you are pathetic," he added, folding his newspaper and setting it aside. "You act as if you're in love, or something."

"Sorry," Ritcherd muttered.

"No you're not. You are thoroughly enjoying yourself, completely oblivious to the fact that I am alone in this world, stuck with a bunch of dusty books to keep me company."

"Not *completely* oblivious," Ritcherd said, and Garret chuckled. "I did tell Kyrah we needed to get to breakfast so you wouldn't be eating alone."

"Well, I'm glad to know you might give me a little thought once in a while."

"Once in a while," Kyrah said, and winked at him before she turned her smile toward Ritcherd.

When the meal was nearly finished, Kyrah told the men, "I'm taking Cetty into town this morning to do a few errands. She's growing out of all her clothes, so we're going to order some new ones."

"How delightful," Ritcherd said. "May I come along?"

Kyrah smiled in surprise at her husband. He'd hardly been out of the house since the funeral. "That would be lovely," she said.

"Perhaps we could have lunch out," he added.

"That would be even lovelier," she said.

"And you will join us, won't you, Garret?" Ritcherd asked.

"Surely I would be intruding," Garret said. "I'll just stay here and—"

"And what?" Ritcherd interrupted. "Dust off your books? You're coming with us. I'd say a family outing is long overdue."

"Indeed," Garret said and chuckled. "It sounds delightful."

Ritcherd thoroughly enjoyed the carriage ride to town with Cetty on his lap and Kyrah beside him. Garret sat across from them, teasing Cetty and making her giggle. The only thing that could have made such an excursion more enjoyable would be to have Celeste with them. Ritcherd ached for her absence, but he forced his mind to the present and focused on enjoying the moment.

Following a few simple errands, Kyrah teased Ritcherd and Garret about going into the dress shop with her and Cetty to offer their opinion. They decided to accept the challenge and went inside, making themselves comfortable while Mrs. Harker fussed over Cetty, taking measurements and talking with Kyrah about different pieces she would like to have made. While Kyrah talked with Mrs. Harker, Cetty became intrigued with the little bell that rang when the door opened. She opened and closed the door three times before Garret picked her up, saying, "I think that's enough of that, young lady." He tickled her and made her giggle, and she scampered to her mother's side.

Ritcherd's mind wandered to an incident that had happened long ago with Kyrah in this very shop. Kyrah had come in to order a gown for the social where they would announce their engagement. Mrs. Harker had been brusque with her, telling her she would do nothing for her without having the money up front. Then Ritcherd had come in and made it clear that anything Kyrah wanted was to be put on his account. Mrs. Harker had changed then, bustling around to accommodate their every wish. It had always been that way with nearly everyone in this community. They responded to him as if he were royalty or something, and would have them beheaded if they displeased him. And he hated it! He'd never wanted to be Lord Buckley, never wanted the title. Money was nice, admittedly. But having everyone know he had it clearly affected the way he was treated. And he hated that, too. While Ritcherd sat there, one memory led to another, leading his mind into dark caverns that frightened him. He didn't realize he was having difficulty breathing until Garret touched his arm.

"Are you all right?" he asked quietly.

Ritcherd glanced down to see his own hand pressed over his chest as he consciously recognized the pain he felt there. "No, I don't think I am," Ritcherd replied just as quietly. "Get me out of here."

"Uh," Garret stood, taking Ritcherd's arm to urge him to do the same, "Captain Buchanan's not feeling well." Kyrah shot an alarmed glance toward them but Garret gave her a stern gaze that seemed to caution her to be discreet. "I think he just needs some fresh air. We'll meet you in the carriage when you're finished."

"Of course," Kyrah said and watched them leave the shop, Ritcherd leaning a little too much on Garret.

While she was trying to ward off her uneasiness, Mrs. Harker asked, "Is your husband not well?"

"Uh . . . no," she said. "He's been ill. I fear he might have overdone it. He'll be fine once he gets some rest." Kyrah returned her attention to her order, trying not to feel concerned.

Garret guided Ritcherd outside where they both leaned up against the storefront, which brought less attention to the fact that Ritcherd was teetering. "What was that all about?" Garret asked quietly. "And bear in mind that you promised to talk to me."

Ritcherd sighed and forced himself to breathe deeply. "I'm better now," he said.

"Better than what?"

"I just . . . sometimes I start thinking about . . . certain things and . . . I don't know . . . I just can't breathe. And my chest hurts. Sometimes I get dizzy. But I'm fine now."

Garret looked so alarmed that Ritcherd wished he hadn't said anything. But he *had* promised to talk about the problems, and he was terrified that if he didn't get some help, he would inevitably slide back into the hellish abyss he had recently emerged from. Now that he'd said what he had, it was easier to say, "I don't want to die, Garret."

"You're not going to die."

"And how do you know that?"

"I just know."

"What makes you such an expert on everything that ails me?"

"Experience," he said. "I'll tell you later. Come on. I'll buy you a drink."

"You made me promise to stop drinking."

"Did I? Well, what I really meant was that you should promise to stop getting drunk," Garret said. "You know my adage: drunk men become dead men. And you just said you don't want to die. But we're just going to have a little drink."

"If you insist," Ritcherd said, walking beside him toward the pub.

Chapter Nine

The Thin Line of Sanity

Ritcherd and Garret chatted casually as they walked the short distance and Ritcherd almost felt like himself, until they entered the door of the pub and many eyes turned toward them. Ritcherd had no conscious reason to feel upset, but he did. Again his chest tightened and his head felt unsteady.

"I can't go in there," Ritcherd said, hurrying out the door.

Garret followed and found him leaning against the wall in the alley. "Why not?" Garret asked.

"I don't know. I just . . . can't go in there." He moved, only slightly unsteady, back onto the street. "I need to get back to the carriage."

Garret said nothing until they were seated across from each other in the motionless carriage. "Are you all right?" he asked.

"I'm fine . . . now," Ritcherd admitted. He met Garret's eyes and added, "You probably think I'm crazy."

"No, I do not. And don't put words in my mouth."

"Well *I* think I'm crazy."

"You're not," Garret insisted, "but I do think it would be better if we have lunch at home."

"I agree," Ritcherd said, and a few minutes later Kyrah and Cetty arrived at the carriage.

"He's fine," Garret said before she could get a question out. "But we are going home for lunch. He just needed some fresh air."

Kyrah looked dubious but she snuggled up close to Ritcherd for the drive home, relishing his nearness while Garret entertained Cetty with a guessing game that frequently made her laugh. Her laughter was contagious, and Kyrah tightened her arms around Ritcherd, grateful to simply hear him laugh.

Ritcherd remained close to at least one of his loved ones through the remainder of the day, and he kept busy enough to keep any negative thoughts out of his mind. But that night, as he lay in the dark with Kyrah sleeping beside him, the inner voices began their emotional torture. Ritcherd prayed himself to sleep, but woke again before morning and was again taunted with horrible thoughts and feelings, luring him against his will toward some hellish inner existence over which he had no control. Again he prayed, but the feelings were less inclined to relent. He forced himself to get out of bed and get cleaned up, determined to enjoy the day and not allow this horrific inner monster to overtake him.

As breakfast progressed, Ritcherd found it increasingly difficult to ward off the thoughts plaguing him. He was actually startled to hear Kyrah say firmly, "Ritcherd!"

"What?" he asked, looking at her.

"Have you heard anything we've been saying?"

He had to admit, "No, I'm sorry. I was . . . daydreaming, I suppose. I'm fine."

He put his attention on his meal, forcing himself to eat when he felt no appetite. A few minutes later, Kyrah asked, "Are you sure you're all right?"

"Yes, of course." He forced a smile. "I'm fine."

"You're lying," Garret said, and Kyrah was grateful to have him say what she'd wanted to say. "You promised you would talk to us about it, that you wouldn't try to bury what's eating at you. It's just the three of us here. So, let's try that again. Are you all right, Ritcherd? You don't seem yourself this morning."

Ritcherd gripped the edge of the table with both hands and watched his knuckles turn white. He wondered why he felt like yelling at them. He wondered why he felt as if a dark shroud was blanketing his mind.

He wondered why he felt completely out of control of his life. But most of all he wondered if he were crazy. He forced back the urge to scream or throw something, but in its place, tears burned into his eyes. He abruptly pushed back his chair, maintaining his grip on the table. He lowered his head, if only in an attempt to hide his emotion.

"Ritcherd?" Kyrah said in a panicked voice, and he heard her standing up. "Are you—"

"No, I'm not all right! There, I said it! I'm *not* myself. But I don't know who the hell I am. I don't know what I'm doing here or what's wrong with me." He heard himself sob and realized why he'd been terrified to be truthful about what was happening inside of him. He couldn't even acknowledge the problem without bawling like a baby. His stomach tightened painfully. His heart raced and his palms turned clammy. His breathing sharpened and he fell to his knees, wrapping his arms around his middle.

"Good heavens!" Kyrah exclaimed and rushed to his side, kneeling beside him, wrapping him in her arms. "Ritcherd, what's wrong? What's happening?"

"I don't know," he cried and clutched onto her. "Don't leave me, Kyrah. Promise me you'll never leave me."

"Never, Ritcherd, I promise."

"What is it, Ritcherd?" Garret asked, kneeling on the other side of him, putting a hand to his shoulder.

Ritcherd only shook his head and a moment later a maid entered the dining room. "Oh!" she gasped. "Should I send for the doctor or—"

"Yes," Kyrah said at the same time Ritcherd said, "No!"

"Yes," Garret added firmly and the maid scurried from the room. Ritcherd scowled at him, but Garret just scowled back.

"Come along," Garret said, helping Ritcherd to his feet. "We're going upstairs where you can lie down, and while we're waiting for the doctor, we're going to have a long talk."

"I don't need a doctor!" Ritcherd growled. "There's nothing wrong with me except what's going on in my head. Tell a doctor that and they'll lock me up." He took hold of Garret's upper arms and looked into his eyes. His voice quavered as he expressed his deepest fear. "I'm losing my mind, Garret. I'm going crazy, and they're going to lock me up in some horrible asylum, and—"

"No, they're not," Garret insisted gently. "Your mind is just fine, and even if you *were* crazy, I wouldn't let them lock you up."

"And what are *you* going to do about it?" Ritcherd demanded with tears in his eyes.

"I'm your brother and I'm going to take care of you, that's what."

Ritcherd took a deep breath, seeming to find some assurance from Garret's promise. Suddenly composed, he moved toward the door and Kyrah asked, "Where are you going?"

"I'm going to my room to wait for the doctor." He paused and glanced at each of them. "I thought we were going to have a long talk."

"We're right behind you," Garret said. He exchanged a concerned glance with Kyrah and they followed Ritcherd out of the room.

In Ritcherd and Kyrah's bedroom, Ritcherd paced the room while Garret and Kyrah sat and watched him. "So, what's the problem?" Garret asked.

"I don't know," Ritcherd muttered. "I just . . . just . . ."

"Just what?" Garret pressed.

"I don't know," Ritcherd said again. "For the first time since Celeste died, I actually feel like I want to live. I don't feel dead inside." He rubbed a hand over his chest. "I actually *feel*. But it's as if the darkness I was lost in is threatening to overtake me again. I feel as if . . ." His voice cracked and he stopped pacing, then squeezed his eyes closed. "Look at me. I'm a mess. It's as if I'm divided, and part of me just wants to go back to the dark oblivion; it feels safer, somehow. The other part of me is terrified to go back there. I don't ever want to feel that way again." He opened his eyes and looked at Kyrah. "I don't want to lose you, and I can't keep you if I don't stay in the real world. But being here makes me . . . afraid."

"Afraid of what?" Garret asked and Ritcherd turned to look at him.

"When my feelings were numb, I could avoid them. Now I'm crying every time I turn around. Are those my choices? To be dead inside or to be falling apart?"

"So cry if you have to," Garret said. "You don't have to do it in front of the servants or the crew of the *Phoenix* or the guys at the pub.

It's just me and Kyrah here. You've got plenty of places to be alone in this house. Just cry and get it out. It's been my experience that you have to feel the pain before you can get rid of it."

Ritcherd's heart quickened over that last statement. Was that what he had to do? Feel the pain? Instinctively he believed that was true, but the very idea was terrifying. He readily admitted, "I don't know if I can do that."

"You can do anything you have to," Garret said.

Ritcherd sighed and moved to a chair, feeling suddenly weak. Following minutes of silent contemplation, he said, "I thought I had worked all of this through before . . . on the *Phoenix,* before Kyrah and I were married. Is this the way my life is going to be? Every few years I lose my mind and fall apart and throw angry fits? I feel crazy . . . like there's something wrong with me; *really* wrong with me." His voice broke again.

"You're not crazy, Ritch," Garret insisted. "It's been my experience that deep-seated hurts have many layers. If you don't go deep and clear it *all* out, it will keep creeping up. Look at it this way. Every time you go through this, you can either heal another layer, or cover it up and let it fester and get worse. Experience tells me you're going to be better off if you just do everything you can to get it all out of your system as much as possible and get on with your life."

Ritcherd looked closely at Garret, trying to read between the lines. A thought occurred to him. "You keep bringing up that word 'experience.' You sound like you know what you're talking about."

Garret's voice became gravelly as he said, "You have no idea."

Ritcherd exchanged a brief, startled glance with Kyrah. She appeared as astonished as he felt. Was there far more to Garret's past than either of them knew? Whatever *experience* he might have, Ritcherd couldn't deny that Garret was a good man—through and through. He was wise and insightful, with strong instincts and a deep trust in God to guide him through every aspect of his life. Most importantly, Garret was a man at peace with himself. If anyone could help Ritcherd get through this, it was Garret. Ritcherd didn't need to know the source of Garret's experience. In truth, he had a fairly good idea. Still, he couldn't help being curious and said, "If I have no idea, then maybe you should tell me."

Garret looked apprehensive but thoughtful, as if he were carefully considering his options. A knock at the door preceded a maid entering the room to tell them the doctor had arrived.

"That was fast," Garret said, sounding relieved to have been freed from the inquiry.

Dr. Ware was shown into the room. He greeted the three of them amiably, then asked to be left alone with Ritcherd. Garret and Kyrah left the room, both pacing the hall with nothing to say.

The doctor closed the door and sat down near Ritcherd, crossing one knee over the other. "So, what's the problem, Captain?" he asked, looking over the top of his glasses.

"I'm fine," Ritcherd insisted. The doctor's glare became dubious and Ritcherd added quickly, "I've just had some trouble . . . adjusting to my sister's death."

Dr. Ware's eyes widened. "So would you say you've been overly preoccupied with grief?"

"I suppose," Ritcherd said, wondering why he felt uneasy.

"And might I guess?" the doctor added. "Have you felt . . . anxious for no apparent reason? Even fearful, perhaps?"

"Occasionally," Ritcherd said.

"Have you felt prone to being alone? Not interacting with others? Difficulty sleeping?"

"Yes," Ritcherd admitted with hesitance.

"Bursts of anger or crying?" he asked with a speculation in his eyes that bristled Ritcherd's nerves.

"Perhaps," Ritcherd said, quivering from the inside out.

"I see," the doctor said, jotting notes down while he made contemplative noises. He then took minutes to apparently read what he'd written and think about it. Then he spoke abruptly. "But I was told you had some physical symptoms." Ritcherd hesitated to answer, and he added, "Might I guess? Shortness of breath? Chest pain? Heart palpitations?"

"What's your point, Doctor?" Ritcherd demanded.

"Getting angry with me will not change the facts, Captain. You have every classic symptom, and you'd do well to make provisions for your family while you still can."

"What on earth are you saying?" Ritcherd asked, barely able to breathe. "You sound as if you're giving me a death sentence."

"Death might be preferable, Captain."

"Just get to the point," Ritcherd said, feeling his palms turn clammy.

"It begins with excessive grief or sadness, which becomes unmanageable melancholia. When the physical symptoms appear, it's readily evident that the mind has become diseased and there is simply nothing to be done. I'm afraid it will only get worse, Captain." He came to his feet and picked up his bag. "I'm sorry to be the one to tell you." He moved toward the door while Ritcherd felt the room spinning. "I'll talk to your wife and brother before I leave."

Ritcherd heard the door close as if it were a million miles away. Then, as if to reaffirm what he'd just been told, his chest tightened painfully and he found it difficult to breathe. "Oh, God help me," he muttered and slid to his knees, wrapping his arms around his middle, wishing he could just die.

Garret sat with Kyrah at his side, across the room from the doctor as he gave his report. He felt Kyrah reach for his hand the same moment he realized what he was hearing. Kyrah began to tremble, squeezing his fingers so hard that it hurt. It was when the doctor used the word 'asylum' that Garret reached his limit.

"That's quite enough, Doctor," he said, erupting to his feet.

"Getting angry will not change the facts, Captain Garret."

"You just spent less than twenty minutes with my brother, and you're sitting there telling us that he's helplessly, hopelessly crazy. You have no idea what you're talking about."

The doctor stood and said tersely, "You can choose to ignore the facts, but one day you will realize that I *do* know what I'm talking about. I've seen this kind of thing many times."

"Oh, I'm certain you have," Garret said with sarcasm. "If you tell someone who is depressed that they are crazy, I'm sure that eventually they will come to believe it. Get out, Doctor. We have no further need of your services. And if any gossip over this is ever spoken in this community, I will hunt you down and beat you senseless. Do I make myself clear?"

"Indeed," the doctor said. "Perhaps insanity runs in the family."

"Perhaps it does," Garret said proudly.

The doctor let out a disgusted sigh and walked toward the door. Garret followed him out and returned to find Kyrah struggling to breathe.

"Kyrah," he said, sitting close beside her, "it's not true."

"How can you possibly know whether or not it's true?"

Garret knew the answer to that question, but he knew it would take time to explain. "Kyrah, you must trust me. We can talk more about this later. Right now, Ritcherd is upstairs believing that he is inescapably insane." Kyrah gasped and attempted to stand, but Garret urged her back to her seat. "Kyrah, listen to me. If we go up there with any degree of belief in what that doctor said, then Ritcherd will be more likely to believe it, too."

"And what if it's true?" Kyrah cried. "Is it right to lead him to believe otherwise if—"

"Kyrah, you must trust me. I know he's not insane. His mind is not diseased. He's going to be all right!"

"How do you know?" she shouted, then sobbed.

Garret sighed and looked into her eyes, resigned to giving her the brief version. "Kyrah, there was a time . . . I was seventeen . . . when I was behaving *exactly* the same way." Kyrah's eyes widened. "And no, that does not mean that insanity runs in the family. I had some help from someone who believed in me and got me through it, the same way you and I are going to get Ritcherd through it. I've never struggled with it since." He hardened his gaze on her and said firmly, "He is not crazy! He's going to be just fine, but not if we don't give him something to hold on to."

Kyrah quickly got hold of her emotions and nodded firmly before she stood and moved toward the stairs. They both seemed to feel the urgency of getting to Ritcherd in the same moment and literally ran to the room where they'd left him. Kyrah paused for a moment to catch her breath, then entered stoically with Garret right behind her. Her emotion threatened again when she found him much as he'd been in the church ruins just yesterday. He was on his knees, curled around his arms, sobbing without restraint. She went to her knees beside him, taking him into her arms. He clutched onto her and cried harder, pressing his face into the folds of her dress.

"Oh," he groaned, pressing both hands over his heart.

"Ritcherd," Garret said, putting a hand on his shoulder, "you've got to calm down. Come on, take a deep breath. Calm down and we'll talk."

Ritcherd struggled to do as Garret said, but it still took him several minutes to be composed enough to focus. He lay on the floor with his head in Kyrah's lap while she gently pressed her fingers through his hair with a soothing touch.

"Now," Garret said, sitting close beside them, "I don't know what that quack told you to upset you so badly. Whatever it was, it's not true."

"How do you know it's not true if you don't know what he said?" Ritcherd asked.

"I know what he told me and Kyrah, and I've never heard such a load of nonsense in my entire life. I told him we no longer required his services. Perhaps he and the vicar could go into business together, making assumptions and gross misinterpretations to make themselves feel powerful and mighty."

"And maybe they're right, Garret."

Garret pointed a finger at Ritcherd. "The only thing that will ever make you crazy is your paying attention to such nonsense when your instincts tell you they're wrong."

"I don't know how to feel my instincts anymore, Garret."

"Well, we're going to work on that," he said, jumping to his feet. "Listen, there's something I need to take care of. I'll be gone a few hours. Why don't the two of you just stay right here and get some rest. We'll talk when I get back." He met Kyrah's eyes and saw fear there, but he nodded firmly toward her, saying gently, "Everything will be all right. I'll be back as quickly as I can."

"We'll be fine," Ritcherd said, holding more tightly to Kyrah.

After Garret left the room, closing the door behind him, Ritcherd asked in a voice of fear, "Do you think I'm losing my mind, Kyrah? Don't lie to me. Don't spare my feelings. We have to consider what's best for you and Cetty. If this is some . . . disease . . . some horrible illness . . . that's only going to get worse . . . I can't expect our lives to go on . . . the way they are."

Kyrah squeezed her eyes closed and felt tears slide down her cheeks. She fought to keep them silent, abruptly wiping them away with her free hand, not wanting him to know how her heart was breaking while she shared his fears. In spite of what Garret had said, she couldn't help wondering if this was one case where his optimism simply wasn't capable of overpowering the problem. Recalling what he'd said about having similar behavior himself in his youth gave her some degree of hope, but at the moment the doctor's words were ringing clearly in her ears, mingled with memories of Ritcherd's despondency, his anger, his volatile emotion, combined with physical symptoms that were frightening. Still, she couldn't give up hope. And she was grateful for Garret's advice. She had to help Ritcherd believe that he was whole.

When Kyrah didn't answer, Ritcherd sat up abruptly to look into her eyes. He wasn't surprised to find them filled with tears. He touched her face and whispered, "Tell me, Kyrah."

"I don't know what's wrong, Ritcherd. But I agree with Garret. Dr. Ware can't possibly make such a diagnosis after talking to you so short a time. Garret seems to believe that we can fix the problem. Why don't you just rest, and we'll talk to him when he gets back." She reached up to touch his face. "Whatever is wrong, Ritcherd, I will stand by you—without question."

"Even if I lose my mind and hurt you again?" he asked with skeptical eyes.

"I won't let you hurt me again, Ritcherd." A little sob escaped her throat. "And I won't let you lose your mind."

Ritcherd looked into her eyes, marveling at her faith in him, her forgiveness, her perfect love. He pressed his mouth over hers, kissing her in a way that made it easier to forget what he was up against. "I don't want to rest," he said and kissed her again—a warm, searching kiss that softened her completely into his embrace. "I love you, Kyrah," he whispered, urging her to her feet and then to the bed.

Long after he made love to her, they held each other in silence while he prayed with everything inside of him that he would come through this trial with his sanity intact. He drifted to sleep with Kyrah in his arms and woke to find the room growing dim with evening. He turned over to find Kyrah sitting in a chair near the bed, just watching him. "I love you, Captain Buchanan," she said when their eyes met. "You will always be the captain of my heart."

"For which I am truly grateful," he said, reaching for her hand.

"Garret could be back soon," she said, coming to her feet. "You should get dressed. I'll check on Cetty and Pearl and be right back."

"I'll be right here," he said, almost terrified to even leave the room.

Kyrah was only gone a few minutes, but she found Ritcherd in the sitting room, leaning against the window frame, looking out at the darkening sky. She lit a lamp and stoked the fire before she stood behind him and pressed her arms around to his chest.

"Thank you, Kyrah," he said.

"For what?"

"For . . . everything. Most especially for loving me, and for your commitment. It means more to me now than you could ever know."

"We've been through struggles before, Ritcherd. We will get through this, and we will live a long, full life together. We will find joy together in our grandchildren."

Ritcherd inhaled the hope she was giving him, wishing it could completely free him of the horrible thoughts rattling around in his head. He was searching for the words to explain what he was feeling when a light knock sounded at the open door, and they both turned to see Garret.

"Is everybody decent?" he asked lightly.

"The door's open, isn't it?" Ritcherd retorted lightly.

"Good," Garret said with a chuckle, "because I brought a friend." Ritcherd and Kyrah both turned more toward the door as Garret stepped into the room and added, "I brought a *real* doctor."

A familiar face appeared beside Garret, and Kyrah rushed toward him. "Patrick!" She spoke his name with joy as she embraced him tightly then looked into his eyes. "Oh, it's so good to see you!"

"And you, my lady," he said, taking her hand to kiss it. "I've gone far too long without feasting my eyes upon you. The *Phoenix* has never been the same without you."

Ritcherd watched the reunion between Kyrah and Patrick Myers, the official medical officer of the *Phoenix*. Next to Ritcherd, he was Garret's closest friend, and he had proven his devotion to Ritcherd and Kyrah many times over. Patrick was also a gifted swordsman, and he had spent countless hours teaching Ritcherd to fence with his left hand after his right had been wounded in the war. His skill as a doctor had saved Ritcherd's life when he was shot in the leg and Patrick had dug the bullet out, quickly and efficiently. Patrick had first met Kyrah when she was in labor with Cetty, and he had helped make certain all was well. Since that time, he had stood by them through many challenges, and Ritcherd couldn't help feeling that Garret's going to get him had been inspired. Already Ritcherd felt more comforted—and comfortable. He knew he could discuss his symptoms with Patrick and get an honest, professional opinion.

When Patrick's greeting with Kyrah was apparently finished, he turned toward Ritcherd. "Hello, my friend," he said.

"Hello, Patrick," Ritcherd replied. "It's good to see you."

"And you." Patrick crossed the room and shook Ritcherd's hand firmly, then he offered a quick, brotherly embrace. Their eyes met and he added, "I'm sorry I didn't make it here sooner. I had some business to take care of when the *Phoenix* docked, and some family that I needed to spend time with. I just got back on board a few days ago and was sitting there twiddling my thumbs when Garret showed up. He told me you had room to put me up if I wanted to join the party."

Ritcherd actually chuckled. "Yes, it's quite a party."

Patrick put a hand on Ritcherd's shoulder. "I was so sorry to hear about Celeste. She will truly be missed. I loved her dearly."

"I know you did," Ritcherd said, recalling well how Patrick had bonded with Celeste the first time they'd met.

"And how are you, Ritcherd?" he asked. Ritcherd hesitated and he added, "I hear you're not doing so well."

"That would be a gross understatement," Ritcherd said. "I hope Garret told you what's going on, which will spare me from having to repeat it all."

"He told me a little." Patrick motioned for Ritcherd to sit down. "Do you want to talk about it now, or—"

"Now is just as good a time as any," Ritcherd said, taking a seat.

Patrick sat down across from him and Kyrah said, "Would you prefer that we go and leave the two of you to—"

"No, please stay," Ritcherd said, reaching a hand toward Kyrah. He nodded at Garret, saying, "Both of you. Close the door."

Garret closed the door and took a chair. Kyrah sat close beside Ritcherd, keeping her hand in his. Patrick scooted his chair closer to Ritcherd and sat to face him directly. He leaned his forearms on his thighs and said in a quiet, gentle voice, "First of all, how well have you been sleeping?"

"Not well at all," Ritcherd admitted.

"Now that's a problem right there. If you're not getting some good sleep, everything is likely to feel worse than it is. We'll work on that. Tell me about the physical symptoms that have you concerned." Ritcherd briefly explained them and Patrick asked, "And when exactly do these symptoms occur?" Ritcherd hesitated and he added, "Garret told me you've been struggling with feeling depressed since you lost Celeste. Are the physical symptoms related to anxiety? Fear perhaps?"

Ritcherd leaned back and sighed. "Yes," he admitted. "And according to Dr. Ware, that's a clear sign—combined with my emotional challenges—that my mind is diseased and I will inevitably lose my sanity."

Patrick chuckled and leaned back as well. "Before we go any further," he said, "I'd like to tell you a little bit about my medical training, and my theories on medicine. May I?"

"Of course," Ritcherd said, marveling at how relaxed he felt in contrast to his visit with Dr. Ware.

"Following my official education, I had the opportunity to work with an elderly doctor who was approaching retirement. He took me under his wing and taught me as much about life as he did about medicine. We got along well because his theories made so much sense to me. He believed that the human spirit and the human mind were greatly integrated into the body and its ailments. He was very conscious of every patient's mood, their emotional well-being. And he'd kept detailed journals of everything he had done medically, from stitching a child's forehead to amputating a gangrenous leg to every baby he'd ever delivered. He left those journals to me when he died. They fill a trunk in my cabin on the *Phoenix;* they are my most priceless possession. Now, there are theories that are taught to doctors, theories that are written about and discussed among the hierarchy of medicine. But the reality is that as human beings we really know so little. My friend taught me that the instincts of a God-fearing doctor were his most valuable tool. He taught me that the patterns established of following patients' lives, their illnesses, their moods, their injuries, were far more valuable than what some stuffy know-it-all doctor might lecture on in some university. Of course doctors need to be educated. We need to know the human body and its functions meticulously. But I was given the marvelous gift of learning what medicine is really all about. I have studied this man's journals over and over, wanting to simply glean his lifetime of knowledge and experience." He chuckled softly. "In defense of Dr. Ware, I could find references in printed medical journals that basically state what he told you."

Kyrah gasped and Ritcherd bristled visibly as he asked, "Are you trying to tell me that I *am* going crazy? That I—"

"Hold on and let me finish," Patrick said. "Now, with that in mind, I'd like to tell you what I *really* believe is going on with you. I'm not going to lie to you. I'm not going to buffer the truth for the sake of your feelings. All right?"

Ritcherd nodded and squeezed Kyrah's hand more tightly.

"You're depressed, Ritcherd. The medical term is *melancholia.* It is more common than you could possibly believe. It is generally brought on by legitimate grief or sorrow or difficult circumstances, and sometimes it just gets out of hand. I could show you at least a dozen detailed cases in those journals, and that's in one relatively small village. Not one of those people ever went insane or lost their mind. Some struggled with it on and off through their lifetimes. Some went through one or more bouts of it, and never had it come up again."

Ritcherd couldn't hold back an emotional noise as a tangible relief washed over him. Kyrah started to cry and pressed her face to his shoulder just as Ritcherd realized his own cheeks were wet with tears. "Sorry," he said to Patrick, wiping frantically at his face.

"It's all right," Patrick said. "Tears are good for you, Ritcherd. Dare I guess that the situation was *really* bad when you felt like you couldn't cry at all?"

Ritcherd nodded and Patrick went on. "Now, about the physical symptoms. Let me explain something to you. Think for a moment about how your body might react to fear. Let's talk about the night the *Phoenix* was attacked at sea when you and Kyrah were with us. I think we were all scared senseless. Do you remember how you felt physically during that experience? How did your body respond when it was afraid?"

Garret said, "That's easy. I remember it well. Quickened heartbeat. Sweaty palms. My stomach was in knots, my mouth dry."

"There you have it, Ritcherd," Patrick said. "When you understand how your body reacts to fear or excitement or joy, it's not so difficult to comprehend that high doses of anxiety would bring on physical symptoms. There's nothing wrong with you that some time and a good listening ear won't cure."

"I can't believe it," Ritcherd muttered, then chuckled. Mentally reviewing the last several weeks, he had to say, "But . . . I've gotten so angry—*irrationally* angry. Surely that's not normal for—"

"Ritcherd," Patrick leaned forward again, "I think if you look inside yourself and figure out the source of your anger, you will likely find the source of your depression. Now, I think Garret's advice might serve you better from here on out, but if it's all right with you, I'm going to stick around for a while. If nothing else, I'm going to make certain you get some decent sleep. Ongoing lack of sleep can affect any person adversely, but it certainly doesn't constitute insanity. I'm going to give you something at bedtime to help you sleep deep and long. After five or six days we'll start tapering it off so you don't get addicted to it, but it will do wonders at helping your body get the rest it needs so you can get past this. Among the three of us, we'll make sure you get the sleep you need." He smirked and added, "We'll lace your coffee with it if we have to."

"He knows how stubborn you are," Garret said to Ritcherd, who scowled at him.

Patrick leaned back and sighed, then motioned toward Garret. "I think it's your turn."

Ritcherd turned toward Garret in surprise, realizing this was something the two of them had discussed.

"Yes, it is," Garret said, "but you'll have to excuse me for a few minutes. There's something I need to get first."

He left the room, and Patrick asked some questions about Celeste's death. He was fascinated with her condition and the things the specialist had told them.

Garret returned and closed the door, holding a leather-bound book. Ritcherd felt relatively certain it was a journal. Garret was a meticulous journal keeper, and he'd passed the habit on to Ritcherd, although he'd not written a word since before Celeste's death.

"I've been thinking a great deal about some experiences of my youth," Garret said, taking his seat. "I briefly mentioned it to Kyrah earlier today, and then I discussed it with Patrick during our ride here. But I was sitting here wondering how I could possibly share one of the most difficult experiences of my life. Then Patrick mentioned the trunk full of journals. Well, it just so happens that my journals are in a trunk that I keep here in my room. The books are in chronological order, so it was easy to find the year I was seventeen, and the pages I need are easy to find because I've reread certain sections so many times that the book falls right open to . . ." He handed the book to Ritcherd and sure enough, it fell open to a certain page. "Read it out loud," he said, meeting Ritcherd's eyes.

Ritcherd eased closer to the lamp and focused his eyes on the top of the page where the date was written. Sure enough, Garret would have been seventeen; Ritcherd would have been eighteen. He cleared his throat and read, "'I am a different man than I was when I wrote in this book a week ago. Today I actually want to live. It seems that Skipper was right all along.'"

Ritcherd glanced at Garret, who explained, "That's what I called my grandfather. We were sailing together when I wrote that."

Ritcherd nodded and continued to read. "'He tried to tell me I wasn't crazy.'" He hesitated, and looked again at Garret while he struggled to keep his composure. He read on. "'Skipper told me I could get through this if I would just trust him enough to talk it through. I didn't believe him. I really thought I was doomed to a life of insanity. What else could I think when I was so consumed with anger, and that was only when I could force myself to get out of bed at all? Skipper finally locked me in his cabin and told me I wasn't leaving until I told him every thought that came to my mind, no matter how angry or afraid or sad it made me. At first, I was so angry with him I actually hit him. I hit my own grandfather.'"

Ritcherd shook his head in disbelief. If he wasn't reading the time-worn page in front of him, he would believe that Garret was making this up just to patronize him. The similarities were unbelievable. "Keep going," Garret said, "just a little further."

Ritcherd read, "'Skipper just hit me back and told me to start talking. So I did, and it was hell, but it was worth it. I feel like a new person. I suppose Skipper got fed up with repairing the holes I kept punching in the cabin walls. If I hadn't talked it through, he probably would have tossed me overboard. There were times when I almost wanted him to. I thought it would have been easier that way. If I could just drown and disappear, then I wouldn't have to feel that way anymore. Well, I'm glad he loved me and believed in me enough to help me get to this point. I really am glad to be alive, and with any luck I can actually make something worthwhile of my life.'"

"All right. That's good," Garret said, taking the book from Ritcherd. He came to his feet and added, "Is that enough expertise for you?" Ritcherd nodded. "Good. Now, if I'm not mistaken, we're late for supper. I told Liza we would be down when we were ready and she said she'd have Mrs. Hawke keep it warm. After we eat a good supper, Patrick's going to give you some of that horrible stuff he gave you after he dug that bullet out of your leg. You're going to get a good night's sleep, and tomorrow you and I are going to have a long talk."

"Are we now?" Ritcherd asked, feeling hopeful but admittedly afraid.

"You bet we are, brother. It might take a week, but rest assured that I remember very well my grandfather's methods for purging the soul. And you will emerge a new man."

"Not too unlike the old one, I hope," Kyrah said.

"Just happier," Garret said and left the room.

Chapter Ten

The Purging

*S*upper was relatively pleasant for Ritcherd, as his depression didn't come up at all, and he felt decidedly relieved to know there was some hope for him beyond the doom of insanity. The conversation was light and full of laughter, reminding him of times gone by that they'd all shared. He felt inexpressibly grateful to have Patrick here—and, as always, for Garret, and for his own sweet wife, and the unconditional love they gave him. He knew in his heart that it was their love and belief in him that actually made him believe he could get beyond all he was struggling with.

After supper they all went to the parlor for coffee, except that Patrick told the maid, "Captain Buchanan won't be having any coffee in the evenings. Could you bring him some warm milk instead please?"

"As you wish," the maid said and left the room.

"Warm milk?" Ritcherd retorted. "I detest warm milk. Some cocoa, perhaps?"

"Cocoa and coffee both have stimulating qualities," Patrick said. "Until you get your patterns of sleep ironed out, you'll be having warm milk in the evenings."

"Yes, sir," Ritcherd said with subtle sarcasm.

While he appreciated their concern, he had a feeling the next several days weren't going to be pleasant. But then, Garret had come right out and said that purging the soul could be hell. Still, could it be any more hellish than living with this inner torment that had plagued him for so long? In truth, looking back over his life, he could see that there had always been some measure of uneasiness inside of him, as if he couldn't be completely comfortable with who and what he was. Perhaps his grief over losing Celeste had just pushed him over the edge enough that he couldn't temper those feelings. Whatever it was, he prayed that he could come to a point like the one Garret had reached when his grandfather had finished with him. Garret was one of the finest men he had ever known. If such strength of character was the result of this purging, then Ritcherd was all for it.

Ritcherd became distracted from the conversation going on around him as familiar troubling thoughts filled his mind. He was startled by Kyrah nudging him.

"Sorry," he said. "I guess I was daydreaming."

"About what?" Garret demanded. "With that expression on your face, it obviously wasn't very pleasant."

Ritcherd looked down, hating the way his heart and soul seemed to be under close scrutiny. He reminded himself that his pride had been shattered long ago, and there was no point in pretenses. "No," he admitted, "it wasn't very pleasant."

"I think," Patrick said, coming to his feet, "that it's time I put my charge to bed for the night."

"You're my doctor, not my nanny," Ritcherd said as Patrick took his arm and urged him to his feet.

"Sometimes the two run fairly close together," Patrick said. "Kiss your wife good night. You're going to bed."

Kyrah stood and gave Ritcherd a long, savoring kiss. "I love you," she said, pressing a hand over his face.

"I love you too, Kyrah," he replied and kissed her once more before Patrick led him from the room, closing the door behind them.

When they were gone, Kyrah wasn't surprised to see Garret stand up long enough to open the door. Once he'd returned to his seat she said, "I want you to know how much I appreciate your willingness to help Ritcherd through this. I've often wondered if he's hesitant to talk to me because I'm such a big part of the struggles of his life. I think he's more likely to be honest with you."

"He won't be afraid of hurting my feelings, that's for sure," Garret said with a little chuckle. More soberly he added, "Yes, I think you're right. I think he has a lot of mixed emotions about many things in his past, and you're tangled into most of them."

Silence fell over the room, and Garret noticed Kyrah looking deeply troubled. "What's wrong?" he asked.

"I was just thinking about those days he holed himself up on the *Phoenix;* those were horrible days, Garret. Is that what this is going to be like?"

"No," he said firmly. "This time I'm going to be holed up with him. And he's not going to stop eating. He'll need his strength. I want you to have meals sent up for us. I want you to ignore anything you might hear. And I want you and Cetty to go shopping and for long walks and have a marvelous time together. If I need you, I'll let you know; otherwise, just let me handle it."

"You do know what you're doing, don't you?"

"I only have my own personal experience, Kyrah, and the belief that God will guide my words and my instincts in order to best help him. I'll be praying very hard."

"As will I," she said.

"Then everything will be fine," he said and smiled, but Kyrah still felt decidedly concerned.

Ritcherd slept nearly ten hours, then was relieved to find that breakfast had been brought to his room when he felt significantly groggy and wasn't certain he could make it down the stairs. By the time he'd eaten and had a few cups of coffee, he felt well rested and alert and ready to face the day.

"Oh, good morning," Kyrah said, coming into the room just as he'd finished his meal. "How are you feeling?"

"Not too bad," he said, and she bent to kiss him.

"Garret's waiting for you," she said, and he felt his countenance falter.

Ritcherd took a deep breath and came to his feet. "I might as well get it over with," he said.

"Yes, I believe so," Kyrah said, fighting hard to keep her emotions from showing.

They went together to the nursery where Ritcherd spent some time with Cetty, then he and Kyrah walked hand in hand to Garret's sitting room, where the door had been left open. Ritcherd hesitated in the hallway, saying quietly, "Why do I feel like I'm stepping into the lion's den?"

Kyrah looked into his eyes and pressed her hands over his chest, "God protected Daniel in the lion's den, Ritcherd. Everything will be all right. Garret loves you."

"Yes, I know. He's also not afraid to bust me in the jaw if he thinks I need it."

Kyrah smiled and touched his face. "And I love you," she said, her voice breaking.

"I love you too, Kyrah. It's my hope of being a better man for your sake that makes me willing to do this."

She smiled and kissed him while tears moistened her lashes, then she hurried to knock at the open door before Ritcherd could hesitate any longer.

"Good morning," Garret said brightly when he appeared. He waved comically at Kyrah and motioned her into the hall before he closed the door. "How did you sleep?" he asked Ritcherd once they were alone.

"Very well, thank you."

"That's good, I believe. As Patrick mentioned, acute lack of sleep certainly does not constitute insanity."

"It's much more than that," Ritcherd said, taking a seat. "But I'm not sure I can explain it. If I could explain it, I wouldn't have to wonder if I'm crazy."

"Well, you're going to have to figure out how to explain it, because I'm not leaving until you do."

Ritcherd sighed loudly as Garret sat down and put his feet up, crossing them at the ankles. They stared at each other a long moment before Ritcherd asked, "Why are you willing to do so much for me?"

Garret's voice was firm with sincerity. "You're my brother, Ritcherd. I had nothing when you came into my life. Now I have everything."

"Not quite everything."

"Well, I'm still looking for the future Mrs. Wentworth. Other than that, I have everything. Enough chitchat. Let's get on with it, shall we?"

"I'm just sitting here waiting for the axe to fall," Ritcherd said glumly.

"All right," Garret said, "here's how it goes. You can either talk, or you can write."

"I'm sorry?" Ritcherd said, not understanding what he meant.

"The idea here is that we are going to completely clean out your mind of every difficult or ugly memory or experience, and the emotions that go along with them."

Ritcherd chuckled. "That could take a while."

"I'm not going anywhere," Garret said.

"And how exactly do we go about that?"

"You can either talk, or you can write," he repeated. "I think some of both would probably be good. So, let's start by talking. You go back as far as you can remember and just start telling me about your life. The important thing, however, is that you don't hold back any thought that comes into your mind. You have to say every word, or this will never work."

"I don't understand," Ritcherd said.

"As I see it . . . as far as it went when I did this, anyway . . . the idea is that we hold too much inside ourselves. Those angry, or painful, or ugly thoughts just churn around year after year and have nowhere to go. You just have to . . . get them out of your head. Simple as that."

"It sounds a little *too* simple."

"Simple, not easy," Garret said with a wise little smirk. "I don't understand it, but there seems to be a connection to the words and the related emotion. If there are things you don't feel comfortable telling me, then you will write them down. But again, it has to be every single word that comes to your mind. No holding back. And of course, if you didn't have anybody you could trust to talk to, you could do this on your own—simply by writing it all out."

"I think I'd rather have you here to make certain I stay sane."

"Glad to be here," Garret said. He lifted a finger and added still again, "But no holding back. You must speak every single word. All right?"

"All right, but . . . do you think you can handle the profanity?"

Garret laughed. "You have no idea."

"No idea of what?"

"How much profanity came out of my mouth when I went through this. Quit stalling and just talk."

"All right," Ritcherd said, "where should I start?"

"What's your earliest memory?" Garret asked.

"Oh, that's easy," he said. "It was the day Celeste was born. They knew right away that something wasn't right with her, but I thought she was beautiful."

Ritcherd spent the morning rambling about his early childhood, the delight he found in his baby sister, memories of his nannies and governesses. Garret pointed out the obvious, that his parents weren't very involved in his care.

"No, they weren't," Ritcherd said. "Of course, it's always been customary that young children dine separately, and I never minded that because as a child I hated the formality of sharing an occasional meal with my parents. I preferred the casual atmosphere of the nursery, and I know Cetty does as well. But my parents *never* came to the nursery. They never played with us, or read to us, or took us anywhere except to church on Sundays. Occasionally when company would come, they'd have the governess dress us up so they could show us off for a few minutes, and then we were expected to remain out of sight. But I really didn't mind."

He went on to talk about how he liked some of the servants better than others, but together they all saw that he and Celeste were well cared for. Whenever Ritcherd hesitated, even for a second, Garret would remind him to speak every word that came to his mind. At first he felt uncomfortable with the theory, but after a couple of hours he was able to spill his every thought without much effort. They shared lunch in Garret's sitting room while Ritcherd continued to talk, almost beginning to believe that this might not be so bad. Then he felt suddenly hesitant. His mind went completely blank. He couldn't form a cohesive sentence, and he felt decidedly uneasy. He explained what he was feeling to Garret, who asked, "What's your next memory?"

Ritcherd had to think about it for several minutes before he finally said, "I remember looking at my parents. They were sitting in the drawing room. I was standing in the hall, watching them while they weren't aware. I remember thinking that they didn't love me. It was as if . . . I'd always just taken their behavior toward me for granted and hadn't cared, but then . . . something had changed, and I realized that they didn't love me."

"What changed?" Garret asked, leaning forward.

Ritcherd looked at him directly. "I don't know." He shook his head again. "I have no idea why one day their feelings didn't matter to me, and the next they did. I honestly don't know."

"All right, well . . . go on from there."

As Ritcherd progressed, it became increasingly difficult not to hold the words back, and incidents came up that weren't easy to talk about. Emotion bubbled out of him as he talked about the day Celeste and her nanny were sent to live elsewhere, and Ritcherd was given no explanation. She had been the center of his life, and she'd been torn away from him as if it were nothing, simply because she was a social embarrassment to their parents because of her condition. He paced the room, hurling angry words, cursing and crying while Garret just encouraged him to keep going. He became calmer as he talked about meeting Kyrah in the church ruins when she was only seven. They talked through supper, then Ritcherd left the room to spend some time with Kyrah and Cetty. Kyrah seemed surprised to see him—or perhaps to see him apparently doing well. He told her about his day, then Patrick showed up with his nighttime concoction and Ritcherd slept long and deep.

The following day, Ritcherd had breakfast with Garret in his sitting room while the course of memories continued. Ritcherd talked in detail of his evolving relationship with Kyrah, many typical experiences of being a young man, and how Kyrah's family had made up for the lack of love he got at home. The memories became difficult again when he spoke of going to war, fighting against the colonists as a captain in His Majesty's army. Ritcherd's struggle with this exercise increased dramatically as he recounted horrid images held in his mind of the battlefields he'd survived, and the army hospital where he had spent many weeks with a wounded arm, while men were dying and having limbs amputated all around him. Then he had returned from the war to the news that Kyrah's father had lost their estate in a card game and had subsequently shot himself in the head. Kyrah and her mother had been left destitute, and Kyrah was working just to survive. But worst of all, Kyrah had initially wanted nothing to do with him.

The story progressed with difficulty and a great deal of heart-ache. Garret heard patterns in the words that came out of Ritcherd's mouth that gave him some significant clues to the internal struggles he was facing. He'd already heard this part of Ritcherd and Kyrah's story before, but not in so much detail, and with so much emotion. It was when Ritcherd's mother had arranged for Kyrah to be illegally deported in order to keep the two of them apart that Ritcherd was assaulted with an intense bout of chest pain that made him cry in anguish. Garret quickly summoned Patrick, and since they'd already eaten supper, Patrick just gave him the usual dosage and stayed with him until he slept in Garret's bed. Garret slept opposite Ritcherd in the huge bed, wanting to be close by. He chuckled to think how they were brothers, and yet they'd not grown up together. If they had, they might have shared a bedroom many times. He fell asleep analyzing what he'd learned about Ritcherd so far and wondering why something seemed to be missing.

Kyrah sat down to breakfast with Patrick, feeling decidedly uneasy that she'd not seen Ritcherd at all since early the previous morning.

"You seem upset," Patrick said.

"I'm just . . . concerned. They've not stepped out of that room since yesterday morning, and—"

"And Garret told you that would likely be the case," he reminded her gently.

"I know. I'm just . . . concerned."

"What you need is a distraction. And some fresh air wouldn't hurt. I would love it if you and Cetty would take me on a tour of the gardens, and then . . . I have a favor to ask you."

"Of course. Anything."

"Would you and Cetty also be willing to take me to Celeste's grave?"

"I'd be happy to," she said. "Perhaps we could do that after lunch."

"I'll look forward to it." Patrick smiled, and she felt immensely grateful for his friendship and the distraction he offered. She longed for her mother to be here, but in truth she was glad for Sarah's absence. All of this would have been difficult for her. The timing of her extended visit to London was in truth a great blessing for all of them.

The day proved to be quite delightful, as Patrick did so well at interacting with Cetty and making her laugh. He even taught her a simple magic trick. But as Kyrah crawled into her bed—alone—having seen no sign of Garret or Ritcherd all day, she could only pray that they were making progress, and that this entire ordeal would soon be over.

When Ritcherd had finally talked through everything he could possibly think of right down to the present, Garret felt enlightened by certain patterns of his thinking. They discussed them rationally, and Ritcherd seemed fascinated with the deductions they had come to. He felt certain that Ritcherd had made remarkable progress, but he felt a distinct uneasiness. Something didn't make sense; something was missing. But another day had come to a close, and Ritcherd was exhausted. He had cried and shouted and raged through the difficult moments of his life, and he was visibly drained. Again he slept in Garret's bed, but Garret left Patrick sitting in the room with the sleeping Ritcherd and a good book while he went in search of Kyrah. He thought it would be well for her to hear of their progress, and he hoped that talking it through with her might help him find the missing pieces. His instincts were practically screaming that something wasn't right.

He found Kyrah just tucking Cetty into bed. Garret kissed his little niece and assured her that her papa would soon be feeling better and would be coming to see her.

"I'll keep praying," Cetty said firmly.

"You do that, my darling," he said and kissed her little brow.

Following Kyrah into the hallway, he asked, "May we talk?"

"Of course," she said. "Where is Ritcherd?"

"He's asleep in my bed. Patrick is with him."

"Is he all right?" she asked intently.

"Yes, I believe he is. I'd like to tell you some things that we've been able to figure out together."

"Oh, yes . . . please," she said and led the way to her sitting room.

Once they were seated, Garret told her the theories and methods that his grandfather had used with him. By listening to Ritcherd talk through memories of his entire life, he'd been able to pick up on a pattern that shed some light on his more recent behavior.

"I don't understand," Kyrah said.

"And it's difficult to explain, but . . . it seems to me that there are attitudes we hold in our minds that we are not consciously aware of that affect our behavior. While Ritcherd could have never seen or believed the reasons for his behavior, it now makes perfect sense. You see . . . it's as if at some level, inside himself, he feels unworthy of being loved, and afraid that any love that comes into his life is only temporary." Garret sighed. "He is terrified of being abandoned."

Kyrah's brow furrowed as she concentrated closely on what he was saying. "First of all," Garret went on, "his earliest, happiest memories are of Celeste, but she was sent away with no explanation. In his early childhood his parents were completely absent in his life, and at some point he came to believe that they simply didn't love him."

"That's no surprise," Kyrah said.

"No," Garret went on, although he still felt confused on exactly what had changed Ritcherd's perception. *Something was missing.* He forced himself to the moment. "So, he met you. Life was better. He came home from the war, and initially you wanted nothing to do with him."

"Good heavens," Kyrah muttered, recalling how confused and difficult she had been.

"Eventually that was worked out, but within days you were deported."

Kyrah's heart quickened as she began to see where this was leading.

"When he finally found you, you had married another man. Eventually that was worked out," he said again. "He reconciled with his mother, finally gained her love and respect, only to have her die in his arms. He got Celeste back, but . . . now she's gone, as well. And the two of you lost a baby not so long ago."

Kyrah felt a tangible ache in her heart as she considered how these events had affected Ritcherd's perspective of life and love.

"Now, it's just speculation," Garret said, "but it seems to me that somewhere deep inside, he was so afraid of losing you that he decided to cut himself off from you instead."

"I don't understand."

"Something in his spirit said, 'I'll leave her before she can leave me. I'll test her love for me to such limits that she will prove me right. She'll leave, and it will prove that I am completely unlovable and unworthy of love. Everyone I love leaves me.'"

"Good heavens," Kyrah said again. "It makes such perfect sense when you put it that way."

"I also believe," Garret went on, "that he has struggled with his own identity. I think a great deal of his confusion and difficult feelings have stemmed from not really knowing who and what he is."

"You've lost me," Kyrah said.

"Well, he was born and raised an aristocrat—old name, title, massive wealth. But he always hated the aristocracy. I think he would prefer to have no connection whatsoever to it, but he *is* an aristocrat. The social barriers are difficult for him, but not in the way you might think. He actually believes that aristocracy is a curse, and that your marrying him has cursed your life—not the other way around."

"He said that?"

"More than once, with fervor."

"Incredible," Kyrah said, feeling deeply comforted without fully understanding why.

"He needs to understand that his value as a human being comes from simply being Ritcherd Buchanan—husband, father, brother, friend. He needs to separate his identity completely from being Lord Buckley, and then perhaps he won't get so testy when people use the title."

Kyrah felt a new level of awareness strike her with poignancy. "Or when his wife calls him an aristocratic snob."

Garret gasped. Kyrah met his eyes. Without saying another word, they both understood now why Ritcherd had responded to those words by hitting her. It had triggered something deeply painful for him.

"Incredible," Kyrah said again, trying to absorb all of this information. "And what about the anger?"

"Well, we're still working on that. He's got a lot of anger bottled up inside of him still. He's made some progress expressing it, but I've got a plan for that—another of my grandfather's methods that will hopefully help him get it out of his system. It's evident that he feels a great deal of anger toward his parents for obvious reasons, but I think he's also angry with people he doesn't want to be angry with, and since he's never been able to express those feelings appropriately, they're eating at him."

"You mean me, don't you. He's got anger toward me . . . for giving up on him."

"Perhaps," he said. "And he's got anger toward me, as well."

"Why would he, when—"

"For being in love with his wife."

Kyrah sighed. "Oh, I see."

Garret went on to tell her his plan for the following day—although he figured it could take much longer than one day to follow through. The timing was really up to Ritcherd. Kyrah went to bed feeling more relaxed to know what was actually taking place with Ritcherd, but she missed him and longed for this to be over.

Before Garret went to bed, he spent some time studying his journal entries from the time he'd gone through such an emotional purging. The following morning, Garret put paper and pen in front of Ritcherd the moment he was finished with his breakfast.

"What is this for?" Ritcherd asked.

"You're going to write a letter."

"To whom?"

"Well, actually you're going to write several. Who you start with is up to you."

"I'm waiting to hear an intelligible explanation, Garret."

"You are going to write a letter to everyone who ever wronged you, or hurt you, or made you angry. You're going to tell them exactly what you think, holding nothing back. You can start with your parents."

"My parents are both dead."

"You're not going to give these letters away, Ritcherd. If these people were actually going to read them, you'd have to be much more diplomatic. These letters are for you. Once you've said everything you need to say, you can read it if you want to, we'll talk about it. That's all."

Ritcherd took a deep breath. He felt good about the progress they'd made and the understanding he'd gained already of the misconceptions that had plagued him. Writing a few letters didn't sound so difficult.

Garret read while Ritcherd wrote a lengthy letter to his father. He admitted about halfway through, "This is more difficult than I thought it would be."

"Why is that?"

"It just feels so . . . callous to be saying such things to someone who was simply human."

"Just say what you have to say and get it over with," Garret said. "We'll work on the other side of it later."

Ritcherd sighed and pressed on. It took him until the middle of the afternoon to finish the letter to his father. "Done," he finally said, and Garret stood beside him.

"May I?" Garret asked.

"Of course," Ritcherd said. "I have no secrets from you—no pride left either, for that matter."

"What are brothers for?" Garret asked lightly and picked up the several pages that comprised the letter. He sat and read it slowly while Ritcherd moved about the room. Garret finally finished and said, "Amazing."

"Is it?"

"Well, he was my father too, you know."

"Yes, I know."

"But I didn't know that until after he'd died. I wrote a letter like this to him myself."

"You did?" Ritcherd asked.

"Funny. It was much the same, and I didn't even live with him."

"That is amazing," Ritcherd said.

"So, what did you learn from this?" Garret asked.

Ritcherd thought about it. "I learned that I was holding more anger toward my father than I'd realized. I forgave him a long time ago for his neglect and his difficult attitudes, but I was still harboring difficult feelings that were affecting me. I think my ill feelings toward him might have even made me afraid of being a bad father myself."

Garret nodded. "Amazing," he repeated. He held up the pages and asked, "Do you want to read it?"

"I already did."

"Do you need it?" Garret asked.

Ritcherd shrugged. "No."

Garret wadded up the letter and tossed it accurately into the fireplace, where it quickly caught the flames and disintegrated into ashes. Ritcherd watched it burn, feeling a little stunned but not knowing what to say. He'd put hours of work into that letter, and now it was gone.

"No need to hang on to that," Garret said. "You told him how you feel, now you can let those feelings go." It took Ritcherd a moment to absorb what he was saying—and how it made him feel. Then he realized he was all right with that.

"Next letter," Garret said, motioning toward the table where the paper and inkwell waited. "This one will begin, 'Dear Ritcherd.'" Ritcherd looked confused and he added, "It will end, 'Love, Father.'"

"You're confusing me."

"I want you to sit in that chair as if you were William Buchanan, and I want you to write a letter to your son."

"How can I do that?"

"You knew him well. Just try to imagine how he would think, how he would have perceived you. Then write it down."

"So you can burn it."

"Maybe," Garret said. "Just write the letter."

While Garret read, Ritcherd had to think for nearly an hour before he could actually begin this letter. When it was finished, Garret read it silently and asked, "What did you learn from this?"

"My father loved me. He just didn't know how to express his feelings."

Garret commented, "It's a beautiful letter, actually. I can really feel what you're saying. He *did* love you."

"Are you going to burn it now?"

"No," Garret said, setting it gently at his side, "I think it would be well for you to keep this one."

The following day Ritcherd wrote a letter to his mother, and one from her to him. This was easier, since he'd made peace with her prior to her death. They had forgiven each other, and she had expressed her love and respect for him. Still, he realized through his writing that he actually felt angry with her for dying and leaving him when they had just started over.

"That's ludicrous," Ritcherd said. "How can you be angry with someone for dying? It was completely beyond her control."

"Yes, it was. But she still left you. A feeling is just a feeling. It doesn't have to have some logical explanation."

Garret burned the letter Ritcherd had written to his mother, but he kept the one she had written to him. As Ritcherd reread the letters from his parents, he truly felt as if they had been written by their hands. He could feel their love for him, and he felt better.

Ritcherd actually enjoyed writing a letter to Peter Westman, and the anger he expressed didn't surprise him in the least. The letter that Peter wrote to Ritcherd simply said, "Dear Captain: I hate you too, but since I'm rotting in hell, you probably don't care. Tell your brother that his swordplay was very impressive."

Garret read the letter, laughed boisterously, and set it with the letters that were to be kept. Ritcherd then wrote letters to Kyrah's parents, a few people in the community, the vicar, and Dr. Ware. That evening they had supper in the dining room with Patrick and Kyrah, and the next morning Ritcherd told Garret he figured they were finished with that exercise.

"Oh, no," he said, putting a fresh sheet of paper in front of him. "This one begins, 'My darling Kyrah.'"

"No!" Ritcherd insisted. "She's my wife. I love her. I'm not going to write horrible things to her and—"

"Yes, she's your wife, Ritcherd, and you love her. She's not going to read this. But you need to write it. She wasn't there for you the way you needed her to be when you came home from the war. And then she gave up on you and married Peter Westman. You need to write her a letter and get all of that out of you. This letter could be the most important of all."

Ritcherd had to admit that Garret was right. He hated it, but Garret was right. It took most of the day to write the letter to Kyrah, and he had to admit that he felt better—especially when Garret threw it into the fire without bothering to read it first.

"Why didn't you read it?" Ritcherd asked.

"I would bet there was stuff in there about me. If there wasn't, then you should write another one."

"Oh, you were in there."

"Good. Now we can move on." Garret motioned toward the pen and paper. "This one begins, 'My darling Ritcherd.'"

"She's down the hall, Garret. She can write me a letter herself."

"Yes, she can, but that's not the point. I want you to sit in that chair and think good and hard about your sweet wife and the way she feels about you. Just close your eyes and *be* Kyrah for a few minutes. Try to see yourself through Kyrah's eyes."

Ritcherd did his best to follow Garret's advice. It had certainly served him well thus far. As he did his best to focus on the relationship he shared with Kyrah from her perspective, he was unexpectedly overtaken with a surge of emotion. With his eyes closed he was surprised to hear Garret say, "Can you feel how much she loves you?"

Ritcherd nodded and wiped the tears from his face. He *could* feel her love for him, and it soothed him, heart and soul. When he'd finished Kyrah's letter to him, Garret put it, unread, with the others that would be saved.

"That's it, then," Ritcherd said. "I'm feeling good about—"

"No, there are a couple more you have to do."

"Who?"

Garret motioned impatiently toward the table. "'Dear Garret,'" he said.

Ritcherd gave a dubious chuckle. "Why on earth would I—"

"Write it down," he insisted. "'Dear Garret.'" Ritcherd sighed and wrote that much. "Now this," Garret added. "'When I first realized you were in love with Kyrah, I wanted to kill you and dump you over-board, but I wouldn't have been able to sail the ship without you. I'm glad I didn't kill you, but there have been moments when I have hated you, simply because I know you love her.'"

Ritcherd stared at Garret, astonished by what he was hearing—and even more so to realize that what Garret had said was true. He had pegged his own feelings so accurately that it was almost frightening.

"Go on, write it," Garret said. "I deserve it, and I can take it."

Ritcherd took a deep breath and wrote a hasty but intense letter to Garret, but he finished it by expressing his love, his gratitude, his deepest respect. He handed it to Garret, saying, "You'd better read this one before you burn it."

"Oh, I intend to," Garret said.

Ritcherd watched him closely while he read, and more than once Garret lifted his eyes from the page to return the gaze. As he came to the end, there was a distinct glisten of moisture in his eyes. He care-fully tore the letter in half, wadded up the top half and tossed it into the fire. He folded the other half and tucked it into his pocket, then he rose and moved to the table, taking up the pen. "I can take care of this one," he said, and Ritcherd aimlessly wandered the room while Garret wrote. He handed the letter to Ritcherd, who sat down to read it, noting that it wasn't very long.

Dear Ritcherd,

I cannot begin to express my gratitude in having you as a brother. You gave me a ship. You've given me a home, and a family to belong to. But most importantly, you've given me your deepest love and respect, even when you knew I was harboring feelings for your wife. No man has ever earned or deserved my trust and highest regard as you have. I know that God exists and He dearly loves us. Your being in my life is evidence enough of that. I wish you every happiness from this day forward, and I anxiously await all the good times we have yet to share.

With love, your brother,
  Garret

With a cracking voice Ritcherd said, "I think I'll keep this one."

"You do that," Garret said. "Now there's only one more, but it's getting late. We should save this for tomorrow."

"Who else could there possibly be?"

"We'll talk about it in the morning," Garret said.

Chapter Eleven

The Hole

*L*ater that night, while Ritcherd snored softly, Garret had trouble relaxing as he puzzled over the uneasiness he felt. *Something was missing.* And he only had two clues. The first was that blank look on Ritcherd's face before he had declared realizing that his parents didn't love him. *Something had changed,* he'd said. But what? The other clue was a statement Ritcherd had made in the letter to his mother. It had been destroyed so he couldn't go back and read it, but Garret remembered it clearly. It stuck in his head with an incongruity that disturbed him deeply. He finally slept from exhaustion, but he woke up knowing that his own troubling thoughts had to be addressed. And with any luck, he and Ritcherd would be able to get some answers that made sense.

Right after breakfast, Garret put Ritcherd in front of a blank page again and said, "This letter begins, 'Dear God.'"

Ritcherd looked up at Garret incredulously. "You want me to tell God why I'm angry with Him?"

"I do. And before you tell me that you wouldn't dare, or that you have no reason to be angry with God, let me tell you that everyone has some anger toward God at one time or another, even if they don't admit it. You've made some poor choices that have brought severe consequences into your life, but you were also dealt some pretty rotten circumstances that had nothing to do with your choices. So tell God how you feel about that. Believe it or not, I think He understands.

And once you get that out of you, you'll understand, too. And then you can write a letter from God to you, and you might actually be able to feel how much He loves you, and how He's always been looking out for you, even if it didn't always feel that way."

Ritcherd did as Garret had suggested, finishing the letter after lunch. His surprise in writing to God was just how much he had to say once he got going. Then he watched the letter burn and did his best to see himself through God's eyes. He marveled that Garret had been right. He *could* feel God's love for him, and that in itself made everything else he'd come to understand through these days all the more amazing. Ritcherd wrote a second letter to God, thanking him for blessings that he listed in detail, and that too was put with those that he would keep. Ritcherd watched Garret fold all of the letters together and seal them closed with wax. He handed the packet to Ritcherd and said, "Read them when you're feeling down. Don't let feeling down lead to being depressed. It's up to you to remember how far you've come and to deal with your emotions appropriately before they get out of hand."

Ritcherd nodded. "Does this mean I'm cured?"

"Do you feel cured?"

"I feel much better, yes," Ritcherd admitted.

"But?" Garret said.

"But what?"

"I could feel a 'but' at the end of that sentence. You just didn't say it."

Ritcherd took a sharp breath. "Sometimes I hate your perceptive nature."

Garret chuckled. "How very honest of you. Sometimes I hate the way you try to pretend that everything's all right when it isn't. You're still feeling uneasy about something, aren't you?"

"Yes, but I have no idea what. I've thought about it until my head aches. It's as if . . ."

"Something's missing?" Garret provided.

"Yes!" Ritcherd said firmly. "It's as if something is missing. And I fear if I don't find out what it is and fix it, I *will* fall again into that horrible black pit. Am I crazy, Garret?"

"I think we've already established that to be a myth. But I must admit that I've felt that something is missing. I have a couple of clues, if you're interested."

"I am," Ritcherd said eagerly, while something quivered fearfully inside of him.

Garret repeated his observation of Ritcherd's declaration that something had changed with regard to his parents. He finished by saying, "But you don't know what."

"No, I don't," Ritcherd said. "It's as if . . . there's a hole." He was silently thoughtful for a minute, then said, "What's the other clue?"

"Something you wrote in your letter to your mother. When you were angry with her for having Celeste sent away, you said, 'Let the thief take anything—even your children if they must.'"

"I did say that, didn't I."

"*Why* did you say that?" Garret asked.

"Well . . . Celeste was gone. My parents had sent her away, and I was angry."

"But that's just it. Your parents sent her away. A thief didn't take her."

"That's true," Ritcherd said, and Garret noticed him pressing a hand absently over his chest. Then, through a few minutes of silence, Garret watched Ritcherd become visibly agitated. His brow furrowed thoughtfully, his eyes became distant, his breathing more shallow.

"Ritcherd," Garret said, and he looked startled, almost afraid. "Why did you refer to a thief? And why did you say 'children?' Celeste is only one child. How many children were there?"

"Just me and Celeste," he said, as if it were obvious. Ritcherd heard his own angry tone and wondered where it had come from.

As if Garret had read his mind, he said, "You sound angry all of a sudden. You seem . . . agitated. Your chest is hurting."

Ritcherd glanced down to see his hand pressed there and realized that Garret was right. He'd been so caught up with a sudden foggy feeling in his head that he hadn't consciously noticed the pain.

In a gentle, quiet voice, Garret said, "Tell me about the thief, Ritcherd."

Garret felt eerily uncomfortable when Ritcherd groaned and squeezed his eyes closed abruptly. Garret's heart pounded, and a sharp chill rushed across his back as the packet of letters fell to the floor and Ritcherd lifted trembling hands to press them over his temples. He groaned again, and then he howled, a noise that filled the room with abject anguish, as if his head had suddenly been filled with unbearable pain. He started gasping for breath, and the word "No!" sputtered out of his mouth several times.

Garret sat beside him, putting his hands on his brother's shoulders. "Ritcherd, what is it? What's wrong?"

"I can't breathe," he muttered. "I can't breathe."

"Yes, you can," Garret said. "Just take it in slowly. Just breathe and tell me what's wrong."

"No. It's not possible," he muttered, clutching onto Garret. "It's not possible."

"What's not possible, Ritcherd?" Garret asked, feeling perhaps more frightened than he ever had in his life.

Through the remainder of the day and all through the night, Garret stayed close to Ritcherd while he cried and screamed and sputtered words that gradually painted a very clear picture—an abhorrent, deplorable picture; a picture that had somehow been neatly locked away in a part of Ritcherd's mind where it had been completely ignored and forgotten.

Night merged into day while Ritcherd refused to eat and got angry at the mere suggestion that he take something to help him sleep. He spilled memories as if he were spewing bile, vacillating from angry to sobbing to despondent—sometimes all in the breadth of a few minutes. Garret watched in horrified amazement as Ritcherd became an eleven-year-old boy, emotionally reliving an incident from that time of his life in grisly detail. When it seemed there were no more memories to be found in the dark caverns of Ritcherd's mind, his anger shifted to repeated ranting about his own insanity. Ritcherd was horrified with the belief that his mind would conjure up such a vile experience. While Garret tried to assure him that surely his mind had blocked out the experience until now, Ritcherd couldn't seem to fathom such a concept. He would only be convinced that he'd gone mad—completely, hopelessly mad. He begged Garret to see that his family remained safe, to lock him up before he did them any further harm, to let him go to the gallows and give him an easy way out.

Through the course of the day and into another night, while neither of them slept even a moment, Garret talked Ritcherd out of killing himself more than half a dozen times.

Finally, exhaustion overtook Ritcherd and Garret was able to calm him down. He curled up in Garret's bed and stared at the wall with glazed eyes. The constant prayer Garret had held in his heart through this entire ordeal became intently focused. He pleaded silently for guidance on exactly what to do now. He couldn't leave his brother alone, but he instinctively felt there was something else he should be doing, and if he didn't get some sleep, he wouldn't be any good to Ritcherd whatsoever. A couple of ideas came to his mind. He thought them through, he searched his feelings, then he went to find Kyrah.

Kyrah lay in a sleepless bed and heard a distant clock strike half past twelve. She couldn't even begin to imagine what was going on with her husband. She'd spent the day trying to keep Cetty distracted and happy in spite of the occasional distant shouting and sounds of anguish coming from Garret's room. She knew that little of the food sent to them had been eaten, and she couldn't recall ever being so frightened in her life. Looking back over certain events she'd lived through, she concluded that it took a great deal of fear to surpass her past experiences.

A light knocking at the door startled her with a combination of hope and fear. Either way, she prayed that this would end her horrible ignorance and distant waiting. She grabbed a wrapper and tied it around her as she hurried to answer the door. In the hall she found Garret, holding a single candlestick, looking more disheveled and spent than she'd ever seen him. "He needs you," was all he said before he started down the hall toward his own rooms. He set the candle down on a hall table and hesitated with his hand on the doorknob, saying quietly, "I couldn't get him to take any of that stuff to help him sleep, but maybe it's just as well at the moment. He feels like he's drowning. You are going to keep him afloat. All you have to do is hold him and tell him you love him—a thousand times if you have to. Don't ask questions. Don't try to reason with him. Just hold him.

Give him tangible evidence of the love you share with him. Distract him with normalcy. Do you understand?"

Kyrah nodded, feeling suddenly terrified.

"I'm going to try to get some sleep. I'll be on the sofa in the sitting room. I'm going to close the doors so you can have some privacy, but all you have to do is shout my name and I'll be there in less than a minute. Do not let him out of that room without telling me. Do you hear me?"

Again she nodded. Garret opened the door to his bedroom and they stepped inside. A lamp had been left burning low near the bed where Ritcherd lay on his side, curled up beneath the covers with only part of his face showing. His eyes were glazed and distant.

Kyrah felt suddenly uncertain and frightened and hurried from the room, motioning for Garret to follow her. He looked distressed as he approached her. "What's wrong?" he demanded with a terseness that made her wonder how difficult this had been for him. How much sleep had he been getting?

"Tell me what's wrong. Tell me why he's like that. I can't do this if I don't know what's going on. Just . . . give me the brief version. Some kind of explanation—*any* explanation."

Garret sighed and looked at the floor. "He just spent hours telling me about an event from his childhood. In essence, he relived much of it today. And it is worse than you or I could have ever imagined." Kyrah put a hand over her mouth to keep from crying out. Garret's voice broke as he added, "Your husband, my dear, is by far the most amazing man I have ever known. To see his strength of character, the goodness of his heart—in spite of living through what he has lived through . . ." He was unable to go on for several seconds while he fought for composure. "I admire him more now than . . ." Kyrah was stunned as she watched Garret crumble into tears. He pressed the backs of his hands over his eyes and turned abruptly away from her. "I'm sorry," he said. "It's been a rough day."

"Garret," Kyrah put her hands to his back, "will you be all right?"

"Yes, of course," he insisted. "He needs you worse than I do. Go." He motioned toward the door. "I just need some sleep. I'll be fine."

Kyrah slipped into Garret's bedroom and closed the door. She uttered a silent prayer and steeled herself to carry her husband through the demonic abyss that threatened to overpower him. She slid beneath the bedcovers and laid her head on the pillow close to his where she could look into his eyes. Gingerly she touched his face, almost fearing he would recoil or be afraid. But he showed no response beyond a glazed blinking of his eyes.

"Ritcherd," she whispered gently. "Ritcherd, it's Kyrah. I'm here with you. Do you hear me? It's Kyrah."

"Kyrah," he muttered, his voice hoarse. She saw his eyes focus on her face. "Kyrah," he repeated. She took his hand into hers and guided it to her face.

"I love you, Ritcherd. Oh, Ritcherd, I love you." She pushed her arms around him and pressed her lips to his brow. Following a moment's hesitance, she felt him take hold of her as if she were a lifeline. Garret's analogy came back to her. *He's drowning . . . Keep him afloat . . .*

Kyrah returned his embrace with fervor. He pressed his face to her throat and cried, "Oh, Kyrah. Hold me. Hold me. Don't ever let me go."

"Never," she murmured and held him tighter as he cried harder. She lost track of the time as he cried and begged her not to leave him. She cried silent tears and told him over and over that she would always love him, always be there for him. He finally slept, and minutes later Kyrah slept as well, holding him tightly in her embrace.

Before Garret went to bed for the first time in more than forty hours, he went to Patrick's room and woke him.

"What do you need?" he asked, pulling on a shirt.

"Uh . . . I'm not sure," Garret said, pressing his fingers over his brow and leaning against the door frame.

"Sit down," Patrick said, urging him into the room. "You look exhausted."

"I am exhausted, and I'm on my way to get some sleep. Kyrah is with Ritcherd, but . . . I need some help. I'm just not exactly sure what and . . . my brain isn't working real well, so . . . give me a little time here."

"All right," Patrick said, sitting across from him.

A minute later Garret said, "I need to prove that an event took place in . . . sixty-six, I believe."

"That's nearly twenty years ago."

"Yes, I know. But . . . if a significant event . . . a crime . . . took place . . . it would be . . . What? Help me, Patrick."

"Would it involve the law? They keep legal records."

"Yes," Garret said with enthusiasm. "Legal records."

"It would be in the newspaper, except . . ."

"Except what?"

"How big of an event are you talking about? If it's local, there might not have been a newspaper back then. But there would have been in London."

Garret thought about it. "I think it probably would have been pretty big news." He focused his eyes on Patrick. "Are you feeling up to a quick jaunt to London?"

"If it would help, I'd take a quick jaunt to Hong Kong."

"You'd never get there without me," Garret said.

"That's true," Patrick admitted. "Tell me what you need."

Garret blew out a long breath. "Autumn 1766. Anything—I mean anything—to do with the Buchanan family of Cornwall. And whatever you find, I need proof. I need something that Ritcherd can look at and hold and know that what happened did not just happen in his head."

"And what if I can't find proof?" Patrick asked.

"Then I fear we will lose him," Garret said. Patrick stood up and grabbed his boots. He was on his way to the stables before Garret got back to his sitting room and curled up on the sofa beneath a couple of blankets, praying himself to sleep. What they needed now was a miracle. No, he corrected, they needed several.

Kyrah felt Ritcherd stirring and came awake to find him watching her in the dim lamplight, seeming more like himself. "Are you all right?"

she asked. He shook his head and looked frightened. She regretted asking even that if it reminded him of the horrors he'd been through. She quickly pressed a hand to his face and forced a smile. "I've missed you. It's nice to have you close."

He sighed as if to agree and eased closer to her. Kyrah tightened her arms around him, recalling Garret's words. *Give him tangible evidence of the love you share with him. Distract him with normalcy.* Impulsively she pressed her lips to his. "I love you, Ritcherd," she murmured and kissed him again. His response was a relief to her, and she eased more fully into his embrace.

Ritcherd felt a sudden desperation to have Kyrah completely, as if their becoming one could somehow erase the horrors that had filled his mind, as well as the absolute belief inside of him that total madness was eventually inevitable. But here in her arms he felt a sweet reprieve, a perfect escape from the fear, the anguish, the absolute monstrosity his mind had conjured up.

The desperation reminded him briefly of the first time they had been together this way. They hadn't been married at the time, and the incident had catapulted them into a series of consequences that were still difficult to comprehend. His memories of their indiscretion were hazy and obscure, and seemed more focused on some consuming desperation to just take her, as if doing so could prevent them from ever being torn apart. Her lack of protest at the time hadn't made him feel any less responsible. In the long run, he believed the emotion provoked by that experience had distracted both of them from the events that had led up to her being deported and months of separation. If he'd minded his manners, the separation might never have happened.

But that was in the past now. With Garret's help, he'd come to terms with those choices. It was the future that concerned him now—now that he knew it was true. He really was losing his mind, and he could only think that such an opportunity to be with his wife this way might soon become a thing of the past. While the desperation he felt reminded him of that first time, the similarities ended there. She was his wife. They had shared years of working together to raise Cetty, facing life's challenges, sleeping in the same bed. He loved her more than he could ever put to words, and in his heart he knew that she loved him too. Within the bonds of holy matrimony they had carried each other through the ins and outs of real life. Given more recent events, he marveled at the depth of her commitment and the conviction behind her love for him. Even now he could see the unmasked adoration in her eyes, the perfect acceptance, the willingness to give all that she had on his behalf. As he held her and touched her in a way that had become warmly familiar, he could almost literally feel her taking his pain into herself, where she sorted it out and sifted it through, giving it back to him buffered and cushioned so that he could almost find it bearable. The rightness of their union gave him the perspective of how this relationship of marriage was created by a loving God to be a strengthening and a pillar of security to those who honored their commitment in spite of life's challenges. Drawing a tangible succor from the love Kyrah gave him, the reality that she had remained true to him filled him with inexpressible gratitude. She loved him, and for the moment, that was all he needed.

Kyrah marveled at the wordless communication taking place between her and Ritcherd as he looked into her eyes, holding her as if she had become his air to breathe. The intimacy they shared was familiar, but she felt it reaching deeper than it ever had, with an emotional intensity that took her breath away. She could almost literally feel Ritcherd's pain seep into her every pore. She cried for his anguish and prayed for his peace while the love they shared put all else into perfect perspective. Long after their lovemaking had ended, they held each other in peaceable contentment, while the difficulties facing them seemed as distant as the stars in the sky.

Ritcherd relished Kyrah's nearness, wanting this oasis of time to never end, for this tranquility to be eternal. But even as he held her, the experiences of the past day and a half tormented him inwardly. In his heart, he truly believed there was only one possibility. His mind had become diseased. Any normal human being would have responded to the healing that Garret had guided him through. But he was doomed to being overtaken with horrific fantasies that consumed him with debilitating emotion. He tried to force the thoughts out of his head and focus on the serenity of the moment. With Kyrah wrapped contentedly in his arms, he drifted off to sleep.

Ritcherd came awake with a gasp, relieved to find the room filled with light when the images of his dreams had been so thoroughly dark. Still, as those images merged into all he'd experienced the past couple of days, a familiar panic overtook him.

Kyrah woke to find Ritcherd frantically pulling on his clothes, gasping for breath as if he were drowning. "What is it?" she asked frantically.

"I . . . don't know. I just . . ." He rushed to one of the doors and found it locked, then the other to find the same.

While Kyrah was wondering why Garret would have actually locked the doors, Ritcherd frantically started rummaging through the wardrobe and the bureau drawers. Kyrah pulled on a wrapper and moved toward him, attempting to soothe him, but he was apparently so intent on finding something that he paid her no mind. Knowing they were in Garret's room and not their own, she couldn't fathom what he was trying to find. She was ready to go and find Garret when Ritcherd stopped abruptly, staring into the bottom of a drawer. Apparently he'd found what he was looking for.

Kyrah sucked in her breath when he lifted the pistol to her view. But it was his expression that spurred her panic. He looked suddenly calm, perfectly content, as if he'd found the answer to his every problem. Kyrah held her breath, praying frantically in her mind.

"Garret!" she screamed before she consciously realized she wanted to. Only then did she recall his telling her that all she had to do was shout his name and he would be there in less than a minute. But what if a minute wasn't soon enough?

Ritcherd turned to look at her, his eyes expressing sorrow and regret.

All Kyrah could think of was the moment she'd been told that her father had shot himself in the head. "Garret!" she called again and heard the door to the sitting room being unlocked.

Garret rushed into the room, then stopped abruptly when he saw Ritcherd standing there with the gun in his hand. From Garret's appearance, Kyrah felt certain he'd been sound asleep until he'd heard her call for him, about forty-five seconds ago. She was relieved when he stood close to her, if only so she could speak to him quietly enough that Ritcherd wouldn't overhear.

"Please tell me it's not loaded," she said.

"It's not loaded," he whispered firmly.

"How can you be sure?" she asked, and felt alarmed when Garret stood directly in front of her, as if to shield her.

He spoke over his shoulder while keeping his eyes tuned to Ritcherd. "Did he leave the room?"

"No."

"I never have it loaded in the house. And there's nothing in the room to load it with," Garret whispered and turned his full focus to Ritcherd while Kyrah gained some measure of comfort. More loudly, he said, "What are you doing with the gun, Ritcherd?"

Ritcherd's breathing became audible. "I can't live like this, Garret. I can't. I can't take it anymore."

"We're going to work this through, Ritcherd. You've made remarkable progress. You've come so far. You can't give up now. We're *so close.*"

Ritcherd shook his head. "It's only going to get worse. I'm losing my mind, Garret. I can feel it. Please, just . . . let me go. Just . . . take Kyrah and Cetty away."

"They need you, Ritcherd."

"They need a man who can be a man. They need a man who is sane."

"You *are* a man, Ritcherd. You are one of the finest, most courageous men I have ever known."

Ritcherd gave a scoffing laugh. "I'm a mess. Haven't you been paying attention? You don't have any idea what's going on inside my head."

"You're right, Ritcherd, I don't. But I know that with some time, and God's help, we can make it go away."

Ritcherd scoffed again, then said intently, "Tell Kyrah to leave." Kyrah grabbed Garret's arm as if to tell him she wasn't going. "Now!" Ritcherd shouted.

Garret turned toward her and looked calmly into her eyes. "Do it. Just . . . leave the room." In response to her panicked expression, he whispered firmly, "Loaded or not, I won't let him pull the trigger. Just go. Close the door on your way out."

Kyrah fought her every instinct and moved toward the door. "I love you, Ritcherd," she said, tears creeping into her voice. "I need you."

He met her eyes with yearning and regret. "And I love you," he said warmly. "Please go."

Kyrah left the room and closed the door. Ritcherd stared at the gun in his hand, saying, "Maybe you should go, too."

"I'm not going anywhere, and neither are you."

Ritcherd abruptly lifted the barrel to his temple. Garret just as abruptly lunged toward him, knocked the gun out of his hand and twisted his arm behind his back. "Did you really think I would let you do it?" Garret growled angrily behind his ear. "Did you really think I would walk out of the room and leave you to die? I know you're hurting and I know you feel desperate, but if you ever pull a stunt like that again I will have no choice but to knock some sense into you."

Ritcherd hung his head and groaned. He slumped forward, and Garret shifted his hold to catch him. He guided him to a chair, then picked up the gun off the floor. Pointing it at the floor, he cocked it and pulled the trigger. Only a hollow click sounded. Ritcherd looked up at him, stunned. "You knew it wasn't loaded!" he said as if he resented it.

"I was relatively certain, but then . . . both you and the gun have been out of my sight for several hours. I couldn't possibly have *known*, now could I." He tucked it into the back of his breeches and added angrily, "We won't be playing any more such games. You're going to eat some breakfast and take a long, hot bath, and then we are going to talk about what happened yesterday."

Ritcherd sighed. "I'd rather die," he snarled.

"That's not an option," Garret retorted in the same tone. "Now, do I have to tie you to the chair while I talk to the servants, or do you think you can sit there and behave yourself for five minutes?"

"I'm fine," Ritcherd insisted, but Garret still locked the door from the outside when he left.

"Is he all right?" Kyrah demanded the moment he entered the hall where she was pacing.

"Yes, but it could be another long day. Could you please get some breakfast up here as soon as possible, and have a hot bath prepared?"

"Of course."

"Good. If you do that, then I can stay with him." He softened his voice and added, "He's going to be all right, Kyrah. Just . . . find something to do and try not to think about it."

"Oh, that's easy for you to say."

"Actually, it's not easy to say, Kyrah, but you must trust me, and you must believe that the greatest thing you can do for Ritcherd right now is to pray—pray very hard."

"I have been," she cried, "every waking minute."

"Then we will surely be blessed with a miracle," he said and went back into the room.

While Ritcherd and Garret ate breakfast in the sitting room, the maids cleaned up Garret's bedroom and prepared a hot bath. Ritcherd said nothing, but he did eat. Later, while he soaked in his bath, Garret got cleaned up in the sitting room with the door open between the two rooms. Garret buttoned a clean waistcoat as he walked into the bedroom to find Ritcherd lying back in the tub, his clean hair hanging over the edge, dripping water onto the floor.

"How are you?" Garret asked, and Ritcherd opened his eyes.

"How am I supposed to be?"

"I didn't ask how you're supposed to be. I asked how you *are*. I would appreciate an honest answer. I haven't kept myself holed up in this room with you all these days to have you clam up now. Surely you have enough respect for me not to allow all the time I've invested in you to be for nothing."

Ritcherd sighed. "Well, since you put it that way . . . I . . ."

"You what?" Garret prodded when he hesitated far too long.

Ritcherd sighed again. "What am I supposed to think, Garret? When I realize what my mind conjured up—out of nowhere—and the way it affected me, it scares me to death. I fear Dr. Ware might be right, that it's just a matter of time before I lose my mind completely, and I would rather die than bring any more grief or heartache to my loved ones. Kyrah and Cetty deserve better than that. *You* deserve better than that. I will not sentence *anyone* to some constant vigil over a madman simply because they love me."

Garret blew out a long, slow breath and sat down, leaning his forearms on his thighs. "I hear what you're saying, Ritcherd, and I think I can understand why you would feel that way. But I have to ask you . . . What if it's real?"

Ritcherd lifted his head to look straight at Garret. "You're serious."

"Yes, I'm serious."

"How could it be real?" Ritcherd countered, chuckling dubiously. "How could something like that just . . . pop into my mind out of nowhere and be real? If it was real, I would have remembered it all these years."

"Maybe," Garret said, "and maybe not. Maybe your mind blocked it out because it was too horrible for a child to accept." He added gently, "What if it's real, Ritcherd?"

Ritcherd leaned his head back and sighed, staring at the ceiling. "I almost wish it were."

"Why?"

"If such a thing had actually happened to me, I wouldn't have to wonder if I was losing my mind. If such a thing had actually been tucked away in the memory beyond my consciousness all these years, it could almost explain why I've been so prone to fits of anger and bouts of depression. If it was real I could almost understand why I am the way I am, and I think I could come to terms with it. But it's really irrelevant because it couldn't possibly be real. I have no reason to base the incident on—nothing. Nothing except this outlandish tale I've come up with in my head with such intensity that I would revert to being a child and scream and cry like a madman." He shook his head and squeezed his eyes closed. "It just can't be real, Garret. It just can't."

"So, what are you saying? That we should take Dr. Ware's advice and make provisions for your family? That we should arrange for you to rot away in some horrible asylum? Is that what you want?"

"It's not what I want, but it might be the only option." Tears trickled down Ritcherd's face. He hurried to wipe them away then added in a facetious voice, "Unless of course you'll let me shoot myself in the head."

"Not in a million years."

"There is the option of confessing to my crimes and dying as a martyr to the cause of freedom. At least I could be a hero that way. At least I could feel like a man again, instead of some . . . withering milksop."

"You are hardly that," Garret insisted. "In my opinion, it takes a real man to have the courage to face up to his inner demons, and to not have his masculinity threatened by a few tears."

"A few tears?" Ritcherd chuckled. "Now you're patronizing me."

"I've never patronized you for a moment since I met you. I'm certainly not going to start now."

Ritcherd sighed loudly. "For that I am truly grateful. If I thought for a moment that you would cloak the truth to spare my feelings, or humor me for any reason, I never could have trusted you enough to come this far."

"You're talking to the guy who has several times belted you in the jaw."

"Only because I needed it—and deserved it."

"Well, yes, but . . ." Garret chuckled. "You'd do well to remember that the next time I belt you in the jaw."

Ritcherd actually smiled. "Of course."

Chapter Twelve

The Bridge

While Ritcherd was buttoning his shirt, Garret handed him his boots.

"Are we going out?" Ritcherd asked. While he typically wore his boots around the house, he'd not worn them for days.

"Some fresh air wouldn't hurt," Garret said. "And I thought you might like to spend some time with your family—if you're up to it." Ritcherd wondered if Garret sensed his apprehension.

"I'd like that, but . . ."

"But?"

"Will you stay with me?"

"I'd be happy to, but what are you afraid of?"

"I just . . . don't know what I might say . . . or do," Ritcherd admitted.

Garret sighed. "You're not crazy, Ritch."

"Prove it," Ritcherd said almost defiantly.

"I'm working on it," Garret said gravely.

The air was cold as they stepped outside, but Ritcherd enjoyed their brisk walk through the gardens, then they spent some time in the stables, just currying the horses and saying very little. On their way back to the house, Garret said, "I think we missed lunch. Are you hungry?"

"Not really. We had breakfast late. I can wait until supper, but if you're hungry feel free to—"

"I'm fine," Garret said.

They hung their cloaks and went upstairs to the nursery. Before Garret opened the door, Ritcherd put a hand on his arm to stop him. "What does Cetty make of all this? How can I face her when—"

"She's your daughter," Garret said and pushed the door open. Ritcherd's eyes first went to Kyrah sitting on the floor, her skirts flowing out around her. *He loved her so much!* She looked up to see him and her expression filled with joy. *She loved him, too.*

While he was contemplating a suitable greeting, Cetty's voice squealed excitedly, "Papa! Papa!" He turned just as she hurled herself into his arms. He lifted her up and held her tightly, praying with everything inside of him that he could share any portion of her life without bringing her grief. "Are you feeling better?" she asked, easing back to look at his face.

"I believe I am," he said.

"Mama said you weren't feeling well." Ritcherd glanced at Kyrah, who was still sitting on the floor. He couldn't imagine how hard it must be to try and explain to a child so young that her father was losing his mind. He glanced back at Cetty as she added, "She said that your heart was hurting, and that's why I could hear you crying." It took all of Ritcherd's strength to keep from crying again. Then, with her perfect love, her genuine innocence, she looked into his eyes and asked, "Is your heart feeling better, Papa?" While he was struggling to answer without losing his composure, she said, "Do you want me to kiss it better?"

Ritcherd chuckled, which helped somewhat to dispel the threat of tears. "I would like that very much," he said. She kissed her hand with a loud smooch and pressed it over the center of his chest. "That feels better already," he said and set her down once he'd hugged her again. He turned toward Kyrah, wondering what she must be thinking when the last time she'd seen him he'd been holding a gun, threatening to kill himself. He held out a hand toward her, saying quietly, "Forgive me."

Kyrah put her hand into his and Ritcherd helped her to her feet, where she immediately pushed her arms around him, pressing her face against his throat. He returned her embrace, aware that Garret had Cetty on his lap and was just opening a storybook to begin reading. Kyrah drew back to look at him, and the emotion in her eyes didn't surprise him. She pressed her mouth to his, luring him to recall the intimacy they had shared in the night—before he'd been plagued with nightmares.

"Talk to me, Ritcherd," she said in a whisper. "Tell me what's troubling you. Let me help you through this. Let me share your burden."

Ritcherd felt himself tremble from the inside out at the very thought of telling her the games his mind was playing with him. "I can't," he whispered back. "Not . . . yet. Please . . . be patient with me."

"Of course," she said and kissed him again.

He sensed that she wanted to leave the room and be alone with him while Garret stayed with Cetty, but he preferred to remain in Garret's presence for reasons he couldn't explain. He urged Kyrah to the sofa and sat close beside her, putting his arm around her shoulders. He relished her nearness while they listened to Garret read stories, making them laugh with his attempt to be dramatic. Gradually Ritcherd began to feel sleepy. He put his head in Kyrah's lap and stretched out, leaving his booted feet to hang over the end of the sofa. He loved the feel of Kyrah's fingers in his hair and concentrated on her soothing touch as he drifted to sleep. His next awareness was sitting up abruptly, gasping for breath, while horrid images littered his mind.

"Are you all right?" he heard Kyrah say. He turned to see Cetty sitting on the floor near Garret, playing with blocks and toy soldiers. She looked mildly alarmed.

"I'm fine," he said, mostly to Cetty. "Papa just had a bad dream. I'm fine now."

Garret deftly distracted her. Ritcherd swung his legs around and looked at Kyrah. Her alarm was more evident. "I'm sorry," he said softly.

"There's no need to apologize," she said. "Just . . . tell me what's going on."

"I . . . can't," he said and hurried from the room.

Garret made a quick apology to Cetty as he jumped to his feet. He gave Kyrah an equally brief assurance that all would be well and hurried after Ritcherd. He came into the hall just in time to see him go around the corner. He rounded the corner to see him disappear into Garret's bedroom. He entered the room just as Ritcherd sat at the desk and dipped the pen.

"Are you seeking sanctuary?" Garret asked, closing the door behind him.

"Probably," Ritcherd said, certain that Garret had realized this was a place he'd come to feel safe—or at least *more* safe.

"Writing a letter?"

"Not really," Ritcherd said, writing frantically. "If I write down everything that my mind seems to think happened to me, will that get rid of it? Will that make it stop plaguing me?"

"I don't know, but it couldn't hurt."

Garret read through some of his old journals while Ritcherd wrote as quickly as he could manage. Occasionally he would get upset and throw the pen down. He would pace the room and get emotional. Garret would make him return to the chair and keep writing. He barely stopped long enough to eat supper, only because Garret insisted. A short while later, he just stopped.

"Are you finished?" Garret asked.

"No, exhausted," Ritcherd said. "Where's Patrick? I think I need some of that stuff. Maybe it will help me sleep deeply enough that I won't dream."

"Maybe. However, Patrick is gone. But he left that nasty stuff in my care."

"Where is he?" Ritcherd sounded alarmed.

"He took a quick trip to London for one reason or another. He should be back in a day or two."

Once Ritcherd was ready for bed, Garret gave him the usual dose of laudanum. As Ritcherd climbed into Garret's bed, he said like a child, "You won't be far, will you?"

"I'll be right here. I promise."

The following morning, Ritcherd woke feeling more exhausted than he ever had in his life. Looking in the mirror, he felt like a stranger was looking back at him. He looked old and spent. A part of him wanted to just crawl back into bed and never wake up, but something deeper compelled him to finish what he had started. Between eating bites of his breakfast, he continued to write the story that had appeared in his mind with such horror. Just as with all the writing—and talking—he had done, he paid no attention to the grammar or punctuation, or even whether or not his penmanship was legible. He just wrote furiously, stopping only to have an occasional fit of anger or tears while Garret stayed near and held his hand—mostly in a figurative sense, sometimes literally.

By the middle of the afternoon, Ritcherd had written all there was to write. He stacked the pages together, thumbed through them, looked them over, then walked to the fireplace and tossed the stack into the flames. The moment they had disintegrated into ashes, Ritcherd took a spoonful of laudanum and crawled into Garret's bed. He prayed that his insanity would not be littered with such horrid images in his head, and his last conscious thought was a prayer in his heart that when he did eventually lose his mind, his family would be spared any further grief.

Kyrah was going over menus with Mrs. Hawke when Liza entered the room, looking distressed. "Forgive me, Mrs. Buchanan, but that Mr. Thayer is here. He insists on seeing the captains—both of them. I told him they weren't available, and he said they could be in a great deal of trouble if they didn't show themselves."

Kyrah felt a little sick to be reminded of Mr. Thayer's existence—and his purpose. But she forced herself to remain calm, knowing this had to be dealt with and there was no one to deal with it but her. Mr. Thayer's timing was atrocious, to say the least.

Kyrah found him pacing the drawing room. He looked surprised when he saw her.

"Lady Buckley, I presume?" he said.

"That's right. I fear the timing of your visit is very poor, Mr. Thayer. My husband is terribly ill, and his brother is keeping a vigil at his bedside."

Mr. Thayer chuckled as if the situation was terribly amusing. "Do you expect me to believe that? Your husband and his brother are both under the scrutiny of the law, and they were warned against trying to run. I will not—"

"I can assure you that they are both on the premises, Mr. Thayer. I resent your implication that I—or they—would be dishonest."

He chuckled again and shook his head. "I will need some proof."

Kyrah sighed. "I will go and talk with Captain Garret. But as I told you, my husband is ill." She left the room and nearly cursed under her breath. She prayed all the way up the stairs, hoping she wouldn't interrupt some crucial element in whatever they might be doing. She knocked lightly at the door, and Garret quickly pulled it open.

"What's wrong?" he asked softly when he saw her face.

"I'm sorry to bother you, but . . . Mr. Thayer is here. He seems to think I'm lying about my husband being ill, and he apparently believes that the two of you have fled the country or something."

"Oh, that's just what we need," Garret snarled. He sighed and added, "Well, fortunately Ritcherd is sleeping. You sit with him. I'll go talk to Mr. Thayer."

Garret hurried down the stairs, attempting to straighten his hair as he went. He entered the drawing room to see Mr. Thayer looking genuinely surprised. "No," Garret said, "I haven't left the country. I'm not trying to hide from you. As my sister-in-law already told you, my brother is severely ill. He is indisposed at the moment."

"I'll need proof of that," Mr. Thayer said.

"You know," Garret said tersely, motioning the man toward the door, "it's not polite to assume that people aren't telling the truth."

Garret led the way up the stairs as he explained, "He is presently sleeping, but we don't know if it's contagious, so you'd do well to keep your distance, I think." They walked in silence to Garret's bedroom. Garret opened the door and peered in to see Kyrah look up at him. He whispered loudly, "Mr. Thayer would like to see that your husband has not left the country." They took a few steps into the room, only far enough for Mr. Thayer to see that it was indeed Ritcherd Buchanan sleeping in the bed." He sighed as if he was almost disappointed to discover that Ritcherd and Garret were both present and accounted for. "Satisfied?" Garret whispered curtly. Mr. Thayer just nodded and walked out of the room. Garret followed him down the stairs and to the door. "I wish I could say it's been a pleasure," Garret said, opening the door.

"I'll be back," Mr. Thayer said.

"I'm sure you will," Garret retorted and closed the door behind him.

"Stupid imbecile," he muttered under his breath and ran back up the stairs to resume his bedside vigil, sending Kyrah back to her menus.

Hours later, Garret still sat with a book open on his lap while Ritcherd slept nearby, but he'd not read a word. His mind wandered helplessly through all he'd learned about Ritcherd these past several days. Tears scalded his eyes as he tried to comprehend the tragedy he'd endured, and admiration burned in his chest as he considered what a fine man his brother truly was. Garret had considered his own upbringing difficult and challenging—and it was. But he'd not lived through a tenth of what Ritcherd had. To live any kind of a normal life, to be able to love and be loved at all with such tragedy in one's heart, was in itself a miracle. And now Garret prayed that Ritcherd would be able to cross this final bridge and find a future filled with serenity and peace. He certainly deserved it.

A light knock at the door startled him and he rose to answer it, finding Kyrah in the hall.

"Forgive me," she said, "but Patrick is here. He's in the library. He wants to talk to you."

Garret's heart quickened with the hope that he had come with something—anything—that might help them through this.

"Is Ritcherd—"

"He's sleeping like a baby. Took some of that stuff this afternoon and he's hardly stirred for hours. He should sleep a while yet, if you wouldn't mind sitting with him while I talk to Patrick."

"I'd be happy to," she said and slipped into the room. She opted to sit on the bed, leaning back against the headboard while she held Ritcherd's hand in hers. In sleep he looked so at peace, and she loved just being with him.

Garret hurried down the stairs and found Patrick leaning back on one of the sofas, his booted feet stacked on a coffee table, a pair of saddlebags at his side. "You look exhausted," Garret said, startling him from a little doze.

Patrick focused on Garret and said, "You don't look so good yourself."

"It's been a long week," Garret said, "or has it been two? I can't remember."

"Somewhere in between, I believe," Patrick said. "But I think I have good news—relatively speaking, that is." His countenance turned grave. "I believe I found what you're looking for." He pulled a bundle of newspapers from his saddlebag. "Is this proof enough?"

"Good heavens," Garret muttered, taking the papers. "How did you get these?"

"Well, the kind gentlemen at the newspaper office told me of another kind gentlemen who had once worked for the paper, who religiously had purchased five newspapers every day and filed them neatly away, certain they would be worth something someday. I found this eccentric man and his house full of paper, and when I offered him a hundred pounds for a copy of every paper related to this particular story, he said it had finally paid off."

"That's incredible," Garret said, moving to a table where he could spread out the papers.

"Yes, it is. Especially since you now owe me a hundred pounds."

"I'll give you two," Garret said absently then gasped when he saw the evidence before his eyes. "Have you read them?"

"I have," Patrick said. "I got a hotel room in London before I started home, and I couldn't help myself."

"So, now you know."

"Well, I know what the papers say."

"And once I have a chance to read them, I can fill in the pieces for you."

With concern in his voice, Patrick asked, "Is Ritcherd—"

"He's sleeping. Kyrah's with him. I'd like to look these over alone. Before you go to bed could you tell her that I'll be up in a while?"

"I'd be happy to," Patrick said and stood, patting Garret on the shoulder before he moved toward the door.

"Patrick," Garret said as he opened it, "thank you. You are the means to a miracle, my friend."

"I'm just an instrument in the Master's hands."

Garret sighed. "Then we are two of the same," he said.

Once alone, Garret turned his attention to the small stack of newspapers. They were already in chronological order, and it soon became evident that Patrick had already marked with a pen any reference to the horrible crime that had occurred in the fall of 1766. He wept more than once as he read, and the pieces fell tidily into place, fitting into Ritcherd's account like a hand in a glove.

When he'd read everything carefully, he took the papers with him upstairs and found Kyrah relaxed next to Ritcherd, but not sleeping. He tapped her on the shoulder and motioned for her to follow him into his sitting room. He left the door to the bedroom ajar and set the papers down except for the first one. He turned up the wick on the lantern and spoke quietly, so as to not disturb Ritcherd. "Sit down, Kyrah," he said.

"What is this?" Kyrah asked as Garret handed her the yellowing newspaper. He purposely gave it to her face down.

"It's a copy of a London paper, from 1766. Read the top of the front page, Kyrah."

She turned it over in her hands and the first words that jumped out at her were, 'Buchanan Child.' She gasped and allowed her eyes to absorb the full sentence printed in bold letters. *Buchanan Child Kidnapped and Held for Ransom.*

"Merciful heaven," she murmured and pressed a hand over her pounding heart. She looked up at Garret. "Is this real?"

"I'm afraid so," he said. "Read on."

Kyrah tried to focus on the tiny, printed words while her mind spun with disbelief.

Ritcherd Christopher Buchanan, eleven-year-old son of Lord and Lady Buckley of North Cornwall, was abducted on Tuesday last and remains missing. The child was taken from his bed and discovered missing early the following morning by his governess. A written message was left on the boy's pillow, clearly stating that the child was being held for ransom, although days have passed and no further word has been received.

The remainder of the article gave a description of Ritcherd as a boy, and where to report any information that might lead to his recovery.

"I can't believe it," she said, still staring incredulously at what she had read. "I knew nothing of this. Why would he not have told me that—"

Garret sat across from her and leaned forward, taking her hand. "Kyrah, he didn't remember. It's as if his mind had completely blocked out the incident, like it had been put into a trunk and locked away—until a few days ago. One moment it was gone, the next it was there." Garret's voice became gravelly as he went on, "I watched him relive it, Kyrah, and now I struggle with horrid images that I will never be free of."

Kyrah didn't realize she was crying until Garret wiped her tears with his free hand. "I'm not going to share those images with you, Kyrah. There are things you simply don't need to know. But you need to have some idea of what he's suffered, and why the memories have affected him—even though he couldn't consciously recall them. To grow up feeling unloved, to have endured the hardships of his life that we have known about, would be enough to break some men, but this . . . oh, this!"

Kyrah swallowed carefully and watched Garret lean back, squeezing his eyes closed while his grip tightened on her hand. "He was taken from his bed in the middle of the night, Kyrah. Bound and gagged and given no explanation. From what he told me and what the papers say . . ." He motioned to a small stack of papers, and Kyrah realized there was far more to read. While a part of her didn't want to know any more, a bigger part wanted to know all she could—even at the expense of dealing with horrid images—if only so that she could do everything in her power to help Ritcherd heal and get beyond this. She was still struggling with the shock of believing it was real at all when Garret went on, struggling for composure. "As I understand it, the kidnappers were two brothers. Thankfully, they were caught and convicted for the crime. They were executed many years ago. One of them had worked as a stable hand for William Buchanan. He had a drinking problem, and he was let go. Soon afterward, his son died of an illness. This man, in his warped mind, blamed the death on the loss of his job and sought vengeance—as well as ransom—from the Buchanans."

Kyrah put a hand over her mouth as bile rose into her throat. She saw Garret's expression turn sour and watched him swallow carefully. He cleared his throat tensely and his voice lowered further. "Three and half months they kept him." She whimpered into the hand still over her mouth, and he continued. "Ritcherd's memories—that have been locked away all these years—are now as clear as if it had happened yesterday. Eighteen years, and he can remember the pattern on his abductor's waistcoat—among other things. I will sum up his experience by saying that young Ritcherd Buchanan became the scapegoat for every injustice done by the British aristocracy—as far as it was viewed through the warped perception of a couple of drunk cretins. I've heard accounts of prisoners of war that were no worse than this." Again Kyrah whimpered.

Garret's voice became angry as he added, "Can you even imagine why the Ritcherd we know and love has such a deep loathing for the aristocracy he belongs to?"

Kyrah carefully removed her hand, unable to keep from sobbing as she said, "And why he flew into a rage when . . . when . . . I called him . . . an aristocratic snob." Her emotion took over completely, and Garret urged her head to his shoulder, where she wept long and hard. When she finally calmed down, she moaned, "I love him so much, Garret."

"I know. I love him too. My respect and admiration for him have magnified tenfold in the last few days, Kyrah. You and I are very privileged to be among those he loves and reveres."

"I'm so grateful we never did anything to . . . betray him . . . when he needed us most."

"So am I, Kyrah," he pressed a kiss to her brow, "more than you can possibly imagine. If I had broken trust with him, how could I ever have expected him to open up such pain and share his burden with me?"

They sat in contemplative silence for several minutes before Garret said, "He's not going to sleep forever, and I need to help him come to terms with this. You need to get some sleep, because when you least expect it, he's going to come back to life, and he's going to need you to be there for him."

"How is he going to react to seeing this in print?" she asked, wiping her nose with her handkerchief.

"I honestly can't say," Garret said, "but I have high hopes that it will be more good than bad."

Kyrah went back into the room where Ritcherd was sleeping and pressed a lingering kiss to his brow. He stirred and opened his eyes, showing a slight smile when he saw her. "Go back to sleep, my love," she said. "It's very late. I'm going to bed."

"I love you, Kyrah," he said, his voice slurred with sleep.

"And I love you, Ritcherd." Her voice broke. "I love you so much."

He smiled, and she kissed him again before she slipped away.

Ritcherd came awake to find a dim glow lighting the room. He turned to see a lamp burning on the bedside table, and Garret sitting nearby, his legs stretched out and crossed at the ankles. The fire in the grate cast strange shadows over the room.

"Hello, my brother," Garret said.

"Hello."

"Did you rest well?"

"I did, actually. That stuff really works—so well that it keeps me from dreaming. That's the best part. Is Kyrah . . ."

"She's gone to bed now, but she was here."

"Oh, good. I'm glad I didn't dream that."

"I have dreams like that all the time," Garret said with a comical lilt.

"I don't want to hear about it," Ritcherd said in the same tone.

Ritcherd sat up and leaned against the headboard. He yawned, then asked, "What time is it?"

"Nearly two."

"Why are you sitting up? You should be sleeping."

"I took a little nap," he said as Ritcherd stood and poured water from the pitcher into the basin then splashed it on his face. "I'm fine," Garret added. "I wanted to talk to you, and I figured that stuff would be wearing off before the night was through."

Ritcherd blotted his face dry, wondering what he might want to talk about. Setting the towel down, he saw Garret's countenance became so severe that Ritcherd felt afraid. Garret came slowly to his feet and moved toward Ritcherd. He noticed that Garret held some kind of paper in his hand. He stopped an arm's length away and looked directly into Ritcherd's eyes as he held the paper up for Ritcherd to take it.

"What is this?" Ritcherd asked, glancing at it hesitantly. He realized then that it looked like a newspaper—a very old one.

"This is the bridge, Ritcherd."

"I don't understand," he said, taking hold of the paper, but Garret didn't let go.

"The bridge to sanity," Garret added, his voice gravelly.

Ritcherd looked down and felt his hands start to shake as Garret let go and the paper was left in his grasp. The implication started to sink in just before he turned it over and unfolded it, then the words jumped off the page into his heart with such force that he teetered and was grateful to find Garret holding him up. He looked again at the words, stunned and overwhelmed. His eyes raced frantically through the brief article before they misted over and he could see nothing. He looked up at Garret as the tears spilled.

"There are several articles," Garret said, "spanning more than three months. It was real, Ritcherd. It happened, just like you remembered."

Ritcherd froze, standing stonelike while information darted around in his mind, attempting to coalesce into something that could make sense of what he'd just learned. And then it did. All at once, everything that had happened to him, all that he'd done and felt and said, came together in one brilliant fact—*he wasn't crazy!*

Ritcherd sobbed, but it rang more of laughter than tears as he threw his arms around Garret and cried like a lost child come home. Garret returned his embrace with a tightness that made it clear that he fully shared his brother's emotion. When Ritcherd finally calmed down, he pulled back and wiped at his face with his shirtsleeve. Glancing at the paper in his hand, he laughed and said, "Where did you get this?"

"Patrick found it in London."

"It's a miracle," Ritcherd said and laughed again.

"Yes, it is," Garret agreed.

Ritcherd insisted on seeing all of the newspapers. The two of them sat together over the same table where Ritcherd had written countless words of anger and difficult memories that had subsequently been burned. Ritcherd read every article more than once, stopping occasionally to shed a few tears and to talk his feelings over with Garret through an entirely different perspective. They talked until nearly dawn, then Ritcherd slept deeply, with no medication and no dreams. He woke to brilliant daylight and squinted against the brightness. As he pondered how far he'd come and how it made him feel, a deep peace filtered through his entire being. Ritcherd recognized this feeling. He'd had a glimmer of it one day in the church ruins, just before he'd set out to search for Kyrah on the *Phoenix*. And he'd felt it more deeply on the *Phoenix* many months later after he'd gone for days without eating while he'd struggled to come to terms with his inner demons. He recalled well the moment when he'd realized that the darkness had been replaced with light, the confusion with enlightenment. And he felt that way now—only more so. He felt suddenly bursting with energy, and left Garret sleeping as he slipped quietly from the room.

Going into his own bedroom for the first time in nearly two weeks, Ritcherd felt like a new man. He hurried to wash up and put on fresh clothes, then he peeked in on Garret. Not wanting to disturb him, he left a note and went to the nursery. Cetty jumped into his arms with laughter.

"Are you feeling better, Papa?" she asked.

"I'm feeling perfect," he said. "I think my heart has finally healed—thanks to all those prayers you said."

She smiled brightly and he asked, "Where's your mother?"

"She went for a walk. She said she needed some fresh air. I think she's worried about you."

"I'm sure she is. So, I'll tell you what. I'm going to go and find your mother, and I'm going to talk to her and let her know that she doesn't need to worry anymore, and then I'm going to come back and we're going to read a dozen stories, and build a new castle, and we can even have tea with all of your dollies."

She laughed and clapped her hands. As he set her down, he added, "I don't know how long I'll be. You just stay patient, and I promise I'll be back."

"I'll be a very good girl," she said and Ritcherd laughed. Oh, it felt good to laugh!

Ritcherd looked quickly in the usual places in the house where Kyrah might be, just in case. He noticed that his wife had obviously been decorating for Christmas in his absence. He checked in the kitchen and received a great deal of attention from Mrs. Hawke and the others, who were apparently very glad to see him feeling better. It was evident that Kyrah and Garret had led the household to believe that his illness had been physical, and that was fine. Still, feeling the way he felt now, he really didn't care if the entire county had believed him to be crazy. He knew he wasn't, and that was good enough.

When Ritcherd admitted he'd not eaten breakfast and it was nearly lunchtime, Mrs. Hawke gave him a couple of buns in a napkin and sent him on his way. He grabbed his cloak and gloves and ate the buns as he perused the gardens and the grounds of the estate, finding no sign of his wife. He bridled his favorite stallion but didn't bother with a saddle as he mounted and galloped over the moors toward the church ruins. The day wasn't terribly cold—as far as December in Cornwall went—and he allowed the fresh air to fill his newly awakened senses. He arrived at the church ruins without seeing her, and he began to feel concerned. He wondered if he might have just missed her by crossing paths in his search. He rode directly into the ruins and saw her just as she stood and turned to see who was there.

Kyrah felt breathless as she absorbed the reality that the man she saw before her was her husband, the same Ritcherd Buchanan she had loved from her childhood. He looked magnificent astride the majestic stallion, his cloak flowing from his shoulders over the horse's back. His gloved hands held the reins with relaxed finesse. He was thoroughly masculine. His eyes were bright and clear, his countenance serene. And just looking at him made it difficult for her to catch her breath. To see him here, now, this way after all he had suffered, was a miracle in itself.

Through the breadth of a long moment, Ritcherd marveled at the reality that this beautiful, incredible woman was his wife, that she had endured so much at his side, that she loved him as much as he loved her. He dismounted and tethered the horse, then he wondered what to say. The first words that came to him were the first words he'd said to her in this very place the day they'd met. She'd been seven. He'd been nearly thirteen. Even then, he'd had painful memories locked away in his mind. For the first time in his life, he felt as if he could see his life clearly. And there she was, right in the center of it—where she had always been.

"This church was built in the fifteenth century," he said, and she smiled widely.

"So I've been told," she said.

"Cetty told me you went for a walk. She said you needed some fresh air, that you were worried about me." He stepped slowly toward her. "I told her I needed to find you, to tell you that there was no need to worry any longer."

She looked up into his eyes as he stood directly in front of her. She didn't need words to know that he was all right. His eyes told her everything she needed to know. Still she had to ask, "Why is that?"

Ritcherd took her hand and pressed it to the center of his chest. "My heart is healed, Kyrah."

"I can see that," she said, pressing her other hand to his face.

"Oh, Kyrah," he muttered and kissed her, drawing her completely into his embrace. With his brow pressed to hers, he said quietly, "Can you ever forgive me, Kyrah, for all that I've put you through, all the grief I've caused you?"

"I already have," she said. "I told you that a long time ago."

"I know," he said, chuckling. "I've just . . . caused you a lot of grief since then."

"No," she said, "you have showed nothing but great courage since then. I have never felt more proud of you, Ritcherd—never more happy."

Tears rose into his eyes and he felt compelled to say, "We must talk. There's something I need to tell you."

Kyrah stepped back and motioned toward one of the few stone pews that hadn't crumbled. They sat side by side and Ritcherd leaned his forearms onto his thighs, pressing his fingers together. He cleared his throat and sounded nervous as he said, "Garret . . . told me you had read the newspapers. And he said he'd told you all you needed to know . . . about what happened, but . . . I need to tell you myself that . . ."

Ritcherd struggled for composure, but it wasn't the frightening, debilitating emotion that he'd been fighting for weeks. Now he only felt an overflowing gratitude and peace. "Just hear me out," he said. "Even though I know that you're aware of what happened, I just . . . have to hear it said between us."

"I'm listening," she said gently.

Ritcherd smiled at her and went on. "Something horrible happened to me, Kyrah, when I was a child. I don't understand how the human mind can completely block out nearly four months in a person's life, but that's what happened. Now that it's all come back to me, I remember the day I was brought home. I know I must have looked horrible, because I felt horrible. Later the doctor came and said that I'd lost significant weight, and I was bruised up pretty badly. But . . . earlier . . . when the constable brought me home, I remember my mother bursting into tears, but then she ran the other way without saying a word. My father just said, 'It's good to have you home, son.' And then he walked away, as well."

Kyrah took his hand and squeezed it tightly as he went on. "From my perspective now, as an adult, I know they simply had difficulty expressing their emotions. I believe they loved me; they just weren't loving people. But from my perspective as a child, I remember thinking that my mother was crying because she would have preferred that I *hadn't* come home. And I remember a few days later coming to a firm conclusion that they simply didn't love me, but at some point before then I must have decided at some level to forget the entire incident. It seemed that my parents were ignoring the fact that it had happened, and I would be better off if I did the same. So apparently, I did. I couldn't talk about it, and I couldn't deal with it, because I couldn't remember it. But I can look back and see how it affected my behavior, even some of my choices, and I'm truly sorry for the way it affected you."

"I understand, Ritcherd. I do."

"I know you do," he said, "and for that I am grateful."

"Go on," she urged.

"When Celeste was sent away, I had assumed that it was due to their embarrassment of her condition. And maybe that was part of it. I remember now that there was talk of protecting her; apparently there had been other threats made, and they feared that Celeste could never survive what I had been through. While I didn't acknowledge it consciously, I think I believed that I had let her down, that I should have been able to protect her—but I couldn't, so they sent her away."

Ritcherd turned to look at Kyrah's tear-filled eyes, and he realized that he had just openly discussed the most difficult experience of his life without screaming or falling apart. He pressed Kyrah's hand to his lips and continued. "Of course, you know the rest of the story, because you came into my life soon after that, but . . ." his voice broke, "I realize now that when you were deported, I blamed myself the same way

I had blamed myself for losing Celeste. I hadn't been able to protect you. And then . . . when we lost Celeste, so soon after we lost . . . the baby . . . I just . . ."

Tears overtook him and he couldn't go on, but Kyrah pushed her arms around him and whispered gently, "I know, Ritcherd. I do. It's all right."

"Yes, it is," he said and chuckled through his tears. "That's what is so amazing. It really is all right. We have each other. We have Cetty. And we have a good life, Kyrah. We have good friends, and good family—even if our family only consists of Garret and your mother."

"But they're so wonderful they make up for our lack of family otherwise."

"Yes, they do. Bless your mother's heart. I'm glad she didn't have to live through all of this with us."

"She would have stood by you, no matter what."

"I'm sure you're right," he said. "She always loved me in spite of myself."

"Ritcherd," Kyrah said, "there's something I need to tell you, if you're finished."

He looked at her intently. "I'm finished," he said. "What is it?"

"Do you remember that day . . . right here . . . When was it? Less than a month ago? We talked and . . ." She blushed slightly and looked away, laughing softly.

"Yes, I remember that, too," he said with a chuckle, knowing well what she was referring to. It was the first intimacy they'd shared since he'd come home from London. "What about it?"

"The church ruins must have a magical effect," she said. He wondered if she was implying something about their being together in the ruins now, until she added, "I'm pregnant, Ritcherd."

Ritcherd took a sharp breath while a burst of joy went through his body. "Are you sure?" he asked breathlessly.

"I had an official visit with Patrick this morning," she said. "He told me there's no doubt. The baby is due late next summer."

"Have you been ill?" he asked.

"Some in the mornings, but if I keep my stomach full it's not so bad. I feel tired a great deal, and a bit lightheaded on occasion—but

I know that's normal. For the time being, I'd like to keep the news between the two of us. Patrick will keep my confidence, of course."

"Of course," Ritcherd said. "I understand. It's between you and me. Oh, Kyrah," he laughed, taking her into his arms. "I'm so happy. I was afraid I could never be happy again."

"I know exactly what you mean," she said, looking into his eyes.

"I pray the baby makes it to the end this time."

"Yes, we'll pray very hard. And if it doesn't, we will get through it and move forward," she said, and he nodded firmly before he bent to kiss her. He kissed her and kissed her, grateful to know that she was his wife and he didn't have to stop with a kiss, which was the same moment she whispered near his ear, "Like I said . . . this place has a magical effect."

"Indeed," he said and kissed her again.

Chapter Thirteen

The Bribe

Ritcherd helped Kyrah onto the stallion and mounted behind her. He wrapped his arms around her to take the reins, and they galloped toward home.

"Wait," she said. "Would it be all right if we go look at the old house?"

Ritcherd was surprised but said, "Sure." He guided the horse down the long drive, between two rows of Cornish elms, to the house where Kyrah had grown up. It had now stood empty for years, and was in sore need of repair. He tethered the horse and helped Kyrah down. They walked together through each room of the house, reminiscing and sharing memories—focusing only on the good. The fact that Kyrah had worked for Peter Westman in this house was completely ignored.

"So, what should we do with it?" Ritcherd asked, standing in the drawing room. "Let me rephrase that. What are *you* going to do with it? It's *your* house."

"What's mine is yours—and the other way around, of course."

"Of course," he chuckled. "So, what should *we* do with it?"

"We should give it to Garret," she said firmly, as if she'd given the matter great thought.

Ritcherd was pleasantly surprised by the idea. But he pointed out, "He'd never take it."

"We'll sell it to him, then. He can afford it since he got that inheritance from your father." She looked around. "Eventually he's going to find the right woman and settle down. He needs a home of his own. But how could we bear to have him live any farther away than this?"

"We couldn't," he said, wondering where he would be now without Garret. He couldn't even imagine. "He keeps telling me that when he *does* find the right woman, he's going to quit the sea for good. If that's the case, he certainly does need a home. I think it's an excellent idea, my dear. I only wish I'd thought of it myself."

Kyrah laughed softly. "I'll let you propose it to him."

"Oh, no," Ritcherd chuckled. "It's *your* house. This is between the two of you."

They returned home, where Ritcherd helped Kyrah dismount in the stable. "Now," he said, "you must excuse me, my dear. I have an appointment to keep with another woman."

"You do?" she asked, pretending to sound shocked.

"That's right. Her name is Cetty, and I promised her many stories, the building of a castle, and tea with all of her little friends."

"How delightful," Kyrah said and kissed him quickly.

"Yes, it certainly is," Ritcherd said and laughed.

His time with Cetty proved to be delightful indeed. Kyrah remained in the nursery as well, just wanting to be close to Ritcherd and bask in the awakening that had occurred in him. In the midst of their play, Garret appeared in the doorway, looking half asleep and disheveled. "So there you are," Garret said.

"Were you worried?" Ritcherd asked.

"Maybe. Call it habit."

"Well, your concern is greatly appreciated," Ritcherd said, "but as you can see, I'm doing well. I'm afraid you're fired."

"Fired?" Garret chuckled.

"Your occupation of being my nanny is no longer applicable."

"Just as well," Kyrah said. "The job didn't pay very well."

"On the contrary," Garret said through a yawn, then he smiled at Ritcherd, "the rewards are superb." He yawned again and asked, "So how are you, really?"

Ritcherd exchanged a smile with Kyrah, then he glanced at Cetty who was humming softly while she pretended to spoon-feed a little doll. Ritcherd met Garret's eyes, saying with conviction, "I feel more sane than I've felt in months—maybe years. And I've never felt so at peace."

Garret returned his gaze, offering a serene smile. "I think that's the best news I've ever heard—at least since I was told that you were going to buy me a ship."

Ritcherd chuckled.

"And since you don't need me anymore," Garret yawned still again, "I'm going back to bed until tomorrow. I'm exhausted."

"You've been working hard," Ritcherd said.

"Oh, but we do need you," Kyrah said, and Garret turned surprised eyes toward her. "Christmas is approaching quickly. We have charity projects, and decorating, and baking to oversee, and gifts to procure."

"Well," Garret said, smirking at Ritcherd, "it would seem we're going to be very busy indeed. I'd better get some sleep."

He turned and left the room. Ritcherd met Kyrah's eyes, saying softly, "I love you, Mrs. Buchanan."

"I can see that," she said and laughed for no apparent reason. Ritcherd laughed with her, then jumped to his feet. He pulled her into his arms, kissing her long and hard before he returned to the floor to play with Cetty.

Through the following days, the Christmas preparations got fully underway according to Kyrah's instructions. She kept Ritcherd, Garret, and Patrick all busy hanging decor that was more easily accomplished by a man wearing breeches. They all worked together to organize a number of charity projects for the community, and the men took a number of trips into town, always with a list from Kyrah of things to be purchased and accomplished. Ritcherd thoroughly enjoyed being with Patrick and Garret. Their commitment to him had gotten him through the worst experience of his life; their presence now helped merge the past with the present by a bridge of deep bonding they had traversed together.

In thinking of times the three of them had shared in the past, Ritcherd commented, "Hey, what's Morley doing these days?"

"He's in charge of the *Phoenix*," Garret said.

George Morley was a childhood friend of both Ritcherd and Garret, and he now served as the first mate on the *Phoenix*.

"That ought to be a tough job," Patrick said with sarcasm, "seeing that she's disabled and grounded."

"It still needs attendance," Garret said.

"Do you think someone else can tend her for Christmas?" Ritcherd asked. "George should be with us for Christmas. If Patrick's going to be here, George should be too."

"Am I?" Patrick asked.

"No," Ritcherd said with light sarcasm, "we just thought we'd use you to help decorate the house, then send you on your merry way. Where else were you going to go for Christmas?"

"The *Phoenix*. I always spend Christmas on the *Phoenix*."

"Well, that's pathetic," Ritcherd said. "This year you're going to have a *real* Christmas."

"I like the sound of that," Garret said.

"Amen," Patrick added.

"And I'm certain that arrangements can be made for the *Phoenix*," Garret said, "so that George can be with us."

"I'll extend the invitation personally," Patrick said, "since I've got to go there in a few days, anyway."

"Good then," Ritcherd said. "It's settled."

"Life would be almost perfect if it weren't for our friend Mr. Thayer," Garret commented, and Ritcherd's heart tightened.

"I'd forgotten all about him," Ritcherd admitted.

"Sorry," Garret said. "He came to visit while you were out cold on laudanum one afternoon. He insisted on seeing evidence that you hadn't left the country."

"The fiend," Ritcherd snarled.

"I could kill him for you," Patrick said and Ritcherd turned to him, astonished. It took a long moment for a subtle smile to seep into Patrick's countenance and make it evident he was joking.

"I really thought you were serious there for a minute," Ritcherd said, and Patrick chuckled.

"Well, I'm certain he'll be back," Garret said.

"And then what?" Ritcherd asked.

"I don't know," Garret admitted. "I suppose we keep praying, and God willing, we'll be spared."

Ritcherd suppressed his own fear over the matter and prayed that Garret was right, that they *would* be spared.

The following Sunday Ritcherd actually went to church with Kyrah, and since Ritcherd was going, Garret came along as well. With the new inner peace Ritcherd had, he found he was even able to listen to the vicar's sermon and gain something from it without any ill feelings toward the vicar himself. When the meeting was over, many people greeted Ritcherd kindly. It was evident that rumors had been circulating that he'd been ill, but the assumption was that it had been a physical illness. A few people even told him they'd been praying for him. He thanked them for their prayers and concern, and realized how good it felt to be a part of the world again.

On their way out of the chapel, Garret nudged Ritcherd with an elbow, drawing his attention to Dr. Ware, who had also attended the meeting. Ritcherd just smiled and bowed slightly before the doctor quickly hurried away and Ritcherd chuckled, whispering to Garret, "He's probably terrified that I'm going to fly into a mad rage and burn the church down."

"Probably," Garret agreed, and they headed for home.

As the holiday drew closer, Ritcherd felt the reality of his healing settle in. No nightmares. No horrible images in his mind. No feelings of anger or fear. No chest pain or difficulty breathing. But he did feel a little down occasionally. He found his mind sometimes wandering through the events of the past couple of weeks, still dumbfounded by the reality of what had happened to him as a child, and the way he had blocked it out—and subsequently discovered it. He continued to talk his feelings through with Garret, and they both agreed that something so traumatic would take time to deal with fully.

An idea occurred to Ritcherd one day and he shared it with Garret, Kyrah, and Patrick over supper. "If I was kidnapped as a child, and everyone knew about it, then why has nothing ever been said about it through all my years of living in this community?"

"I don't know," Garret said. "Maybe you should ask someone and see what they say."

"And if you can get through the conversation without having trouble breathing," Patrick said, "then you'll know you're cured." He chuckled and Ritcherd realized he was teasing, but Ritcherd wasn't so sure it would be that easy.

He didn't give it much thought until the following day when Garret and Ritcherd went with Kyrah to pick up some of Cetty's new clothes from Mrs. Harker's shop. Ritcherd was standing in the shop before he recalled that the last time he'd been here he'd been attacked with horrible trauma. He was just thinking that he didn't feel uncomfortable in the slightest when Garret whispered to him, "Now's your chance. I bet Mrs. Harker remembers the kidnapping."

Ritcherd's heart quickened as he gazed at Garret, feeling as if he'd challenged him to jump off a cliff. For a moment he feared that in spite of the proof of newspapers, the experience really had been a product of his imagination. For a moment he imagined Mrs. Harker looking at him askance and suggesting that he might be mad. But Garret nudged him with an elbow and he knew he had to bring it up. It truly was a perfect opportunity. There was no one else in the shop, and Mrs. Harker had been here as long as he could remember. He didn't necessarily like her, but she could be a great source of information.

"Mrs. Harker," he said before he lost his courage.

She turned toward him, seeming surprised. "What might I do for you, Captain?"

"I wonder if you could answer a strange question for me."

"I'll do my best," she said, giving him her full attention.

"Were you aware of my being kidnapped as a child?"

Mrs. Harker's eyes widened, and Ritcherd's heart threatened to pound out of his chest. He could almost hear her calling him a crazy fool. Her eyes filled with something close to compassion before she said, "Of course I remember. Who could forget such a horrible thing? There are few people around here who *wouldn't* remember."

Ritcherd breathed in one more piece of evidence in favor of his sanity. "Then why," he asked, "through all these years, have I never heard anyone talk about it?"

"My dear Captain Buchanan," she said in a gentle voice that he never would have attached to Mrs. Harker, "your father made it inescapably clear that the trauma had been so great for both you and your mother that if anyone so much as breathed a word about the incident, there would be the devil to pay."

Ritcherd sighed as a new level of understanding settled into him. "I see," he said and was surprised when Mrs. Harker went on.

"I can't even imagine how you ever survived such an ordeal to become such a fine man." While Ritcherd was still stunned from hearing such a comment, she went on to say, "It was such a horrible thing; the way your parents suffered. They say your mother couldn't bring herself from her bed the entire time you were missing—and then some. And your father, God bless him, he holed himself up with his liquor—couldn't eat or sleep for days at a time. The servants said his grief was inconsolable; he blamed himself, they say. In a way, I don't think they ever got over it. Neither of them ever seemed quite the same, even after you were brought home. It was a miracle, you know, that you would be alive after all that time. The entire community had been praying for you, my boy. If you must know, every time I see you, I still think what a miracle it is that you're alive and well. And you are doing well, aren't you, Captain? You have a beautiful family." She glanced toward Kyrah and Cetty.

"Yes, Mrs. Harker," he said, barely able to speak, "I'm doing very well, thank you. It's been a pleasure talking with you."

Ritcherd felt so overtaken with emotion that he rushed out of the shop, well aware of Kyrah's panicked expression. He walked quickly up the street toward the carriage, willing his tears back before he made an utter fool of himself. He'd only gone a dozen steps before Garret caught up with him.

"Are you all right?"

"I'm fine," Ritcherd insisted. "I'm breathing and I'm still upright. I'm fine. I just . . ." He hurried into the waiting carriage.

Garret followed and sat across from him. "You just what?" he asked.

"Did you hear what she said?" he asked, and the tears flowed.

"I heard her."

"They loved me—they really loved me. They just didn't know how to show it."

"I'm sure you're right," Garret said. "Our father was not a warm man, Ritcherd."

Ritcherd looked at Garret, feeling a new layer of validation and a new level of connection between them. "You knew him well."

"Well enough, but I didn't necessarily like him. I didn't know he was my father until after his death, and then I was angry. You knew all of that."

"Yes, but I'd forgotten."

"Still," Garret said, "I've come to realize that, in his own way, he loved me as well. Knowing now that he was my father, I can look back and see that he was mindful of me, watching out for me. But as I said, he was not a warm man. You're right when you say that he didn't know how to express love. And our mothers were both much the same, I believe. Mine was more quiet and passive. Yours was hot-headed and aggressive. But neither of them knew how to express their feelings. Still, they loved us. I'm certain of it."

"Yes, I finally found my mother's love the day she died, but now I know she'd loved me all along. But when she died, I . . ."

"What?" Garret asked, seeing Ritcherd's eyes become briefly distant. "Are you with me, brother? You're not having some horrible new memory, are you?"

"No," Ritcherd chuckled, "I'm with you, but . . . I did just remember something that . . . never made sense before. Something my mother said just before she died. I remember feeling confused, perhaps uneasy, but then she went on to say something else, and she died, and I didn't give it much thought."

"What did she say?" Garret asked.

"She said there was one more thing she had to say, and then she told me she was sorry for what happened. I asked her what had happened; I thought she meant sending Kyrah away, or Celeste, but she'd already apologized for those things. Then she said, 'When you were a boy . . . it was so horrible. And I didn't handle it well. I'm so sorry.'" He turned to Garret and said in a hushed voice, "Now I know what she meant."

"It's incredible," Garret said, "and I must say I agree with Mrs. Harker."

"How is that?"

"She said, 'I can't even imagine how you ever survived such an ordeal to become such a fine man . . . It's a miracle.' I agree with her."

Ritcherd gave a dubious chuckle. "She doesn't even know me."

"*I* know you," Garret said, "and I agree with her."

Kyrah and Cetty arrived at the carriage with their purchases. "Is everything all right?" she asked as Ritcherd helped her step inside and Garret picked up Cetty.

"Everything is fine," Ritcherd said, "I just got a little emotional."

"I think that's understandable," Kyrah said and kissed him.

"All right, you can stop that now," Garret said with mock disgust.

"We need to find him a woman," Ritcherd said and kissed Kyrah again as the carriage eased toward home.

Later that day, Patrick left with the intent of being gone a week to see to some business and to check on the *Phoenix*. He promised to bring George back with him, estimating that they would arrive sometime the day of Christmas Eve. Ritcherd found that he missed Patrick, but he knew that wasn't the reason he felt a little down. While he and Garret and Kyrah were loading items into dozens of gift baskets that filled the formal dining room, he sat down with no warning, pressed his face into his hands, and wept.

"What is it?" Kyrah asked, sitting beside him.

"I think I'm digressing," he said with a chuckle that was a futile attempt to get control of his emotion. "I just miss her so much. She loved helping us do this project. In fact, she loved everything about Christmas."

"I know she did," Kyrah said, pressing a hand to his face. "We all miss her."

"Yes, we do," Garret said, leaning against the table and folding his arms over his chest. "And I don't think you're digressing. This is normal grief, Ritcherd. I think your mind was too clouded before to truly grieve her loss. So, go ahead and cry, my brother. I've certainly cried my share of tears over losing her."

"You have?" Ritcherd felt genuinely surprised.

"I have," he admitted. "Life will never be the same without her."

Kyrah stood up and busied herself, and within a few minutes the men were following her example. While they worked, Garret commented, "It's nice to be with you for Christmas, I must admit."

"It's good to have you here," Kyrah said.

"Yes, but maybe I should start paying rent or something."

"That's the most ridiculous thing I've ever heard," Ritcherd said. "You're family. It's not like we don't have the room—or need the money."

Garret chuckled. "It's the principle, I suppose."

Ritcherd passed Kyrah an encouraging nod and felt certain she knew his implication; she'd never get a better opportunity to bring up her proposal. She smiled slyly and cleared her throat.

"Garret," Kyrah said, "there is something I've been meaning to talk to you about."

"Yes, my love?" he said in a simpering voice that made Kyrah giggle—and Ritcherd comically hit him in the shoulder.

"Stop that," Ritcherd said. "She's taken."

"Oh, I'm well aware that she's taken—heart and soul." He winked at Kyrah. "What is it that you've been meaning to talk to me about?"

"Well, you *are* family, Garret, and we always want you close. When you do find the right woman and settle down, we want you to be nearby so we can see each other often, and raise our children together."

Garret smiled. "What a pleasant thought."

"Indeed," Ritcherd added warmly.

"So, the logical solution is that you take my home—the house next door. It's just through the garden, and—"

"I know where it is," Garret interrupted, his astonishment evident. "It's a beautiful home."

"It's been empty and it needs some work," Kyrah said, "but yes, it is a beautiful home, more than adequate for a family. There's also the cottage on the estate. I was thinking that you could hire someone to look after the property while you're away—and help you while you're here—and they could live in the cottage. My mother and I lived there for years. It's really quite lovely and—"

"I know how lovely the cottage is, Kyrah. I have fond memories of being there with you and your mother."

"But?" Ritcherd said.

"What do you mean 'but?'" Garret asked.

"There was a 'but' at the end of that sentence, you just didn't say it." He smirked and pointed at Garret. "See, I can be perceptive, too."

"So you can," Garret said. He turned to Kyrah and added, "I would love to buy the home from you, Kyrah. I just want to know your reasons for selling it, and if this is *really* what you want to do with it."

Kyrah looked at him firmly. "I want you and your family to live in that house and grow old right alongside me and Ritcherd. You're family, Garret. You're the only family we've got besides my mother. There's plenty of room here for you and a whole brood of children, but I'm certain you'd prefer having your own place—that's the way it should be. But we want you nearby. It just *feels* right. It feels to me like the house should be yours." She hesitated. "But it's not for sale. I'm giving it to you."

"Oh, no." Garret chuckled and shook his head. "You will do no such thing. I will buy it for a fair price or I will not take it at all."

Kyrah sighed loudly. She threw a cautioning glance to Ritcherd then approached Garret, taking his upper arms into her hands. "Listen to me, Garret. This house we're talking about is the home of my childhood. Ritcherd and I grew up together within its walls. But the memories became tainted when Peter bought it and I had to work for him just to survive. I inherited the house when he was killed. I know you know all of that, but it's important for you to understand what this house means to me. It's a symbol of my triumph over Peter and what he did to me—to all of us." She lowered her voice to an imperative whisper. "You freed me from Peter. You killed for me, Garret."

"Not only for you," he said firmly.

"I know, but I was the one with his wedding ring on my finger. No one but the three of us here in this room could ever fully understand what that house symbolizes. How could I let anyone but you live there? Buckley Manor is my home now. I've grown to love it here. This is where I belong." She glanced at Ritcherd. "This is where my heart is." Looking back into Garret's eyes, she added with a quavering voice, "But you must understand, Garret, that were it not for the love I share with Ritcherd, I would give you so much more."

Garret's eyes widened. She glanced at Ritcherd to gauge his reaction. He seemed pleasantly surprised. She turned back to Garret. "And were it not for you, I would have lost Ritcherd. You guided Ritcherd to me when I was lost in Virginia. And you guided me to Ritcherd when he was lost right here at home. We owe you our deepest love and respect, Garret. What I am offering you is a home."

Garret glanced at Ritcherd, then at Kyrah. He took hold of her shoulders and pressed a lingering kiss to her brow. "You are too precious, my dear. I'll take it." Kyrah smiled and he added, "For a fair price." He stepped back. "We'll find out what it's worth and I'll give you a check." He lifted a finger. "But it will be *your* money, not his." He pointed comically at Ritcherd.

"I told her a long time ago that I didn't marry her for her money," Ritcherd said. "I certainly don't want it now."

"Garret," Kyrah said, "I have no idea of your financial circumstances, and it's none of my business, but . . . when you settle down, and quit the sea, I want you to have enough to live comfortably, to fix up the house, to have a good life. I don't want to take money for the house that could be put to better use elsewhere. I don't need the money." She glanced again at Ritcherd. "I'm Lady Buckley, you know."

Garret smirked. "Yes, I know." He took her hand and kissed it. "And I can assure you, my dear, that the inheritance I received from the former Lord Buckley was more than ample to live comfortably for the rest of my life. I can afford the house, Kyrah. And if you must know, I had considered talking to you about buying it. I agree with you completely. It just *feels* right."

"Well, I'm glad we've got that settled," Ritcherd said. He stood and took Kyrah's arm. "Just remember, she has *me* so she won't be giving you anything more."

Garret chuckled. "I wouldn't be expecting her to." He followed them out of the room, feeling a deep joy and peace to see his brother restored to his former self—although there was a brightness to his eyes that had never fully been there before. To hear him actually joke about the sensitive situation of his feelings for Kyrah let him know that everything was indeed all right. They had come far.

The following morning, Ritcherd and Garret went into town. It didn't take long to gather enough information to establish a reasonable value on the house. Garret had a check drawn up for Kyrah and presented it to her over the lunch table, where she signed the bill of sale, and the transaction was complete. After lunch, Ritcherd and Garret went to Garret's new home and wandered through it together, discussing plans for fixing it up. They determined that it wouldn't take much beyond some serious cleaning to make the main part of the house livable, and Garret decided that on his next visit home he would begin putting it in order.

Ambling through the dormant gardens, Garret asked, "So, how are you feeling?"

"I'm all right," Ritcherd said, but he didn't sound convincing.

"Not completely, I take it."

"No, not completely," Ritcherd said. "But comparatively, I'm doing significantly better, so I must keep perspective."

"Yes, perspective is a good thing," Garret said. "But what's wrong?"

"I just feel . . . down at times. Sometimes I fear that the depression will overtake me again."

"You've come to terms with much of what was weighing you down," Garret said, "but I would guess that it's possible for some people to simply have a tendency to such moodiness. I think you've just got to do something about it when it's a matter of feeling 'down' and not let it get out of control."

"And how would you suggest I do that?" Ritcherd asked.

"First of all, you need to look inside yourself and find out if there is something legitimately bothering you, and if there is, you've got to talk about it, fix what's fixable, and let the rest go."

"That makes sense. I think I actually know how to do that now."

"I believe we develop habits in the way we think, and it might take some time to retrain your mind to believe the truth that you've come to learn about yourself, as opposed to the myths that you grew up believing."

"Such as?"

"Well, for instance, you grew up with the belief that you weren't lovable because you believed your parents didn't love you. When discouragement tempts you to believe you're not lovable, you need to remind yourself that such thinking is merely a bad habit, and you have to tell yourself the truth."

Ritcherd inhaled Garret's wisdom. "That makes sense," he said again.

"And then I think you need to stay busy. Being a gentleman, as you are, it's easy to become idle when you feel no motivation. So, maybe it would be good for you to assign yourself certain tasks and do them. You used to stay busy. Muck out stables if you have to. Just don't allow yourself to be idle."

"That's good advice. I'm sure you're right. I hated the way my parents never did anything. I love the way Kyrah works *with* the servants."

"You're not afraid of hard work yourself. But you also know that if you don't do it, someone else will. So it takes more discipline to stay busy."

"I'll work on that," Ritcherd said.

"May I make another suggestion?" Garret asked.

"I'm always open to suggestions from you."

"Why is that?"

"Because they're usually good."

"Usually?" Garret said, pretending to sound insulted. They both chuckled and he added, "Well, if you can't find any work to do, there are always people in need. You've been blessed with a great amount of time and wealth. With some prayer and ingenuity, I'd bet you could find many ways to help others—even anonymously, perhaps. My grandfather always taught me that getting outside of myself was the best way to get outside of feeling sorry for myself."

Ritcherd sighed loudly. "I would have liked your grandfather."

"He would have loved you," Garret said with nostalgia.

Ritcherd stopped and looked up at the house. "My memories here before the war are very dear. Stephen and Sarah took me in like one of their own, loved me in spite of myself."

"They raised a fine daughter."

"Yes, they certainly did," Ritcherd said. He sighed again and said, "Maybe I could put some of my energy to use helping you fix this place up, eh?"

"Sounds like a great idea," Garret said, and they started for home.

While they were caring for the horses in the stables, Ritcherd said, "May I ask you something?"

"Of course," Garret said. "Anything."

Ritcherd glanced over his shoulder toward a couple of stable hands, then walked outside with Garret following. Walking together through the gardens, he found the privacy he wanted.

"What is it?" Garret asked.

"I've been thinking about Celeste; thoughts I had soon after she died—thoughts that gradually became swallowed up in everything else I was struggling with. Now that the rest has been sorted out, I've been thinking . . ." He sighed, searching for the right words. "Well, I suppose losing someone to death naturally brings up certain questions about life. I just . . . can't help wondering . . . where she is now? Is she still the same? Will her condition be a part of her eternal existence? And then I wonder about my parents, as well. They both led questionable lives in some respects; they made a lot of mistakes. My mother turned her life around at the end, but there are some who believe that's not good enough. And my father was . . . unfaithful, among other things."

"I know about that," Garret said severely.

Ritcherd sighed. "I can't imagine how difficult that must be for you."

"What?"

"Knowing you're the product of an affair. At least I know I was conceived within my parents' marriage."

"Yes," Garret said, "but I have every reason to believe my parents loved each other, which was not necessarily the case with your parents."

"That's a good point," Ritcherd said. "Either way, it's . . . difficult, I suppose. The thing is, I just can't help wondering . . . what we're really doing here, and where we'll end up when this is all over. Beyond Kyrah and Cetty, you're the only family I have left, Garret. Will we ever see them again? Or be with them? If I can't get any answers that make sense from my religious leaders, then where exactly do I go for answers?"

"Well," Garret said, "I'd say if you need answers, you should go straight to the source. I firmly believe that God hears and answers our prayers."

"Yes, I'm living proof of that." Ritcherd was silent for a minute, then went on to say, "Instinctively I believe that what the vicar said wasn't true, Garret. But there's a part of me that can't help wondering . . . Is she all right? Is she happy? Are my parents happy? They weren't bad people—a little misguided, perhaps. But Celeste was . . . Well, in a word, she was perfect, Garret. She brought nothing but happiness into this world. She was completely without guile. Surely she would be given the greatest blessings of heaven."

"Yes, I believe she would," Garret said.

"But how can I know?" Ritcherd asked.

"I'm not certain you can *know*. But you can have faith. And that can bring you peace."

Ritcherd sighed and made no comment.

Garret went on to say, "I've thought a lot about what the vicar said to you, and an idea occurred to me."

"Yes?" Ritcherd said, immediately interested.

"He told you that paradise is reserved for a select few, yet Jesus said to the thieves on either side of him, while he was hanging on the cross, that they would be together in paradise. They were thieves, being crucified for their crimes. It seems evident to me, according to His teachings in the Bible, that it is the intent of our hearts, as well as our actions, that determine what we earn in the life beyond this one. In my heart, I really believe that Celeste truly is happy and at peace. And I believe our other loved ones are the same. They struggled with imperfections and mistakes, but some things are a result of upbringing or circumstances. We *all* struggle with imperfections and mistakes. That's just my opinion."

"It makes sense to me," Ritcherd said. Then he gave a scoffing chuckle. "I can't help thinking," he added, "that the vicar's opinion of those who will be in paradise probably has a lot to do with who has the oldest names and the most money."

Garret chuckled. "I'm sure you're right."

They laughed together and moved toward the house.

Not long after returning to the manor, a maid came to the kitchen, where Ritcherd and Garret were teasing Kyrah and Mrs. Hawke about stealing dessert before supper.

"What is it, Liza?" Kyrah asked, noticing her first.

"Mr. Thayer is here to see the captains," she said and curtsied.

Kyrah, Garret, and Ritcherd all sighed in unison, exchanging silent, concerned glances.

"Thank you, Liza," Ritcherd finally said. "Tell him we'll be right there."

"I'm suddenly wishing that you *had* left the country," Kyrah said, "both of you."

"I think I agree with her," Garret added. "Come on, let's get it over with. We haven't had a trial yet." He moved into the hall.

Ritcherd and Kyrah followed until Ritcherd stopped and said to her, "Maybe you should just wait in the—"

"No, I'm coming with you!" she insisted and hurried to catch up with Garret.

At the door of the drawing room, they all three hesitated and Kyrah whispered, "Why do I feel like I did before I was deported?"

"I don't think I like the comparison," Ritcherd said, taking a step back from the door.

"Like I said," Garret turned the doorknob, "we haven't had a trial yet. We are innocent."

The three of them entered the room to find Mr. Thayer sitting comfortably, one leg crossed over the other. "Ah, gentlemen," he said. "Mrs. Buchanan."

No one responded. Garret closed the door.

"You're looking much better, Captain Buchanan. I trust you feel the same."

"I do," he said, "but I'm growing tired of these visits. When your accusations and implications are completely nonsense, I see no reason for us to put up with your repeatedly dropping in unannounced."

Mr. Thayer chuckled and made a sweeping motion with his arm. "Have a seat, gentlemen, my lady."

They were all seated and Garret growled impatiently, "Come to the point, Mr. Thayer. You're ruining our Christmas preparations."

Mr. Thayer chuckled again. "The fact that I am going to allow the two of you to spend Christmas with your family before you are carted off to prison is something you should be thanking me for."

"What are you implying, Mr. Thayer?" Kyrah snapped. "These men are innocent, I can assure you."

"I'm not implying anything, Mrs. Buchanan. I'm telling you—all of you—that I have more than enough evidence to have you both arrested." He shook his head at Kyrah. "It always amazes me how little women really know of their husband's activities—especially when they're illegal."

In a cool voice that defied his inner distress, Garret said curtly, "I'd like to know more about these charges, Mr. Thayer. I would like to know exactly what ridiculous fabrication has been created to implicate us in these crimes."

"It is no fabrication, Captain. And the proof is sound enough." Ritcherd and Garret exchanged a firm glance then looked back at Mr. Thayer, while Kyrah pressed a hand over her mouth and held tightly to Ritcherd. "But you don't need to worry about the proof until your case actually comes to trial. It's over, gentlemen. The two of you are bona fide turncoats, and I've got enough proof to send you both to the gallows. I would advise that you quickly put as much property as you can in your wife's name so that she will not be left destitute by this unfortunate turn of events."

"My wife already has plenty of property in her name," Ritcherd said sharply. He fought to keep his fear from showing, fought to suppress the utter horror he felt at what he was hearing. "But that's really irrelevant. I am not going to the gallows for a crime I did not commit."

"I have proof otherwise, Captain, and that is what the judge will base his decision on."

"This is absolutely preposterous," Garret insisted.

"Perhaps," Mr. Thayer said, "but that does not change the facts." Following a long minute of silence while Kyrah cried silently against Ritcherd's shoulder, he added, "Apparently you have nothing to say."

"I'm stunned, Mr. Thayer," Ritcherd said. "Stunned that our activity in the colonies would be so utterly misconstrued. It's evident that you are convinced of this notion. I can't contest these alleged records that I haven't even seen, but there is no possibility beyond . . . I don't know what. Someone is obviously fabricating this lie to implicate us in these crimes. We are innocent, Mr. Thayer. But you expect us to just hold out our hands and let you lead us away to the gallows? It's absurd!"

Mr. Thayer sighed loudly. He looked hard at Ritcherd, then at Garret. Both men boldly returned his stare. "You know," he said, "I've been in this business a long time, and . . ."

"And what?" Garret demanded sharply when he hesitated.

"I'd almost believe that you *are* innocent."

Ritcherd and Garret exchanged a discreet glance. Knowing their own guilt, the statement had the ring of a potential miracle. "How very perceptive of you, Mr. Thayer," Garret said.

"You know," he went on, glancing at Kyrah as if her tears were too much for him to bear, "this investigation is completely under my control. It's up to me to go back to my superiors and report that there is either sufficient evidence against you, or there is not. I could just . . . destroy what I've found. It would never turn up again."

Again Ritcherd and Garret exchanged a glance, this time skeptical and suspicious. "And to what would we owe this mighty change of heart?" Garret asked.

Mr. Thayer sighed again, looking carefully at each of them, as if to size up their character. "I'm getting on in years. I work hard for a living. An early retirement is starting to look awfully good. A hundred thousand pounds could ease all of our burdens immensely."

Kyrah, Garret, and Ritcherd all gasped in unison. "That's bribery," Kyrah blurted as if the others might not know the obvious.

"And what guarantee would we have that the case would truly be dropped for good?" Ritcherd asked.

"You'd have to take my word for that, as an officer of the law."

"Your word?" Ritcherd retorted. "As an officer willing to take an exorbitant bribe?"

"I'm willing to take your word that you're innocent—in spite of evidence otherwise," Mr. Thayer said, and again silence ensued. He abruptly came to his feet as he added, "I'm giving you until the day after Christmas at noon, gentlemen. The house will be watched. If you leave you will be followed. You are as good as under arrest. If it was any other time of year, I would be arresting you now. I'll be back, and I will expect a decision. It will either be the money or the two of you in bonds. Don't bother packing anything. You won't need it."

Chapter Fourteen

The Guest

*O*nce Garret had escorted Mr. Thayer out of the house, he returned to the drawing room and closed the door, leaning against it. Ritcherd and Kyrah's expressions were as stunned and horrified as he felt. He also felt furious.

"That is unbelievable," he finally said, if only to stop the torturous silence. "We ought to turn the imbecile in to his superiors and *he* would go to the gallows."

"Oh, that would be just grand," Ritcherd said with sarcasm. "Let's go tell the authorities and put someone else on to the fact that we're guilty of treason."

"I can't listen to this," Kyrah said. "I can't bear to lose either one of you, let alone both of you. As I see it, there's only one possible option. The two of you talk about it and let me know if life will actually be worth living once Christmas is over." She stood and took hold of the doorknob before she turned and gazed at Ritcherd. "God did not bring you this far to let you die now. We all know that He endorsed the cause you were willing to aid. Surely He would help you through this now." She hurried from the room, closing the door behind her.

Ritcherd sighed and said, "She's right. Maybe this is the miracle we've been praying for. We'll just pay him the money."

"A hundred thousand pounds?" Garret countered, astonished.

"That's what he said the going rate is for our lives."

"I don't have a hundred thousand pounds. How can I—"

"I'll pay it," Ritcherd said and Garret's eyes widened.

"You have a hundred thousand pounds?"

"I do."

"A hundred thousand pounds that you could part with and not miss?"

"Well, I'd certainly miss it, but it's not going to change my lifestyle, if that's what you mean."

"I can't believe it," Garret said. "I knew you were rich, but . . . that's incredible."

"Is it?" Ritcherd asked nonchalantly. "I didn't do anything remarkable. I just happened to be born to Lord and Lady Buckley."

"A happenstance that also got you kidnapped as a child," Garret said gently. "I'd say you earned whatever you've got."

"Perhaps," Ritcherd said. "If it will save our necks now, I'm grateful to have it."

"Yes, so am I," Garret said. He added facetiously, "Sure makes my inheritance look rather paltry though, doesn't it."

Ritcherd laughed. "Do you want more?"

"Yes, I want fifty thousand pounds to save my neck from treason."

"Done," Ritcherd said and chuckled.

Ritcherd and Garret went directly to the bank and took out the money. They returned home and tucked it safely away. Through the remainder of the day, Garret tried to tell himself he was grateful to have the money and to believe they had a way out, but he realized that something didn't feel right. Something uneasy nagged at him. He'd learned long ago to rely on his instincts, and he didn't like what they were telling him now. When bedtime came and he knew he couldn't sleep, he knocked lightly at Ritcherd's bedroom door. Ritcherd answered, thankfully not dressed for bed yet.

"Can we talk for a few minutes?" Garret asked.

"Would you be surprised if I said I was about to come and find you?"

Garret looked him in the eye. "No, I don't think I would be surprised."

Ritcherd peered around the door into the room, saying to Kyrah, "I'm going to talk to Garret. Don't wait up for me."

He stepped into the hall and closed the door behind him. "So talk," Ritcherd said as they started walking slowly toward the stairs.

"Why don't you tell me what you wanted to talk about?" Garret prodded.

Ritcherd sighed. "Something doesn't feel right. Something is not what it seems to be."

"Exactly," Garret said.

"Kyrah was right when she said it feels the same way we felt before she was deported. It's as if we knew something horrible was going to happen, but we ignored it and . . . it became a nightmare. I'd like to think I've grown older and wiser, and that I could pay attention to—and trust—such feelings."

"Amen," Garret said.

"I also remember feeling this way when Peter Westman was trying to blackmail Kyrah."

"You know what I'm reminded of?" Garret asked.

"What?"

"I'm reminded of the time that Peter Westman sold us information, then sold us out. I lost my ship and twenty-three men."

They stopped walking and stared at each other incredulously for a long moment before Ritcherd pointed out the obvious, "But Peter Westman has been dead for years. This has nothing to do with him."

"Logic would make us think so."

"But our instincts would tell us otherwise?" Ritcherd suggested.

Garret shook his head. "I don't know. This can't have anything to do with him. Can it?"

"I wouldn't think so, but . . . something's not right. I don't trust this Mr. Thayer. I would bet my life that he's the kind of man to take the money and still send us to the gallows."

"Your life is exactly what you will lose if we don't go about this the right way."

"One way or another, we need to get to the bottom of this."

"How do you propose we do that?"

"We pray very hard," Ritcherd said.

"That's what I was going to say."

"I learned such concepts from you, my friend. If we've ever needed a miracle, we need one now."

With only three days left until Christmas, Kyrah insisted that Ritcherd take her into town early to see to some necessary errands, and then to spend the bulk of the day delivering Christmas gifts and charity offerings throughout the community. Garret declined going along, thinking the two of them could use some time together. He saw no evidence of the house being watched or anyone following the carriage that left with Ritcherd in it, but he felt sure that whoever was working with Mr. Thayer would be well trained at being especially discreet.

Feeling the need for some fresh air, Garret went to the stables right after breakfast. He found no servants there and took his time with currying his stallion, enjoying the relaxation of the simple task. Hearing an unusual noise, he stopped his chore and listened carefully. A slight rustling was followed by even, loud breathing, as if someone had shifted in their sleep to a position where their breathing became more audible. Garret set down the currycomb and turned to look around. He walked stealthily toward the sound and peered over the sides of three stalls before he found a man sleeping in the straw, curled up in a long, shabby coat as if he were freezing.

"Good heavens," Garret muttered, wondering who he might be—and what he was doing here. This huge country estate, many miles from the nearest town, was not a likely place for vagrants or beggars to come looking for a handout or seeking unsolicited work. It was too long a walk with no guarantee of achieving any gain.

He wondered whether or not to wake the man, but he thought it might be best for him to deal with the situation now, as opposed to having one of the servants come upon him. He also felt certain the man would prefer sleeping in a warm bed inside the house. Garret could at least see that he got a good meal and some decent rest before sending him on his way.

Garret slid carefully into the stall and squatted beside the sleeping man. He nudged his shoulder gently, wondering if he might be drunk and it would take great effort to bring him around. But the man started immediately, sitting up abruptly with blatant terror showing in his eyes.

"Forgive me," Garret said, putting a gentle hand to the man's arm. "I didn't mean to alarm you. I just thought you might sleep better someplace a little warmer."

The man's expression softened in response to Garret's kindness, but he said nothing. His eyes cautiously absorbed Garret in a way that made him certain he was being assessed by his attire and manner. Garret asked gently, "Are you hungry? I know you must be cold."

"I am, yes," the man admitted.

"Come inside, then." Garret stood up straight and offered a hand. The man took it and came somewhat unsteadily to his feet, but Garret knew he wasn't drunk; more likely ill, or just exhausted and starving.

The man was in his early fifties, Garret guessed, with reddish hair going gray. He was close to Garret's height and lean to a point that didn't look healthy. He wore a scraggly beard that looked more as if he'd not had the opportunity to shave for a few weeks. The beard was mostly gray with only hints of dark red. Garret sensed a goodness about this man, while his eyes held a sad, almost despondent quality. While he took a moment to gain his footing, Garret asked, "May I ask your purpose for coming to Buckley Manor? You've come far."

"I have," the man admitted as they moved toward the house. "I'm looking for the lord of the manor. Would that be you?"

"Are you in need of work, then?" Garret asked, wondering if he might be interested in sailing on the *Phoenix*. It wouldn't be the first time he'd hired hands who were in desperate need with nowhere to go.

"Perhaps," the man said. "Are you offering work?"

"Perhaps."

"You are the lord of the manor, then?" he said with a certain disappointment in his voice.

"Actually no. I am his brother."

The man stopped walking a moment as if to absorb this information. The disappointment deepened so intently that Garret almost wondered if he would cry. Was this man looking for Ritcherd Buchanan, unaware that he even had a brother? While he was wondering how to clarify the situation, the man said, "I may well be in the wrong place, then."

"Whether or not you are," Garret said, putting a hand to his shoulder and moving on toward the house, "you'll not leave without some rest and a few decent meals. And perhaps I could give you transportation to wherever you might need to go."

"Thank you, sir," the man said, his voice cracking subtly. "You are most kind."

They went into the house through the side door, while the man took in his surroundings with complete awe. Garret had to assume he'd never been inside such a magnificent home. They entered the kitchen, where Mrs. Hawke, the head cook, looked up, showing a smile when she saw Garret, and puzzled concern when her eyes moved to the stranger with him.

"Good morning, Captain," she said, wiping her hands on her apron.

"Good morning, Mrs. Hawke," he replied.

"And who do we have here?" Mrs. Hawke asked, moving toward them.

When the man didn't offer a name, Garret simply said, "I'd be most grateful if you could give this good gentleman something to eat."

"I'd be happy to," she said with a warm smile.

"I'll be back for you in a short while," Garret said, and the man nodded. "Let Mrs. Hawke know of anything you might need in the meantime."

"Thank you," the man said. "I don't know what to say."

"You already said 'thank you.' That's good enough for me." Garret left the room, feeling subtly intrigued with this visitor.

Following a conversation with the housekeeper, Garret dug some clothes out of his own closet that he'd not worn since they'd been put there a few years earlier. He returned to the kitchen to find that the man was just finishing his meal. Mrs. Hawke quietly told Garret that he'd said hardly a word, but had eaten ravenously, as if he'd been starving. Garret thanked her for her help, then crossed the kitchen to find the man just setting his napkin on the table.

"Did you get enough to eat?" Garret asked.

"I did, thank you," the man said, and Garret recognized a natural refinement to his manners and speech that didn't ring true with a penniless vagrant.

"A room has been prepared for you so that you can get cleaned up and get some rest," Garret said. "I'd be happy to show you the way."

Again the man looked as if he might cry, but he said nothing. They walked slowly up the stairs, and Garret sensed his lack of strength. When Garret showed him into one of the more conservative guest rooms, the man gasped audibly. He turned to survey the room, his eyes lingering on the tub filled with steaming water, the shaving items on the bureau, and finally the clothes left on the bed.

"The clothes were mine," Garret said. "I think they'll work, we're near the same height. You're welcome to keep them; I'll not miss them. Feel free to rest as long as you like. If I'm not in the room across the hall, I'll be somewhere around the kitchens if you need anything."

"Thank you," the man said.

Garret just nodded and closed the door. He made himself comfortable in his own sitting room across the hall, leaving the door open. Settling into a good book, he figured he'd not likely see the man for hours if he took a long bath then slept, but he felt compelled to stay nearby. He didn't feel prone not to trust the man, but he had taken a complete stranger into his brother's home, and he felt it best to stay close and take full responsibility for him. Less than an hour after he'd left the stranger alone, Garret heard a door open across the hall, then looked up to see him standing in the open doorway. He looked considerably better with his wet hair combed back off his face, which was clean-shaven. The clothes were a little baggy, but did well otherwise. Even the boots Garret had left apparently worked, since he was wearing them.

"Feeling better?" Garret asked, setting his book aside.

"Better than I've felt in years, thank you," the man said.

"I thought you'd be wanting some rest."

"I'm fine, actually."

"May I ask your name?" Garret said.

The man looked overly cautious, almost afraid. "Forgive me for my hesitance, sir. It's difficult for me to tell you my reasons for not wanting to disclose my name. I could be dishonest and give you a false one, but I would prefer to just save formal introductions for another time."

Garret watched him closely, liking the deep honesty he sensed in this man. Thinking about the reasons he himself had chosen to use Garret as his only name, and not to be known by his official surname, he felt some measure of understanding in this man's plea. He pressed forward by simply saying, "So, what might I do for you?" Garret motioned him to a chair. The man sat down while his eyes took in the room, but he said nothing. "I have to assume, from what you said earlier, that you are looking for the lord of the manor. You're familiar with Buckley Manor, then?"

"I am," he said and Garret wondered if he might have worked here years ago, or one of his relatives perhaps. "But I've not been here for many years. In fact, I don't recall ever actually coming inside."

Garret found that odd. A stable hand perhaps. But wouldn't he have at least come into the kitchens if that were the case? He didn't want to be too nosy, but his curiosity was growing steadily. He asked carefully, "You know the lord of the manor, then?"

The man's eyes became intense. "I knew him at one time," he said carefully, almost as if he feared he might get into trouble and be tossed out if he said the wrong thing. "But I'm having to assume the manor has changed hands. The Lord Buckley I knew had no brother."

Garret smiled. In all the time he'd known Ritcherd, he'd only heard him called "Lord Buckley" a handful of times, by people in the area. He far preferred his military title to the aristocratic one, and it was terribly uncommon for his name to be put that way. Garret folded his arms over his chest and said, "Lord Buckley didn't know he had a brother until just a few years ago."

The hope that filled this man's eyes was so stark that Garret felt chilled. The chill intensified when he said with a cracking voice, "Then perhaps we *are* talking about the same man."

"Perhaps."

"How long has he been lord of Buckley Manor?"

"Since his father died in his youth," Garret said. "He inherited the manor. He did not purchase it."

Hope and recognition burned brightly in this man's eyes just before he said, "If you tell me we're talking about Ritcherd Buchanan, then I will know I've not lost all hope of finding him."

"We are," Garret said.

The man leaned forward eagerly. "And is he well?"

"He is," Garret said, unable to keep from smiling. "I'm afraid he's not at home right now, but he'll be back this afternoon sometime."

The man made an emotional noise and leaned back. Then a new darkness clouded his expression. "With any luck he will actually want to see me, and not have me thrown out on my ear."

Garret searched carefully for his words. "I don't know what past you share with Ritcherd, but he's not the kind of man to throw anyone out on his ear."

"That's good, then. Perhaps he'll at least be willing to hear what I have to say."

"I would assume," Garret said.

The man glanced down at himself and muttered, "Thank you again for the clothes . . . for letting me get cleaned up. It will be easier to face him this way."

"I'm glad I could help," Garret said.

Following some minutes of silence while this man seemed to be contemplating the fact that he'd found Ritcherd Buchanan, he looked up at Garret and asked, "Is Lord Buckley married?"

"He is," Garret said. "In truth, he is married to the finest, most beautiful woman I have ever known. My temptations to steal her away have been many," he added lightly.

"Tell me about her."

Garret looked toward the window and couldn't help the dreamy tone he heard in his own voice as he said, "Kyrah Buchanan is magnificent. She is as kind as she is beautiful. She has suffered much but come through brilliantly. I only hope to find such a woman myself one day and . . ." Garret stopped when he heard a strange sound. He turned to see this man with a hand pressed over his mouth and tears streaming down his face. What had been said to provoke such emotion? Had this man lost his own wife, perhaps? Had Garret's tender words touched something difficult in him? Garret looked away and graciously allowed him to regain his composure. When minutes passed and he continued to cry, Garret handed him a clean handkerchief and said, "Would you like some time alone?"

"That would be well, I believe. Thank you. Perhaps I am tired, after all."

"Get some rest. I'll be close by if you need anything."

"You've been too kind. And I don't even know your name."

"Garret Wentworth," he stated.

"And you're Ritcherd's brother?"

Garret was taken a little aback. Who was this man that he would call the lord of the manor by his given name, so naturally? "Half-brother," he said, "and scandalously at that. I must confess I am the result of an affair between my mother and the previous Lord Buckley."

"Ah," the man said, wiping at his face. "Well, it is a pleasure to meet you." He hurried from the room as if he feared his emotion might overtake him again. Garret attempted to return to his book, but he found his mind wandering speculatively through the conversations he'd had with this man. He felt impatient for Ritcherd to return to see if he might know or recognize him. He finally forced himself to read until lunchtime. He went to the kitchen and fixed a tray with enough for two and took it back to his sitting room. He'd barely finished eating his own lunch when the stranger appeared again, looking a little sleepy but more composed. They exchanged greetings and Garret invited him to sit and eat, while Garret pretended to read and avoided expressing his curiosity.

It became evident that he wasn't the only one suffering from inquisitiveness when the man said, "Forgive me if I'm being too bold, but . . . you said that Mrs. Buchanan had suffered much but come through brilliantly. May I ask exactly . . . how . . . she has suffered?"

Garret knew the question was a difficult one to answer, and he wondered if this man truly had a right to know. He tested him by saying, "You knew Kyrah?"

The man took a deep breath. "I knew both Ritcherd and Kyrah very well at one time, but it was many years ago, before the war. They were both very young—and very much in love, as I recall. It's been a great relief to learn just today that they have endured the years and remained together. But apparently the years have not been easy."

"There have been many challenges," Garret said, "but most of that is in the past." Testing this man's knowledge a little further, Garret asked, "Might I ask the last time you saw Ritcherd Buchanan?"

"Before he left for the colonies to serve his commission. Until today, I honestly didn't know if he'd even lived through the war. I'm glad that he did—for many reasons."

"Indeed," Garret said. "And Kyrah? When did you see her last?"

"Some months later," he said, looking down.

"Would that be before or after her father died?"

The man looked up abruptly, a horrified shock etched into his expression. "Died?" he squeaked. "How?"

Garret's heart quickened with sympathy. His subtle suspicions melted into pure compassion. This man had obviously known Stephen Payne, and for whatever reason he'd been away from Cornwall these many years, learning of Stephen's death was a shock. When Garret hesitated, knowing the answer was difficult, the man growled imperatively, "How did he die?"

"He shot himself in the head," Garret said, and wasn't surprised when this man stared at him in horror for a long moment, then erupted to his feet and began to pace the room, breathing sharply.

"No," he muttered, more to himself, "it's not possible."

"I'm afraid it is," Garret said gently while the man continued to pace, seeming more angry than anything. But Garret knew well enough that anger was often the first response to learning of a loved one's tragic death. Perhaps this man had been a friend of the family, or even a relative. He became distracted by the sound of footsteps on the stairs and approaching the door. He was vaguely aware of the man moving away from the view of the door to stand behind the chair he'd been sitting in.

Kyrah appeared in the doorway, looking vibrant and happy. "There you are," she said. "Before Ritcherd comes up, I need to hurry and ask you if—" Kyrah hesitated when she caught movement from the other side of the room. "Oh, I'm sorry," she said, tossing a brief glance toward the man standing there, then turning back to Garret, "I didn't know you had company. I . . ."

Garret watched Kyrah closely as she stopped speaking and seemed to freeze. Her cursory glance toward this man had obviously spurred significant recognition, but there was something confused—perhaps frightened—in her eyes. For a moment Garret wondered if he'd been graciously entertaining someone who was in truth an enemy to Ritcherd and Kyrah; someone from their past whom he'd never been told about. He expected her to turn again and look at their guest, but she fixed her eyes firmly on Garret. Her breathing sharpened and she pressed one hand over her heart, wrapping the other around her middle. "Is there a man standing in the room?" she asked.

Garret felt startled by the question. "Yes," he said with a dubious chuckle. "Do you know him?"

"He . . . looks like someone . . . I once knew. Too much like him, in fact." Her voice became raspy, her breathing more shallow. "What is his name?"

"He didn't tell me, but . . ."

Kyrah turned abruptly to face their visitor, as if doing so had taken great courage. Garret saw her teeter slightly and moved to her side to steady her. She leaned heavily against him, her breathing turning to a subtle whimper. She turned to face Garret, clutching onto his arms as if he might save her from death itself. She squeezed her eyes closed tightly while Garret tried to understand what was happening. Kyrah's fear of this man didn't ring true according to all that Garret had felt in their conversations. She looked up at Garret and muttered, "Who is this man, Garret? Tell me who he is and why he looks so much like . . . like . . ."

Garret glanced over Kyrah's head at the man, hoping to silently apologize for Kyrah's behavior, but he seemed to understand by the compassion in his eyes. While Garret was wondering how to answer her, the man said gently, "I know this must be a shock, Kyrah." She squeezed her eyes closed at the sound of his voice. "But it's me," he added.

Garret's heart jumped into his throat when Kyrah let out a scream that threatened to bring the house down. His entire focus turned to Kyrah as she sobbed and screamed and held to him more tightly. Her behavior reminded him very much of Ritcherd's response to uncovering a horrid memory that had been locked away for years. He wrapped her in his arms and attempted to soothe her, but there was no calming her down. He finally took hold of her shoulders and shook her gently, looking into her eyes. "It's all right, Kyrah. Whatever is wrong, it will be all right."

She looked into his eyes as if she'd been confronted with hell itself, then with no warning she slumped into his arms, losing consciousness. He picked her up and carried her to the sofa, laying her there gently, sitting on the edge of the sofa beside her. A quick glance at the man who had caused this scene showed him to be visibly upset, but apparently too stunned to speak. Garret was about to demand some answers when Ritcherd literally ran into the room. He rushed to Kyrah's side, demanding, "What happened? Why was she screaming?"

"She's all right," Garret said. "She just . . ." He glanced toward their visitor, not certain how to explain. Ritcherd's eyes followed, and Garret heard him suck in his breath. He sidestepped abruptly, as if he had lost his ability to stand, and clutched onto the back of a chair as if it might save him from certain collapse. Garret's heart thumped audibly as he glanced between the two men, absorbing the disbelief and shock in Ritcherd's expression and the compassion and fear looking back at him.

"It's not possible," Ritcherd muttered between a series of sputtering breaths.

"I'm afraid it is," the man said.

"Is it really you?"

"It is," he replied, "and my deepest prayer is that we can clear up this horrible misunderstanding, and undo all the damage that's been done."

Ritcherd let out a noise that sounded more like laughter than a sob, but a moment later he let out another that was more sobbing than laughter. He took a tentative step forward. "It *is* you," he said. "I can't believe it."

"Well, that's understandable." The man shook his head and tears showed in his eyes. "Oh, Ritcherd, my boy, how can I ever begin to explain what's happened? I'm not certain I even understand it myself."

Ritcherd shook his head slightly and took another step. "It doesn't matter what happened."

The remaining distance between them closed in an instant as Ritcherd swept toward this man and they wrapped their arms around each other. Ritcherd wept like a baby while this man pressed a loving hand to the back of Ritcherd's head, soothing him as a father would his son.

Kyrah moaned as she began to come around and their attention was drawn to her. "I'm afraid I scared Kyrah nearly to death," the man said, keeping his arm around Ritcherd, who chuckled and embraced him again tightly as if he couldn't bear the thought of letting go—or perhaps to further convince himself that this was real. Silently observing this drama unfold, Garret couldn't begin to imagine who this man was, but he was looking forward to finding out. Garret watched the man take Ritcherd's face into his hands, murmuring with emotion, "You can't know how grateful I am to know that you made it home alive and well, that you've been taking care of Kyrah."

Ritcherd just let out an emotional laugh, unable to speak. The man's expression sobered and he asked, "Where is Sarah?"

"She's gone," Ritcherd said, and the man's countenance fell dramatically. Ritcherd quickly added, "No, I mean . . . she's in London. She'll be back in a couple of days."

The man let out a delighted laugh, then hugged Ritcherd tightly while they both cried fresh tears. Garret's attention was drawn to Kyrah when she gasped and took hold of his hand. He turned to see her looking at him fearfully. She seemed to be orienting herself to the events that had led up to her fainting. When her eyes made it clear that she'd remembered, she squeezed them closed and sat up abruptly, clutching onto Garret and muttering breathlessly, "Tell me I was dreaming, Garret. Tell me he wasn't real."

Garret replied quietly, "Whoever he is, he looks pretty real to me."

She opened her eyes just before he glanced over his shoulder and her gaze followed while her grip tightened. Seeing Ritcherd holding tightly to this man, still weeping, Kyrah gasped. "It's not possible," she muttered, turning their attention toward her.

"Forgive me, Kyrah," the man said, holding out a hand toward her. "I had no idea until a few minutes ago that you had believed I was . . ." He seemed hesitant to say it.

"What?" she demanded, sounding skeptical, almost angry as she came unsteadily to her feet and Garret stood close beside her—just in case she threatened to lose consciousness again. She took hold of his arm tightly as if she shared his concern.

The man seemed reluctant to answer her. Kyrah stared at him, visibly confused and disoriented. Ritcherd finally said, "That he was dead?"

Garret felt something coming together in his mind, but he still felt far too ignorant. He finally filled the ongoing silence and said, "Forgive me, but . . . given the drama, I would really like to know who this man is."

Ritcherd turned toward Garret, keeping an arm around this man he obviously loved and revered greatly. He chuckled and wiped his face with his sleeve. "I'm sorry," Ritcherd said. "This is my brother Garret Wentworth. Garret, this is Kyrah's father—Stephen Payne."

Garret took a sharp breath as the events of the day suddenly made perfect sense—and the events of the past suddenly made no sense at all. He startled himself to the moment and held out a hand without moving away from Kyrah's grasp. "This is indeed a pleasure then," he said, and Stephen gripped his hand tightly.

"The pleasure is mine," Stephen said, then more to Ritcherd, "Your brother has been very kind to me."

"As he should be," Ritcherd said.

Kyrah stood frozen, observing the exchange with wide eyes. She took a step forward without letting go of Garret. Stephen moved away from Ritcherd and held out both of his hands toward her. "Oh, how I missed you!" he said. "You've grown up since I saw you last . . . and so beautifully; so much like your mother."

Kyrah sobbed and reached toward his hands as if she were trying to touch a wild animal and feared it might bite her arm off. Stephen took another step forward and took hold of her hands, making her gasp. Their eyes met for a long moment, then he pulled her into his arms where she wept uncontrollably. Stephen wept silently, holding her as if his life had begun again in that moment.

Ritcherd stood beside Garret while Kyrah wept in her father's arms. "Unbelievable," Ritcherd muttered.

"Indeed," Garret added in a whisper. "It would seem there has been some foul play going on in your lives; more so than we ever imagined."

"It would seem so."

"And I would bet my life that Peter Westman had a lot do with it."

Ritcherd looked at Garret sharply, knowing he was likely right.

Chapter Fifteen

Renaissance

Kyrah finally calmed down enough to ease back and look into her father's eyes. *She couldn't believe it!* Taking his face into her hands, she murmured, "How can this be possible? All this time . . . we were told you had . . . died."

"I realize that now," Stephen said. "And that certainly answers a great many questions for me, but there is still a great deal I don't understand."

"It would seem we all need to have a long talk," Ritcherd said, "whenever you feel up to it."

"I'm fine," Stephen said. "As I said, Mr. Wentworth has taken very good care of me."

"Please, call me Garret," he said.

Kyrah eased onto a sofa, feeling suddenly too drained of strength to stand. She kept hold of her father's hand, almost afraid to let go, as if this moment might disappear into a dream. She wondered if it was her hand or his that was trembling, then she realized it was both. Stephen smiled at her as he sat close beside her. He put his arm around her and pressed a kiss into her hair, provoking fresh tears that spilled down her face.

Ritcherd sat down and Garret moved toward the door. "Where are you going?" Ritcherd demanded.

"I thought I'd just leave you to get reacquainted and—"

"You're family," Kyrah said. "Please stay."

Garret sat down while Ritcherd gazed at Stephen, feeling completely stunned and dumbfounded. While there were a hundred questions he wanted answered, he felt too in awe of the moment to even think straight. After several minutes of silence while they all just seemed to accept the circumstances, Ritcherd finally said, "Obviously you're not dead, so . . . where have you been all this time?"

Stephen sighed. "I was in prison for seven years."

"No!" Kyrah insisted, lifting her head to look at him. "Prison? All this time? But . . . why?"

"I've never known," Stephen said. "I just . . . woke up there with no explanation."

"But . . . surely," Kyrah protested, "they would have notified us, or . . ."

"They told me they had notified my family," Stephen said with a helplessness that was heartrending. "When I heard nothing . . . I naturally assumed that . . ." He became too emotional to speak.

"What?" Ritcherd asked gently. "You assumed what?"

"I had lost the estate," Stephen muttered. "I had to assume that my family wanted nothing to do with me, that they figured I was where I deserved to be."

"No!" Kyrah cried. "If we had known . . ." She became visibly upset again. "Oh, I can't believe it. Prison, all this time. But . . . why?"

Ritcherd said angrily, "I'd wager it had something to do with Peter Westman."

Stephen turned to him sharply. "How did you know that?"

"Practically everything rotten that's happened in our lives since then has had to do with Peter Westman." Ritcherd paused and asked, *"Did* your going to prison have to do with Westman?"

"The last thing I saw before I blacked out was Westman putting a gun to somebody's head and pulling the trigger."

Kyrah gasped. Ritcherd and Garret gave each other a hard stare then looked back at Stephen. "And apparently," Ritcherd said, "that someone you saw killed is buried beneath a gravestone with your name on it."

"I can't believe it!" Kyrah gasped. She sat up straight and looked at her father. "We were told you'd been found in a hotel room in

London. The casket came sealed and stayed that way because of the damage. Your papers were sent to us, including the letter."

"What letter?" Stephen asked.

"The letter you wrote to Mother. You said you would not ask her to forgive you, that you wouldn't try to explain what happened because it made no difference now. You wrote that you did not leave her with nothing." She sobbed and tightened her hold on his hand. "We had every reason to believe that you had written that note to her and then put a gun to your head."

Stephen moved to the edge of his seat, closer to Kyrah, taking both her hands into his. "But I didn't, Kyrah. I wrote your mother that note to offer some form of apology for losing our home. There was still business in London I had to see to. I wanted her to know there was still money so that she would have hope to hold on to until I got home. I would not have left you and your mother destitute, Kyrah. I wouldn't have!"

Kyrah cried a steady stream of tears and pulled her hands away to wipe them with trembling fingers.

"Please tell me you found the money," Stephen said. "You can't imagine how I prayed that you would find that money."

"We found it eventually," Kyrah said, sounding angry, "but not until I'd spent years working for Peter Westman just to keep food on the table."

"No," Stephen muttered under his breath, his expression turning to horror.

Kyrah erupted to her feet and started pacing while a thousand thoughts and memories darted around in her mind—foremost, all of the horrible, vile things Peter had done and said to her. One statement stood out prominently and she stopped to face her father. "He . . . he told me that . . ." She pressed her handkerchief over her face, attempting without much success to get control of her emotion. "He told me that . . . I was going to have to accept that my father had put my security on the table and gambled it away, and then that . . . he'd taken the cowardly way out . . . and left us to fend for ourselves." She sobbed and added the obvious, "It was a lie. It was all a huge, horrible lie."

Stephen spoke vehemently. "I did *not* gamble away our security, Kyrah. I *knew* I could win that game. He cheated. You have to believe me."

"Oh, we know he cheated," Ritcherd said, and Stephen turned toward him. Ritcherd exchanged a poignant glance with Garret before he added, "Maybe we'd better start at the beginning."

"That would be well, I think," Stephen said, sounding understandably upset. "But there's one thing I have to know. Where is Westman now? Please tell me it is possible to find this man and see him pay for what he has done to us."

"Westman is dead," Garret said firmly.

Stephen looked doubtful. "Are you certain?"

"I'm absolutely certain," Garret added. "I killed him myself. Ritcherd and Kyrah can both testify to that."

Stephen sighed. "Then I owe you my deepest gratitude."

Ritcherd chuckled without humor. "And that isn't the half of it. What Garret has done for us is incomprehensible."

Garret looked at Ritcherd. "God brought us together. I just did what I believed He wanted me to do."

"That about sums it up," Ritcherd said. "Nothing short of divine intervention could ever explain the miracles we have encountered."

"And Peter Westman was a man in league with the devil," Garret added. "There's no other explanation for the way hell just followed him wherever he went."

Stephen leaned back and sighed, pressing a hand over his mouth. Kyrah gasped and said, "Good heavens. I told Cetty I would . . ." She turned to her father. "I'll be back in a few minutes. Forgive me. I just need to—"

"It's all right," Stephen said. "Do whatever you need to do. I'm not going anywhere."

She laughed and moved toward the door. Garret said, "Kyrah, I can see to it if—"

"No, thank you," she said. "It's all right. I'll only be a few minutes. Don't say anything important until I get back."

When she was gone, Stephen said, "It could take me that long just to accept what I've heard so far."

"Yes, I know what you mean," Ritcherd added. "It's unbelievable."

"Perhaps it would be good to take the conversation slowly for that very reason," Garret suggested. "It could take days to catch up."

"You're probably right," Ritcherd said, "but I have to leave for London in the morning to bring Sarah home."

Stephen let out a loud sigh. "Is she well?" he asked, anguish showing clearly in his eyes.

"She is," Ritcherd said. "Losing you was terribly hard on her." Stephen squeezed his eyes closed. "But she has come far."

"I wonder if getting me back will be equally hard," Stephen said. "I don't know if . . ."

Kyrah came into the room, holding Cetty's hand in hers. Stephen looked up at Kyrah, then down at the child, his eyes widening. "Father," Kyrah said, "this is our daughter, Cetty." She laughed softly. "Of course you can easily see that she's Ritcherd's daughter—she looks just like him."

"And she's adorable in spite of that," Garret said lightly, and Ritcherd chuckled.

"Good heavens," Stephen said breathlessly and moved to the edge of his seat, his eyes sparkling as he took in the beautiful child standing beside Kyrah. Looking a bit nervous, he glanced up at Kyrah and asked, "Does she know who I am?"

"I gave her a very brief explanation," Kyrah said. "I'm certain it will take time for her to adjust."

"As it will for all of us," Ritcherd said.

Stephen smiled at Cetty and she smiled in return. "Hello, Cetty," he said.

"Hello," she replied. "Are you my grandfather?"

"I am," Stephen said with pride in his voice.

"I've never had a grandfather before," Cetty said, and they all chuckled comfortably.

"And I've never had a granddaughter before," Stephen said. "We will have a marvelous time getting to know each other better."

"Do you like to play toy soldiers?" she asked.

"I do," he said with enthusiasm.

"Papa and Uncle Garret like to play that, too. You could come to the nursery and play soldiers with me, and we could read stories together."

Stephen got tears in his eyes. He glanced at Ritcherd, then Kyrah, saying, "She's beautiful."

"Yes, she is," Ritcherd said proudly.

Stephen looked again at Cetty and gingerly reached a hand toward her. With no hesitation Cetty stepped forward and took the outstretched hand. "I'm very pleased to meet you, Cetty," he said. "I remember when your mother was exactly your size. She was very beautiful, too." He smiled up at Kyrah. "She still is." He put an arm around her and asked, "How old are you, Cetty?"

"I'm four and a half years old," she said proudly.

Stephen smiled and went on to say "Tell me all about yourself, Cetty."

Cetty began chattering about her favorite toys, her governess, her music lessons, and the friends she visited with occasionally. Kyrah sat close to Ritcherd and put her head on his shoulder, unable to hold back an ongoing flow of tears as she observed the sweet interaction between her father and her daughter. She heard Ritcherd sniffle and knew that he, too, was emotional. His voice cracked as he whispered close to her ear, "It's unbelievable. I'm still not certain it's real."

"I know what you mean," Kyrah whispered in reply.

A few minutes later, Pearl came into the room and gave a slight curtsy. "Pardon the interruption," she said, "but Miss Cetty's piano teacher is here. It's time for her lesson."

"You run along," Stephen said to her, "and later I should very much like to hear you practice the piano, and then we'll read together and play with those soldiers."

Cetty nodded with enthusiasm and pressed a quick kiss to Stephen's cheek, which made him laugh as she scurried from the room with Pearl. Stephen's eyes sparkled as he looked to Ritcherd and Kyrah, saying with reverence, "What a remarkable child!"

"She has brought us a great deal of joy," Kyrah said. Their eyes met with a heartfelt gaze while Kyrah attempted to accept the reality that what she had believed for nearly eight years simply wasn't true. She knew by her father's expression that he too was having trouble accepting that they were together again.

"I can't believe it," Ritcherd said, turning their attention toward him. "If we had only known where you were, we could have . . ."

"What?" Stephen asked. "What could you have done?"

"I don't know, but . . . surely we could have cleared up this horrible misunderstanding. If you were in prison under a false identity . . . if we had known . . ."

"There's no good to be found in regret," Garret said. "Although I think it would be well to try and understand what happened, if only so that you can all come to terms with it."

"I'm sure you're right," Stephen said. "At the moment, however, I simply feel overwhelmed to just . . . be here."

"I'm still having trouble accepting that you're actually alive," Ritcherd said.

"So am I," Kyrah added. "When you believe something to be true . . . for so long . . . it's just . . ." She shook her head but couldn't find any words to explain.

Following a long moment of silence, Stephen said to Ritcherd, "The last time I saw you was the night before you left for the colonies. How long did you end up serving there?"

"About three years," Ritcherd said. "It probably would have been longer, but I was wounded and they sent me home after I spent far too much time in some pathetic army hospital." Stephen's brow furrowed, and Ritcherd held up his right hand. "I was shot through the arm at close range." He briefly demonstrated the limited use of his fingers, then lifted his sleeve to show the hideous scar.

"Good heavens," Stephen muttered. "It's a wonder you didn't lose your arm."

"It's more of a wonder that he wasn't killed," Kyrah said with fervor. "As I heard the story, it was his chest they were aiming for and he dodged the bullet just in time."

"Then it's a miracle you made it home alive," Stephen said with emotion tinging his voice. "My prayers were answered."

"They were indeed," Kyrah said quietly, taking hold of Ritcherd's hand.

"And that's not the half of it," Ritcherd said. "The real miracle happened long before that when . . ." He stopped abruptly and took a sharp breath.

Garret watched Ritcherd's expression become dazed and distant. He leaned toward him, asking quietly, "Are you all right, Ritch?"

Ritcherd started at the sound of Garret's voice and turned toward him. "I don't know," he admitted. Garret and Kyrah exchanged a concerned glance and Garret knew she was wondering, as he was, if Ritcherd might have been confronted with some difficult thought or memory. Ritcherd pressed a hand over his chest; his gaze grew more distant, his breathing sharper. Garret saw panic appear in Kyrah's eyes the same moment his own heart quickened with concern.

Ritcherd felt his surroundings become hazy as he was taken back in time to a life-altering experience. It was not the unearthing of some horrendous memory, like his being kidnapped as a child. It wasn't frightening or ugly. Rather, it was one of the clearest, brightest memories of his past. It was an experience that had let him know beyond any doubt of God's existence, of His mindfulness of mankind. The experience had actually occurred in two separate moments, years apart; two moments that had become linked irrevocably together in his heart. There had been the incident itself that had occurred in the midst of a battle in the colonies when he'd nearly lost his life. And years later, there had been the moment when he had been given absolute knowledge and understanding of that event. For long moments Ritcherd ingested the memories, then he turned abruptly to gaze at Stephen. What he'd believed had occurred was suddenly shaken. He felt Stephen's gaze penetrate his own, as if he could understand, with no words spoken, what Ritcherd might be feeling.

"What is it, Ritcherd?" Stephen asked gently. "Tell me what's troubling you."

His tenderness and sensitivity took Ritcherd back to his youth, to a time when Stephen Payne had been more of a father to him than his own had ever been. Their relationship had been close and strong. They'd shared a friendship completely independent of his relationship with Kyrah. They'd gone hunting together, and shared long talks. Ritcherd knew that the majority of the values he'd grown up with had come from Stephen's careful tutelage, as opposed to the neglect and harshness he'd endured in his own home. The closeness they'd once shared came rushing over him as their eyes met. But Ritcherd still had difficulty putting his thoughts to words.

"I . . . heard your voice," he finally muttered. "Or at least . . . I thought I did. But . . . I couldn't have, because . . ."

"I don't know what you mean," Stephen said.

Kyrah gasped as she realized what Ritcherd was talking about. "I remember," she said, "your telling me how . . . good heavens."

"What?" Stephen pressed.

Ritcherd shook his head. "It made so much sense; now it makes no sense at all."

"Don't try to make sense of it," Stephen said. "Just tell me what happened."

Ritcherd tried to take Stephen's advice and focus his thoughts. He cleared his throat and said, "In the colonies . . . the first time we went into battle, I came into a wooded area where I realized that I could possibly get a vantage point to see what the enemy was doing. I was completely alone, moving through the trees, when I heard a voice say, 'Get your head down, boy. There's one coming right at you!' That was it. I immediately ducked and heard a bullet whistle past. I knew I would have been dead if not for that warning. But when I turned around, no one was there. I figured whoever it was had run for it. But looking back, I know that there was no sound there beyond my own breathing. I went over and over it in my mind. From where I was, it would have been impossible to see whoever was shooting at me. There is no way that someone behind me could have possibly seen him."

Ritcherd sighed and went on. "Years later, after I'd returned to Cornwall, I was struggling with my feelings for Kyrah because . . ." He hesitated and gave her a cautious glance.

"Just tell him," she said. "I was being completely difficult and wanted nothing to do with you."

Stephen's eyes widened but Ritcherd continued, "For reasons we will get into some other time. I can only say that while I was praying very hard to know what to do, that experience came back to me, and I knew—I *knew*—that my life had been spared that day so that I could come home and care for Kyrah and Sarah." He looked directly at Stephen. "It sounded like your voice. At the time it happened the idea had been preposterous, but then . . . when I thought you were dead, it all seemed to make sense. But now . . . well, you weren't dead, so . . ."

Stephen offered a subtle smile. "It was a miracle, Ritcherd. Can we question the means by which a miracle occurs? Is it not possible that the voice of the angel who saved you that day somehow reminded you of me because it was a voice you would trust?" Stephen put his forearms on his thighs and leaned closer to Ritcherd. "My dear boy, I could never tell you how hard I prayed for that very thing."

"What?" Ritcherd asked, unclear of exactly what he meant.

"I prayed night and day with all the energy of my soul that you *would* be spared, that you *would* go safely home and take care of Sarah and Kyrah for me."

Ritcherd felt Kyrah squeeze his hand tightly the same moment he felt a tangible warmth rush over his shoulders and down his back. He saw tears in Stephen's eyes only a moment before his own vision clouded with mist.

"My prayers were answered, Ritcherd," Stephen said. "I felt so completely helpless, so . . . cut off. I knew the only thing I could do for my family was pray; and pray I did."

"Evidently it worked," Garret said. "Ritcherd's life being spared was only the beginning of many miracles."

"Yes, that's true," Kyrah said, wiping fresh tears from her face. "Your prayers were surely heard all these years."

Stephen sighed and said, "That's not the first clue I've heard that these years have been difficult for you. I'm almost afraid to ask exactly how they were difficult, but . . . I need to know."

A heavy silence fell over the room while Kyrah, Ritcherd, and Garret all exchanged rueful glances. Ritcherd finally gave a humorless chuckle and admitted, "I don't know where to start."

"Well, there's no hurry," Stephen said. "We'll have plenty of time to catch up."

"Of course we will," Kyrah said brightly.

"And it's obvious you've had good times, as well," Stephen said, smiling at them both. "You're happily married. You have a beautiful daughter." He smiled at Garret. "And I can't wait to hear about your discovering you had a brother."

"That story just kind of ties into everything else," Ritcherd said.

Another silence was broken when Stephen said, "So, as close as I can figure, if you served in the colonies for three years, you must have been married right away once you got home."

Ritcherd knew the alarm was evident in his expression by the way Stephen's eyes widened. Ritcherd felt his chest tighten and his palms turn sweaty. Kyrah met his eyes with perfect acceptance showing through her concern. He turned to look again at Stephen and felt sick to his stomach. He told himself he could handle this like a man, that he could face his father-in-law with an honest explanation of what had happened and why. But he suddenly felt so overcome with grief that he couldn't even speak. Unable to look Stephen in the eye another second, he shot out of his chair and moved abruptly toward the window. He pressed his hands over the sill and leaned heavily against them, finding it difficult to breathe. He closed his eyes and prayed silently for the strength to face this moment. In the midst of his prayer, a gentle hand came over his shoulder. He looked up to see Stephen standing beside him.

"Did I say something to upset you?" he asked gently.

Ritcherd shook his head and looked out the window. "Forgive me," he said, then struggled through moments of silence for what to say next. He shook his head again and muttered, "I cannot even count how many times I imagined you looking down from heaven at me and wondering what kind of imbecile you had entrusted your daughter to." Ritcherd swallowed carefully and forced himself to look Stephen in the eye. "I never imagined having to actually tell you this. I figured that you would be aware, somehow, of what was going on in our lives, and if we ever saw each other again in another life, there would be no need for explanation." He took a deep breath and forced himself to just say it. "No, Stephen, we were not married right away. We were not married until months after Cetty was born."

Stephen's eyes showed surprise, even alarm, but he kept his hand on Ritcherd's shoulder and said nothing, as if he would wait for an explanation.

"I broke trust with you, Stephen." Ritcherd's voice cracked. "I made some horrible choices . . . deplorable mistakes. I hurt her so deeply."

"You searched the world for me," Kyrah interjected firmly. "Your love for me brought me back to life."

Stephen looked deeply into Ritcherd's eyes, then he glanced at Kyrah. "She looks pretty happy now. It seems everything worked out all right."

"Eventually," Ritcherd said and shook his head. "I don't know how you could ever understand why I did what I did, and the regret that's eaten at me. I don't know how you could ever forgive me."

"Ritcherd, listen to me," Stephen said. "How can you look at me and think that I wouldn't understand? I abandoned my wife and daughter to fend for themselves, leaving them at the mercy of that . . . cretin."

"It certainly wasn't your fault that you ended up in prison with no—"

"I put my home on the table in a game of cards, Ritcherd. I let Westman coerce me into playing that game against my better judgment and my every instinct. The results were disastrous; the consequences are still before us. How am I supposed to live with that?"

"You're here now," Ritcherd said. "It's in the past and forgiven."

"Don't patronize me by telling me it's in the past and forgiven, and then try to convince me that I could never forgive you for any pain you may have caused Kyrah and Sarah. It's evident that you have righted the wrong. Your commitment to your family is plain to see." He lowered his voice and put his hands on Ritcherd's shoulders. "It's in the past, Ritcherd. It's forgiven."

Ritcherd sighed and absorbed the words into his heart. Then he chuckled tensely and added, "Maybe you'd better hear the whole story before you say something like that."

"From what was said earlier, I'm guessing that Peter Westman plays a big part in this story. If that's the case, then I am more to blame for the circumstances than anyone."

"No," Garret said, "Peter Westman is more to blame than anyone. If not for his evil manipulation, every other circumstance would have worked itself out a hundred times more easily. I'll tell you what I once told Kyrah. Peter Westman was a man who knew no honor. He lived for his own gain and would stop at nothing. He killed callously, sold his allegiance to the highest bidder, and cheated men out of their lives. No one is at fault here except for Westman. We were all just pawns in the sick game he played."

"You obviously knew him well," Stephen said.

"I knew Peter Westman long before I met Ritcherd and Kyrah," Garret said. "I had my own score to settle with the man. It was no coincidence that my grudge against him had a great deal to do with *your* grudge against him."

"What do you mean?" Stephen asked.

"I mean that God brought Ritcherd and me together through miraculous means and for many purposes to be served."

Stephen's eyes showed intrigue. "I think it's time I heard exactly what happened in my absence."

"It probably is," Kyrah said, coming to her feet. "But it's nearly time for supper, and I believe we've got plenty to think about for a while."

"I'm certain we do," Stephen said as he stood and pressed Kyrah's hand to his lips before laying it over his arm.

Kyrah walked toward the stairs, holding tightly to her father, still unable to believe that his presence was real. She felt as if she were in the center of a dream, swirling in the midst of a huge mixture of emotions. Her joy in having her father alive and with her was indescribable. But the reality of their separation and the grief they'd endured caused her a deep sorrow that was equivalent to her happiness. She noticed how he took hold of the stair rail firmly and moved carefully down the stairs. A couple of times he hesitated, seeming subtly unsteady.

"Are you not well?" she asked quietly.

"Oh, I'm fine," he insisted almost lightly. "I fear they didn't feed us very well in that dreadful place. I've been a little . . . weak. I'm certain it will improve with time."

Kyrah fought back the reality of what he was saying, fearing she'd burst into tears otherwise. She simply said, "Of course," and they moved on down the stairs, going slowly, with Ritcherd and Garret coming behind them. In the dining room, Stephen moved toward the fire and lingered there while the others were seated.

"Cold?" Ritcherd asked.

"Not at the moment," Stephen said. He chuckled and said, "First time in nearly eight years that I haven't been."

Ritcherd exchanged a concerned glance with Kyrah. The implication was difficult to accept, but they said nothing.

"Your home is beautiful," he said, looking around the room. "I've never been inside before today."

"Well," Ritcherd chuckled, "there wouldn't have been much incentive for you to pay my parents a visit."

"No," Stephen's voice darkened, "they weren't very impressed with me—for good reason."

"No, not for any good reason," Ritcherd insisted. "My parents were self-righteous and judgmental—an issue that brought a great deal of grief into our lives."

Stephen cleared his throat tensely and sat down at the table. "Ritcherd," he said, "you were in love with a gambler's daughter."

Ritcherd smirked. "I still am, if you must know."

Stephen remained serious. "Perhaps they had good cause to be concerned."

"Their only concern was your lack of aristocratic blood," Ritcherd said, "and the fact that your money wasn't *old* money. But that's all in the past. I'm happy to say that my mother eventually came around." Stephen's eyes widened as Ritcherd went on. "She actually apologized to Kyrah, and to me. She told me that Kyrah was the best thing that had ever happened to me."

"A miracle, indeed," Stephen said. He turned to Kyrah and added, "Of course, I agree with her."

"So do I," Ritcherd said.

"I don't know," Garret interjected. "I think Kyrah's the best thing that ever happened to *me*."

Ritcherd chuckled. "Kyrah is a thorn in your side, and you know it."

Stephen didn't seem to know how to take the statement. Garret laughed softly and winked at Kyrah. "Oh, but a thorn from such a beautiful rose is well worth the pain it causes."

"Now you're just being silly," Kyrah said.

The first course of soup was brought in and served. After the maid left, Stephen asked Ritcherd, "So, where is your mother now?"

Ritcherd's countenance became grave. "She was killed."

Stephen looked up with his spoon halfway to his mouth. "How?"

Ritcherd exchanged a rueful glance with Garret, then Kyrah, before he looked straight at Stephen. "Peter Westman shot her." Stephen's spoon fell noisily against the edge of his bowl. "Although he had the gun pointed at Kyrah. My mother stepped in between them."

Stephen took a sharp breath and looked at Kyrah, as if to silently question if it was true. When her eyes told him it was, he gripped the table with both hands and hung his head. "I'm not sure I even want to know what might have led up to such an event. Through seven years in prison, my most prominent nightmare was seeing him shoot that man in the head—whoever he may have been. If I had known that such atrocities were taking place . . ." He shook his head.

"It's probably well that you didn't know," Garret said with compassion.

Stephen glanced at him then looked firmly at Ritcherd. "Well, I'm here now and I need to know. Tell me what happened."

"And ruin your supper?" Ritcherd said, attempting a light voice.

"I can't eat wondering what else he did to my family."

Ritcherd sighed and set down his spoon. When it became evident that he intended to tell Stephen what had happened, Kyrah said abruptly, "No, it can wait." She looked at her father. "Forgive me, but . . . it will ruin *my* supper. We can talk about it later, and we will—I promise. But not right now."

"Very well," Stephen said, and they ate in silence for a few minutes until he added, "There's something I need to say."

"All right," Ritcherd said.

"It's wonderful to be here—more wonderful than I could ever tell you." He smiled at Kyrah, but he seemed nervous. "When I got out of prison, I debated over whether or not I should come here at all."

"But why would—" Kyrah began, but Stephen put up a hand to stop her.

"You must understand that until today I didn't realize you believed I was dead. You can imagine my surprise when Garret asked me if I'd last seen Kyrah before or after her father died."

"That . . . would be a surprise," Ritcherd said.

"Having spent seven years in prison with no indication that my family wanted anything to do with me, I simply assumed you were better off without me. When I got out, I found work enough to get by, but as you can see, my health is not conducive to being worth much. I'm doing better, but it's slow. Finally I reached a day where I realized I could keep working at the mill, or I could at least find my family and find out for certain where I stood. So, here I am. I am more grateful than I could ever tell you to realize that, in spite of gross misunderstanding and obvious heartache, my family is glad to see me—those of you who are here, at least." He sighed and looked directly at Ritcherd. "Your hospitality and generosity are very touching, Ritcherd. I'm certain you can afford to feed me and give me a room, and I don't wish to be impertinent. But I must make it clear that I do not intend to be a burden to you, Ritcherd. I did not come here seeking a handout."

"A burden?" Ritcherd echoed, then he countered firmly, "You could never be a burden to me, Stephen. *Never.*"

"That's easy to say, your being one of the wealthiest men in Cornwall. But if—"

"And were I not," Ritcherd interrupted, "you would still never be a burden to me. You're family. You are my father, in the truest sense of the word. If I had to work every waking hour to see that my family's needs were met, I would do it, and I would consider it a privilege to count you among those I provide for. It has been a privilege to care for Sarah, and now that you will be here with her, we will all be the happier for it."

"Being here with all of you would give me the greatest pleasure," Stephen said. "But you need to know that I am capable of providing for myself. I will get my strength back and I'll do whatever I have to do. You've cared for Sarah for many years, and I am grateful beyond words for that, but I'm here now and I intend to take responsibility for my wife."

"Stephen," Ritcherd said gently, "we are family. If I didn't have the money, we would have to work together to do whatever needed to be done. But I have it, and I didn't do anything magnanimous to get it. So just be gracious, and enjoy the fact that you're home."

Stephen sighed and looked down. "I don't know what to say."

"You don't have to say anything," Ritcherd said. "You made me a part of your family and gave me a home when I had no place of refuge or comfort. You believed in me and taught me the difference between right and wrong." Stephen looked up and Ritcherd gave him a hard stare. "And you loved me and forgave me even when I disappointed you. Your place is with us, for as long as you live. And that's final." He smirked and added, "There's plenty of room. I'm sure you can avoid us if we get on your nerves, but . . . I think my children ought to grow up with a grandfather under their roof."

"I agree completely," Kyrah said. "Mother loves it here. When she gets back, you can ask her yourself."

Stephen sighed and looked down again before he said, "I have no doubt that your mother loves it here, Kyrah, but perhaps we should ask her whether or not she wants me here with her."

Kyrah gasped. "And why would she not?"

"I've been dead to her for nearly eight years, Kyrah. I'm grateful to know she didn't marry someone else or . . ." He hesitated and looked momentarily nervous. "She didn't, did she?"

"No, of course not," Kyrah said. "And she will be happy to see you. I'm absolutely certain of it."

Stephen took a deep breath. "Why don't we just talk about this again after your mother comes back. Once she recovers from the shock, we'll discuss what's best."

"Very well," Kyrah said, and the subject was dropped.

A few minutes into the main course, Garret said, "Speaking of Sarah coming home, I was thinking that perhaps I should go to London to escort her home, Ritcherd, so that you can spend some time with Stephen and get reacquainted."

"That's a marvelous idea," Kyrah said. "Are you certain you want to?"

"I'd be delighted," Garret said. "So, I'll plan on leaving after breakfast."

"Very well," Ritcherd said. "I know better than to argue with you."

"Also," Garret added, "if I may offer an opinion?"

"Of course," Ritcherd said with an expression that clearly said his asking was ridiculous.

"I think it might be best if I say nothing to her about what's happened. Although I think *someone* should tell her before she actually *sees* Stephen. I just don't think it should be me."

Stephen looked visibly nervous. Ritcherd said, "I'm sure you're right. Once you get back with her, we can tell her . . . as delicately as possible." He looked at Stephen and chuckled.

"What's so funny?" Stephen demanded.

"I can't wait to see the look on her face when I tell her the resurrection has occurred."

"Well, not *the* resurrection," Garret said.

Kyrah added, "I'm glad you're willing to tell her, Ritcherd, because I'm not sure I want to."

"You can keep me from going mad while he's telling her," Stephen said.

"Everything will be fine," Kyrah assured him and laughed softly, but Stephen didn't seem convinced.

Chapter Sixteen

The Evil Deeds of Peter Westman

"There is something else I need to say," Garret said over dessert.

"And what is that?" Ritcherd asked. "If you're going to tell Stephen you're in love with his daughter, you're wasting your time. She's taken."

Again Stephen looked unsure of how to take the comment. But Garret laughed and Stephen seemed to relax, even when Garret said to Ritcherd, "Just watch yourself, boy. You can't get too comfortable with a woman like that."

"No worries," Ritcherd said, lifting his glass toward Kyrah. "Her heart is all mine."

"As it should be," Garret said more seriously. "Now, if you'll stop trying to change the subject, there's something I need to say."

"And what is that?" Ritcherd asked again.

"I think perhaps we should reconsider the situation with the house," Garret said.

"The house?" Ritcherd echoed, confused.

"The house that I just purchased from Kyrah. Now that Stephen is back, maybe it should belong to him."

"That house is yours, Garret," Kyrah insisted.

"Yes, I know, Kyrah," he said. "I have the deed. But I'm saying that I am willing to sell it back to you so that your parents can live there, if that's what they would prefer."

All eyes turned to Stephen. "What house?" he asked.

"The house," Ritcherd said. "The house you were living in before the war."

Stephen's eyes widened. "You own it?" he asked Ritcherd.

"No, Garret owns it," Ritcherd said. "Kyrah sold it to him. It never belonged to me. It was *her* house."

Stephen looked at Kyrah. "How did you get the house back if Westman owned it?"

Kyrah glanced at Ritcherd, biting her lip. She met her father's gaze and said, "That's part of the story we promised to tell you later. Suffice to say that I inherited the house. Of course, it's been sitting empty since then because . . ."

She stopped when Cetty came running into the room, going directly to Ritcherd. "There's my princess," he said with laughter, lifting her onto his lap.

"Thank you, Pearl," Kyrah said, and the governess slipped away.

Stephen's eyes sparkled as he observed Cetty with her father. Ritcherd teased her and made her giggle, then he chased her around the table and tickled her while she giggled harder, provoking laughter from Stephen as he observed. When Ritcherd declared that Cetty had exhausted him, she went directly to Stephen and took his hand. "Do you want to see my toy soldiers and my dolls and my books?" she asked.

"I would love to," Stephen said, coming to his feet.

They all went upstairs and made themselves comfortable in the nursery while Cetty showed her grandfather all of her favorite possessions. Kyrah sat on the sofa between Ritcherd and Garret, holding each of their hands, observing her father playing with Cetty. She felt so overwhelmed and in awe that she could have observed them together for hours. It was evident that Ritcherd and Garret were equally entranced.

"Do you want to play toy soldiers?" Cetty asked Stephen.

"That's my favorite," he said, sitting on the floor beside where they were lined up in two rows, facing each other. Stephen glanced at Ritcherd. "I assume you've trained her well in this respect."

"Oh, extremely," Ritcherd said facetiously.

With great seriousness, Cetty told her grandfather, "Garret likes the blue ones because that's the color the colonist soldiers wore in America. Papa uses the red soldiers because he used to be a redcoat, but he's not a redcoat anymore. Now he's a turncoat."

Stephen looked up at Ritcherd in astonishment. Garret muttered, "Goodness. Don't let the child talk to Mr. Thayer or we'll hang for certain."

Ritcherd noted Stephen's furrowed brow and said, "I'll tell you later."

"I hope you're keeping a list of everything you're going to tell me later," Stephen said, then returned his attention to Cetty.

After Cetty had reluctantly gone off to bed with the promise that Stephen would play with her tomorrow, the adults gathered in Ritcherd and Kyrah's sitting room to visit.

"All right, it's later," Stephen said.

Kyrah said, "Surely you must be tired, and—"

"I had a nap," Stephen said. "And I will never be able to sleep, wondering what happened in my absence. Now, out with it."

"All right," Ritcherd said. "I'll give you the brief version, and we can fill in the details later. I'm certain it will take some time to catch up on everything. Before I begin, however, I want to say that we had some very good things come out of all that happened. Reconciling with my mother was one of them. Finding Garret was another."

Garret and Ritcherd exchanged a warm smile before Ritcherd sighed loudly and turned toward Stephen. "Kyrah didn't write and tell me that the estate had been lost and you were dead—or so she believed. I came home from the colonies to hear the news from my mother. By that time, Kyrah had been working for Westman for more than two years. She and Sarah were living in the cottage on the estate."

"The one where Sarah lived in her youth?" Stephen asked.

"The very same," Ritcherd said. "Sarah took your loss very hard. Her health was poor, and Kyrah was working every waking hour just to keep Westman off their backs. It took some effort upon my return to convince her that the changes in her life had not altered the way I felt about her. When she finally agreed to marry me, my mother was furious. She made some veiled threats, I got angry and scared, then things got out of hand between me and Kyrah. That's when Cetty was conceived." Ritcherd sighed loudly and looked askance at Stephen. His voice betrayed his shame when he added, "I know I said this would be the brief version, but I have to stop and say that . . . my regret is indescribable."

"It's in the past," Stephen said. "Obviously the results were good."

"Eventually," Ritcherd said. "But maybe you'd better hear the rest of the story before you reconcile it so easily."

"I'm listening," Stephen said.

"Well, my mother made good on her threats. She framed Kyrah, claiming she'd stolen jewelry from her. She was arrested. The constable promised me if she spent a night at the station, he could get it straightened out. Before morning she had been knocked out and taken aboard a ship, where she—"

"What?" Stephen interrupted. "Did I hear you right? A ship?"

"That's what I said. She was deported, Stephen. I had no idea where she was going or how to find her."

Stephen stared incredulously at Kyrah, then at Ritcherd. "Good heavens," he muttered. "Deported?"

"That's right," Kyrah said. "But the clever twist to all of this is that Peter Westman was on that ship. After being drugged and locked in a cabin for weeks, his company actually began to seem pleasant."

Stephen pressed a hand over his mouth and shook his head. He motioned for them to go on.

"When I arrived in Virginia," Kyrah said, "Peter seemed certain that I'd never be able to make it on my own. That was his first attempt at getting me to marry him."

"*Marry* him?" Stephen shouted quietly, and Kyrah turned dark eyes toward Ritcherd before she turned back to face her father.

"Fortunately," she said, "Ritcherd had given me some diamond jewelry, and I had it with me. I sold the earrings and lived off the money for several weeks. But time passed. I couldn't get passage home because there was a war going on. And I was pregnant. I kept hoping and praying that Ritcherd would come, but he didn't. I got scared. Against my better judgment, I eventually accepted Peter's proposal."

Stephen's gaze tightened on Kyrah, his eyes turned fearful. "What are you saying, Kyrah?" he asked, his voice hard and cautious.

Kyrah swallowed carefully and drew the courage to say what she needed to say. "I married him." Stephen gasped and she hurried to add, "Fortunately it didn't last long, but it didn't take him long to do his damage. Although he didn't even stick around long enough for a wedding night. He told me he'd be back when Ritcherd Buchanan's brat was no longer a problem." Stephen's expression seethed with anger. Kyrah went on. "By the time he came back, Ritcherd *had* found me, and we were soon on our way to England. I tried to divorce him, but it would have taken years. We're all grateful that he was foolish enough to put himself in a position where Garret was justified in killing him in a fair fight. As his widow I inherited the estate, and the bounty money as well."

"The bounty?" Stephen questioned, his voice sour.

"That's where my mother twists into the story," Ritcherd said. "She and Peter were in this together. She put a bounty on Kyrah. Fifty thousand pounds for a marriage certificate that could prevent her from marrying me."

"Good heavens," Stephen muttered, aghast.

"Of course Peter had his own incentives on top of that," Garret said. Stephen turned to him with wide eyes. "Apparently there was a promissory note in that game you played."

"Yes, there was," Stephen said, "but there should have been no way that Westman could have found that money."

"Well," Garret said, "apparently he figured with Kyrah as his wife, his ability to find it, and his right to it, increased immensely."

"The filthy . . ." Stephen hesitated and glanced at Kyrah, as if he would refrain in a lady's presence.

"It's all right," she said. "There is no profanity that could offend me after what he put me through. And there are no words vulgar enough to describe him."

Garret leaned forward and continued. "A friend of mine—a man who sailed with me—was actually—"

"You sail?" Stephen asked.

"That's right."

"Then . . . you're a sea captain, not a military captain like Ritcherd."

"That's right," Garret said.

"I heard Mrs. Hawke address you as 'captain,' but I didn't get a chance to ask." Stephen motioned with his hand. "Forgive me. Please go on."

"Well, this friend of mine," Garret said, "actually witnessed the game you played with Westman." Stephen's eyes widened. "He knew Westman was cheating. He took the promissory note from the table, hoping to hold some leverage over Westman to undo what had been done. He tried to find you but never could. He confronted Westman, which eventually led to Westman's double-crossing me, since this man was sailing on my ship."

Garret's expression turned cloudy and Stephen asked gingerly, "What exactly did he do?"

"He sold my position to a British Letter of Marque. I lost the ship, a full cargo, and twenty-three men."

"Good heavens!" Stephen said with anger permeating his voice. "Would the man stop at nothing to get what he wanted?"

"Nothing," Ritcherd growled.

"So, you see," Garret went on, "when I met Ritcherd, I was already hunting for Westman, but I had no idea that Ritcherd's quest was leading us in the same direction."

"And how exactly did you meet?" Stephen asked.

Ritcherd chuckled. "This was supposed to be the brief version."

"We're catching up on several years here, Ritcherd," Stephen said. "Anything less than staying up all night would be the brief version."

"That's true," Kyrah said.

Ritcherd tossed Garret a sideways smile as he said, "How did I meet Garret? Where do I begin?"

"You were half dead with a hangover when Morley gave you a proposition," Garret said.

"So I was," Ritcherd said. "When I got back from the colonies, my friend George Morley—you remember George."

"Of course," Stephen said.

"Well, George kept trying to get me to hold still long enough to talk to me about something, but I was busy trying to convince Kyrah that she loved me. After she'd been deported, I got blind drunk and woke up to find George insisting that he would talk to me then and there. To state it succinctly, George had become a privateer, smuggling arms and ammunition to the colonists." Stephen's eyes widened but he said nothing. "He told me their ship had been shot down, they'd lost everything, and he was asking me to buy a ship to aid their cause. I'm ashamed to say I felt reluctant until I realized it could serve my own purposes. George knew that the only ship that had left dock the night Kyrah was deported was also a privateer vessel, headed for the colonies. So I told George I would buy the ship if I could go with them. We took care of the transaction, and while they were preparing to sail I made certain that Sarah had everything she needed. Then I went aboard the *Phoenix* and met this . . . scoundrel here," his voice picked up a facetious lilt, "who told me I stuck out like an aristocratic sore thumb, and I wasn't sailing on *his* ship until I did something about it. Once I was dressed like some second-rate pirate and had my ear pierced, he let me on board."

Stephen showed a subtle smile. "Did he now?" His brow furrowed and he added, "But . . . the two of you are brothers? Surely that can't be coincidence."

"I don't believe in coincidence," Garret said. "It's plainly evident that God brought our lives together. Of course, George had been a friend to each of us for years, even though Ritcherd and I had never met prior to that time."

"Tell him the truth," Ritcherd said with mock anger. "Tell him how you *knew* I was your brother long before I came on board, but you didn't bother to tell *me* until a year later."

"It just didn't seem important," Garret said with a smirk. He turned to Stephen. "When I had hoped he would buy us a ship, I had never dreamed he'd actually sail with us. But the more I got to know him, the more I actually liked him—when I had expected to hate him. After all, I hadn't liked our father much."

"But then, neither did I," Ritcherd said.

"So," Stephen said, "you sailed for the colonies."

"That's right," Ritcherd said. "But we were blown off course by a nasty storm, and had a number of setbacks. By the time we got to the port where Kyrah had arrived, we knew she had been there, but we couldn't find her. She was married to Westman by then and hiding away. Ironically, Kyrah met Garret through other means and arranged passage home with him. When we were ready to sail, he sent me to get her. And that's when I finally saw her again. She was in labor with Cetty."

Stephen shook his head. "Incredible," he muttered. "But I take it that's not the last you saw of Westman."

"No, he made his presence known soon after the baby was born—before we left port. Then the *Phoenix* was boarded at sea by Westman's thugs, trying to steal Kyrah back. Fortunately they didn't get away with her, but they did leave the *Phoenix* burning. It took us several days to repair her enough to get us home."

"You're leaving out the best part," Garret said.

"And what is that?" Stephen asked.

"The fact that in the skirmish Ritcherd got shot," Garret said. "There he was, bleeding all over the deck while the sails were turning to ash. It was horrible. Fortunately, I have a good crew who fought well and scared the enemy off, then they got the fire out. I also have a good doctor who got the bullet out of Ritcherd's leg and took very good care of him. Eventually we got back to England, where Westman continued to make a nuisance of himself. But he got really nasty when he heard rumors that Kyrah had found that money. When she didn't give in to his threats, he showed up at the manor with a gun. And you know the rest."

Stephen shook his head. "Incredible," he muttered again. "It's evident that God was with you, that you were blessed with many miracles."

"Yes, that's true," Ritcherd said fervently.

"I can never express the depth of my regret," Stephen said. "I never would have imagined that becoming involved with Westman to such a minimal degree would have brought so much trouble to my loved ones." He pressed a hand over his eyes, and it quickly became evident that he was crying. He gave an embarrassed chuckle that didn't slow the tears. "Forgive me," he said, wiping the tears from his face. "I just can't seem to stop crying."

"Your life has changed significantly in the last several hours," Garret said. "I think some emotion is understandable."

"I just feel like such a baby," Stephen chuckled.

"Oh, the men around here never cry," Ritcherd said with light sarcasm. "Except for me, of course. I've cried enough the past few months to fill a bathtub twice over."

Stephen looked surprised. "Why is that?"

Ritcherd hesitated and Garret answered for him. "Ritcherd's had a pretty rough time since his sister's death in October."

Stephen looked at Ritcherd, astonished. "You have a sister?" He chuckled. "I've known you since you were less than thirteen, young man. I thought you were an only child. Now you not only have a brother, you have a sister who died in October."

"That's right," Ritcherd said. "I'm just full of surprises."

Minutes of silence made it evident that they were all tired and overwhelmed.

Stephen shook his head again, visibly stunned. "There's so much I want to say . . . questions I want answered, but . . . I can't even put a thought together."

"I'm certain it will come together with time," Garret said.

"Well, it's certainly been an eventful day," Stephen said. "It could take weeks just to let my head catch up with all I've learned today."

"I could agree with that," Ritcherd said.

"We've got a lifetime to catch up," Kyrah said, coming to her feet. Stephen stood to meet her, taking both her hands into his. "It's so good to have you back," she said, unable to hold back her tears.

Stephen smiled and moisture rose into his eyes. "It is so good to *be* back, my dear. I never imagined that I could ever be where I am now."

Kyrah smiled and embraced him tightly. "Do you have everything you need until breakfast?" she asked.

"I do, thank you," he said.

Ritcherd embraced Stephen as well, holding to him tightly, reluctant to let go. "We'll see you in the morning, then."

Garret shook Stephen's hand firmly, saying, "It's been more of a pleasure to meet you than I could ever say." He glanced toward Ritcherd and Kyrah then back to Stephen, "These children of yours are two of the finest people I have ever known. Now I can see why."

Stephen looked dubious, but too emotional to speak. In a broken voice he finally said, "The pleasure is all mine, Garret. I look forward to getting to know you better, as well."

Kyrah left with Stephen to walk him to his room. Garret turned to Ritcherd and chuckled. "Amazing."

"I still can't believe it," Ritcherd said. "It's a good thing Peter Westman is dead, or I'd . . . ooh, what I wouldn't like to do to that man." He took a sustaining breath. "As it is, I think I'll just write him another letter."

Garret chuckled. "Good idea. I think I might write him one myself."

Ritcherd put a hand on Garret's shoulder. "Are you sure you're all right with going to London for Sarah?"

"Absolutely," Garret said. "You and Kyrah need some time with Stephen, I think."

"Yes, I admit that would be a good thing. And I appreciate your insight on how to handle the situation with her. We can tell her about Stephen once she's home. However . . ."

"What?" Garret pressed when he hesitated.

"I would really appreciate it if you would catch her up on what's happened to *me* since she left." Ritcherd sighed. "She's as good as my mother, and she needs to know, but I don't want to be the one to tell her. I know that you'll know how to tell her what's important."

"I can do that," Garret said.

"I know you can, but will you?" Ritcherd asked.

"Of course. I love Sarah almost as much as I love Kyrah."

"Well, they're both taken," Ritcherd said, and Garret laughed.

"I think she'll be glad to hear that," Garret said.

"What?"

"That she's taken."

"Yes," Ritcherd laughed, "I'm sure she will."

Kyrah hesitated at the door of her father's room, almost afraid to let him out of her sight, as if he might disappear into a dream. He took her hands into his and kissed them each in turn. He paused over her left hand and took a good, long look at her wedding ring. He met her eyes and she realized what he was thinking even before he said, "That's your mother's wedding ring."

"It is," she said. "She told me that . . . she couldn't bear to wear it after you'd . . . died. She gave it to Ritcherd the day we announced our engagement. But . . . she should have it back now and—"

"No," he said with a tender smile. "I'd say it's appropriate that you have it. Very sweet, in truth. If your mother wants anything to do with me, then . . . we will make a new start, and I will buy her a new ring."

Kyrah felt concerned over his obvious doubts about his relationship with his wife. She wondered how she could ever explain the undying love that Sarah felt for her husband, even believing all these years that he'd been dead. She felt certain that once her mother recovered from the shock, her joy at having Stephen back would be beyond all imagination. Rather than trying to convince her father of that now, she simply said, "You'll be seeing her soon enough, and then you'll know that all will be well."

He smiled. "I do hope so."

They talked for a few more minutes, then she kissed him good night and went to her own room to find Ritcherd sitting on the edge of the bed, pulling off his boots. She closed the door and leaned against it. "Never in a million years," she said, "would I have imagined such a day as this."

"Amen," Ritcherd muttered.

They prepared for bed as usual, but neither of them could sleep. They lay close together in the darkness, holding hands, talking about the incredulous circumstances they'd been confronted with this day. The conversation finally ran down and they both slept, but Kyrah woke from a strange dream that provoked deep emotion in her. She was surprised at the torrent of grief that rushed out of her, and she pressed her face into the pillow, not wanting to wake Ritcherd.

Ritcherd came awake to a strange sound. It took him a minute to orient himself in the darkness of their room, then he realized Kyrah was crying. Her obvious attempts to muffle the noise with her pillow failed miserably.

"Kyrah, what is it?" he asked, wrapping his arms around her.

She turned abruptly toward him, murmuring through her tears. "I tried not to wake you."

"It's all right," he said, holding her close. "Tell me what's wrong."

"All these years," she cried, "he was alive, and . . . suffering. I found some measure of peace in believing that at least *he* was at peace, in spite of the way I'd believed he'd died. Now. . . to think of him alone and . . . cold and hungry and . . . believing that we had . . . abandoned him there. Oh, Ritcherd, I can't bear it. I can't even think about it without . . ." She became too emotional to speak.

Ritcherd just held her, whispering soothing words. He pressed a kiss into her hair and eased her closer. When her crying had quieted to an occasional sniffle, he said softly, "Are you going to be all right?"

"Eventually," she said. "I just . . . can't think about . . . what he's been through without . . ."

"And how do you think he feels about what *you've* been through, Kyrah?"

"But he had no control over what happened, and—"

"Exactly. And you had no control over what happened to him. It's horrible and ugly, Kyrah, and we all need to grieve for what's been lost. But we need to concentrate on the miracle." His voice lowered to a brilliant whisper. "He's alive, Kyrah. He's here. He's real. He's going to grow old right here in our midst. It's a miracle, Kyrah, and we are going to enjoy every minute of it."

Kyrah felt laughter rush through her tears. "Oh, you're right," she said. "I only wish that—"

Ritcherd put a finger over her lips. "No wishing," he said. "We can talk about what's happened, and we can cry over it if we must, but we will not wish for the past to be any different than it was. It's been difficult; some of it was hell. But we're here, we're together, we're happy. And think of all we *wouldn't* have gained had it not worked out the way it did."

Kyrah took a deep breath, inhaling Ritcherd's words, feeling them soothe her spirit. "You almost sounded like Garret."

Ritcherd chuckled softly. "You mean . . . Garret. Wise, sensitive, at peace with himself. *That* Garret?"

"That's who I mean," she said, pressing a hand to his face.

"Then I'll take that as the highest compliment," Ritcherd said. "I must admit that I've come far—thanks to Garret."

"He's a good man," she said, "but he's not you. You are the most incredible man I have ever known, Ritcherd Buchanan. I love you, and I love the way you love my father."

"That's not hard," Ritcherd said. "It's almost as easy to love him as it is to love you." He kissed her warmly. "You are the most beautiful and amazing woman in the world, Lady Buckley." She laughed softly and he added, "Now, as I was saying . . . we have to be grateful for all we've gained. Bear in mind that Garret would not be a part of our lives if you had not been deported."

"That's true," Kyrah said. "And I am grateful. I only wish that—"

Ritcherd stopped her by pressing his lips over hers. "There is nothing to wish for, Kyrah," he whispered. "The past is behind us. The present is perfect. And the future is something we will take on together." He chuckled. "We'll have a house full of children, with your parents here to help keep them safe and happy."

"What a delightful thought," she said and kissed him. Before their kiss ended, he eased her completely into his arms.

"Now," he said and kissed her again, "I've got some lost time to be making up for."

"So you do," she said and felt his kiss turn warm and passionate.

He eased back and said lightly, "You're not thinking about Garret, are you?"

"Garret who?" she asked. Ritcherd chuckled and kissed her again.

Ritcherd and Kyrah entered the dining room for breakfast, holding hands. Stephen was already there, standing close to the fire. He smiled when he saw them. Kyrah rushed toward him, taking him tightly into her arms. "Oh, you are real!" she said, looking into his eyes.

"I was thinking the same about you," he said, laughing softly.

Garret arrived a moment later. They were all seated except for Stephen, who lingered near the fire until the maid came in to serve the meal.

"How did you sleep?" Ritcherd asked.

"Very well," Stephen said. "Best night's sleep I've had in years."

Conversation at the table remained light. When Garret rose and announced he was leaving for London and would be bringing Sarah back with him, Stephen looked visibly nervous.

"Go safely," Kyrah said, taking both of Garret's hands and pressing a kiss to his cheek.

"Of course," he said, pressing a lingering kiss to her brow.

On the other side of the room, Stephen whispered to Ritcherd, "Kyrah and your brother are apparently very close."

Ritcherd chuckled. "Yes, they certainly are."

Stephen turned to him. "Is that a problem?"

"Not anymore, it's not," Ritcherd said.

"Am I being too nosy?" Stephen asked.

"No, you're family. We don't have any secrets in this house." He looked at Garret and Kyrah. "We're all well aware that Garret is deeply in love with your daughter."

Stephen looked astonished. "You mentioned that yesterday, but I thought you were joking."

"Oh, we treat it as a joke, which makes it easier for all of us to keep the matter open and light. The truth is that Garret struggles with his feelings a great deal."

"And Kyrah?"

Ritcherd smiled and blew out a long breath. He realized how far he'd come in a short time when he was able to answer with no difficult feelings whatsoever. "Kyrah's love for me is strong and true—as mine is for her. As long as I remain as devoted to Kyrah as she deserves, I have nothing to worry about. Garret is one of the most decent, honest men I have ever known. He would never do anything to hurt Kyrah—or me, unless of course I deserved it. He has given me a fat lip more than once, but I most definitely deserved it."

Stephen chuckled. "Sounds like he's been good for you."

"Well, you weren't here to keep me in line," Ritcherd said lightly. "Somebody had to do it."

Ritcherd glanced at Garret to see him kissing Kyrah's brow once more. "All right," he said loudly with mock anger, "that ought to be good. You're only going to be gone a couple of days."

Garret laughed and tossed a mischievous glance toward Ritcherd. "Her heart belongs to you, Buckley," he said. "She's just humoring me."

"Yes, I know," Ritcherd said. "So leave, and get it over with. We'll be expecting you tomorrow before supper."

"And we will be here," Garret said and left the room.

"So, now what?" Stephen asked.

"There's nothing pressing," Kyrah said. "I have some Christmas preparations to see to, but the two of you could do whatever you like."

"Christmas?" Stephen echoed.

Kyrah laughed softly. "Surely you've noticed the decor in the house and . . ."

He looked around. "I hadn't thought about it. When is Christmas, exactly?"

"The day after tomorrow is Christmas Eve," Ritcherd said.

Stephen took a deep breath. "I haven't had Christmas for . . . years."

Kyrah forced a smile but couldn't hold back her tears. "Then this Christmas will be especially good for all of us."

Stephen hugged Kyrah tightly. "Yes, it will."

A minute later Stephen said, "I promised Cetty I would play with her this afternoon, but . . . I wonder, Ritcherd, if I could get you to help me with something this morning."

"Of course, anything," Ritcherd said. "What is it?"

"Well . . . first of all, I'd like to go see the old house. Let's start with that."

"All right," Ritcherd said with a little laugh, "let's start with that."

Chapter Seventeen

Exhuming the Past

*R*itcherd gave Stephen a good coat and a pair of gloves before they went out. In the stable Stephen asked if they could take the trap, since he wasn't certain he was up to riding. "Not a problem," Ritcherd said and harnessed the vehicle.

He grasped Stephen's arm to steady him while he stepped in. "Thank you, my boy," he said, sounding subtly embarrassed by his need for help.

Little was said as they made the short drive to the house where Stephen had lived before he'd made that fateful trip to London nearly eight years earlier. Ritcherd pulled the trap up in front of the house, and Stephen sighed loudly. "When I arrived the other night," he said, "it was dark and I didn't bother stopping. Of course, I assumed someone was living here. I assumed Westman would be living here. That thought alone has given me nightmares."

"Seeing him live here was difficult for all of us," Ritcherd said. "But he's been gone more than four years now. We're doing our best to put the past behind us."

"As we should," Stephen said.

"Shall we go inside?" Ritcherd asked. Stephen nodded hesitantly.

Ritcherd helped steady Stephen's descent from the trap, and they went together into the house. They reminisced some but said little as they walked from room to room. In the drawing room, Stephen pulled away the sheet covering a small sofa. He pressed his hands over the tapestry fabric, then sat there and crumbled in tears. Ritcherd sat beside him and put a hand on his shoulder, letting him cry for a good, long while.

Stephen finally calmed down and leaned back, shaking his head. "Forgive me," he said.

"It's fine," Ritcherd said. "I've learned that it's better to have a good cry than to hold all that emotion inside."

"I lost so much," he said, looking around. "He took everything from me."

"Not everything," Ritcherd said. "He's gone, and you're still standing. Your spirit is strong. Your heart is good, as it always was. He didn't take your integrity or your conviction. And he didn't take away the love you have for your family—or theirs for you."

Stephen smiled. "You've grown into a fine man, Ritcherd. I knew you would."

"Did you?" Ritcherd chuckled. "I had doubts, myself."

"Well, I'm grateful for you now . . . for saying what I need to hear."

"I'm only telling you what's true," Ritcherd said.

They went together into the yard and wandered idly, talking some and contemplating the memories in silence. They walked together to the cottage where Sarah and Kyrah had been living when Ritcherd returned from the war. Ritcherd knew that Sarah had lived there when Stephen had courted her, which had been his purpose for acquiring this estate to begin with. But he didn't seem nostalgic as he entered the walled garden and looked around. In a businesslike tone he asked, "Where exactly did you find the money?"

Ritcherd pointed to the biggest tree in the center of the garden. "Buried next to that tree, beneath the hearts you carved in your youth."

Stephen chuckled. "So I did."

He walked to the far corner of the garden and went to his knees, brushing dead leaves from around a small tree. Ritcherd was about to question him when he looked up and asked, "Is there a shovel around here somewhere?"

"I believe so," Ritcherd said, wondering if this meant what he thought it meant.

Ritcherd quickly found a shovel and returned to find Stephen sitting on the ground as if he were exhausted. "I assume you want me to dig a hole," Ritcherd said.

"You're a smart lad," Stephen said with a chuckle. "You can start right there." He pointed to a specific spot with conviction.

Ritcherd started to dig, and only removed a half-dozen shovelfuls of dirt before he hit something hard. "A rock?" Ritcherd asked.

"Not likely," Stephen said.

Within minutes Ritcherd had uncovered a small metal box. He knelt on the ground and lifted it out with his hands. Stephen let out a delighted laugh and knelt beside Ritcherd to open the box. Ritcherd gasped when the money appeared.

"There now," Stephen said. "As I told you, I'm capable of caring for myself, and of supporting my wife." He closed the box and handed it to Ritcherd. "It's yours."

"I don't need it," Ritcherd said.

"I know you don't need it. Consider it Kyrah's dowry, or some paltry attempt to pay back all you did for my wife and daughter while I was incapable of caring for them myself." Stephen stood up and took hold of the shovel. "Come along, son."

Ritcherd carried the box and followed Stephen out of the walled garden. "How much is there?" he asked.

"Somewhere between two and three thousand pounds, I believe," Stephen said.

"And it was here all along," Ritcherd said, struck by the irony of Kyrah and Sarah's poverty while he'd been fighting in the colonies.

"It was, yes," Stephen said. "If I had known I was going to prison, I could have told them where to find it. If they had let me write to my family, it could have solved many problems. Now I can at least pay you back for all you've done."

"You don't need to pay me anything," Ritcherd said. "This is your money, Stephen, and—"

"Ritcherd," Stephen stopped walking and turned abruptly, "this transaction is just between you and me." He put his hand on top of the box Ritcherd was holding. "Please take this and allow me to regain some measure of pride. I assure you that your taking it will not leave me destitute."

He turned and walked away. Ritcherd followed, not knowing what to say. It was true that he didn't remotely need the money, but he certainly understood a man's need to have his pride in providing for his family.

"So," Ritcherd finally said as they returned to the yard of the big house, "are you trying to tell me that you're actually rather well off?"

"No," he chuckled, "but I can certainly get by." He led the way to a little stone path in the overgrown garden and started trying to move some of the stones with the shovel.

"Here," Ritcherd said, setting the box aside and taking the shovel from him. "Enough pride for one day. Sit down before you fall over."

"Yes, sir," Stephen chuckled. "Move those four stones there, and dig."

"Yes, sir," Ritcherd mimicked him and did as he was told. While he was digging, Stephen said, "My profession may not have been admirable, but I was good at what I did, and I never cheated. I hope that counts for something when I do end up facing the good Lord."

"I'm certain it will," Ritcherd said.

"And," Stephen drawled, "I always made a point of putting away a percentage of everything I won, so that we would never be destitute."

"Very wise," Ritcherd said, and the shovel struck metal. "But you never trusted banks, I knew that much."

Half an hour later, while Ritcherd was opening the *third* box of money, he reverted to the accent he'd carefully learned to blend in with privateers at sea. The words rolled effortlessly off his tongue as he muttered, "Ye're no better than a bloomin' pirate, mate."

Stephen looked at him as if he'd turned green. "What did you say?"

"I said ye was no better than a—"

"I heard *what* you said, but . . ." Stephen hesitated, and Ritcherd could almost feel information coming together in his mind. Ritcherd just shrugged his shoulders. Stephen's face filled with enlightenment. "You *are* a turncoat!"

Ritcherd chuckled. "Yes, I am," he said proudly. "Guilty as charged. I bought a privateer vessel and helped smuggle goods to the colonists."

"But you did it to find Kyrah."

"Initially," Ritcherd said, "but it didn't take me long to see that what the colonists stood for was right and good, and I know beyond any doubt that God was behind their cause. What I did, He wanted me to do. Even after Kyrah and I were married, I spent a great deal of money funding their cause. I bought the goods and Garret delivered them."

"But you fought for His Majesty's army. You were nearly killed by those colonists . . . more than once."

"I'm well aware of that," Ritcherd said. "I did what I had to do at the time, but I didn't know then what I know now. Sometime I would very much like to share with you what I learned—and how I feel about it."

"And I'd very much like to hear it," Stephen said, "but we should be careful, don't you think? We can thank God that no one ever found out."

Ritcherd sighed as the dark cloud he'd been able to ignore descended over him. The excitement and emotion of Stephen's return had made it easy to forget the impending doom. He knew he'd get no better opportunity to tell Stephen what they were up against. "Actually . . ." he drawled, "someone does know about it . . . or so it seems. We honestly can't figure what proof they've found against us, but Garret and I have been investigated for treason. They told us we are being watched, and they're coming the day after Christmas to arrest us."

Stephen stared aghast for a full minute before he said, "You're serious."

"Quite serious."

"Are you telling me that I've come home just in time to lose you to a hangman?"

Ritcherd took a deep breath, noting the emotion in Stephen's eyes, the horror in his expression. "I certainly hope not," Ritcherd said. "We've held to the story that we're innocent, that it's a misunderstanding. This Mr. Thayer actually said he believes us, in spite of the evidence. In fact, he's offered us the opportunity to bribe our way out of the charges."

"Really?" Stephen said, his eyes narrowing.

"He said it's up to him to tell his superiors whether or not the evidence against us is valid, and he's willing to destroy the evidence.

He'll be here the day after Christmas at noon. He said it's either a hundred thousand pounds, or we'll be arrested."

Stephen's eyes narrowed further. "I don't like the sound of that."

"Neither do I," Ritcherd said.

"Do you have the money?"

"I do, and I'm willing to pay it. But Garret and I both feel . . . uneasy. I'm not so sure we can trust this guy. I fear that he'll take the money and still send us to the gallows."

"We'll just have to pray for a miracle," Stephen said, and Ritcherd smiled.

"That's what we've been doing," Ritcherd said.

"If God was with you in your actions, surely He will protect you now. You have a family to care for."

"Yes, I do," Ritcherd said, "and I've come too far to lose them now."

Stephen looked hard at Ritcherd, then chuckled and shook his head. "My son-in-law is a turncoat."

Ritcherd chuckled, then his accent kicked in again. "Don't be tellin' Mr. Thayer that, or 'e'll 'ave me neck at the end of a rope 'afore th' year's out."

Stephen laughed. Then he became distracted, suddenly seeming far away with his thoughts.

"Is something wrong?"

"Mr. Thayer, you say?"

"That's right."

"That name rings a bell, but I can't think where I've heard it. Of course, it could be a common enough name. I'm sure it will come to me if it's important."

"Of course," Ritcherd said. "Perhaps we should get home. Lunch should be ready soon. And I'd wager Cetty's watching out the window for her grandpapa to come home."

"What a delightful thought," Stephen said, and they got into the trap and headed back to the manor. They took all the money straight to a safe in Ritcherd's office, then they got cleaned up and met Kyrah in the dining room just as lunch was being served.

Kyrah was delighted to see them, and her eyes sparkled with curiosity when Ritcherd said in his sailor's drawl, "Yer father's a bloomin' pirate, missy."

"How is that, Captain Buckley?" she asked with laughter.

"'E's got a flair for buryin' treasure," Ritcherd added.

"I knew that," Kyrah said, smiling toward her father.

"Well," Ritcherd said in his normal voice, "I just got a healthy dowry that apparently goes along with my wife."

"Really?" Kyrah said with obvious delight.

"That makes me a rich man," Ritcherd said, winking at Kyrah.

"That dowry isn't likely to make much difference in your fortune," Stephen said.

"I wasn't talking about the dowry," Ritcherd said. "I was talking about the wife."

Kyrah laughed and blushed prettily. Ritcherd couldn't help thinking how good it was to see her so happy.

"However," Ritcherd added, "since I do have that dowry, I can afford to pay off Joe Thayer and still keep a wife."

Kyrah's countenance faltered. "Oh, don't even mention the name. I don't even want to think about Mr. Thayer. At least I can find some measure of peace in knowing that you *can* pay him off."

Ritcherd forced a smile. He didn't want to admit that something didn't feel right, and he wasn't sure that paying the man off would be enough to save their lives. He caught a subtle glance from Stephen that let him know their concerns were mutual. But Ritcherd changed the subject by asking Kyrah about her Christmas preparations, and they spent the meal talking about their plans for the holiday. Stephen seemed enchanted with the idea of spending Christmas with them, but every time Sarah's name came up, he looked decidedly nervous.

Stephen spent a couple of hours in the nursery with Cetty while Ritcherd helped Kyrah with a project. He slipped away to go upstairs and peek in the nursery, where he found the two of them getting along famously. On his way to find Kyrah again, she met him at the foot of the stairs.

"What's wrong?" he asked, noting her countenance.

"Nothing . . . really," she said. "I just feel . . . disoriented."

"Why is that?" he asked, taking her hand.

"The Christmas wreaths I ordered were just delivered," she said. "The ones we always take to the cemetery. I ordered an extra one for Celeste." Ritcherd felt momentarily taken aback, as he always did at the evidence that his sister was gone. Then Kyrah added, "But I really didn't need to. Now we have an extra." He lifted his brows in question and she clarified, "I think we could get my father something a little more practical for Christmas this year."

"Yes," Ritcherd said, "that would be a good idea." He put his arms around her. "We'll figure out something appropriate to do with his wreath."

He sighed and she asked, "What's wrong?"

"I miss her," he murmured.

"Yes, so do I."

"Do you think she's happy, Kyrah? Do you think she's all right?"

"Why wouldn't she be?" Kyrah asked with concern.

"I don't know. I just . . . worry about her. Does she understand how we love her and miss her? In her childlike perspective, could she possibly . . ." His voice broke and he swallowed carefully. "Never mind," he said. "There's no point asking questions that have no answers." He cleared his throat and forced a smile. "Why don't we take those wreaths to the cemetery right now? It's relatively pleasant out at the moment."

"I'd love to," she said.

"And why don't we take your father with us? I think he might find it a rather enlightening experience."

Kyrah took a deep breath. "Yes, I'm sure he would."

Ritcherd returned to the nursery to find Pearl helping Cetty into her coat so they could go to the gardens for some fresh air. Ritcherd said to Stephen, "Kyrah and I are going for a little ride. Would you like to come along?"

"I'd love to," Stephen said.

"Good," Ritcherd said. "There's something we think you should see."

Again Ritcherd harnessed the trap, and Kyrah laughed as she squeezed in between Ritcherd and her father. "How thoroughly delightful," she said as they set out.

"Indeed," Stephen said, and Ritcherd laughed.

Ritcherd halted the trap beside the cemetery, and they walked in silence to where Ritcherd's parents and Celeste were buried. Ritcherd reverently laid wreaths over his parents' headstones, then he stood solemnly over Celeste's while Kyrah held his hand tightly. "I still can't believe she's gone," he said.

"It will take time to adjust," Kyrah said gently.

"It's a beautiful stone," Stephen commented.

"Yes, it is," Kyrah agreed, brushing a gloved hand over Celeste's name and the angel carved above it. Across the top it read: *Our Darling Angel.*

"The angel was Ritcherd's idea," Kyrah said proudly. "It's perfect, really. She was as much of an angel as any human could possibly be in this world."

"Why is that?" Stephen asked, showing genuine interest.

They wandered idly through the cemetery while Ritcherd told Stephen about his sister. He talked of her condition and the reasons why she hadn't been around through the years of Ritcherd's youth during the time that he had known the Paynes. As Ritcherd spoke, he realized that it felt good to talk about her. He missed her, but he felt a little better. They stopped at a certain place while Ritcherd finished telling Stephen about his sister. He was so focused on Ritcherd that he didn't pay any attention to his surroundings until Ritcherd said, "We ordered a wreath for this grave, as well. Now, we're not sure what to do with it."

Stephen glanced down abruptly and took a sharp breath. There it read:

Beloved Husband and Father
Stephen Payne
1734–1777

"You all right?" Ritcherd asked.

"I'm not sure," Stephen said. "I don't think I like the way this feels."

"Well, I sure didn't like the way it felt the first time I saw it," Ritcherd said.

"Mother wanted a nicer marker," Kyrah said, "but it was all we could afford."

"It would have been a shame," Stephen observed, "to spend any more money on something so . . ."

"Temporary," Ritcherd provided. "In your case, at least."

"And fairly useless, in anyone's case," Stephen said.

"Well, the gravestone is not for the one who's dead," Kyrah said. "It's for us poor souls left behind to have some tangible connection." She put her arms around her father and hugged him tightly. "I'm just grateful to have you back."

"Amen to that," Stephen said. He contemplated the stone, then added, "Maybe we should find out who is *really* buried here, and have a stone made with *his* name on it. Since I spent seven years in prison, apparently with his identity, I think we have a certain bond." His voice softened. "Seeing him die has haunted me for years."

Kyrah said with a sour voice, "I've been haunted for years by imagining your dying that way."

"Well, now you don't have to think about it anymore," Ritcherd said. "Come on. Let's go home. Tomorrow is Christmas Eve. We've got work to do."

"Like what?" Stephen asked with the excitement of a child.

"I don't know," Ritcherd chuckled, "but I'm certain we can find something that needs doing."

"I'm certain we can," Kyrah said and laid the wreath over the grave before leaving, her father's hand in hers.

Back at the manor, they found Cetty in the kitchen with Mrs. Hawke, engaged in some baking project. Kyrah pitched in to help, and Ritcherd eagerly joined them, teasing Mrs. Hawke while he attempted to keep Cetty's efforts from creating havoc. Stephen sat near the work-table observing, and occasionally laughing for no apparent reason.

After supper, Kyrah met with Mrs. Hawke and the head house-keeper to discuss final Christmas preparations while Ritcherd and Stephen sprawled on the nursery floor to build block castles then knock them down with imaginary cannons. Cetty supervised the battle with great expertise and kept the men laughing.

Once Cetty was put to bed, Stephen and Ritcherd went to the library to visit. They were barely seated when Stephen said, "There's something I need to ask you."

"Anything," Ritcherd said.

"I've had some time to digest everything I've been told about the years I missed. There are several holes in the story of your ongoing struggle with Westman. I'm sure it will take time to fill them all in. I'm disturbed most by his apparent need to have some kind of warped control over my daughter in my absence."

Ritcherd stood and absently perused the bookshelves. "Yes, he certainly did."

"Do you think it was the money? Or was there more?"

Ritcherd sighed. "How does one begin to understand such a distorted mind? From what I could add up, money spoke very loudly to Westman. But there was more. I offered him a significant bribe on more than one occasion if he would just give Kyrah the divorce and get out of our lives. He didn't take it, so obviously it was more than money. The day he was killed, he said some things that made me believe he had some distorted hatred toward the aristocracy."

"But Kyrah's not an aristocrat."

Ritcherd turned to face Stephen. "She is now—technically, at least. She is Lady Buckley. But I believe that it was me Peter hated. He wanted Kyrah so that I couldn't have her. He actually said something to the effect that men like me always got what they wanted, and he felt sure I would miss Kyrah more than any amount of money. He was right about that."

Ritcherd turned his attention back to the bookshelves. "Kyrah grew a great deal through those experiences. You would have been proud of her. She learned how to stand up to him." He chuckled. "She learned how to stand up to me, too. She's very good at putting me in my place when I need it."

"As any good woman would do."

"Indeed."

Ritcherd chuckled again. "I was especially proud of her the day she stuck a paring knife in Peter's shoulder."

"Did she now?" Stephen said. "Well, I would have liked to see that."

"It's incredible that she could stop with that. There were times when it took everything inside of me to not kill him with my bare hands. When I think what he did to her . . . the pain he caused her . . ."

Ritcherd's voice drifted into a silence that was broken when Stephen said, "Which brings me to something else that's disturbed me."

"What's that?"

"How exactly did he hurt her?"

Ritcherd turned abruptly, feeling startled. Stephen's expression made it clear he expected an answer. "When Kyrah told me she'd married him, she said something about it not taking long for him to do his damage." Stephen cleared his throat tensely. "What damage did he do, Ritcherd?" Ritcherd hesitated and he pressed, "I need to know."

"It's in the past and Westman is dead," Ritcherd said, again turning his back to Stephen to pretend to be looking for a particular book.

"I need to know, Ritcherd," he repeated.

"You probably do," Ritcherd said, turning toward Stephen, "but I really don't want to be the one to tell you."

"Who else should I ask? Kyrah?"

"No!" Ritcherd insisted so firmly that Stephen looked startled. In a softer voice he added, "There's no need for her to ever talk about it again."

"Talk about what?" Stephen asked.

Ritcherd sat down and crossed an ankle over his knee. He idly rubbed the leather of his boot while he tried to come up with a delicate way to say it. Then he realized there wasn't one. He sighed and began, "I initially learned what had happened from a good woman named Daisy who befriended Kyrah while she was living in Virginia. Daisy told me she'd been aware that the man she'd seen coming and going from this particular house would be bringing home a bride. She noticed him come home with a woman, and she noticed the screaming that came from the house afterward."

"You mean they were arguing?"

"That's what I thought when she said it. But . . . no. Days later, Daisy finally went to the door and met Kyrah for the first time. She said Kyrah's face was dark purple with bruises." Stephen groaned and squeezed his eyes closed. "She said that for weeks Kyrah had trouble walking, sitting, lifting a fork to eat." Ritcherd made a disgusted noise. "He beat her nearly to death, Stephen. He was apparently angry because she was pregnant with my baby. The irony is that he told her he wouldn't be sharing a bed with her until she was no longer pregnant. So, the baby saved her in that regard."

"I'm grateful he's dead," Stephen snarled, "or I'd . . . I'd . . ."

"You don't have to say it," Ritcherd said. "I know exactly how you feel. The most difficult aspect of all this for me is the fact that if Kyrah hadn't been pregnant, she wouldn't have felt desperate to marry the fiend and give her baby a name. While I am eternally grateful for Cetty's existence, I had a difficult time coming to terms with the horrendous price we paid for that one mistake—an indiscretion that was clearly my fault."

"Have you come to terms with it?" Stephen asked.

"I have," Ritcherd said easily.

"Then there's hope for me?" Stephen's eyes hardened. "Is it possible for me to find peace with the fact that I made choices that left my wife and daughter in such unspeakable circumstances?"

"They are very forgiving women—I can testify to that. Truthfully, Stephen, there have been times when I have not treated Kyrah very well. There have been moments when my behavior was atrocious. I had a great deal of anger inside of me that I didn't understand. I often felt unworthy of her but responded badly to those feelings. I worked very hard to come to terms with such feelings, and she has forgiven me."

"She's a good woman, much like her mother."

"Yes, she is," Ritcherd said.

"So . . . how did you come to terms with it?"

"That's a long story," Ritcherd said.

"Is there somewhere else you need to be?"

"No," Ritcherd said, "but . . . you might find it tedious to hear how thoroughly maudlin your son-in-law really is."

"Try me," Stephen said.

Ritcherd settled more deeply into the sofa and told Stephen of the depression that had followed his sister's death, and the strain it had put between him and Kyrah. He told him how his belief that Kyrah and Garret had been intimate had snapped him back to his senses, and how Garret had helped him work through his anger and false perceptions. Stephen asked some questions and seemed intrigued with the purging process Ritcherd had gone through. But Ritcherd was left completely speechless when Stephen said, "Is it possible that some of these difficult feelings you have stem from your being kidnapped as a child?"

For a long minute Ritcherd tried to imagine how he might be feeling right now if he'd not uncovered those suppressed memories before now, if he'd not read about the incident in newspapers. He honestly couldn't fathom how he would have responded. He could only be grateful that he *did* know about it, and that he'd worked through the memories. He was grateful to realize how sane he felt, and how validating it was to hear one more piece of evidence that the experience of his youth had indeed happened.

Ritcherd was finally startled to the moment when Stephen said, "Are you all right?"

"Yes, of course," Ritcherd said. "I just . . ." He narrowed his eyes on Stephen. "You knew?"

"Knew what?"

"That I'd been kidnapped?"

"Of course I knew. Everyone knew."

"How . . . did you know? You didn't even live in the area when it happened."

"No, but . . . we lived in London. Sarah noticed it in the papers. She'd grown up in the area; she knew of the Buchanans. She took a special interest in the story. I remember her praying daily for the safe return of a child who was a perfect stranger. The very first day you came to the house with Kyrah, Sarah whispered to me that you were the child who had survived that horrible kidnapping incident."

Ritcherd shook his head, stunned beyond words. "But . . . why . . ." he stammered, "why . . . did you never . . . say anything to me about it?"

"We figured if you wanted to talk about it, you would."

"Well, I couldn't talk about it," Ritcherd said, "because I didn't remember it—at all—until earlier this month." Ritcherd went on to explain how the memory had come back to him, and how he'd been convinced of his own insanity.

Their talk shifted to details of what had happened to Stephen after he'd played that fateful card game in London. The reality was still difficult to swallow, but Ritcherd felt it gradually beginning to settle in. Stephen was alive.

When the conversation ran down, Stephen said, "Well, we've lived a very colorful life, my boy."

"So we have," Ritcherd chuckled. "The amazing thing is that we've lived to tell about it."

"That *is* amazing," Stephen said.

The following morning, Stephen helped Ritcherd gather some pine boughs and holly that Kyrah wanted for her Christmas decor. Ritcherd noted that Stephen had already gained significant strength in the few days he'd been with them. His face had more color, and he was steadier on his feet.

When the gathering was done, Kyrah took a long walk in the gardens with her father while Ritcherd spent some time with Cetty. After lunch, with all their preparations underway, Stephen asked Ritcherd if he would mind taking him into town.

"You're not thinking of putting your money in the bank, are you?" Ritcherd teased.

"Of course not," Stephen said, "I was thinking I might spend some of it."

"Well, I've got some money to spend myself," Ritcherd said. "We'd better go do it before your wife comes back."

"Oh!" Stephen said and put both hands over his middle. "When will she be here?"

"Around five, I believe, if the carriage makes adequate time."

Stephen took a deep breath. "Then it would be well for me to buy her a Christmas gift, I think."

Ritcherd smiled. "What a delightful thought."

Their time in town together went well. They split up to do some shopping, and Ritcherd was able to get some gifts for Stephen that he and Kyrah had discussed. They went together to the pub and talked back and forth over a drink, while memories rushed over Ritcherd with a tangible quality. In the space of a heartbeat, years vanished. He'd been barely a man, less than twenty years old, and helplessly in love with little Kyrah Payne, a young lady just blossoming into womanhood. He'd been her brother and her friend for many years, but as time passed, the more he'd envisioned a future with her when she was all grown up. And through those years, Stephen and Sarah had taken him in as their own. While he'd found no love in his own home, they'd loved and nurtured him in a way that Ritcherd truly believed had saved his spirit from crumbling. But beyond that, Stephen had befriended Ritcherd. They'd spent many hours together talking and laughing. They'd gone hunting together and had shared many outings. Stopping at the pub to share a drink had become common once Ritcherd was old enough. And now here they were, all these years later, talking in a way that made all they'd gone through seem nonexistent and irrelevant. The roads they'd traveled had been littered with horror and pain, but they had survived, and they were family still. Ritcherd had found the future he'd always dreamed of with Kyrah, and now there was an added joy to know that Stephen and Sarah would be at the heart of it, as he'd always believed they should have been. They'd come far. And he was grateful.

Chapter Eighteen

Reunited

*D*uring the carriage ride from town, Ritcherd watched Stephen become visibly anxious.

"What's wrong with you?" Ritcherd asked, startling him.

"What if she . . ."

"What if she what?" Ritcherd pressed when he didn't finish.

"What if she . . . wants nothing to do with me?"

"That's the most ridiculous thing I've ever heard," Ritcherd chuckled. "She loves you beyond comprehension."

"I can't imagine her loving me at all," Stephen admitted.

"Now, why would you even think such a thing?"

"When I lost the estate in that game, I was scared to death to come home and tell her. Well, I'm still scared to death."

"When I came home from the war, she told me if you'd only come home, she would have told you that it didn't matter. She told me it was you she needed, you she loved."

Stephen inhaled Ritcherd's words, but still he said, "My choices have caused her a great deal of grief."

"You were a victim, Stephen, just like the rest of us."

"In many ways, yes, but my choices still started this mess, and I wouldn't blame her if she couldn't forgive me."

"Of course she'll forgive you."

"All right, so let's say she forgives me. I've been dead to her for nearly eight years. Perhaps she would prefer that I stay that way."

Ritcherd chuckled. "Why don't you just relax. If she tells you to go away, we'll deal with it later."

"Oh, that's comforting," Stephen said with sarcasm, and Ritcherd chuckled again.

A minute later, Stephen asked in a tender voice, "Has she changed, Ritcherd?"

"That's difficult for me to answer when I've been with her every day for years. When I came home from the colonies, she'd changed. She looked much more than three years older. She was weak and tired. It was as if losing you had drained the life right out of her. But gradually she became more like herself. She became vibrant and healthy again. I've heard people ask Kyrah if Sarah was her sister. Kyrah usually tells them that she is."

Stephen chuckled, then turned nostalgic eyes toward the window—while he wrung his hands nervously.

At home, Kyrah met them when they came through the side door.

"She hasn't come yet, has she?" Stephen questioned, a tremor in his voice.

"No, of course not," she said. "They're not due for an hour or so."

Kyrah questioned her father about his nerves. He told her the same things he'd told Ritcherd—and she told him the same things Ritcherd had told him. But he paced the floor and muttered his concerns over and over. Ritcherd and Kyrah just listened, glancing at the clock frequently, hoping the carriage would make good time and they could get this over with.

When the time drew near, Kyrah suggested they wait in the upstairs hall where Sarah wouldn't see Stephen until Ritcherd had had a chance to talk to her. The sound of a carriage coming up the long drive incited an audible moan from Stephen.

"Calm down," Ritcherd said. "She loves you."

Stephen nodded but said nothing.

Kyrah said to Ritcherd, "You take her to the drawing room, and then we'll wait in the library."

Ritcherd nodded and hurried down the stairs to meet her. Kyrah guided her father to the window where they could see the drive below through the sheer draperies. They watched the carriage come to a halt below the window. Garret stepped down, then turned and held up his hand to help Sarah. Kyrah heard her father take a sharp breath when Sarah stepped from the carriage, but she was wearing a cloak and bonnet and it was impossible to see her face.

"It will be all right," Kyrah said and embraced her father. She could feel him trembling and held to him for several minutes, until she knew that her mother would be in the drawing room with Ritcherd. Then she urged her father down the stairs and to the library where they could wait comfortably for the reunion to take place.

Ritcherd was waiting in the entry hall when Garret and Sarah came through the door. Garret laughed as Sarah flew into Ritcherd's arms and he twirled around with her, lifting her feet off the ground.

"Oh, you're more beautiful than ever," Ritcherd said, setting her down.

"That's what I told her," Garret said.

"You're both a couple of flattering scoundrels," she said, handing her cloak and bonnet to a maid who hurried away.

"We are both virtually honest men," Garret said firmly, making Sarah laugh.

"Where is Kyrah?" Garret asked in a careful voice that let Ritcherd know he was really wondering where Kyrah and *Stephen* were.

"Upstairs hall," Ritcherd said quietly.

Garret slipped away and ran up the stairs. Sarah took Ritcherd's face into her hands. "I was hoping for a moment alone with you," she said. "Garret told me everything. I'm so sorry for what you've been through, my dear."

"Your concern is appreciated, Mother," he said, "but as you can see, I'm doing well."

"I knew about the kidnapping," she said. If Ritcherd hadn't heard this already from Stephen, he would have been surprised. As it was, he simply let her tell him. "We were living in London, and it was in the papers. I had known of the Buchanans in my youth. I prayed for you, Ritcherd, and I remember feeling such relief when the papers reported that you'd been returned safely home. The day I met you, I knew you were the one, but we didn't feel it was important to talk about—unless you wanted to. Now I realize that you didn't even remember the incident."

"Incredible, isn't it," Ritcherd said.

"And you're really all right?"

"I really am," he said. "In fact, I think I'm better than I've ever been—in spite of losing Celeste."

"Oh," she said tenderly, "sweet Celeste. I wish I could have been here."

"I wish you could have been, too—but maybe it's better that you weren't." She seemed to expect an explanation, but he simply said, "We can talk about it more later. We should—"

"Is Cetty upstairs with Kyrah?" she asked. "I just can't wait to—"

"Sarah," Ritcherd said, taking her arm, "I was hoping to talk to you alone first. Would that be all right?"

"Of course," she said, seeming concerned.

Ritcherd motioned toward the drawing room and followed her in, closing the door behind them. After they were both seated, Sarah asked, "Is something wrong? Is everyone all right?"

"Everyone is fine," he said. "Nothing is wrong . . . in a manner of speaking. But something has happened that's been rather shocking. We have learned that something has been wrong for many years, and it's finally being made right—but it's not easy to face."

"You're frightening me, Ritcherd."

"Forgive me, Sarah. There's nothing to be afraid of. I've been trying to plan how I would tell you this, but it's not coming very easily. Please be patient with me. We have learned that the games Peter Westman played with our lives were far worse than we'd ever imagined."

Sarah gasped and put a hand over her heart. It was evident that just hearing his name bristled her nerves. "I should have known it would have to do with him."

"Yes, and as you know, it was Stephen's association with Peter that started all of our problems." Her eyes widened but she said nothing. Ritcherd continued. "Sarah," he took her hand and leaned toward her, "we have learned something about what took place between Westman and Stephen."

"What?" she demanded, and Ritcherd could almost imagine her instincts responding to all of the little nagging doubts she'd felt through the years; all those little things that never quite made sense in light of Stephen's character.

Ritcherd took a deep breath. "Stephen did not commit suicide, Sarah."

Sarah gasped, then stared at him as if to be sure she'd heard him correctly. "I never believed he could have done it, but . . . how can you possibly know?" she demanded.

"I'll get to that in a minute. You see he actually—"

"Are you saying he was murdered?" she asked, and Ritcherd shook his head. Her eyes narrowed with confusion, her brow furrowed. "What *are* you saying, Ritcherd?"

Again he drew in a deep breath. "Sarah, you have to understand that when we come to believe something, we tend to piece everything around that belief, whether it's true or not. We've all believed for many years that Stephen lost that card game and shot himself in the head. It's difficult to accept any other possibility."

"Well, if he didn't shoot himself, and he wasn't murdered, then . . . what? What other possibility is there?"

"Only one," Ritcherd said. "It was a case of switched identity, Sarah. The casket was closed because the man in it was beyond recognition, but it was not Stephen Payne."

Sarah's grip tightened on Ritcherd's hand before her fingers began to tremble. "What are you saying?"

"Stephen is not dead, Sarah."

She stared at him, dazed and disbelieving. In a quavering voice she asked, "How can that be?"

"The simple version is this," he said. "Stephen played a card game and lost the estate, because Westman was cheating. Stephen went back to his hotel room and wrote you a note to apologize for what he'd done and let you know that there was money left so that you would have hope until he could finish up some business and return from London. With that note in his pocket, he thought about what had happened and became angry. He went to Westman's hotel room to confront him. He overheard three men arguing—including Westman—and learned a great deal about their illegal activities. The argument became fierce; Westman shot one of the other men in the head at close range. When Westman and his friend realized that Stephen had witnessed the crime and heard of their criminal doings, they knocked him out, put all of his personal papers on the body of the man they'd killed, and put him in Stephen's hotel room. This man's papers were put on Stephen. He woke up in prison, with a seven-year sentence."

"Prison?" Sarah gasped, and then she could hardly breathe. She cried and gasped for breath while Ritcherd just held her. When she gained control enough to speak, she asked gingerly, "Where is he now?"

"I'll get to that in a minute. There's something else you have to know . . . that he wanted me to tell you . . ."

"You've spoken to him?" she said through another rush of emotion.

"I have," Ritcherd said. Sarah clutched onto him tightly, as if doing so might bring her closer to Stephen.

"He didn't know until a few days ago that we had believed he was dead; he didn't know his identity had been switched. He believed that his hearing nothing from any of us was an indication that we wanted nothing to do with him because he'd lost the estate. He was afraid to come back. He's afraid now, as he was then, that you will be angry with him for the choices he made that caused you so much grief. But I told him what you once told me."

"What's that?" she asked, wiping at her ongoing tears.

"You told me if he'd only come home, you would have told him that you could make it through, that you didn't need the big house or the fancy things. You told me that you only needed *him,* and if he'd just come home, you could have convinced him that it was not so terribly serious."

"I did say that, didn't I," she said. "I said it over and over." She held more tightly to Ritcherd. "Oh, I can't believe it. I can't believe it." She cried again for several minutes with an emotion that was surely reminiscent of her initial belief that he was dead. Ritcherd just held her until she became silent, seeming too much in shock to even move. He wasn't surprised when she finally sat up straight and looked into his eyes. "Where is he now?"

Ritcherd sighed. "I believe he's in the library with Kyrah, likely pacing the floor, praying you will . . ."

Sarah flew off the sofa and out of the room. With the energy of a woman thirty years younger, she lifted her skirts and fled down the hall. "Stephen!" she shouted with the obvious intention of letting her voice penetrate every corner of the house. "Stephen, where are you?" she called.

Ritcherd moved into the hall just as Stephen appeared from the library, gripping the doorframe tightly. "I'm here," he said breathlessly.

Sarah hesitated and just looked at him, pressing her hands over her flushed cheeks, making an emotional noise. Kyrah appeared beside him just as Sarah hurried those last few steps and flung herself into her husband's arms, laughing and crying. He swung her around with more energy than he'd shown since his return. When he set her down, she touched his face, his hair, his face again, as if to convince herself that he was real. He did the same to her while tears coursed down his cheeks. And then he kissed her. Ritcherd smiled and met Kyrah's eyes to see her smiling too—and crying. Garret appeared and leaned in the doorway, smiling complacently. Ritcherd stood beside Kyrah and put his arm around her, pressing a kiss into her hair just as she murmured, "That is the most incredible thing I have ever seen in my life. It's a miracle."

"It is indeed," he said. "It's how I imagined they would greet each other in heaven when Sarah finally left here to be with him again."

Kyrah laughed softly. "This way, we get to be here to see it."

Ritcherd chuckled and tightened his embrace.

Stephen took both Sarah's hands and looked her up and down. "You're more beautiful than I could have possibly remembered," he said.

Sarah laughed through her ongoing tears and pressed her hands to Stephen's face. "You're alive. You're real. I can't believe it. It's a miracle."

"At least she didn't scream and pass out like Kyrah did," Garret said.

"She did have fair warning," Ritcherd added.

"Oh!" Sarah said and wrapped her arms around Stephen, holding him as if she would never let him go. "I love you, Stephen," she declared. "I love you so much!"

Stephen laughed through his own tears and returned her embrace. "And I love you, my darling." He looked into her eyes. "Can you ever forgive me for the grief I've caused you?"

"I forgave you a long time ago, my darling," she said. "Oh," she gasped again, "you must tell me everything—*everything!*"

As they all moved into the library to sit down, Ritcherd whispered to Stephen, "And you were nervous for what?"

"Watch your mouth, boy," Stephen said facetiously.

Stephen and Sarah sat close together on one of the sofas, holding tightly to each other while he answered Sarah's questions. She wept openly through the entire conversation, and occasionally tears came to his eyes, as well.

When supper was announced, they all moved to the dining room. Stephen and Sarah held hands and ate very little. They were more preoccupied with just staring at each other, obviously in awe of being together. Before dessert was served, Stephen rose from the table and helped Sarah with her chair. With his arm around her he said, "If you will excuse us, it's been a long day, and I think my wife and I have a great deal to talk about."

"Of course," Ritcherd said. Kyrah rose and kissed them each good night. They were nearly to the door when Ritcherd asked, only a bit facetiously, "Would you like breakfast brought to your room?"

"Yes, thank you," Stephen said quite seriously.

"We'll be in *my* room," Sarah added, and they left together.

"I still can't believe it," Kyrah said. "I have to keep pinching myself to be certain I'm not dreaming."

"I know what you mean," Ritcherd said. "But I felt the same way when I learned he was dead, or should I say, *believed* he was dead. At least this is a good dream."

"It is indeed," Kyrah said, and they exchanged a warm smile across the table.

The following morning, Stephen and Sarah didn't show up for breakfast. When Ritcherd mentioned their absence, Kyrah commented, "I'm certain they have a lot to talk about."

Garret chuckled, saying with light sarcasm, "Yes, I'll just bet they're talking. If I were Stephen, I wouldn't be talking." Kyrah glared at him, and he added, "Well, not *only* talking."

Kyrah smiled and glanced away. "You're embarrassing me, Garret."

"Forgive me," he said facetiously. "I should never discuss such things in the presence of a lady."

"You have before," Ritcherd said. "Why stop now?"

It took Kyrah a moment to realize what he meant, then she *did* feel embarrassed. She felt certain he was referring to the conversation he'd overheard when he'd believed that she and Garret had been intimately involved. Kyrah's embarrassment deepened when Ritcherd obviously picked up on her disconcertment. "It's all right, my dear. I was only teasing." She glanced up and found him smiling, but she was still relieved when he changed the subject.

While Ritcherd and Garret bantered lightly about trivial things, Kyrah took a good long look at these two men she loved so dearly and felt a little sick to think of the pending treason charges. The excitement of her father's return had relegated the issue to the back of her mind. When it had come to her thoughts, she'd pushed it away, not wanting anything to mar her happiness at being with her father and seeing her parents reunited. But now her parents were happily enjoying each other's company, and in little more than forty-eight hours, Mr. Thayer would be returning with an ultimatum. She honestly didn't know what Ritcherd and Garret had decided to do. She'd heard nothing about it except when Ritcherd lightly mentioned that he could afford to pay Mr. Thayer off. Beyond that, neither of them had said a word to her since Mr. Thayer had proposed his willingness to accept a bribe. Now she almost brought it up, but they were laughing and enjoying each other's company, and she didn't want to mar the mood. Still, her heart felt heavy. Time was running out. She felt certain they would give this man the money he wanted. But would that truly be the end of it?

As soon as breakfast was over, Ritcherd and Kyrah took Cetty with them in the carriage to deliver gifts and Christmas offerings throughout the community. The day was especially cold, but the sky was bright and clear. Once the deliveries were made, Cetty begged to go to the church ruins.

"It's awfully cold," Kyrah said.

"Just for a short while," Cetty pleaded. "I've not been there in such a long time. Please, Mama. Please . . ."

"Oh, all right," Kyrah said, and Ritcherd smirked at her.

The carriage stopped by the side of the road, and Ritcherd helped his wife and daughter step down. Kyrah made certain Cetty was bundled up as much as possible in her hat, coat, and gloves before she let her run toward the ancient structure. Ritcherd and Kyrah walked more slowly, arm in arm. They were mostly silent until they arrived at the church, where Cetty was exploring what was left of a series of stone archways. While Kyrah felt hesitant to say anything, Mr. Thayer's impending visit had been weighing on her. If she didn't talk about it, she would never be able to relax and enjoy the holiday.

"Forgive me," she said. "I don't want to dampen the mood, but . . . you never told me what you'd decided to do about Mr. Thayer."

Ritcherd looked so disarmed from the comment that her fear deepened for reasons she didn't understand. He chuckled, albeit tensely, and glanced away. "Forgive me," he said. "With all the excitement, it slipped my mind. We got the money out of the bank. We're prepared to pay him off."

Kyrah breathed deeply. "Then everything will be all right."

"Of course it will," he said, but he didn't look at her when he said it, and there was something guarded in the tone of his voice that led her to believe he wasn't being completely honest.

For a long moment she debated whether or not to confront him. A part of her preferred ignorance, but the reality was that she could irrevocably lose Ritcherd—and Garret—in another two days.

"Ritcherd," she said, and he looked at her. There was no denying the fear in his eyes. In a trembling voice she asked, "Now, why don't I believe you?"

"I don't know, why?" he asked coolly.

"Because I know you better than anyone, and I know you wouldn't lie to me, but you're keeping something from me. I can feel it."

Ritcherd sighed loudly and looked to where Cetty was running between the few remaining stone pews. "I'm trying very hard to have faith and believe in miracles, Kyrah. I've certainly been blessed with miracles in my life—more than my fair share, perhaps. I can only tell you that neither I nor Garret feels wholly comfortable with the situation. We don't trust him. But what can we do? I've been praying night and day that we *will* know what to do, that our lives will be spared, and the matter can be dropped for good. In the meantime, I am doing my best to enjoy this time with my family, and I'm counting on being here *next* Christmas."

He put his arms around Kyrah and held her tightly, while she willed her own fears away. *Faith,* she reminded herself. They just had to believe in miracles. *They had to!*

Cetty soon became cold and asked to go back. They returned to the manor just in time for lunch, and found Garret, Stephen, and Sarah all waiting in the dining room. Kyrah couldn't help but notice how her parents were beaming with happiness, and their love for each other was evident in their eyes. Garret mentioned that George and Patrick would likely be arriving before supper, which steered the conversation to telling Stephen the significant part these two men had played in Ritcherd and Kyrah's lives during his absence.

When lunch was finished, Stephen and Sarah excused themselves for a walk in the garden. "And then I'll probably take a nap," Sarah said. "We didn't get much sleep." She smiled at her husband and added, "We had a lot to talk about."

Kyrah caught a subtle smirk passing between Ritcherd and Garret just before Ritcherd said, "The two of you have a lot to catch up on."

"Yes, we do," Stephen said and ushered Sarah from the room.

Once they were gone, Garret's smirk deepened and Ritcherd said, "Not *only* talking."

They both laughed and Kyrah said, "You're just a couple of scoundrels."

"Guilty," they said at the same time and laughed again. Kyrah soaked in their laughter, praying it would forever be a part of her life.

She stood from the table, saying, "I promised Cetty she could help decorate the mantel in the drawing room right after lunch. I hope the two of you will join us."

"I wouldn't miss it for the world," Garret said, coming to his feet.

"Oh," Ritcherd said, walking beside him as they left the room, "but you *have* missed it for the world, and you will miss it again. Next year at this time you will be sailing the world, and it just won't be the same."

"My heart will always be here for Christmas," Garret said.

"If you would find a woman and settle down," Kyrah said, "we could always be together for Christmas—all of us."

"I'll keep working on that," Garret said.

Kyrah appreciated their easy talk of the future, and she prayed that their hopes were not fruitless.

A short while later, they were gathered in the drawing room. Garret and Ritcherd took turns tickling Cetty and making her giggle while Kyrah carefully arranged pine boughs and holly over the mantel. Quite accidentally, it had become her favorite aspect of the Christmas decor. Her first Christmas at Buckley Manor, she had become fairly obsessed with warming the huge, beautiful home with holly and evergreen branches, according to tradition. While she'd been arranging the greenery, intermixed with red berries, on the drawing room mantel, Ritcherd had come into the room and presented her with a gift. It had been a little porcelain replica of the baby Jesus in a manger, and there were separate pieces of Mary and Joseph. Kyrah had set them in the middle of the greenery on the mantel, along with some white candles. Before she was finished, a package was delivered from Garret. The note inside had simply said, "Just a little something that reminded me of my family, to let you know my heart is with you for Christmas." The package had contained a little golden bird that was obviously meant to be hung on the wall, but Kyrah had set it among the greenery instead. And the tradition had begun.

"It's all done except for what's in the box," Kyrah announced, carefully setting the candles in place around the nativity pieces.

"Can I help?" Cetty asked, wiggling out of Ritcherd's arms.

"Of course you can," Kyrah said and sat down, holding a little box on her lap. "Here are the Christmas keepsakes that Uncle Garret has sent to us. One each year since—"

"Oh, that reminds me . . ." Garret said and hurried from the room.

Cetty put her attention to the little box as Kyrah removed the lid. There, carefully laid in a bed of tissue, were four unique and beautiful ornaments. Kyrah lifted the first, saying, "This is the one he sent the first Christmas after you were born. Do you know what it is?"

"It looks like a bird," she said, carefully touching the gold filigree.

"Yes, it does. I told you how I love birds, especially sea birds."

"And you named me after a bird," Cetty said proudly.

"That's right," Kyrah said. "Your real name is Avocet."

"I like Cetty better," she said, wrinkling her nose.

Ritcherd chuckled. "I do, too."

Ritcherd lifted Cetty up so she could set the golden bird carefully into the greenery on the mantel. She let out a little laugh as he set her down, and she returned to the box just as Kyrah lifted out the second item. "This is my favorite," Kyrah said. Cetty gasped with pleasure to see the little ship carved from wood with little canvas sails. "It looks like the *Phoenix*," Kyrah said. "You sailed on the *Phoenix* when you were just a tiny baby."

Cetty grinned as she took the little ship from her mother and Ritcherd lifted her up so she could set it on the same side of the mantel as the bird, but some distance away. Garret entered the room just as Kyrah was reaching into the box for the third trinket he had sent. "Sorry," he said and sat down. "Go on."

Kyrah pulled out an intricately crocheted lace snowflake. It had edges that moved out in different directions, and was starched in order to hold its shape. "This one is very special," Kyrah said. "This was made by a very good friend of mine—and of Uncle Garret's. Her name is Daisy, and she lives in Virginia. She is the one who helped me when you were born. She took very good care of us. Garret went back to visit her whenever he went to Virginia, and—"

"Until she got married, that is," Garret interjected lightly.

Ritcherd chuckled. "You had your chance."

"She's very happy," Garret insisted.

Kyrah smiled and turned her attention back to Cetty. "Daisy gave this snowflake to Garret, and he sent it to us for Christmas."

"He sends us something for the mantel every year," Cetty said with enlightenment.

"Yes, he does," Kyrah said and smiled at Garret. "Although I think it's much nicer to have Garret here with us himself for Christmas."

"I agree with that," Garret said.

Garret lifted Cetty up this time to set the snowflake on the side of the mantel opposite the ship and the bird. As he set her down, he commented, "How lovely. I've never actually seen them on the mantel."

"They are lovely," Kyrah said, "especially since they all have meaning for us." Cetty returned to the box and Kyrah said, "There's one more." She lifted out a brass star. "This one he sent last year. The war was over, and Garret started sailing all over the world. This star was made in India."

"It's like the star that Father in Heaven sent to tell us Jesus was born," Cetty observed.

"That's exactly right," Ritcherd said with pride in his voice.

With Garret's help, Cetty put the star on the same side as the snowflake, making the decor symmetrical. Garret set her down, saying, "There's one more. I bought it last spring, but I didn't bother shipping it since I knew I would be here." He held a little package out for Cetty.

"I think I like having you deliver them personally," Ritcherd said. "You should make a habit of it."

Garret shrugged. "I do have to do enough world trade to make some money occasionally, or my vast Buchanan fortune could dwindle quickly."

Cetty pulled away the tissue and made a gleeful noise as she held up a little white angel, trimmed with gold. "It's an angel," Cetty declared brightly, "just like Aunt Celeste."

Ritcherd was suddenly overcome with emotion as just hearing her name brought home how very much he missed his sister. He reached for Kyrah's hand and squeezed it tightly while he attempted to get control of his tears before they fell.

"It's beautiful, Garret," Kyrah said, "and very appropriate, I'd say."

"I suppose it is," Garret said. "Funny that I bought it months before we lost her, but it does remind me of her."

"She was always an angel," Ritcherd said, his voice cracking only a little.

"But she's a real angel now," Cetty declared as Ritcherd lifted her up and she set the angel between the ship and the bird. While she was still in Ritcherd's arms, she added with conviction, "She told me she was an angel now, and she would watch over me while your heart was hurting."

Ritcherd gasped at the implication and hurried to sit down, feeling a little unsteady. Cetty slipped off his lap and stood beside him while he reminded himself that Cetty was a four-year-old child with a vivid imagination. He was attempting to brush the comment aside when Kyrah asked, "What did you say, darling?"

"Celeste told me she was an angel now. She said her name was like the word *celestial* and that means heavenly, and when I thought of her name, I would always know that angels are watching over me."

Ritcherd exchanged a glance with Kyrah, then Garret, wondering if they were feeling what he was feeling. Their expressions implied that they were, but still, Ritcherd tried to convince himself that *he* was letting his imagination run away with the whimsy of a child. Surely her governess had told her the meaning of the word *celestial*. Surely she had just merged the concept of angels with a childish fantasy. He almost had himself convinced when Cetty added, "She said to tell you that Mother and Father are fine and they're happy in paradise."

Ritcherd heard an emotional noise come from his mouth before he put his hand over it. *Paradise?* Any talk of life after death with Cetty had always been related to heaven.

Kyrah leaned forward and reached out a hand for Cetty. She stepped forward to take it and Kyrah asked gently, "What are you saying, Cetty? Are you saying that you saw Celeste and spoke with her . . . after she died?"

Cetty nodded firmly. Kyrah glanced at Ritcherd, then back to Cetty.

"When did this happen, Cetty?" Kyrah asked.

"When Papa's heart was hurting. I woke up in the night and I heard him crying, and I was afraid, and I said a prayer just like you told me to do if I was ever afraid. And Celeste sat with me until I went back to sleep. She was gone in the morning."

"Did she look the same?" Kyrah asked.

"Yes, but . . . different."

"Different how?" Garret asked when Kyrah suddenly became too emotional to speak.

Cetty turned toward him and said matter-of-factly, "When she lived with us, she was like a little girl in a grown-up body. That's what Papa told me. That's why she liked to play with me so much."

"But she looked different when you saw her?" Garret asked.

"She was like a grown-up lady. She didn't talk like a little girl. She talked like a grown-up lady."

"Good heavens," Kyrah muttered, tightening her grip on Ritcherd's hand. During a long moment of silence, Ritcherd digested the implication that Celeste's infirmity had not been carried with her into the next life. Kyrah said to Cetty, "Did she say anything else?"

"Just a secret for Papa," Cetty said and stepped toward him. With no hesitation, she took Ritcherd's face into her tiny hands and kissed him on the nose. "Angel kisses," she whispered, and Ritcherd sobbed as he pulled his little daughter into his arms, holding her close while a tangible peace filtered through his entire being. He knew beyond any doubt that there was no one living who knew the words Celeste would whisper to him when she kissed him on the nose that way. It had been a secret between them. *He couldn't believe it!*

Cetty drew back and wiped at his tears with her fingers. With concern on her little face, she asked, "Is your heart hurting again, Papa?"

"No, my darling Cetty, my heart has never been happier. Now I know that Celeste is happy and doing well, and everything is perfect."

Cetty smiled brightly and Ritcherd laughed, hugging her once more. *It was truly a miracle.*

Chapter Nineteen

The Swindler

Ritcherd, Kyrah, and Garret were barely seated in the dining room for supper when Liza came in, saying, "The doctor and Mr. Morley have just arrived."

"Thank you, Liza," Ritcherd said. "Show them in here."

Ritcherd and Garret came to their feet as Patrick and George entered the room. Kyrah watched the four of them exchange greetings like a pack of little boys. When their salutations were apparently finished, Patrick looked into Ritcherd's eyes and asked firmly, "How are you, my friend?"

"I'm very well, thank you," Ritcherd said.

George lightly slapped Ritcherd's shoulder. "Patrick told me you hadn't been feeling well, but he didn't tell me what was wrong."

"Nothing's wrong anymore," Ritcherd said. "Come. Sit down. You came just in time."

"You even had a place set for us," George said, moving toward the table.

"We were expecting you," Garret said.

George and Patrick both halted in the same moment when they saw Kyrah sitting there. "Well, look at you, Mrs. Buchanan," George said in his typical playful way. He took her hand and kissed it gallantly. "You're looking radiant, as always. Although it's been far too long since my eyes have feasted upon you."

"I've missed you too, George," Kyrah said brightly. "It's always good to see you."

George bent to kiss her cheek, then he moved aside for Patrick to greet her. "It *has* been too long," Patrick said, kissing her hand as well.

Kyrah laughed. "In your case, it's only been a few days," she said.

"Still too long," Patrick said, taking his seat.

"Stop flirting with my wife," Ritcherd said with mock anger.

"You let Garret flirt with your wife," George countered lightly.

"That's different," Garret said. "She's practically a sister to me."

Ritcherd chuckled. "If I actually believed you loved her like a sister, I could possibly trust you enough to sleep at night."

"You may not trust me," Garret said, "but you can trust Kyrah. She's got no interest in me when she's already got the best."

"That's true," Kyrah said, smiling at Ritcherd. He returned her smile and lifted his glass toward her, holding her eyes while he took a long sip of his wine.

After the first course was served and George had finished teasing the maids, he commented, "There are two empty places. Are we expecting someone else?"

"Kyrah's mother, of course," Patrick said. "I assume she's returned from London."

"She has," Ritcherd said.

"And is she well?" George asked.

"She is," Ritcherd repeated. "She should be here soon, and you can see for yourself."

"And the other place is for—" George was interrupted by Stephen and Sarah coming into the room. The men all came to their feet.

Ritcherd watched George closely as his eyes came to rest on Stephen. He could see George struggling to remember how he knew this familiar face, just as Stephen said, "Hello there, George."

"You know me?" George asked.

"I do," Stephen chuckled. "I recall several times in your youth when you followed Ritcherd into my kitchen."

George took a sharp breath, which provoked a giggle from everyone but Patrick, who was obviously baffled. "But you're . . ." George began but couldn't seem to finish.

"Not to worry, George," Ritcherd said. "You're not looking at a ghost. It really is Kyrah's father. Sit down and eat. It's a long story."

While George stood frozen and dazed, Sarah approached him and kissed his cheek. "It's good to see you, George," she said. She laughed softly when he didn't respond, then she approached Patrick and kissed his cheek, as well. "Hello, Patrick," she said. "It's good to see you."

"And you," he said, squeezing both her hands. "You're looking lovely as ever."

"You're too kind," she said, then she turned to Stephen, who was standing at her shoulder. "This is my husband, Stephen," she said, and Patrick shook his hand firmly while his eyes showed intrigue.

"It is an unspeakable pleasure," Patrick said.

"The pleasure is mine," Stephen said. "I've heard wonderful things about you."

Stephen helped Sarah with her chair, then lightly slapped George on the shoulder, startling him from the daze that still held him dumbfounded. "Sit down, George," Stephen said, "and I'll tell you all about it."

The conversation jumped around the table while George and Patrick were informed of all that had happened since Patrick had left the manor only days ago. Long after supper was over, they remained at the table, talking and laughing and marveling at the ironies of life. Cetty was brought to the dining room, where George and Patrick each teased her, then she took turns sitting on the laps of her uncle, her grandfather, and her father.

Kyrah observed her family and closest friends, feeling a profound sense of gratitude. The conversations faded briefly while she tallied all she had been through with these people, and how far they had come together. A burst of laughter brought her back to the moment. She joined in, even though she wasn't certain what they were laughing about. But she felt happy, and as long as she chose not to think about Mr. Thayer, she was almost perfectly happy.

Through the course of their Christmas festivities that evening and the following day, a deep impression of gratitude hovered with her. She thoroughly enjoyed having Garret sharing Christmas with them, and it was a thrill to see George and Patrick having such a good time when she knew that they had no strong family ties. The deepest thrill of all, however, was just seeing her parents together and the obvious love they felt for each other. Occasionally she would look at her father and simply wonder at the miracle. And often he would meet her eyes and smile, as if what they shared as father and daughter was as priceless to him as it was to her. She loved the way he would spontaneously put his arms around her and hug her tightly, as if he too had to be convinced that they were actually together.

Of the Christmas gifts that were exchanged, the most memorable was the gold wedding ring that Stephen gave to Sarah. She wept as he slid it onto her finger, vowing to be by her side for the rest of his life. The way they kissed with everyone looking on, it was almost like a wedding. Kyrah felt the moment was appropriate as a new beginning for her parents.

The most unique gift was the box of expensive cigars that Garret gave to Kyrah. While she was laughing Ritcherd looked into the box and said, "You're giving my wife cigars? Has she taken up smoking without my knowledge?"

"I should hope not!" Garret said with mock astonishment, then he smiled. "No, this is an admission that I've given it up."

"I didn't know you'd ever started," Ritcherd said.

"I was discreet," Garret said.

"He told me if he didn't have a woman, he'd keep company with a cigar," Patrick said. "I've been trying to get him to quit for months."

"You don't have the influence that Kyrah does," Garret said.

"Obviously not."

Garret added, "After I'd spent several days holed up with Ritcherd and hadn't smoked once, I figured I could let it go. But I'm still looking for a woman."

"And we'll all be glad when he finds one," George said plaintively, and the gift opening continued.

Kyrah hated to see Christmas Day coming to a close, even though she'd not given a thought to Mr. Thayer's imminent visit for hours. She was trying to convince Cetty that she needed to go up to bed when George announced, "Look, Kyrah. You and Garret are standing under the mistletoe. You need to kiss her, man."

"Take the chance while you can get it," Patrick encouraged lightly.

Garret comically lifted his eyebrows toward Ritcherd, who smirked and said, "Go ahead, but bear in mind that I'm watching."

"And were you not," Garret said, "it would be no different."

Garret took Kyrah's shoulders into his hands and pressed a lingering kiss to her brow. "Merry Christmas, Lady Buckley," he said.

"Merry Christmas, Sir Garret," she replied and kissed his cheek.

"That ought to be good," Ritcherd growled lightheartedly. Then he playfully nudged Garret from under the mistletoe, took Kyrah into his arms, and gave her a tender kiss.

In a dreamy voice Kyrah said, "Merry Christmas, Lord Buckley."

"And to you, my lady," he said and kissed her again.

After Cetty had given everyone in the room a hug good night, she left with Pearl.

"She is so precious," Sarah commented.

"Yes, she is," Ritcherd said with pride.

"She reminds me of her mother at that age," Stephen said.

"Even though she looks nothing like me?" Kyrah laughed.

"She may look like her father," Stephen said, "but she behaves very much as you did."

"And she's smart like her mother, too," Sarah said.

"Well, I'm glad she looks like me," Ritcherd said lightly, "or I'd wonder if she got anything from me at all."

A brief lull fell over the room as the laughter died down. Patrick broke the silence by saying, "Forgive me, but . . . I have to ask if you're still expecting a visit from Mr. Thayer tomorrow."

Ritcherd and Garret exchanged a disconcerted glance. "We are," Garret said.

"Who is Mr. Thayer?" Sarah asked, apparently sensing the tension that fell over the room when his name had come up.

Ritcherd answered when it became evident that no one else was going to. "Mr. Thayer is the man who believes that Garret and I are guilty of treason. He will be coming tomorrow to either arrest the both of us or collect a significant amount of money to drop the investigation."

Sarah gasped. "Why . . . that's preposterous? *Treason?* You and Garret! It's—"

"It's true, Mother," Ritcherd said solemnly. "Of course, we don't want Mr. Thayer to know that."

Ritcherd and Garret took turns filling in the pieces of the story for Sarah, and aspects of it that Stephen hadn't yet heard. When there was nothing more to tell, Sarah asked, "So do you believe that paying this Mr. Thayer off will end the whole affair?"

"That's what we're praying for," Ritcherd said, wishing he didn't feel so uneasy over the matter.

Stephen said, "I knew a Thayer once."

"You mentioned that before," Ritcherd said.

"I just can't quite place him," Stephen went on. "His first name was . . ." He snapped his fingers. "It started with a J."

"Joe?" Ritcherd asked.

"That's it," Stephen said, pointing at him.

Garret and Ritcherd exchanged a wary glance.

"So, who is he?" Garret demanded.

"I have no idea," Stephen said. "Sometimes I think those years in prison with nothing to do and too much to think about caused some kind of brain damage. Hopefully I'll remember how I know him."

"Well, when you do," Garret said, "I hope you remember something that will give me a good excuse to run him into the ground."

"Before he runs *you* into the ground," Ritcherd added.

"Exactly."

A harsh silence fell over the room until Ritcherd felt compelled to say what he felt certain everyone was thinking. "It's nothing personal, Stephen, but considering your history of the past several years, knowing you know Joe Thayer makes me even more suspicious than I was before."

"I couldn't have said it better myself," Garret said. "If he—"

Garret stopped when Pearl came into the room. "Forgive me," she said, curtsying slightly. "Cetty is insisting that she can't go to sleep until she tells her parents something very important, but she wouldn't tell me what."

"It's fine, Pearl. Thank you," Ritcherd said as he came to his feet and held out a hand for Kyrah. "We'll be back," Ritcherd said to the others, then left the room with Kyrah's arm over his.

About halfway up the stairs, Ritcherd impulsively stopped Kyrah and took her into his arms, kissing her long and hard. When the kiss had left her breathless, he looked into her eyes and murmured quietly, "I love you, Mrs. Buchanan."

Kyrah felt herself melt from the inside out. It hadn't been so long ago that she'd felt half dead when Ritcherd had shut her out of his heart. Now, with the ongoing evidence of his love for her, she felt alive and real and fulfilled. She felt as if she could fly. Returning Ritcherd's gaze, she prayed with all her heart and soul that they *would* be granted a miracle, that she would have him by her side for the rest of her life.

"Come along," Ritcherd said with a smile, moving on up the stairs. "Her majesty is waiting."

Kyrah laughed softly and wrapped her arm around Ritcherd's waist as she walked by his side. They found Cetty sitting up in bed, looking anxious.

"What is it, darling?" Kyrah asked, sitting on the bed beside her. Ritcherd squatted next to the bed and took Cetty's hand.

"There's something I forgot to tell you . . . that Celeste said."

Ritcherd and Kyrah exchanged a quick glance. "What is it, Cetty?" Ritcherd asked gently.

Looking directly at Ritcherd, Cetty said, "She told me it would be a very long time before you would see her again, but she would be watching over you. She said you would need to stay in this world to take care of my brothers and sisters."

Kyrah abruptly reached for Ritcherd's hand, squeezing so tightly that it hurt. She fought for a steady expression and sensed that he was doing the same. Cetty had no idea of the threat hanging over her father's head, and the turmoil it had created in their household. Kyrah was fighting to steady her voice enough to speak when Ritcherd said with a cracking voice, "Thank you for sharing that with us, Cetty. I'm so glad you remembered what Celeste told you." He urged her to lie down and kissed her little forehead before he stood up straight.

"You go to sleep now," Kyrah said with a barely steady voice. She kissed Cetty and tucked her in tightly. Cetty smiled and rolled over as if she could now sleep peacefully.

Kyrah barely managed to keep her tears back until they were out of the room. In the hall Ritcherd quickly urged Kyrah some distance from Cetty's room and around the corner before he pulled her tightly into his arms and she realized that he was crying, too.

"Oh, Kyrah," he murmured, "tell me you believe in miracles. Tell me you believe that Cetty has truly spoken with an angel who knows more than we do."

"I do believe in miracles," Kyrah said, taking Ritcherd's face into her hands. "And I know that everything is going to be all right. Somehow, I know."

Ritcherd nodded and laughed softly through his tears before he kissed her. "Oh, Kyrah, I love you, and I don't want to die. I know I said that I did . . . before. But I wasn't myself then, and . . . I want to share a long life with you. I do. I want to be with you forever."

"Forever," she murmured and kissed him again.

It took them both several minutes to gain control of their emotion and look presentable enough to return to the drawing room, where they found the others chatting and laughing.

"How is the little princess?" Garret asked when they entered.

"Queen, more like," Ritcherd said, and they all chuckled. "She's fine. She just wanted to tell us something."

Ritcherd sat on one of the sofas with Kyrah close beside him, barely aware of the ongoing conversation. His mind was more preoccupied with the tangible hope he'd just been given. The relief he felt made him realize that he'd been much more terrified than he'd wanted to admit—even to himself. At this point, he had no idea how this was all going to work out. But somehow, he knew that it would. Seeing the sparkle in Kyrah's eyes, he knew that she felt the same peace he did, and he knew that his time in this world was not yet over. *Brothers and sisters,* Cetty had said. What a delightful thought. Pressing Kyrah's hand to his lips, he couldn't think of anything he would rather do with his life than raise a house full of children with this incredible woman that he loved beyond his own comprehension. Life just couldn't be any better than that. And with any luck—and God's blessings—his life might be numbered in years, not days.

Ritcherd found it difficult to sleep while his fear of what Joe Thayer was capable of doing to his life battled internally with the tangible hope he'd felt from Cetty's innocent words. He could find no logical explanation for the things Cetty had said beyond the one she'd given. She'd spoken to Celeste. Still, it seemed so difficult to believe. And the threat of the charges against him and Garret were real.

Ritcherd finally slept, praying in his heart that Cetty's presage of his future was genuine, and they would indeed be blessed with a miracle. He came out of a deep sleep to the sound of someone knocking at the bedroom door.

"Good heavens," Kyrah murmured, half asleep. "Who could that be?"

"I'll get it," Ritcherd said, reaching for a dressing gown. He pulled open the door to see Stephen, looking disheveled, holding a lamp.

"What's wrong?" Ritcherd demanded.

He seemed more excited than distressed as he said, "It hit me like a lightning bolt out of nowhere. I know who Joe Thayer is."

"Who is he?" Ritcherd asked.

Stephen's countenance became severe. "I think we should wake your brother and have a long talk."

"What's wrong?" Kyrah demanded, appearing at Ritcherd's side.

"Nothing's wrong," Ritcherd said. "We just need to have a little talk. Go back to bed."

Kyrah watched Ritcherd and her father leave the room. She was reminded of the evening Ritcherd had come to her home and he and Stephen had holed themselves in the library for what seemed hours. Ritcherd had emerged with the announcement that he had been asked to serve his country, and he would be going to war. And Kyrah felt the same dread now. Whatever they needed to talk about at five in the morning could be no small thing, and she couldn't help feeling afraid. She reminded herself of the hope she'd gotten from Cetty's innocent words. Surely this situation would work itself out and all would be well. It just had to be!

Kyrah never went back to sleep. When she arrived at the dining room for breakfast, she found only her mother there.

"Where are the men?" Kyrah asked.

"Liza just told me they were all holed up in the library and asked for breakfast to be brought to them there."

Kyrah sighed and sat down, wishing she had the nerve to just burst into the library and demand to know what was going on. As it was, she sat through a long, silent breakfast with her mother, glancing at the clock frequently, counting the hours until Mr. Thayer would arrive and demand a hundred thousand pounds. But would that be enough to spare Ritcherd and Garret's lives?

An hour after breakfast was over, Kyrah couldn't stand it any longer and went to the library to find out what was going on. Finding the room empty, she discovered that all five men had left the house while Sarah and Kyrah had been eating breakfast.

Kyrah's nerves heightened. It wasn't like Ritcherd to leave without telling her. Rather than feeling angry with him, she simply wondered what could consume his thoughts. She went upstairs, where Sarah and Cetty were reading together. She tried to relax and tell herself that all would be well, but she still glanced at the clock every few minutes, both wishing the morning would hurry past and longing for it to last forever.

When it was past eleven, Kyrah went out to the stables to find that the men hadn't returned. The stable hands assured her that their horses were still missing. As eleven-thirty approached, Kyrah paced the main hall, knowing that Ritcherd and Garret could not meet their noon appointment with Mr. Thayer in the drawing room without first crossing her path. The minutes ticked by mercilessly. Eleven-forty-five. Eleven-*fifty*-five. Where could they be? She gasped to hear a door closing in the distance and more than one set of footsteps approaching on the marble floor; in fact, it sounded like several. She turned to see Ritcherd, Garret, her father, and a gentleman who looked vaguely familiar.

"Good morning, Kyrah," Garret said and rushed past her, along with the other man, who simply nodded quickly and hurried on.

"Hello, my dear," Stephen said and hurried on as well.

Kyrah caught Ritcherd's arm. "What's going on, Ritcherd?" she demanded quietly. A door closed in the distance and they were alone in the hall.

"There isn't time to explain right now," he said gently. "I apologize for leaving you in the dark, but . . . just know that we have some hope, and with any luck it will all turn out in our favor."

"And what if it doesn't?" she asked, holding to him more tightly.

"We're praying for a miracle," Ritcherd said and kissed her quickly.

As he attempted to move away, she said, "Just . . . tell me what my father has to do with all of this. How can—"

"Kyrah," he said, taking her shoulders into his hands, "we have every reason to believe that Joe Thayer is the man responsible for sending your father to prison." Kyrah gasped and he added, "A friend of Peter Westman's."

"That certainly puts a new light on the situation," she said, her voice betraying the sudden anger she felt.

"Yes, it certainly does." He kissed her again. "Now, just . . . stay out of sight and let us handle this. It will all be over soon." Ritcherd hurried away, adding under his breath, "I hope and pray it will all be over soon." He entered the drawing room with a prayer in his heart— as it had been all morning—that they were not simply treading into territory that would be better left uncharted.

Ritcherd closed the door and leaned against it. Garret was there alone, leaning back comfortably in an overstuffed chair, his ankle crossed over his knee. Ritcherd glanced toward the door of the adjoining music room, noting that it was slightly ajar. "Are we ready?" he asked.

"We are," Garret said coolly.

Ritcherd attempted to quell his nerves. "Why do I feel like we're engaged in some form of . . . acting here? Like we're in some kind of satirical tragedy?"

"We are," Garret said. "So sit down. Act calm, even though you're not."

Ritcherd sat down, sighing loudly. A minute later he asked, "And what if this is not the same Joe Thayer? What if the name is simply coincidence and we have nothing to—"

"We've already discussed this, my dear brother," Garret said. "I've told you a hundred times. I don't believe in coincidences. And there are just a few too many strange elements going on here. The fact that there has been no evidence whatsoever of either of us being watched or followed is a good indication that this is not what it appears to be. The fact that this exorbitant bribe has come into the situation is a *really* good indication that Joe Thayer is not who he is pretending to be."

"So, why didn't he use a false name? Wouldn't he be concerned that we'd find out who and what he really is?"

"No. He knew human nature enough to know that we would be so preoccupied with saving our own necks that we wouldn't dare question him—or bother to look into his past."

"And if he is who we think he is, would he not know the connection between my wife and the man he sent to prison illegally?"

"Yes, I think he would," Garret said. "But I don't think he would have believed in a million years that Stephen Payne would ever show up in our lives again. If he . . ."

Garret stopped when noises from the hall indicated that a visitor was coming through the front door. "Here we go," Garret said and took a sustaining breath. Ritcherd did the same, using every ounce of self-discipline to appear calm.

Liza showed Mr. Thayer into the room. Ritcherd and Garret remained seated as the maid left the room and closed the door. "I wish I could say this was a pleasant surprise," Ritcherd said. "Unfortunately, it is neither a surprise nor pleasant."

"Indeed," Mr. Thayer smirked.

"You came alone?" Garret asked. "I expected you to bring some of your intimidating friends to drag us away in shackles."

Mr. Thayer chuckled and took a seat. "And I expected that the two of you would have the good sense to accept my offer and prevent me from having to resort to such atrocities. I think that I will be able to carry away a hundred thousand pounds on my own."

"Well, you're right about one thing, Mr. Thayer," Ritcherd said. "We do have the good sense to avoid being led away in shackles."

"So . . . where is the money?" Mr. Thayer asked, glancing around.

"Oh, it's here in the house," Ritcherd said. "Someone will be bringing it in any minute now. However, before we hand it over, we need some kind of guarantee that we are purchasing complete and irrevocable innocence. How do we know you won't take the money and still turn us in on the evidence you claim to have?"

"You're going to have to take my word for it," Mr. Thayer said.

"Your word?" Garret echoed cynically. "Your word as a lawman willing to accept bribery? Forgive me, Mr. Thayer, but I'm not wholly comfortable with that. Perhaps we should—"

Garret stopped when the door came open and Stephen entered the room carrying a large satchel. "Here it is," he said to Ritcherd, who stood to take the bag from him. "I counted it again. It's all there. I can . . ." Stephen hesitated as his eyes took in Mr. Thayer. Ritcherd knew from the gleam in his eyes that it was indeed the same man Stephen had remembered from their encounters in London. Ritcherd's relief turned to something almost delightful as he observed Stephen's unadulterated acting skill. With perfect innocence, he turned toward Thayer and said, "Don't I know you from somewhere?"

"Not that I recall," Mr. Thayer said, sounding irritated.

"No, I'm sure of it," Stephen said, taking a step toward him. "I'm terrible with names, but I never forget a face. I'm certain we've met before, but I just can't quite . . ."

"Well," Ritcherd said, coming to his feet, "allow me to make the introductions official. Maybe that will jog your memory."

"Stephen, this is Joe Thayer. Mr. Thayer, my father-in-law, Stephen Payne."

Mr. Thayer barely nodded an acknowledgment while his mind was obviously stirring with a name that sounded familiar. Stephen looked at him closely and said, "So, you do remember me. I can see it in your eyes."

"Actually," Mr. Thayer said, "the name sounds vaguely familiar, but I can't seem to place it." He stood and added, "This is all very quaint, but if you gentlemen don't mind, I'll just be taking the money, and hopefully we will never see each other again."

"That's a pleasant thought," Garret said.

"Wait a minute," Stephen said, stepping closer to Mr. Thayer. "Before you go, I'd like to have a word with you. It's just come to me how I know you, and the very fact that you don't remember me is more than a bit disconcerting." Stephen's voice picked up an edge that seemed to make Mr. Thayer subtly uncomfortable. "It's amazing to me that you could go to so much trouble to destroy a man's life and not even remember his name."

Mr. Thayer chuckled, but it had a nervous ring to it. "I have no idea what you're talking about."

"Well, let me refresh your memory," Stephen said, stepping still closer to Mr. Thayer. "Does the name Peter Westman stir up anything for you?"

Mr. Thayer's eyes betrayed a clear apprehension that he covered quickly as he glanced at Ritcherd, then Garret, then back to Stephen. His countenance became confident and his voice cool as he said, "The name means nothing to me."

"It should," Stephen said, "since it was only you and I who were standing in the room and saw Westman shoot a man in the head. Of the two of us who witnessed that crime, I'm the only one who went to prison, while Westman went free, subjecting my family to hell while they believed that I had shot myself in the head."

Thayer chuckled in a visible attempt to cover his nervousness. "I have no idea what you're talking about."

Stephen chuckled as well—with complete confidence. "And I could testify otherwise," he said. "In fact, the conversation I overheard before Westman put a gun to that man's head would probably send you to prison for a good many years. That *is* why I went to prison, isn't it? And from that conversation I gathered that you were actually working with the law at the time—double-crossing them, no doubt. Obviously you had the right connections to switch my identity with the murder victim and see that I wouldn't be a problem to you or to Westman. Is this story sounding more familiar to you, Mr. Thayer?"

Ritcherd felt downright gratified to see the cornered frenzy in Joe Thayer's expression just before he cleared his throat carefully and said, "So we meet again, Mr. Payne. I must say I'm terribly surprised to come upon you here—or at all. Most people die or go crazy in that prison long before their sentence is complete."

Stephen made a bored noise. "Good thing I didn't know that, or I might have died or gone crazy. As you can see, I'm alive and well— and my memory is intact." He glanced at Garret, then at Ritcherd, who was holding the satchel of money. "And obviously you are still using your connections to the law to threaten and swindle innocent people." He glared at Mr. Thayer. "I think it's about time such non-sense came to an end. I'm absolutely certain that I could get these two young men to physically prevent you from leaving until we got a *real* lawman out here to arrest you. I'm certain they would be interested in hearing my story. I'm certain I could come up with names and dates enough to prove that what I'm saying is true." Stephen glanced obtrusively at the satchel containing the money. "Or . . ." he drawled, "a hundred thousand pounds could go a long way toward keeping the matter quiet."

Mr. Thayer chuckled nervously. "Listen," he said, "let's just drop this whole thing right now. I'll keep my mouth shut. You keep yours shut. We'll all be happy."

"What an excellent idea," Garret said. "However, considering what I just heard, I think I'll be wanting all of this evidence you claim to have that will convict my brother and myself of treason." He smirked and added, "One good turn deserves another."

"There is no evidence," Thayer blurted. "There's nothing. I haven't worked with the law for years. I saw the *Phoenix* come into port and recalled Westman's interest in following her at one time, and what he'd told me. I saw an opportunity to make some easy money. That's it. Let's just . . . drop the whole thing and forget we ever saw each other."

"An excellent idea," Ritcherd said, motioning toward the door. "I can't tell you how happy I am that I will never have to see you again. Although it doesn't seem quite right to just let you go after what you did to my family all those years ago."

"I agree," Garret said. "In fact, I'm reminded of Peter Westman. He just couldn't leave well enough alone."

"I'll keep that in mind," Mr. Thayer said and hurried toward the door. But when he opened it, he was met by two officers of the law. Thayer gasped and stepped back into the room while the officers clearly blocked the doorway. He turned around, glaring at Ritcherd, then Garret, and Stephen. Then his eyes came to rest on the man who had just entered the room from the adjacent music room, where the door had been ajar.

"Yes," Garret said, "you've been swindled, Mr. Thayer."

"We were on to you," Ritcherd added. "Fortunately, my father-in-law has an excellent memory—once he can connect the name with the event. But then, he's had a lot of time over the last several years to think about his encounter with you."

Stephen motioned to the man standing in the room and said, "Mr. Williams here is the local constable, and he overheard our entire conversation."

Thayer gasped, then his eyes turned angry. "You'll never prove *anything,*" he snarled.

"We'll let that be determined in a court of law," Mr. Williams said. "You are under arrest for more reasons than I care to itemize at the moment."

Mr. Thayer's attempt to protest was halted by the burly officer at his side who warned him boldly against saying a word, while the other one snapped his wrists into handcuffs behind his back. After Mr. Thayer was taken from the house, Mr. Williams said, "Well, this has certainly been an eventful morning, gentlemen. My superiors will be very impressed to learn that I have apprehended a man wanted for many crimes."

"But you say he actually was a lawman at one time?" Garret asked.

"He was," Williams said. "According to the records I have which I looked over earlier, and what I've heard through the grapevine, he was dishonorably discharged some years ago due to questionable activity, and his criminal doings have been on the rise ever since."

"Well, we can't thank you enough," Ritcherd said, shaking Mr. Williams's hand.

"I'm glad it worked out so well," Williams said, shaking Garret's hand as well, then Stephen's. "Imagine even implying treasonous activities when you were simply searching for the woman you loved among such horrendous circumstances."

"Imagine," Garret said, meeting Ritcherd's eyes behind Mr. Williams' back.

"I wonder," Mr. Williams said, "if I might have the opportunity to speak with Mrs. Buchanan before I leave."

"Of course," Ritcherd said and stepped out of the drawing room to find Liza in the front hall. He asked her to find Kyrah and bring her to the drawing room. The men chatted comfortably until she appeared only a minute later.

"Mrs. Buchanan," Williams said with obvious delight, bowing slightly, "this is indeed a pleasure."

"Mr. Williams is the local constable," Ritcherd said in an effort to alleviate Kyrah's obvious confusion.

"Allow me to explain," Mr. Williams said. "I was one of the officers on duty when you were illegally deported some years ago."

"I see," Kyrah said, realizing why he looked familiar.

"I simply want to tell you that while I knew something was not as it should be, I was not made aware of the circumstances enough to be able to do anything about it until it was too late. I have often thought of you and regretted what happened. I was thrilled to see your husband this morning and hear that all had worked out well in the end. I simply wanted to offer my personal regret for what happened, and to tell you that it was a pleasure to take over Constable Killeen's position and do my best to see that the law is adhered to in every matter."

"That is good to know, indeed," Kyrah said. "Thank you for your kind words."

"And thank you for your help today," Ritcherd said.

"I am only too glad to be of service, Captain," the constable said. "It has been a pleasure, I can assure you. I can also assure you that you will never be bothered by Mr. Thayer again."

"How is that?" Kyrah asked.

"He was just arrested," Garret explained.

"We'll tell you later," Ritcherd added when Kyrah's eyes widened.

Ritcherd and Kyrah walked the constable to the door, and once it was closed Kyrah turned to her husband and said, "You may tell me now."

"Very well," Ritcherd chuckled and motioned her toward the drawing room.

Chapter Twenty

The Arrival

Ritcherd and Kyrah entered the drawing room to see Garret just taking a seat, and Stephen leaning back comfortably in an overstuffed chair, looking rather complacent.

"I must say," Stephen chuckled, "that was likely one of the most gratifying moments of my life."

"As it should be," Garret said.

"You swindler, you," Ritcherd added facetiously.

"Gambler by profession," Stephen said proudly. "It takes a certain amount of acting to keep the opponent guessing. Although my gambling days are done."

"I'm glad to hear it," Ritcherd said. "But I'm glad you still have the ability to be a good actor."

"And a good swindler," Garret added and they all laughed, except for Kyrah, who was obviously frustrated by her ignorance.

"Any time now," she said impatiently, taking a seat across the room from her father. Ritcherd sat close beside her.

"This is your story," Ritcherd said to Stephen. "I think you owe your daughter an explanation."

"Well, to put it simply, my dear, Joe Thayer is someone I often encountered casually in London. He loitered around the gaming tables. We were vaguely acquainted. Occasionally we shared a drink. But he was also in the room when Westman shot the man whose identity I apparently went to prison with. I heard enough of their conversation to be a threat to them—as if witnessing the crime weren't enough."

"So, what has all of this got to do with the accusations of treason?" Kyrah asked.

"Apparently Thayer was a good friend of Westman's, and was aware of his interest in tracking the *Phoenix* at one time. He likely suspected that we'd done some privateering, but certainly would have had no proof. He admitted that he saw the *Phoenix* and envisioned an opportunity to make some easy money."

"So . . . it was simply a ruse . . . all along?" she asked, clearly appalled.

"It was," Ritcherd said. "When Stephen told me who he was, we talked it through very carefully, then we took a chance and went to the local constable. Turns out he remembered me from the time I had a very unfriendly encounter with his predecessor the morning after you were deported. We had a good visit. He looked up some records. He now has Mr. Thayer in his custody."

"Incredible," Kyrah said. Following a long moment where she allowed all of this information to settle into her, she laughed softly and added, "It's a miracle."

"It is indeed," Ritcherd said. "But I think we might have had more than our fair share. From now on, I think we'll be very careful about admitting that we're turncoats."

"We never admitted it to anyone but family," Garret said. "Although, it might be wise to retrain your daughter on your political preferences."

"Yes, I'll do that," Ritcherd chuckled.

"Where are Patrick and George?" Kyrah asked.

"They're outside," Garret said. "They were just helping the officers make certain that Mr. Thayer didn't have any friends loitering about. But I don't think they'll find any. Thayer probably hired the two men who initially came on board the *Phoenix* with him, and since that time he's been completely acting on his own."

Kyrah came to her feet. "I see. Well, do you think we could have lunch now? I'm starving."

Garret and Stephen headed toward the dining room, but Kyrah stopped Ritcherd with her hand on his arm. She lifted her mouth to his and gave him a long, savoring kiss.

"What was that for?" he asked, chuckling.

"I'm just grateful I get to have you around *next* Christmas."

He chuckled and kissed her again. "Yes, you will. In fact, I think I'll die in your arms as a very old man."

"I'll count on it," she said, and they walked hand in hand to the dining room.

With the help of a local investigator, the identity of the man buried beneath Stephen's gravestone was brought to light. It was determined that this man had no family connections whatsoever, which explained why the mistake of Stephen's imprisonment under his name was never discovered. The decision was made to leave the casket buried where it was, but Stephen's headstone was removed and destroyed, and an appropriate marker was put in its place for the man who had taken Stephen's place in death for several years.

Proving that Stephen was alive was not so easy. Long after Garret sailed with the *Phoenix,* Ritcherd and Stephen were still working hard to straighten out legal and religious records and prove that Stephen Payne was indeed among the living. The people of north Cornwall were stunned by the news of this horrible misunderstanding, and most people accepted Stephen graciously back into the community. Ritcherd and Kyrah were just happy to have him a part of their lives— but not nearly so happy as Sarah was. Stephen and Sarah took to a habit of travel, and were frequently gone on lengthy vacations. They always came back full of laughter and glowing with happiness, and they were never gone long enough to let Cetty forget who her grandparents were.

Months passing enhanced Ritcherd's happiness as he recognized a deep inner peace that had never been with him before—and had not gone away with the passing of time. His joy only increased as Kyrah passed the time in her pregnancy when she had lost the last baby, and their hope swelled that this baby would make it into the world healthy and safe.

With less than three weeks left until the expected arrival, Ritcherd sat close beside Kyrah in the nursery while Cetty demonstrated how well she was learning to read. While Cetty ran to get another book, Kyrah asked, "When is it that you have to go to London to take care of that business you mentioned?"

Ritcherd blew out a heavy breath. "I should probably go tomorrow and get it over with. I don't want to wait any longer with the baby coming."

"I don't want you to go," she said, "but I do want you to get it over with." A moment later she added, "When did my parents say they would be returning from France?"

"According to the last letter, they should be here in the next few days." He kissed her hand and added, "They don't want to miss being here when the baby comes. After all, they missed the last one."

"Everyone did except you," Kyrah laughed softly.

Ritcherd sighed. "That seems like a hundred years ago."

"Yes, it does," Kyrah said. "And look how far we've come. I never dreamed I could be so happy."

"Nor did I," he said, wrapping his arms around her.

Cetty came back into the room and climbed onto her father's lap with a book in her hands. She stopped before she was fully situated and looked over Ritcherd's shoulder toward the door. "Uncle Garret!" she squealed and ran across the room.

Garret's laughter filled the room. "Oh, I missed my little princess," he said, twirling Cetty around.

"What are you doing here?" Ritcherd laughed, rising and moving toward him. "We didn't expect you for weeks yet."

Garret set the child down. "We made good time," he said. "Had a good wind."

Ritcherd and Garret both laughed as they wrapped their arms around each other in a firm brotherly embrace. Garret drew back and looked into his eyes. "How are you, my brother?"

"Never better," Ritcherd said. "How are you?"

"Glad to be home," Garret said, then he looked down to where Cetty was tugging at his coat. "Oh, I almost forgot," he added, reaching into his pocket. He squatted down and pulled out a closed fist.

"What do I get?" he asked, and Cetty gave him a loud smooch. He laughed and opened his fist.

Cetty gasped with pleasure as she lifted a set of five brass bracelets. "Oh, thank you, Uncle Garret," she said brightly.

"You're welcome," he smiled.

"Where did they come from?" she asked.

"Your favorite place," he said.

"The place with the elephants!" she said and slid them over her arm, showing them with pleasure to her father, then to her mother, who was still sitting down.

"I'm going to show Pearl," Cetty said and ran from the room.

Garret's eyes moved to Kyrah and she smiled. "Hello, my lady," he said, stepping toward her.

"Hello," she said and reached out both her hands.

He took hold of them and helped her to her feet, but as he leaned forward to give her the standard kiss on the brow, his eyes moved downward. "My dear Kyrah, what *have* you been doing?"

"I don't think we should discuss such things in polite society," Ritcherd said.

"I'm not polite society," Garret smirked at Ritcherd. "I'm your brother." He turned back to Kyrah and laughed with pure delight. "You look terribly happy, my dear sister."

"I am," she said.

"And you are terribly pregnant," he added.

"He's observant," Ritcherd said.

Garret chuckled and leaned closer to Kyrah. "Has he been keeping his promises, my dear?"

Kyrah smiled at Ritcherd. "Every hour of every day," she said with conviction.

"Good then," Garret laughed again. "I won't be needing to steal you and your babies away from here."

"No, there won't be any need for that," Ritcherd said.

Garret finally got to kissing Kyrah's brow, then they were all seated. "I brought Patrick with me," Garret said. "He's downstairs flirting with Mrs. Hawke in the kitchen."

"How delightful," Kyrah said.

"I'm not certain Mrs. Hawke thinks so," Garret said lightly.

"She loves Patrick," Ritcherd added. "And you. We weren't expecting you, but I'm glad you're here. I have to leave for London in the morning. I'll only be gone a few days, but I will feel better knowing she has you here to look out for her."

Ritcherd and Garret exchanged a subtle smile, and Ritcherd hoped that Garret understood and appreciated—as he did—the level of trust between them. "It would be an honor," Garret said.

"With the baby coming soon, I hate to leave at all," Ritcherd said, "but it has to be done. If I want my investments protected, I occasionally have to show my face and sign my name."

"No worries, my friend," Garret said. "Patrick and I will take very good care of her."

"Yes, I know you will," Ritcherd said, then he pointed at Kyrah. "But don't you be having that baby while I'm gone."

"It's not due for more than two weeks," she assured him.

"You never know," Ritcherd said. "I'm just glad to know you have the best medical care in the world on hand, and someone who loves you and will watch out for you."

Ritcherd met Garret's eyes and they exchanged a poignant smile. "We'll take very good care of her," Garret said.

"I know you will."

"Where are Stephen and Sarah?" Garret asked, glancing around.

"France, actually," Ritcherd said. "They've been on one long honeymoon ever since you left here in January."

"As they should be," Garret said.

"Speaking of honeymoons," Ritcherd said, "are you—"

"No!" Garret said tersely. In a more cordial voice he added, "I have not found a woman to take my breath away—but not for lack of trying."

"It will happen," Kyrah said. "After all, we are people who believe in miracles."

"So we do," Garret said.

The first two days of Ritcherd's absence, Kyrah shared her meals with Patrick and Garret, and otherwise spent much of her time resting. Either Garret or Patrick checked on her regularly, but she insisted that her fatigue was simply a matter of not getting much sleep with the baby kicking her all the time. Patrick gave her an official examination and declared that everything seemed fine.

On the third morning, Kyrah mentioned at breakfast, "I forgot until this morning, Garret, but I need you to accompany me to Mr. Hatfield's office."

"The solicitor? Why?"

"Just a formality with the deed for the house," she said. "I told him we would both come in as soon as you returned, but then it slipped my mind. If it's all right with you, let's take care of it this morning."

"That would be fine," Garret said.

"And," Kyrah added, "since I would like to do some shopping and the two of you have been assigned to take care of me, I assume you'll both be joining me for the better part of the day."

"How delightful," Patrick said. "Rarely has serving under Captain Garret presented an opportunity for such pleasant duties."

The errand at Mr. Hatfield's office went smoothly, then they rode some distance farther in the carriage to a particular cobbler's shop that was situated in a farm home that Patrick declared was out in the middle of nowhere.

"Yes," Kyrah agreed, "but he's a fine man and no one does a better job, it's worth the extra drive. We can stop back in town on our way through to finish my errands."

Kyrah picked up some shoes for Cetty that had been ordered a few weeks earlier, while Patrick and Garret waited outside. Walking back to the carriage, Kyrah hesitated, feeling a twinge of pain.

"Are you all right?" Garret asked, his attention drawn to the way her hand was pressed low on her belly.

"I'm not certain," she said. "Perhaps it would be well to save the rest of my shopping for another day."

"Very wise," Patrick said.

Kyrah put her hand into Garret's so he could help her step inside the carriage. A strange sensation made her hesitate. She tightened her grip and he asked again, "Are you all right?"

Kyrah glanced down, lifted her skirts slightly and took a step back to see a large wet spot on the ground where she'd been standing. She turned toward Patrick, who was standing just behind her. "My water just broke."

"Oh my," Patrick chuckled.

"What does that mean?" Garret questioned.

Patrick chuckled again, apparently amused by Garret's distress. "It means we're going to have a baby."

"Not here we're not," Kyrah said, stepping into the carriage just as a sharp pain grabbed her. She groaned and teetered, grateful for Garret's hands that steadied her.

"Are you all right?" he asked yet again.

"No, I don't think I am," she said, easing carefully onto the seat. Garret sat beside her and she grabbed his hand, squeezing tightly as another pain assaulted her.

Patrick shouted orders for the driver to get them home as quickly as possible, then he got in and sat down across from them and the carriage moved forward. "That's two pains already," she said to him.

"Whoa," Patrick said. "That's moving a little faster than last time."

"A *little* faster?" she snapped. "I didn't reach this point for hours last time."

"Second babies tend to get here more easily," Patrick said as if it were nothing.

Less than a minute later, Kyrah groaned and gasped for breath.

"Slow down," Patrick said. "Come on, breathe, Kyrah. Slow breath in. Slow breath out."

She tried to follow his lead, but the pain came on again and she almost slid off the seat.

"Good heavens," Garret said, easing her into his arms just as Patrick took hold of her feet and swung her legs gently over Garret's lap. He rolled up his coat and put it behind her head. She moaned and hissed and clutched onto Garret so hard that she left fingernail prints in his arms.

"What's wrong with her?" Garret demanded of Patrick.

"She's having a baby!" Patrick growled.

"I can see that, but—"

"Not in this carriage, I'm not," Kyrah snapped.

"I'm afraid that's up to the baby," Patrick said. "We've still got nearly half an hour's drive home."

"No!" Kyrah howled and moaned again.

"Why is she in so much pain?" Garret asked. "What's wrong with her?"

"There's nothing wrong with her, Captain," Patrick said, apparently amused by Garret's ignorance. "She's having a baby. Have you never seen a woman in labor before?"

"No, I haven't, actually," Garret said.

"Well, now's your opportunity to see firsthand what life is really all about."

Garret saw something in Patrick's eyes—something cautioning and fixed—that made Garret wonder if this would be an opportunity or a trial from his perspective. Already he felt terrified to see the evidence of Kyrah's suffering.

Another ten minutes passed while her pain intensified, and Garret's fear deepened. While Kyrah held to Garret's arms, Patrick knelt on the carriage floor beside her, guiding her through her breathing so she wouldn't pass out, and offering gentle encouragement.

Five minutes later, Kyrah felt a dramatic difference in the pain. It took on a constancy and a severity that she recognized. "Oh," she groaned, "it's getting worse."

"We're more than halfway home, Kyrah," Patrick said. "I'll check you as soon as we get there, and—"

"No, you check me *now!*" she shouted, then threw her head back in anguish.

Garret met Patrick's eyes, feeling a fear that he couldn't begin to express. Never had he imagined that childbirth entailed such horrible pain. Focusing on Kyrah's face, he was only vaguely aware of Patrick discreetly putting a hand beneath her skirts. A minute later he heard Patrick let out a quiet gasp. Garret met his eyes again, seeing a concern there that didn't match his gentle, even voice as he said, "It is getting close, Kyrah, but it's not ready to come yet. Don't start pushing until I tell you."

"Pushing?" she screamed. "I can't . . . I can't . . . have this baby here. I can't."

"Wherever you have this baby, Kyrah, we're going to take very good care of you."

She screamed and tightened her hold on Garret. She met his eyes with a silent plea that nearly cracked his heart wide open. "I can't do this," she muttered. "Don't make me do this."

He wanted to ask her what he was supposed to do about it. Instead, he said gently, "It's going to be all right, Kyrah."

She screamed again, then muttered hoarsely, "Don't leave me, Garret. Please don't leave me."

"I'm right here," he said, praying that they could get her home and someone—anyone—else could be with her through this.

They were still five minutes from the manor when she let out a loud wail and shouted at Patrick. "It's coming. Oh, heaven help me. It's coming."

Patrick checked her and almost chuckled. "Yes, it is," he said, then he spoke close to Kyrah's face. "Just let it come, Kyrah. It's all right."

"No, I want to be home," she cried.

"We're almost there, but . . ." Patrick abruptly lifted her skirts above her knees and Garret shot his eyes the other direction, focusing intently on Kyrah's face.

He wiped sweat from her face with his handkerchief and kissed her brow. Then he realized the carriage was slowing. A quick glance out the window prompted him to exclaim, "We're home, Kyrah. We made good time."

"All right, get her in the house," Patrick said. "Carefully now."

Patrick had the carriage door open and had stepped down before it came to a complete stop, then he helped steady Garret's descent with Kyrah cradled in his arms, moaning and gasping for breath. Patrick ran and threw the front door open, shouting at Liza, "Lady Buckley's having a baby. I'm taking her to the library. We'll never get her up the stairs. I need blankets, clean sheets—now! And once I get those, you have someone bring me plenty of water, and you go to my room and get my bag. Do you understand?"

"Yes, Doctor," she said and scurried away.

Patrick led the way into the library and motioned Garret toward the floor. "The sofa's not big enough," he muttered. "She won't be comfortable." He grabbed a sofa pillow and stuck it beneath her head as Garret laid her gently on the floor.

"Oh, it's coming!" Kyrah shouted then groaned.

"Garret, you kneel there and—"

Garret interrupted Patrick, his voice a panicked whisper. "I shouldn't be with her through something like this. It's not . . . proper."

Patrick retorted quietly in a voice that oozed with authority. "Propriety has nothing to do with it, Garret. She's giving birth, and she needs you. This is the way God sends babies into the world, but I don't think He intended for them to arrive on their own. Now you just look Kyrah in the eye and talk her through this. I'll do what a doctor does and handle everything else."

Garret took a deep breath and knelt beside Kyrah just as she attempted to sit up, groaning and hissing as if she were being split in half. "Help her," Patrick said. "If her back is elevated it will come easier."

Garret did his best to hold her in a half-reclined position while she grabbed onto his arms and looked into his eyes with a silent intensity that sent his heart pounding. The maid plopped blankets and sheets down beside Patrick and rushed from the room. He gracefully lifted Kyrah up enough to get a folded sheet beneath her then pushed her skirts up over her knees just as she groaned and bore down, and a moment later Garret heard Patrick laugh. "The worst is over, Kyrah," he said. "The head is through—it has your dark hair. One more push and—" She bore down again, and again Patrick laughed. "It's a girl," he said the same moment that Kyrah collapsed against Garret and started to cry. A moment later, the baby's healthy wail penetrated the room.

Liza entered the room with Patrick's bag. She fussed over the baby while Patrick gave her instructions on what to get out of the bag for him and how she could help him. Garret just held Kyrah in his arms, relishing the miracle of life he'd just been privileged to witness.

"She's beautiful, Kyrah," Patrick said as Liza wrapped the baby in a little blanket and put her into her mother's arms. The baby's crying quieted while Kyrah's tears increased.

"I fetched a little blanket from the nursery for her," Liza said.

"Thank you, Liza," Kyrah said, then she laughed and cried as she looked at her little daughter. "Oh, look at her, Garret. She's beautiful."

Garret caught his breath at how tiny the baby was. "She *is* beautiful," he said, bravely reaching out to touch her tiny little hand. "She has a beautiful mother."

Kyrah met his eyes for just a moment before she turned her attention back to the baby. "Thank you, Garret," she said, "for helping me get her here. I couldn't have done it without you."

"You're amazing, Kyrah," he said softly. Watching her with the baby, he couldn't help but recall how she'd been significantly pregnant with Cetty when he'd first met her. She'd gone into labor the night the *Phoenix* was setting sail, and Ritcherd had stayed with her through the ordeal. Ritcherd had told him later how difficult it had been, but he'd had no idea what a woman went through to have a baby. As hard as it had been for him to see her suffer that way, he felt deeply privileged to have shared this experience with her.

"And thank you, Patrick," Kyrah said to him. "I'm so grateful that you were here."

"A privilege, I can assure you," Patrick said.

Kyrah's attention turned fully to the baby while she wished that Ritcherd could have been there. She wondered how long it might be before he could see his new daughter.

"What's her name going to be?" Patrick asked, sitting on the floor beside Kyrah while he wiped his hands on a wet towel. "You named Cetty after a bird, didn't you?"

"That's right," Kyrah said proudly. "Avocet is her real name."

"And this one?" Garret asked. "Will she be a bird as well?"

"Yes, actually," Kyrah said. "And Ritcherd agreed it would be a fine name. Linnet Buchanan."

Garret smiled. "I like it," he said.

"Look, Linnet," Kyrah said, smiling at him, "there's your Uncle Garret. Someday he will read you stories and play toy soldiers with you, and he'll bring you gifts from exotic ports."

"I'll accept the first two," Garret said, "but I think I'd prefer being settled down as opposed to sailing exotic ports by the time she's old enough to care."

Kyrah smiled again and sighed. "Yes, that would be nice, wouldn't it." She lifted a hand to touch Garret's face. "She's out there somewhere, Garret, needing you as much as you need her."

Kyrah saw a hint of moisture brim in his eyes as he admitted, "That's what I'm praying for."

"And what about you, Patrick?" Kyrah asked. "When are you going to quit the sea and settle down?"

"When Garret quits the sea, I suppose. I don't think I could live a sailor's life without him around to keep me company."

"Well, let's pray that the two of you don't end up being eternal bachelors," Kyrah said.

"Ritcherd could never handle the stress created by Garret's being a bachelor," Patrick said with a smirk toward Garret.

Garret chuckled. "My being a bachelor keeps Ritcherd humble—and on his toes."

"So it does," Kyrah said.

The moment Ritcherd arrived home, he headed up the stairs in search of Kyrah. He peeked in the nursery to find no one there, and he wondered if the governess had taken Cetty for a walk, or if perhaps she was elsewhere with Kyrah. He checked the bedroom next and found the door ajar. Pushing it open he felt his heart quicken with panic before he consciously absorbed the scene before him. He could see Kyrah's dark hair on the pillow, although her back was turned toward him. She was beneath the covers, but it was still evident that she was wearing a nightgown, and her hair was down. Patrick was sitting close beside the bed, and Garret was standing at the window, looking out. He wondered what would keep her in bed this time of day, with the doctor and Garret keeping a bedside vigil.

"What's wrong?" he demanded, and both men turned abruptly toward him.

"Good, you're here," Patrick said, coming to his feet. "She's been asking for you."

"What's wrong?" Ritcherd repeated, moving toward the bed. "What's happened?"

"Nothing's wrong," Patrick said, putting a hand on Ritcherd's shoulder. He chuckled and added in a whisper, "It's a girl."

Ritcherd looked at him closely to be assured that he wasn't teasing. "Really?" he squeaked.

"Really," Patrick said, and Ritcherd chuckled. "And she's perfect. Now I'm going to get some exercise. I won't be far if Kyrah needs anything."

"Thank you," Ritcherd said. He met Garret's eyes, seeing clearly that he shared the joy Ritcherd felt. Focusing on Kyrah, he eased onto the edge of the bed. She turned to look at him and his joy deepened. She was so beautiful! And there was an added serenity in her expression that magnified her beauty beyond description.

"Ritcherd," she said with a tired ring to her voice.

"So I missed it, eh?"

"I'm sorry," she said. "It happened so fast. We almost didn't make it home."

Ritcherd's eyes widened, but before he could ask, Kyrah added, "Look at her, Ritcherd. She's beautiful." Kyrah eased the sheet back to reveal a little head of black curls and a chubby little face pressed to the bed.

Ritcherd chuckled and leaned closer. "She *is* beautiful," he said. He tossed a smirk at Garret and added, "Especially since she doesn't look at all like her Uncle Garret."

Garret wondered if there was some hidden undertone in the statement, but Ritcherd's eyes were genuine, full of trust and acceptance. "No chance of that," Garret said. "Although . . . I did help get her here," he added proudly.

"Really?" Ritcherd said, glancing back and forth between Garret and Kyrah. "What happened?"

"She was almost born in the carriage," Kyrah said. "Thankfully, Patrick was with us. I had her on the floor in the library."

Ritcherd's voice betrayed his astonishment. "Are you all right?"

"I'm fine," Kyrah laughed softly. "I'm sore and tired, but I'm fine. They took very good care of me, just like they told you they would."

Ritcherd laughed as well, then carefully lifted the baby into his hands. He held her little face close to his own while his laugh deepened. "She looks like her mother," he declared. In a silly voice he added, "Hello, Linnet Buchanan. Welcome to the world. You and I are going to have a marvelous life together, my little darling. And with any luck, we'll be able to keep Uncle Garret away from the sea."

"I think it will take someone quite a bit older than Linnet to keep Garret away from the sea," Kyrah said. Garret smiled at her, and she added, "And then we shall all live happily until the end of time."

About the Author

Elizabeth D. Michaels began writing at the age of sixteen and has since immersed herself in the lives created by her vivid imagination. Beyond her devotion to family and friends, writing has been her passion for the majority of her adult life. While she has more than seventy published novels under the name Anita Stansfield and is the recipient of many awards—including two Lifetime Achievement Awards—she boldly declares the historical novels published under the Michaels name to be dearly close to her heart. She is best known for her keen ability to explore the psychological depths of human nature, bringing her characters to life through the timeless struggles they face in the midst of exquisite dramas.

For more information on the author and her books, follow her on Instagram or go to anitastansfield.com.

Scan to visit

www.anitastansfield.com